HEARSE

OF A

DIFFERENT COLOR

.

.

OTHER BOOKS BY TIM COCKEY

The Hearse You Came In On

HEARSE

OF A

DIFFERENT COLOR

·

TIM COCKEY

HYPERION

New York

This book is a work of fiction. The characters described in these pages are fiction. Even the dog is made up. Some of the buildings are real.

Mass Market ISBN 0-7868-8963-2

With love
to
Florence Louise Hinman Ames Cockey
Merryman Harrison

(I find it easier to call her "Mom.")

ACKNOWLEDGMENTS

A number of people graciously took the early drafts of this book out for a test run, reporting back to me on some of its wobbles, pings, minor misalignments, pullings to the left . . . that sort of thing. Chief among my truly superior test-drivers were Wendy Barrie-Wilson (wobbles), Battlin' Jim Mc-Greevey (pings), Ted Manekin (pulls to the left) and Lorna Aikman Mehta (minor misalignments). Thanks one and all; and I'm glad nobody got seriously hurt.

If banging out this book was half the fun, the other half was certainly kicking it all the way into shape with the relentless help of my pitch-perfect editor, Peternelle van Arsdale. Also at Hyperion, Martha Levin, Bob Miller, Ellen Archer and Jane Comins have each hoisted me up onto their shoulders at numerous points over the year. The kind of support that money can't buy. Many thanks to you guys. Big old nod, too, to Alison Lowenstein and April Fleming.

A tip of the toupee must also go to Gabrielle Maloney, Jeff Promish, Chris Fisk, Amy Schraub, Shelly D'Arcambal, Michelle Felten, David Gottlieb and Ann Megyas—avid all—

as well as to my partner in these crimes, my agent, Victoria Sanders. And my collective thanks go to damn near everyone at the Foundation Center (go to them to seek grant information!).

Finally, a very special acknowledgment to my niece, Arianna Jarvis, mystery novelist-in-training. Keep an eye on this one.

HEARSE

OF A

DIFFERENT COLOR

•

CHAPTER

1

The dead waitress had beautiful eyes. Large, chocolate and lovely. Of course, this was something I couldn't possibly know until some time later, once I had the chance to see them in a photograph. As usual with me, I get them when the spark has gone out and they're already losing their looks. Aunt Billie has a term for this. She calls it "occupational disappointment."

The waitress couldn't have arrived at a more inopportune moment. Baltimore was right in the middle of an unscheduled pre-Christmas blizzard and Aunt Billie and I were right in the middle of a wake. A heart surgeon from nearby Johns Hopkins Hospital had gone out in a blaze of irony two days previous, struck down by a heart attack, no less, while in the middle of performing a triple bypass. His name was Richard Kingman. Dr. Kingman had been in his late fifties, played tennis several times a week, hadn't touched a cigarette for decades, ate sensibly, drank politely and all the rest, and yet there it was. The needle suddenly skidded across his heart, and he collapsed in the operating room. He had been a robust fellow, judging by the photograph provided to me by the man's widow. Ruddy. Expansive smile. Big healthy mop of rust red hair as wavy as a small ocean. The photograph had been snapped during a skiing vacation the family had taken out west some fifteen years previous. It featured the now-dead patriarch in the center, flanked by his then-teenage son on one side and his daughter and wife on the other. Everybody looked nurtured and well fed. The son bore only a thin resemblance to his father, his face a little longer and his smile considerably less natural. Unlike his sister's smile, which—like Father's—was wide and exuberant. As for Mom, her bland expression revealed nothing. Or, for that matter, in its nothingness, everything.

"Everybody loved Richard," the widow said flatly when she handed me the photograph. She made it sound like a bad thing.

This weather of ours, it wasn't simply bad. It was a wet, ugly, bitter, nasty and thoroughly crappy, stinking god-awful slop of a miserable night. A cold front from hell (if you can withstand the oxymoron) had skidded into town without warning. Poor Bonnie, over at Television Hill, was probably in tears. Again. During the six o'clock news—pinwheeling her arms all around the map of Baltimore and the vicinity—she had promised that the real shit (my term, not hers) would be passing well to the north. But no sooner had the anemic December sun packed it in for the night than the bottom fell out of the thermometer and huge amoebas of sleet began dropping out of the sky, accompanied by crisscross gusts of wind that were flinging the mess in all directions at once. Now Bonnie would have to come back on at eleven and hold on to an iron smile as her on-air colleagues jovially ganged up on her.

Again.

On my way up the street for the doctor's wake, I slipped on the fresh ice and landed knees-first in a slush puddle. Then my elbow took a hard hit on the iced sidewalk as I slipped trying to get up. The pain ran up and down my arm like a frantic hamster.

"What in the world happened to you?" Billie asked as I came through the door. From the knees down I was a joke.

"Uncontrollable urge to pray," I muttered, reaching down to flick the stray bits of ice from my pant legs.

"Are you going to change them before the people start arriving?"

"I'm not going back out in that slop to change my clothes," I said. "Maybe you'd like to lend me one of your dresses."

My aunt clucked at that. "Oh, I'm too zaftig, dear."

"Meaning?"

"Big fanny. You're way too svelte for my wardrobe." Billie sighed. "You could always hide behind a floral arrangement," she suggested.

"No flowers please, remember? Send condolences in the form of a contribution to the Heart Association?"

Billie sniffed. "What's wrong with flowers *and* a contribution? Hitchcock, when I go I want that room in there glutted with flowers, do you understand me? I want a jungle."

"Yes ma'am."

"Don't 'yes ma'am' me, I'm serious. The funeral of an undertaker should be exemplary in every way." Billie stepped over to straighten my tie. "You give me flowers. Irises. Orchids. Lilies. Even mums. You can make entire blankets of mums." She smoothed my lapel.

"Duly noted," I said, fluffing the silk scarf under her chin. Billie gently slapped my hand away.

"And no black-eyed Susans. I have never understood why people do that."

"It's the state flower."

"I don't care. This isn't a constitutional convention, it's a funeral. The black-eyed Susan is strictly a roadside flower. It has no business at a funeral. At least not mine. Understood?"

I nodded. Billie turned to the wall mirror and began poking her silvery do. My aunt is a handsome little chippy, who would gently slaughter me if I revealed her age (she's sixty-three). A daughter of the South, she was born with a silver spoon pretty near her mouth but developed fairly quickly into a frustrating disappointment to her high-toned Confederate family. Billie was a socialite rebel. She pretty much ripped it with her aristocratic papa when she showed up at her own cotillion in a pair of riding britches and puffing on a short-stem pipe. It was an offense that she swore—albeit without much vigor—was intended to pay homage to the twin economic pursuits of her dear southern father, namely horse rearing and tobacco farming.

They have a term for this: black sheep.

Billie finished with her hair—it looked exactly the same as before—and turned from the mirror. I had removed my jacket and was rolling up my sleeve to have a look at the elbow.

"Would you like some ice for that elbow? Ice might help, if it's swelling."

"Ice is *why* it's swelling."

Billie's nose twitched like a rabbit's. "Well then, how about some brandy?"

A half hour later, and just after I had salted the sidewalk and the front steps, the friends and relatives of the dead doctor started arriving. We had laid out newspapers beneath the metal coatrack in the front hallway, to catch the runoff. Billie and I were expecting a somewhat smaller than usual turnout on account of the piss-poor weather. My aunt was working the front door. I took up my position near the coffin. I admit, I like to drink in the compliments.

"He looks very nice, Mr. Sewell," the doctor's widow said to me, after spending approximately five seconds gazing down at her husband. Her name was Ann. She had arrived with her husband's brother, along with her daughter and son-in-law, the three of whom immediately set themselves up at the parlor door to start greeting the arriving guests. Ann Kingman was around fifty, short and stocky, a formerly pretty woman gone hard in the eyes and tight around the mouth. She was as heavily made-up as her husband.

"I have your photograph in my office," I told her. "I can give it back to you before you leave."

She gestured vaguely. "Keep it. It's a copy. I have dozens more. We used it for a Christmas card that year."

"It's a very good photo. You have a handsome family."

The woman gave me a frank look. "I know that it is your job to be solicitous, Mr. Sewell. You're very gracious. But if it is all the same to you, I'd feel better if you would drop the effort."

She said all this without a trace of bitterness in her voice. "It's not that I don't appreciate it. I do. But to be honest with you, I'm angry with Richard . . . I know it sounds cold. But the effort of being polite to all the well-wishers tonight is going to exhaust me." She paused to see if I would react. I didn't.

"You and I have a strictly financial relationship," she went on. "And I am officially releasing you from the obligation to tell me that I have a handsome family. The truth is, I have a daughter who hates me and a son who hated his father. Don't let the photograph fool you."

I was tempted to tell her that it hadn't, but I remained silent. She gave me a humorless smile then stepped over to join the daughter who hated her. The son was just arriving. I could see him in the front hallway, shrugging out of his parka.

As expected, the storm did keep the turnout somewhat small, though not as small as I had thought. What with Hopkins being so close, a fair number of the doctor's colleagues did manage to pop in to pay their respects. From what I could tell, the widow was not requesting polite indifference from anyone but me, and was receiving the sympathies of her guests with apparent authenticity. Her smile was weary and sincere;

her occasional laugh was tinged with effort. The daughter, on
the other hand, was a slobbering mess. Her husband was duti-
fully feeding tissues to her from a stash in his jacket pocket.

The son was a little more difficult to read. He was in his
late twenties, slender, pale, sandy-haired. He wore a pair of
wire-rim glasses. I observed that he looked even more like his
mother in real life than he did in the ski-vacation photograph,
right down to the thinly disguised look of scorn that he was
wearing. His indifference to his sniffling sister was remarkable.
After ten minutes or so of meeting and greeting, he broke away
from his family and wandered over to take a look at his father.
As he reached the coffin he pulled his hands out of his pockets, as if suddenly ordered to—for the umpteenth time—by
the imperious old man. His eyes narrowed as he gazed down
at his father. I tensed. If a person is going to do something loud
and embarrassing at a wake, this is where it will usually happen. At the coffin. I had positioned myself against the wall, trying my best to look like a potted plant. Just as the son's face
was collapsing into tears, I was distracted by a commotion
coming from the front hallway. I glanced toward the parlor
doors, and when I looked back, the son was reaching his hand
into the coffin. The commotion from the front was spilling
into the room. I took one step toward the coffin, then the
scream rang out. High and shattering.

Our dead waitress had arrived.

CHAPTER

2

She was folded unceremoniously on the top step. A bloodstain about the circumference of a drink coaster covered her left breast.

The scream had come from the dead doctor's secretary, who had been on her way out. "I just pulled open the door and . . . there she was," the woman said to no one in particular as we all gathered around the open doorway.

Assessments came swiftly.

"She's been shot."

"Stabbed."

"She's dead."

"She might be alive."

As if by an invisible signal, a half dozen doctors suddenly surrounded the woman and confirmed, with a check of her neck and her wrists, that there was indeed no pulse. One of them said, "Let's get her inside," and over the protests of a few who cautioned that we should wait for the police, the woman was lifted by four of the medical professionals and carried inside and laid out on the couch in the front hallway. I went back over to the front door. Before I closed it I peered into the darkness. The various sets of footprints in the slush and snow were—to my eyes—indistinguishable. I saw none that bore the peculiar imprint that said: MURDERER. Maybe if Alcatraz were there he could have put his nose to some use. But I sure as hell wasn't going to get down on my knees and start sniffing. I glanced across the street at St. Teresa's. Their Nativity scene was looking out of place, all those folks dressed for desert climes standing around in snow. A yellow North Star on a pole behind the manger had a bad electrical connection and was flickering erratically. Like Morse code: *S-E-N-D M-Y-R-H-H-!*

The wake was a bust. Everybody was crowded into the front hall, leaving the dead doctor to his own devices. One of his colleagues was kneeling in front of the couch, gingerly lifting the bloodstained front of the dress and peering inside. He meant well, but it was a perverse sight.

"Looks like a bullet wound," he said, confirming the previous guess. "Has anyone called the police?" A half dozen cell phones were suddenly whipped out, but a man off in the corner announced that he had just made the call. He flipped his phone shut and slid it smugly back into his pocket.

The dead doctor's daughter was standing near the couch. She had a grip on her husband's lapels and was weeping into his shirt. Who could blame her? I looked about and found the widow and her son standing near the parlor door. Shock had loosened the poor woman's skin. She looked ten years older. Her brother-in-law stepped over to them. He didn't look too peachy either.

"We've got to get these people out of here," I muttered to Billie.

"The police will want to talk with them, won't they? I think everyone should stay put."

She was right. I looked about to assess the scene. I'm six-three, so I have a decent vantage point for assessing. My instinct was to herd everybody out of the hallway, away from the gruesome new arrival and back into the parlor. But, of course, there was a dead body in there as well. What a mess. I had to take command. The buzz of voices was rising to a din. I hated to do it, but I clapped my hands together loudly, like a school-teacher harnessing an unruly class. The room fell instantly silent. Impressive. The only sound was the continued soft sobbing of the daughter.

"I'm terribly sorry about this, but I'm going to have to ask everybody to hang tight until the police get here. Make your-selves at . . . If you could all please be patient, I'm sure that we'll—" Billie was tugging on my sleeve. She pulled me down to her level and whispered in my ear. Brilliant tactician. I straightened and cleared my throat.

"Would any of you care for a drink?"

A dam of relief burst.

As a certified undertaker and overseer of funerals, I'm deft at crowd control when need be. Aunt Billie had taken the doc-tor's immediate family upstairs to her apartment in order to get them away from the nonsense below. I was bartending and butlering the other guests. Doctors are largely a Scotch and soda crowd, though personally I've never much cared for the perfumey aftertaste of Scotch. I'm a bourbon man. But then, I wasn't drinking.

I had fetched a thin blanket from Billie's linen closet and placed it over the dead waitress. Before I did, I paused and took a long hard look at the woman. I've seen plenty of dead bodies, so it wasn't from morbid fascination that I stared over-long at her. I couldn't place her. She was from none of the restaurants that I frequented in the immediate neighborhood, unless she was brand-new. She had shoulder-length hair, thick and black, which had been gathered up at the back of her head and held there with one of those oversize plastic clips that you can also use to close up a bag of potato chips. With all the jostling she had undergone, the clip was crooked and only holding back a portion of her hair. The loose strands were glued with melted snow against her cheek and her neck. The young woman—I was placing her in her early- to mid-twenties—had high cheekbones, a very distinct widow's peak and a slightly turned-up nose. She was about five-five, probably around a hundred and twenty or so. She had a small scar on her chin, roughly the same as the one I have just below my lip. Mine came from a sledding fiasco in my youth which, next to bicycle mishaps, probably accounts for 90 percent of the tiny scars on the faces of America's men. Of course, I had no idea where the dead waitress got hers.

One more thing: How did I know she was a waitress? Simple. She was wearing a short, pale green dress, a pair of white sneakers and a brown-and-white checked apron with a plastic tag attached that read: HELEN.

The police weren't happy that the body had been moved. The snow still hadn't let up and the impression that the body had left was already vanishing. The first policemen to arrive were a mixed pair: The older one was large and gruff, his partner skinny and sour.

"Why did you move the body?" the older cop asked me, shining his flashlight on the front steps. Only the slightest trace of blood remained.

"It's cold out," I said. "It was still sleeting. She wasn't wearing a coat." I didn't have a good answer.

"The crime scene has been breached," the skinny guy said.

I scratched my head. "How do you know it's a crime scene? Nobody here heard any shots."

A general mumbling of assent from the assembled chorus just inside the door backed me up on this point. The two cops exchanged a look.

"We're going to have to question everyone here," the skinny cop said. "I hope you didn't let anybody leave."

His partner looked past me at the milling guests. "Why are they drinking?"

I shrugged. "It's the holidays."

"No more drinks, please. Gather them up."

While I collected everyone's glasses, the two cops moved inside and took a look at the victim. It seemed like a pretty indifferent look, but I suppose I give some ho-hum once-overs at corpses myself. The skinny cop gestured toward the parlor.

"What's in there?"

"Another body," I told him.

"Man or woman?"

"Man."

"How'd he die?"

"Heart attack."

"When?"

"Not tonight, if that's what you're asking."

"You got some sort of table, Mr. Sewell?" the older cop asked. "And a chair?"

I fetched a card table from upstairs and set it up for him. I rolled in my own chair from my office. Command post. The skinny cop pulled the blanket back down so that the waitress's face was showing, then he had everyone line up and walk slowly past her to take a good hard look at her before then stepping over to the card table to be questioned by his partner. The dead doctor's family was still upstairs with Billie. I decided to wait until all of the guests had been interviewed and allowed to leave—out the side door to avoid further "breaching" of the so-called crime scene—before letting the police know about the others. The two cops were as unhappy with this information as they had been with the body's being moved.

"What are they doing upstairs?" the gruff cop demanded.

I indicated the parlor. "That's their loved one in there. It's been upsetting enough for them even before the arrival of our mystery guest. I was giving them a little peace."

"We have to talk to them too."

"Of course you do."

The gruff cop glared at me. Fetch.

The rest of the investigating unit was arriving, everybody grumbling the same thing about the body having been moved. The person with the yellow crime-scene tape wasn't sure if she should even bother. The photographer took a few pictures of the sidewalk and the front steps then came inside and snapped off a dozen portraits of the waitress. The medical examiner arrived, and after some poking and prodding, announced that the waitress had been dead between two to five hours. "Fresh kill" was how he put it.

I went up to Billie's living room to fetch the dead doctor's family. I led them back downstairs where they each took a turn looking down at the face of the dead woman. No one recognized her.

"Her name is Helen," the skinny cop said. "Does the name Helen mean anything to anyone?"

"Her face launched a thousand ships," the widow said wearily, then turned and went into the parlor to be with her husband. She was joined by her brother-in-law. The daughter detached herself from her husband's arm and stepped over to me. Her eyes were puffy from crying. Even so, I could tell that she had her father's eyes. Unfortunately she had his jaw too. And perhaps even at one point the nose, though I suspected she had had this doctored sometime back. The woman was handsome at best. She wore her straw-colored hair coifed into a perfect bowl. Good skin. Pearl earrings and matching necklace. A well-maintained Guilford housewife. She took my hand—my fingers really—and pinched lightly.

"Thank you for all you've done, Mr. Sewell," she said in a

voice just barely above a whisper. She withdrew her fingers and joined the others in the parlor.

A short, stocky man with yellow hair and the demeanor of a congenial bulldog was coming through the front door. He was wearing a Humphrey Bogart trench coat and a Humphrey Bogart sneer. He stepped directly over to the body. I met him there.

"Dr. Livingstone, I presume?"

Detective John Kruk let out a soft grunt, from which I was able to extract the words, "You again." He was looking down at the woman on the couch.

"Did you know her?"

"I've never seen her before in my life."

"Any idea why she was left here?"

"Well, we're a funeral home. She's dead. Maybe someone was tossing us a bone?"

Detective Kruk looked up at me. "You still a smart aleck, Mr. Sewell?"

"One can never really climb all the way out of the gene pool, Detective."

He grunted again and returned his gaze to the dead waitress. He got down on one knee—a short trip—and pulled the blanket back further, down to the woman's waist. Without taking his eyes off her, he asked me a series of questions.

"Was she on her front or her back when you found her?"

"Her side, actually."

"Left? Right?"

"Right."

"Which way was she facing?"

"Sideways, I guess. Is that what you mean?"

"When you opened the door. Head to the left? The right? Facing the door? What?"

"I see. Um . . . her head was to my left. Her right. That would be, facing south."

"Feet?"

"Excuse me?"

"Her feet. Her legs. Was she in a fetal position or was she stretched out?"

"Like did someone dump her off or lay her down gently?"

"You can't know that. You weren't present. I'm asking what you observed."

Kruk's warm and fuzzy style was all coming back to me now. He had moved the blanket all the way down to her feet and was looking closely at her legs. The cad.

"I'd say somewhere in between fetal and laid out," I said.

Kruk got back to his feet. Aunt Billie had just come into the hallway. A smile blossomed on her face as she came forward.

"It's Sergeant Kruk, isn't it? Why hello."

"Lieutenant. Hello, Mrs. Sewell."

"We meet again. Isn't it terrible? The poor girl. Can I offer you anything to drink, Detective?"

"No. Thank you." Kruk told us that he and his gang would be there another hour or so. "You might as well go on about your business," he said. I stepped over to say my good-byes to the dead doctor's family, who were finally leaving. They all looked terrible. The widow summed it up.

"It's a rotten night all around."

The dead doctor's brother gave me a lousy handshake as they were leaving. He took one final glance back toward the coffin, then joined his family at the door. They left, huddled together like a family of turtles. I watched them disappear into the snow. Forty minutes later the dead waitress was hoisted onto a gurney and taken away. She was being referred to now as "Jane Doe," though it seemed to me that "Helen Doe" would have been—technically—closer to the truth. Kruk's minions began drifting away. I went into the parlor and battened down the hatches on the doctor's coffin. That's when I discovered what the son had been doing when he had reached into the coffin. There on the dead man's chest was a silver dollar. One of the old ones. This one was dated 1902. I had no idea of the significance, but I'm accustomed to people dumping various memorabilia into their loved one's coffins at the last minute. My favorite was a small alarm clock, set to go off every day at four in the morning. Billie and I debated all through breakfast the morning of the funeral whether or not to turn off the alarm. In the end, we left it.

I replaced the silver dollar on the doctor's chest and closed the lid of the coffin, then I shut off the lights and left the doctor to his last night on Earth. Billie was looking tired and I sent her off to bed. "I'll lock up," I told her. Which I did. Then I put on my coat and headed back down the dark street to my place. The wetness had finally gone out of the snowfall. It was down to wind-whipped flurries, silver brush strokes in the gusty night air. And *cold*. God*damn* it was cold.

There was a leggy blond woman in my bed when I climbed the stairs to my place. She had a big, sad, bruised look on her face.

"I hate my goddamn job," she pouted.

I shrugged, getting out of my clothes as quickly as possible. "Oh you know, you win some, you lose some."

I slid between the sheets. The warmth coming off her body was a rapture. She turned to me.

"I didn't just 'lose some,' Hitch. I called for light fucking flurries and lows in the upper twenties. Have you seen it out there? It's a goddamn disaster. I fucking stink."

I love a woman who swears like a sailor. Bonnie Nash rolled into my arms. Fronts collided. High pressure dominated. We were in for a wild one.

CHAPTER

3

The following day was gray and bitter. Greenmount Cemetery was painted in apocalyptic tones. Chalky tombstones angled out of the dingy snow like disordered teeth. Black trees against a gray sky. Low, transparent clouds and a spastic wind slicing hard scars in the air. It was ugly.

Bone cold, with a threat of vultures.

Nobody at the doctor's funeral mentioned the incident of the night before, but it was in everybody's eyes. Huddled together against the cold on the side of a shallow hill, the mourners looked hungover, unfocused and detached. The coffin hovered above the grave, and next to it was a pile of earth, covered with a tarp, too frozen now to shovel into the hole. After the guests left we'd be calling on the cemetery's John Deere.

We zipped through the service and got the hell off that hill. The doctor's brother escorted Ann Kingman to her car, and she never looked back. I declined the post-funeral bash. I usually do.

Bonnie was still there when I got back home. Her disposition hadn't improved much from the night before. She was wearing my white plush bathrobe and standing at the window when I returned. The robe has a curlicue *H* embroidered on the front. On a drunken lark a few years ago I checked into the downtown Hilton for the night. A hundred and twenty-five dollars later, I came away with this robe. I could have snagged one at Sears for half that.

"Looks like a beautiful day," Bonnie sniffed, looking out the window at the unquestionably lousy weather. "What do you think? Sunny and warm? Highs in the low eighties? Oh! Is that a fucking *rainbow* I see over there?"

"Don't be so hard on yourself," I said, giving her a pat on the bumper and a nip to the back of her neck . . . to show that *I* wasn't going to be hard on her. I'm sometimes accused of being patronizing, and I guess I am. But only with people I already like.

Bonnie turned from the window. "I'm a fucking joke in this town. I might as well stand before the camera and tap dance for two minutes."

I stepped into the kitchen to feed Alcatraz. "I didn't know you could tap dance," I called out. I filled my dog's bowl with hard, chunky nuggets, poured in a touch of milk, a half cup of water and mixed the stuff up into an ersatz gravy. I topped it with a garnish of crushed doggie vitamin. Bonnie appeared at the kitchen door. She didn't appear there amused.

"I don't. But I'd probably *predict* that I was going to tap dance and then break into a goddamn Charleston."

Uh-oh. This wasn't going away. I skidded the food bowl across the floor to Alcatraz and took Bonnie by the shoulders. She tried to look away, but I bobbed and weaved and finally got her to lock on.

"Look at me. Read my lips," I said. "Astrolo*gist*. Psycholo*gist*. Meteorolo*gist*. The root word 'gist.' Do you know what that means?"

She shook her head.

"The gist. The general idea. It means 'guess.' Sometimes right, sometimes wrong. The word is imbedded in the profession. You are a prognosticator, not a soothsayer."

Bonnie's big, beautiful blue eyes narrowed. "How much of this are you making up?"

"Nearly all of it."

"God, it almost sounds legit."

"I know. Scary, isn't it."

She smiled. Cold front passed. Crisis over. I asked, "You want to walk the pooch?"

She looked at me with mock suspicion. "Is that something kinky?"

"It could be. But actually it means I've got to take Alcatraz out to pee as soon as he finishes his breakfast. Maybe after we walk the pooch we can come back and walk the pooch. Whatever that turns out to be."

She stepped into the bedroom to change. Alcatraz padded over to sit next to his master and watch. There can be little that is sexier than a woman letting a bathrobe drop from her naked body. You see it in the Bond movies all the time. I turned to my dog and growled. "You and your bladder." He paid me no nevermind.

I made a special effort to not say anything about how godawful cold it was outside. A bastard wind kicked out of the harbor a block away and slapped us in the face the moment we stepped outside. Even Alcatraz tensed. I unleashed my best friend and let him skid around on the ice and snow as he sniffed out locales on which to leave his love letters. Bonnie and I linked arms, as much for the combined body heat as for affection, and picked our way down to the harbor. All was calm, all was gray. The seagulls hovering above the docks were barely distinguishable against the dull sky. A bright red tugboat bobbed in the oily water. Opposite the tug, the Screaming Oyster Saloon—capped with a frosting of ice—clung to the side of the pier like a worn old man about to lose his grip.

Bonnie and I walked along in silence, our only sound the crunch of snow under our feet. The frost from our breathing was like dialogue balloons in a comic strip . . . but without words. I had no idea where her thoughts were. Mine were on the dead waitress. Helen. I could guess where she was by now. Not all that far away, in fact. She would be out of her black body bag, stretched out on a cold aluminum table in the basement of the medical examiner's office over on Penn Street. By now the M.E. would have cracked open her breastbone and opened her up to have a look around. The contents of her stomach would be excavated and various tests run to determine what her last meal had been and when it had been eaten. There were organs to be removed and weighed and, of course, a bullet to be extracted. In my mind's ear I heard the little *ping* as the bullet was dropped onto a metal tray. *Ping.* A far cry from the sound it must have made when it came out of a gun sometime last night and slammed into the woman's chest. A chill spiked my spine.

Alcatraz was enjoying his romp, which featured several four-legged splits—like Bambi on ice—as he trotted about in search of love. I've done a few splits myself in search of love. Who hasn't?

"Everybody loves my father."

I was jerked from my reverie. Bonnie and I hadn't spoken for several minutes. I looked down at her lovely profile.

"*You* love your father," I reminded her.

"But I don't want to *be* him," she said. "I don't want to follow in his footsteps, damn it. It's just so frustrating." She made as if to count off on her fingers, but she was wearing mittens, so it didn't work so well. "One. Everybody loved him, and he's an impossible act to follow. Two. I'm not doing what I want to be doing anyway. Three. I'm not doing it well. In fact, I'm doing it horribly. *Look.*" She spread her arms to take blame for the entire world. "*He* would have called it right."

And there was the rub. Lewis Nash. Bonnie's father had been Baltimore's preeminent television weatherman since before the Stone Ages. The man started back when bow ties were a fashion, not a fad. *That* long ago. You can scour a Boy Scout manual to come up with the adjectives you need for what a loyal, trustworthy, congenial, caring, honest guy Lew Nash was. Baltimore loved Lewis Nash. He had been everybody's favorite uncle.

Bonnie never intended for the weather slot to be anything but a rung on the ladder. She wanted to cover hard news not light flurries. But we live in a patronizing and capitalizing culture and Bonnie Nash is a drop-dead darling of a palomino blonde. Genetically perky face. Bright blue schoolgirl eyes. And a body like Everyman's dream of the perfect stewardess. From the moment the station tried her out at the tender age of twenty—the perky blonde in the pumps and tailored suits— the glass ceiling was immediately lowered into place. The fact that Bonnie couldn't forecast a sneeze in a pepper factory didn't mean a damn thing.

"Everyone wants me to be Daddy's little goddamn girl, Hitch. I'm fucking sick of it."

"Why don't you just quit?" It wasn't the first time I had suggested this.

She snapped right back. "And do what? I'm pigeonholed. I'm Lew Nash's kid. I'm a pair of breasts that tells you what the weather is going to be tomorrow. *Maybe.* And the more I screw that up the less likely I'll ever be taken seriously as a reporter anyway. I'm so fucking *frustrated.*"

She drew up short from her fit and gave me a plaintive look. Bonnie was wearing one of those dead-animal Russian caps. Her cheeks were as red as the tugboat in the harbor behind her, and her lips were quivering.

"We should get back," I said. "You're freezing."

She snapped. "Don't try to change the subject!"

I tried to point out to her—gently—that there was no subject. "Are you trying to make an actual decision here or are you simply lamenting?"

Her expression grew vulnerable. "You're tired of hearing me complain, aren't you? You think I'm just a whiny girl."

"I don't think you're a whiny girl. I think you're a frustrated young woman."

Bonnie came back to me and pretzeled our arms together. Alcatraz was melting some snow over near the Oyster. I tried to whistle to him, but my whistle was frozen. And a clapping of gloves—especially impeded by Bonnie's arms—didn't amount to much either. Bonnie curled her tongue under her teeth and brought forth a piercingly loud whistle. Alcatraz nearly snapped his neck at the sound.

"I didn't know you could do that," I said.

"There's a lot about me you don't know."

I lowered my nose into the dead Russian animal. Bonnie squeezed my arm. Unfortunately, this was all the foreplay we could afford. A noon whistle from across the harbor pierced the air. My Bonnie lass had to get back to work.

Just before we got back to my place I told Bonnie about the events of the previous evening. I suppose it might seem peculiar that the fact of a dead waitress being dropped at my front door hadn't been the first thing I blurted out when I got home the night before, but you can blame Bonnie's loving embrace for that.

Bonnie's mouth dropped open. "You're kidding. She'd been *shot*?"

"I don't think she was shot there. I think someone brought her there and dropped her off."

Bonnie's eyes were as wide as saucers. "Absolutely. The murderer! That's who dropped her off! Oh my God. Do the police have any leads?"

"I can't say. As of last night all they knew was that she was a waitress named Helen."

"Do they know what restaurant?"

"Her name tag didn't say. They've probably figured it out by now though."

Alcatraz was across the street at a mailbox, nosing around. Bonnie was practically beside herself.

"Hitch! We've got to find out what restaurant she worked at. And what shift she was working yesterday. Or last night. We've got to find out her name!"

"Her name is Helen. I told you that."

"Helen *who*? Helen from *where*? Hitch, for God's sake, a murder victim was dumped off at your fucking *door* last night. We have to investigate!"

We had reached my place. I've got a narrow formstone house in the middle of a row of narrow formstone rowhouses. Sewell & Sons is at the far end of the block. It's a great commute.

"The police are investigating," I reminded her.

Bonnie looked at me like I had four ears. "Screw the police! Aren't you *curious*? I mean, she was dropped off at your goddamn door! What did she look like?"

I gave a cursory description.

"Was she pretty?"

"She was dead."

"Don't hide behind that. You're an expert in dead people. You know if she was pretty."

"She appeared to have been a nice looking woman."

"Hitch. I want to solve this murder. I want this more than anything. This is a golden opportunity. I want to find out who killed that woman."

"But—"

"I want you to help me. Please. Do this. I want you to go inside right now and write down everything you can remember from the moment the body was discovered. Everything. Every detail."

"Aren't you getting just a little too excited at the expense of a murder victim?"

Her eyes flashed. "Yes!"

I guess you couldn't fault her for honesty.

Now who knows. Maybe it would have all ended in another minute or two. Flared up and sizzled out. But just then the Fates, the Muddling Chessmen, the old S.I.B. (Supreme Ironical Being) himself, stepped in. In the guise of a dog. My dog. Alcatraz trotted over to us and Bonnie bent down to see what he was carrying in his slobbery chops. She took what appeared to be a small pad of paper from Alcatraz's mouth. She straightened and waved it triumphantly in my face.

"Oh Hitch. How can you say no?"

It was an order pad. The kind a restaurant uses.

I pictured the woman curled up dead on my doorstep.

I said yes.

Helen Waggoner was a month shy of her twenty-sixth birthday when she was killed. She had worked at a place called Sinbad's Cave, which was a restaurant lounge out by the airport. She had lived in the Woodlawn section and "had attended" Northern High School. No mention of having graduated. She was survived by a sister and a three-year-old son. No husband.

I hadn't gleaned any of this information from sleuthing; I got it from the *Baltimore Sun*. City Section. Front page, below the fold.

MURDERED WAITRESS FOUND
ON FUNERAL HOME STEPS
by Jay Adams

The story continued on page B9, alongside an article about a man biting a dog. No lie. The dog was pictured. A German shepherd named Rosie. Rosie was up for adoption and had already received over two dozen offers. The SPCA was sifting through the calls. The man was not pictured.

Neither was Helen Waggoner.

I handed the paper to Billie. "Do you want to see your name in print?"

We were in Billie's kitchen. It was two days after the unexplained drop-off. Jay Adams, the *Sun* reporter, had been out the day before and had spoken with Billie. I had met him as he was leaving. A delicate looking fellow with olive skin and jet black hair slicked back in large comb grooves, he didn't look so much like an Adams as maybe an Adamapadopolis, but anything's possible in this great melting pot of ours. Jay Adams had wanted to know if I would talk to him about the dead waitress, and I told him no thanks. I trusted that Billie had given him the pertinent details.

"Do you have any idea why she was dumped off here?" His notebook was open. His pen was poised.

"Nope."

"And you've never seen her before? You don't know her?"

"Nope."

"Have you ever been to Sinbad's Cave?"

"Nope."

"So you have nothing to add to the story."

"Nope."

He had flipped his notebook closed with a prissy snap.

"Did you see this about the dog?" Billie folded the paper in half. She looked over at Alcatraz in the corner. He was curled up in his tail-chasing posture, dreaming doggie dreams. "Do you think Alcatraz would like a friend?"

"He has a friend. Me. Dog's best friend."

"I mean Rosie."

"I know you do. And no. Alcatraz likes the spotlight. He wouldn't want to share it. Especially with a dog that has had her picture in the paper."

Billie was wearing a thin flannel robe and a pair of those old fuzzy slippers that used to be so popular. Maybe they still are. Hers were pink. Alcatraz had a pair as well, handed down from his godmother Billie. His *used* to be pink. If I ever want to hear my dog's primal growl I simply insert one of those slippers between his teeth. Never fails.

"The article says here that you had no comment," Billie said. She looked up from the paper. "That sounds a tad sinister."

I shrugged. "I had nothing to add." I'm sure that Jay Adams would simply say that he was being thorough in adding that fact that "Hitchcock Sewell, co-proprieter of the funeral home where the body was delivered, had no comment." But I suspected he was also taking a little jab at me for my chorus of nopes.

"I'm still not comfortable with our conducting this poor girl's funeral," Billie said. "It smacks of opportunism. It feels disrespectful somehow. Am I just being batty?"

I looked across the table at the woman in the flannel robe and pink fuzzy slippers, dipping a Bordeaux cookie into her rum-laced tea. Batty? Come, come.

I reminded her, "We didn't lobby for the job. It was Kruk's idea. The sister went along."

"Do you really think that the killer is going to be so foolish as to show up? Isn't your detective friend asking for a bit much?"

"When did he become my detective friend?"

She ignored me. "If you killed someone, would you show up at their funeral?"

"Kruk is figuring it a couple of ways. If Helen Waggoner knew her killer well, then he or she *has* to show up. Their absence would put the spotlight right on them. That's one thought. Another thought is that whoever did it took the effort to bring the body to a funeral home, which would possibly suggest some level of compassion."

"Not killing her in the first place would suggest some level of compassion."

"Okay then. Remorse. Maybe something got out of hand, and the next thing you know someone shot her who really hadn't intended to and then freaked out. I can buy the argument that a person with a guilty conscience would at least deliver the body to a funeral home. It doesn't exactly make up for them killing the person. But it's a gesture."

Billie made a gesture herself. Of dismissal. "They could turn themselves in."

"Sure. And they still might. That's also part of Kruk's thinking. Hold the funeral right where the killer dropped off the body, and maybe the killer will show up. Maybe he'll attend the funeral and then turn himself in."

Billie nibbled at her Bordeaux. "I hope we don't have a drama right in the middle of the service." She picked up her teacup. "Shall we play for it?"

I shook my head. I had already been thinking about this. "I'll do it."

Billie's cup was raised to her lips. She held it there and eyed me over its rim. "Oh?"

"Yes. Oh."

"As you wish."

As a rule, Billie and I play a round of cribbage to determine which of us is going to prep the cadaver and be the front man for the funeral. Not always. Sometimes we have back-to-back-to-backs, and we simply divvy things up equitably and that's that. But otherwise, we play for it. Billie taught me cribbage after my parents were hit by the beer truck and I had moved in to be raised by her and ugly Uncle Stu. She's a good player and a good teacher. And I'm a good learner, so we're pretty even. I've scoured antique shops all over the city and have come up with over a dozen different cribbage boards that I've presented to my aunt over the years. There's one in the shape of a figure-eight, one with mother-of-pearl inlay, a triangular one with a large glass eye embossed in the center and a fairly rustic one fashioned out of gouged domino pieces, built by a blind auctioneer from Ellicott City. My best find was a board that is actually a full-size coffee table. Teak. Rivets of rhinestone (six hundred and seventy-one; I counted them once during a deep and relentless funk). The actual board within the table is sort of paisley-shaped, like the inside curl of a conch shell. The table's legs are rippled and they taper to near-stiletto points, capped in red glass. Goddamn thing set me back eight hundred dollars and is as gaudy as Liberace's Steinway, but I couldn't pass it up. Billie calls it Milton, after Milton Berle. Billie names a lot of her possessions. The mirror in her bedroom is Clark. She has a favorite armchair named Hecuba. Her phone is George.

Billie set her teacup back down on its saucer. Lo and behold, George rang. Billie got up and took the call. It was a short call. She returned to the table and dropped heavily into her chair. She picked up her teacup and intoned exactly like Boris Karloff, "The body arrives at noon."

My ex-wife was being hung in Druid Hill Park, and I had promised to come watch. This might sound like the gloating of a vindictive ex-husband, but that just goes to show how slimy our perceptions can be.

Julia is a painter. She is wildly popular in all sorts of concentric circles, not only in Baltimore but also in New York and Los Angeles and—peculiarly—in Scandinavia, where, in certain pockets, she has achieved the sort of ill-proportioned cult status that Jerry Lewis enjoys all over France. The brooding suicidal masses just seem to love her. Julia wings off to Stockholm, Oslo or Copenhagen at least once a year to bask in the blond, blue-eyed spotlight. It's something akin to taking the waters, though in her case with a lot of sex thrown in. Julia has a lover in every Scandinavian port. "My Swede. My Dane. My

Norwood." She returns from these jaunts refreshed and ener-
gized and always with a colossal appetite. Still, no amount of
gorging in Baltimore's finest restaurants or lowliest hash
houses seems to have any effect on Julia's salamander figure.
Suss out what it is Audrey Hepburn's got that Sophia Loren
ain't got, and then vice versa. Mix in a little Irish and a faint
strain of Cherokee blood, pour it all into a long shapely
beaker . . . and then step back, Jack.

Julia's hair is coal black. Today it was cut in short spikes
and she was wearing a sixties era Carnaby Street cap. The rest
of her ensemble was like something out of the Beatles's *Yellow
Submarine* cartoon, only on Julia the god-awful polka dots and
bell-bottoms looked just swell. She was, as usual, barefoot.
Luckily for her we were inside.

"Oh Hitch, I'm really glad you could make it." Julia's eyes
were made up like a B-movie scream queen. And *still* she
looked gorgeous.

"I always like to support your little hobby."

Without their ever closing, she batted her eyes at me.
"Sweet man. I'll have to remember to drop by one of your little
funerals sometime soon. It's been a while."

Julia had been commissioned to paint a canvas for the new
visitors center at the Baltimore Zoo. The zoo had fallen into
neglect back in the late seventies and eighties but as part of the
city's trumpeted resurgence has since received several
facelifts. The new visitors center was one of them, and Julia
had been tapped to add her two cents to the look of the place.
She was paid ten thousand dollars for her two cents, which is a
dizzying return on the dollar if you think about it.

Julia had painted a huge triptych. Three separate canvases
to be hung side-by-side-by-side up on the visitors center's dom-
inant wall. Along with an array of shapes and colors that play-
fully suggested a menagerie of animals in near-Biblical
harmony, each canvas featured in the foreground a portion of

a hippopotamus in profile, trotting. Front, middle and rear. Julia's conceit was that the canvases were to be rotated monthly so that only occasionally would they actually line up in the logical order of the trotting hippo. On any random month the hippo's face might be staring at it's own tail or it's midsection. Or the rear end might be trotting right out of the scene.

Today, for the unveiling, all three sections were lined up in order. A reception of finger foods and champagne was underway when I arrived. The new visitors' center features huge glass walls all around, one of which looks out onto a dirt pen where the deer and the antelope play. A curious antelope stood at the glass throughout the reception, staring in with its yellow eyes.

I took a flute of champagne from an expressionless young girl and mingled. It's wonderful how many people have time on their hands in the middle of the day to attend these sorts of events. I'm so glad I'm one of them. The crowd was a mix of zoo officials—the board, the staff, etc.—some financial bigwigs and people from the mayor's office. The mayor himself was home with the flu, but he was being represented by his culture czarina, a hawkish woman who stood well over six feet tall and whose face revealed not a tendril of animation. She spoke with aristocratic lockjaw when she stepped to the podium beneath Julia's canvases and read her spiel. Julia stood demurely behind her and off to the left. She caught my eye once and giggled. The hawk droned on nasally about the zoo and the city and the world. She couldn't seem to find much to say about Julia's paintings except—at the end of her spiel—to elevate a mannish hand in their direction and call them "nice paintings." It sounded like nice *kitties.*

I offered Julia a ride home after the affair. Julia doesn't own a car. She takes taxis or is otherwise squired about. All the drivers at Jimmy's Cabs know her. I told her I had to swing by the police station on my way home. I had phoned Detective Kruk the day before, after Alcatraz had found the restaurant order pad. Bonnie and I figured that it had likely belonged to Helen Waggoner and that it must have fallen from her apron pocket when she was being delivered to the funeral home. Kruk had merely sighed heavily into the phone when I told him that my dog had fetched the pad from underneath a mailbox on the street.

"You're telling me it's been moved from where it was located, right?"

"That's right."

"Just like the body. Do you do this on purpose, Mr. Sewell? Just to drive me crazy?"

"It was my dog," I reminded him.

"Dogs can be taught," he said. Whatever that was supposed to mean.

Julia was giving the inside of my car the once-over. She was wrapped in an ankle-length leather coat. She wasn't barefoot now but wore a pair of Army boots.

"You must have the most boring car in America," Julia said as we took the North Avenue exit off the beltway.

"I don't believe in one's car as an extension of who they are," I answered her.

"I can see that."

A car in front of me braked suddenly. I jerked the wheel of my Chevy Nothing and hit the brakes. We skidded on an ice patch and slid deftly past the stopped car at a diagonal. I let off the brake and hit the gas and we shot through the intersection a full five inches in front of a slowly skidding city bus. Julia laughed.

"But it's got your moves."

I pulled the order pad out of my pocket and tossed it onto her lap.

"Does this belong to your dead girl?" she asked.

"I don't know. It seems likely."

Julia squinted at the pad. "Turkey club. Cobb salad. Some sort of soup."

"I think it's split pea," I said. Actually it was Bonnie who had made the deduction.

"Was she pretty, your dead waitress?"

"Everyone keeps asking me that. Why is that?"

"Oh Hitch, come on. Everyone cares more about a pretty corpse than a plain one. Don't be coy."

"You'll be a beautiful corpse one day, Julia," I said, sliding gently through a yellow light.

"Thank you, Hitch. That's sweet." She looked down again at the order pad in her hand. "Shot in the heart, isn't that what you said?"

"Yes."

"That could be symbolic, couldn't it? It could point toward a lover."

"Or just someone with smart aim."

Julia looked over at me. "You disappoint me, Hitch. You used to be more of a romantic. A girl gets shot directly in the heart, and you want to go out looking for a sharpshooter. Are you getting to be a pragmatist in your old age?"

"I'm thirty-four."

"Bad habits now can be difficult to shake later, you know."

"Not to worry. I plan to get all my pragmatism out of the way as quickly as I can. When the time comes, I wouldn't want anything to get in the way of the full blossoming of my senility."

Julia leaned her head against the window. "I'm just kidding about your not being a romantic, you know. I see behind your curtain."

"Sweetie pie, you have a backstage pass. You always will."

She looked over at me and grinned. "Ditto, dodo." She waved the order pad in the air. "So. Pretty? Good enough to shoot?"

I nodded. "Pretty."

"And right on your doorstep. Mr. Sewell, you are some kind of magnet."

"They do sort of flock to me, don't they."

Julia tossed the pad onto the tilted dashboard. It slid to the floor.

"You don't even have a real dashboard. It's a marvel I ever married you, isn't it?"

"Real men have dashboards?"

"Please. There aren't any real men. Just fantastic boys."

I turned left on Charles Street. The snow had been plowed off to the sides of the road burying the cars that were parked there. The road surface was scarred with salt, like Jackson Pollock with a box of chalk. Julia's head was resting against the window.

"I could use some sex. Are you still seeing that weather girl?"

"Yes I am."

"And you're faithful, even though it's just a fling?"

"Who said it was just a fling?"

"I did. So you're still a serial monogamist, I assume?"

"Sorry to disappoint you."

"No you're not."

Kruk wasn't in, so I left the order pad with the cop at the front desk.

"What's this?" he asked.

"It's possible evidence in a murder case," I said.

The officer frowned. "Why isn't it bagged?"

Helen Waggoner was waiting for me when I got back. So was a little piece of information provided by the medical examiner.

"She was pregnant," Aunt Billie whispered to me as I was taking off my coat.

"Pregnant?"

"Yes," Billie whispered. "Two months. It was discovered during the autopsy."

"Billie, why are we whispering?"

The answer rose from the couch. The same couch where two nights before we had laid out Helen Waggoner. Billie cleared her throat.

"This is Helen's sister."

If I said that the woman was a dead ringer for her sister, I might be accused of making a cheap joke and, for that matter, getting it wrong. She wasn't. But she was close. Same widow's peak. Same general shape of the face. Same nose. Of course, she was alive, which put more color in her cheeks. She had a small birthmark, or maybe it was a tiny mole, on the side of her nose, a little blueish blemish, vaguely star-shaped—up near her left eye. Like her sister, she was full-figured. Of the two, this one was probably the slightly more *zaftig*, though "Rubenesque," I suppose, is the more accurate description. Or, as we simple folk say, "built." I sensed the promise of an alabaster cello beneath her highly touchable wool sweater and simple brown skirt as she moved forward to shake my hand.

"Mr. Sewell? I'm Vickie Waggoner."

She squeezed off a smile of sorts as she took my hand. It appeared to take all the energy she could muster. Vickie Waggoner's hair was lighter than her sister's, a sort of bronzy brunette that fell without much fanfare to just above her shoulders. Her lips were painted a ruby red. Her large green eyes faltered as she released my hand. The difficult smile drained away.

"And this is Bo."

A three-foot tall human appeared from behind her. Blond bangs. Red corduroys. The little boy wore a politely blank expression, tinged with uncertainty. I squatted down on my haunches as Vickie Waggoner added, "Bo is Helen's son."

"Hello, Bo. My name is Hitchcock. That's a funny name, isn't it."

"My mommy's dead," the boy said.

"I know that. I'm very sorry."

"She's getting married tomorrow."

"Oh?"

I glanced up at the sister. Vickie Waggoner was mouthing the word *buried* even as the tears started down her face.

Bonnie was running through her weather routine. "Now, moving to the latest satellite pictures, we see . . ."

Sally pointed the remote and turned up the volume on the television set mounted up over the bar. "Let's see what sort of fantasy your girlfriend has in store for us this time." She turned to me with a chuckle. There isn't a mean bone in the woman's gargantuan body. Sally is my ex–mother-in-law. Julia's mom. She loves me both like a mother and like a shrewd barkeep who cherishes her paying regulars. On the television, Bonnie was calling for "a clear and cold night." Sally sang out, "Heat wave!" then whooped like a crane.

Forty minutes later, Bonnie came into the bar. "Nice to see you, Miss Nash," Sally said to her as she was shrugging out of her coat. "What'll it be?" Bonnie ordered a draught. Sally's eyes twinkled as she pulled back the sticks. "Here you go, hon. Clear and cold."

Bonnie and I took a table near the back. There was a couple off in the corner making out and another two tables away, arguing vehemently. Ah, the humanity.

"I wish I had been there for the questioning."

Bonnie ran a lacquered fingernail around the rim of her glass. I reminded her that it hadn't been a "questioning."

"She came by to view her sister."

"You didn't let the little boy see his mother like that, did you?"

"Of course not."

"That's good. How old is the tyke, anyway?"

"Around three."

"Poor kid. So what did you learn from the sister? Did she have any idea who might have killed Helen?"

"She didn't really say much on the subject."

"So what did you two talk about?" Bonnie cocked an eyebrow. "The weather?"

I gave Bonnie the gist of what I had picked up from Vickie Waggoner. Helen Waggoner was the younger of the two sisters, by about two years. Half sisters actually. Different fathers, both absent. Their mother had been, among other things, a dancer, though not of the Martha Graham variety. Ruth Waggoner's résumé read like a tourist map of The Block, which is the three to four block section of Baltimore Street that in its bygone heyday had been the city's vibrant and naughty little strip of topless joints and vaudeville fun clubs, but which has since withered to . . . well, in fact, a block. And a dreary one at that. A mere shadow of its former bump and grind. Ruth Waggoner, as I gathered from her surviving daughter's terse account, had danced during the decline. Gone down with the ship and then finally bailed, forced to take her trade around to any number of the windowless booze joints around Charm City. The tiny runways. The disco balls. The ubiquitous metal pole. Vickie Waggoner hadn't gone into any great detail about any of this and, more than once, stopped herself to mutter an apology to me for even going into it at all. She told me that her mother had died just this past summer, a washed up stripper, eaten away by cancer at the age of fifty-six. I gathered from the way she talked about her that Vickie Waggoner had not had a whole lot to do with her mother for quite a number of years. But death can leave a hole where a person once stood, and sometimes the ones who have been left behind find the need to pour the details of the person's life back into it. That's what Vickie Waggoner had been doing. And now on top of this, her sister. Vickie Waggoner had *two* holes opening up in front of her. She had stood next to me down in the basement, staring at the drained face of her murdered sister and speaking in a low monotone not so much about Helen, but about the woman who had brought her sister into the world. My take was that she wasn't anywhere near ready to make sense of her sister's death. Not until she had tackled the unfinished business of putting her mother to rest.

"She blames the mother," I said to Bonnie, taking a sip of my beer. "She just kept coming back to the mother. How the woman dragged the two girls from club to club. How there was always a strange man at the breakfast table. Or sometimes no man, just a bruised look on her mother's face and a very, very short fuse. I wasn't exactly hearing 'happy childhood.' "

"Fine. We've all got parents," Bonnie said. "But that's ancient history. What's any of that have to do with her sister getting murdered?"

I shrugged. "Nothing. People tend to ramble when they come into a funeral home. This one had a lot to unload."

"But it sounds like she didn't unload much about her sister. Did she have any guesses why someone would shoot Helen?"

"If she did, she didn't tell them to me."

Bonnie was tapping her fingernail on the rim of her glass. "What about the boy's father?"

"What about him? He seems to be out of the picture."

"You asked?"

"That's a quote."

"Well, maybe it was him," Bonnie said. "Maybe he came back into the picture, and he found out that Helen was pregnant again. Maybe it rubbed him the wrong way. Men can get weird. I've seen it."

"Maybe the second kid was his too and *that* rubbed him the wrong way."

Bonnie sneered at me over her glass. "And so he killed her. Only a man would come up with that."

I shrugged. "It's a wacky world, Wanda."

"Poor kid, huh?"

"He's too young to understand what's going on," I said. "It'll hit him later." Like a meteorite.

Bonnie reached across the table and set her hand atop mine. "Okay then. So the killer could possibly be the father of the little boy, or whoever it was who got Helen pregnant. That would be two suspects right off the bat. So come on, Hitch, did the sister say *anything* about Helen that might give us a clue?"

"I got the sense that she really didn't have much to do with her sister. In fact, I'd guess that as soon as she could, Vickie Waggoner hightailed it away from her little family altogether. She didn't come right out and say it, but I got the sense that Helen's dying young has come as no great surprise to her."

"So that's the eulogy."

I shrugged. "That's the eulogy."

Bonnie finished off her beer and set the glass down on the table slowly, like a spacecraft coming in for a soft landing. Her soft face molded into a question mark.

"Hitch? What do you think of me?"

My gears didn't even grind; they simply sheared right off. "Um. Could you narrow the scope a little?"

"Sure. What do you think of me? Do you think I'm being silly about wanting to solve this murder? Do you think I'm just trying to prove something?"

"You're trying to prove that you can investigate a story," I said, picking my words carefully.

Bonnie smirked. "Very diplomatic. But come on, Hitch. Level with me. You know I'm tougher than I look. Is there a part of you that sees a blond bimbo who's throwing a hissy fit because everybody is patting her on the head and calling her a good little weather girl?"

I didn't think this was the time to point out that people weren't exactly calling her a *good* little weather girl. "You've got a chip on your shoulder. I don't blame you for that."

"I'm too cute," she said sourly.

I held my palms up to the ceiling. "You're too cute. It's a hell of an albatross, but there it is."

Bonnie skidded her chair away from the table. "We'll see about that." She stood up. "Come on."

"Where are we going?"

"You'll see."

As we headed out of the bar, a fat guy by the jukebox called out, "What's the weather, honey?"

Bonnie snapped back, "Screw you, dirtbag!" She turned to me. "Cute, huh?"

Bonnie and I took the Baltimore-Washington Parkway south to the airport exit. A long time ago the airport went by the name Friendship Airport. It was ten times smaller then, as was the world it serviced. As things developed, the demands of the hemorrhaging population along the Baltimore-Washington corridor required that little old Friendship be swallowed by a gigantic glass and girder terminal along with a whole new pinwheel of departure and arrival gates, the entire affair given a snappy new name: Baltimore-Washington International Airport. BWI to most. "Bweee!" to a few.

Bonnie and I followed the airport tradition of misreading

the signs on our first pass, and we found ourselves cruising by the passenger pickup area not once, but twice. At this hour it was pretty much empty. We read the traffic signs out loud this time, pointed left and right and finally took an exit that swung along past the commercial hangers and out onto a frontage road. Once we had passed the Ramada, the Marriott and the Airport Sheraton, things took a turn for the dingy, and we pulled up in front of a motel that time had forgotten. The Charm Inn appeared to have started life as a Holiday Inn, back in the days when their wedge-shaped signs were as ubiquitous as the golden arches. Now the word "Holiday" had been replaced with the big fib, "Charm." The rooms were laid out in a two-story, single horizontal strip looking out onto a parking lot and a metal fence-enclosed swimming pool that was covered with a tarp for the winter. Or possibly forever. The curtains in all the rooms were pulled shut. The fluorescent light on an ice machine was blinking spasmodically.

"Lovely. I'll have to remember this place the next time I'm contemplating suicide."

Some thirty feet to the left of the motel—sharing its parking lot—was a rectangular, windowless stucco cube, trimmed with brown plastic shingling and landscaped with dead dwarf shrubbery. A yellow spotlit sign on the side facing the frontage road read SINBAD'S CAVE, painfully spelled out in letters resembling sabers. Below this the sign promised "Music, Dining, Entertainment."

"Are you ready for Señor Sinbad?" I asked.

Bonnie was smearing off most of her makeup. She gobs it on for television. She found an Orioles cap in my glove compartment and put it on, tucking her hair in it as best she could. She pulled up the collar on her Burberry coat and popped a piece of gum into her mouth. She gave me a thumbs-up.

"Let's do it."

If I were expecting a motif—some sort of Arabian pirate

decor—I was disappointed. Sinbad's Cave looked like any other uninspired restaurant lounge out on any other airport's frontage road. Dim lighting. Drop ceiling. Several dozen tables on the main floor, half as many in the small, elevated section to the left as you walked in. The bar ran along the far wall, lit in ugly amber lighting. Muffled music pulsed from a jukebox.

"Up or down?"

Bonnie chose up. "The view." For what it's worth.

We took a table at the railing. At the far end of the main floor stood an electric piano, a pair of amplifiers and an empty stool with an acoustic guitar propped up against it. I pointed this out to Bonnie.

"You know those old movies where the couple go to the nightclub in New York or Los Angeles and sit at their table and watch the floor show?"

"Yes."

"I think this is going to come up short."

The place was half empty. Or half full. Depending on your mood. Here and there I spotted some locals, some big-haired gals, some Budweiser boys. But primarily the clientele appeared to be businessmen, out-of-towners from the nearby Ramada and Marriot and . . . shudder, Charm Inn. Loud talking and loud laughing is a big part of the game when businessmen get together to unwind on the company's expense account, as is the clinking of glasses and a never-ending spiral of meaningless toasts. Plenty of this was going on. A beefy fellow at one of the tables was giddily stacking a pyramid of empty glasses to the forced amusement of the poor man's Ivana Trump who was clinging to his shoulder. A few tables over a triad of business buddies were swapping war stories at a fever pitch. A mute redhead packed into a tight paisley dress was seated at the table, patiently tracing circles with her fingernail around the rim of her glass. I watched as one of the waitresses—

dressed exactly as Helen Waggoner had been dressed the night she was dumped off at my door—lingered over at the bar to chat up two salesman types. One of them told a joke. Funny or not, all three laughed.

I turned to Bonnie, whose eyes were also darting everywhere at once, and asked, "Do you see it?"

She nodded. "Meat Market. The people here are way too pumped up."

Tucked into practically every other table being occupied by these garrulous minions of industry was at least one woman who didn't quite look like she belonged. Or rather, *did* look like she belonged. They were easy to spot. The large, false laugh. The long steady stare. The touchy-feely . . .

Our waitress came over to take our order. She too was dressed exactly like Helen Waggoner had been the other night. The similarity ended there. She had bad skin, a round flat face, steel-wool hair and a boxy figure. Apparently she had some dust in one of her contact lenses. Her mouth hung open as she stood poking her finger into her eye. She looked like the village idiot. Her name tag identified her as "Gail."

"Something to drink?" *Poke. Poke.*

I ordered a whiskey. So did Bonnie. I realized I was hungry, so I also ordered a grilled cheese with bacon and an order of fries. Bonnie ordered a salad. Gail wrote down our order and left. She was still poking her eye.

"Your heart's going to love you in about ten years," Bonnie said.

When Gail brought our drinks, her gaze snagged on Bonnie.

"I know you. You look familiar." She was flattening her empty tray against her breasts and rocking slightly. Bonnie tugged on her cap, avoiding eye contact.

"I don't think so."

"Yes I do! You're the one does the weather on TV, aren'tcha? Wow."

Bonnie conceded that she was.

"Wow! That's cool. Were you like, on TV tonight and all?"

"I was."

"Cool."

Gail continued to stand there, hugging her tray and staring at Bonnie as if this was her brand-new occupation. The waitress was probably around the same age as Bonnie—twenty-five—which was both a sad and frightening thought. Bonnie made a silent appeal to me from beneath the Orioles cap. I downed my whiskey in a single burning gulp. Ouch. House brand. Sinbad's finest rot. I held my empty up to the hypnotized girl.

"Gail, how about another whiskey. And could you make this one a Wild Turkey? For that matter . . ." I reached over and slid Bonnie's untouched drink to the edge of the table. "How about we upgrade Miss Nash while we're at it?"

"Sure." Gail scooped up our glasses and set them on her tray. "Two Turkeys," she said, then left. I cocked an eyebrow at Bonnie.

We went back to scanning the room. I spotted four other waitresses, all dressed like Helen. It was a little creepy. The waitresses each wore nylon fanny packs, in this case used as money belts, to make change right at the tables. I pointed this out to Bonnie.

"Helen wasn't wearing a money belt when we found her."

"I hardly think somebody killed her for a handful of cash. Those things can't carry all that much."

I agreed. Whoever killed her might have grabbed the money belt because it was there, but that certainly couldn't have been the motive. At least I hoped not. I looked about the room again. I've always heard that after the first or second business trip, the luster evaporates. It all becomes TV at the bar or cable in the room . . . long-distance calls back home and an early night with a John Grisham. Apparently though, for the more lusty and indiscriminate, it is also places like Sinbad's Cave with its low lights and working gals. I had no doubt that for all the smiles and coos going on down there on the floor, these were strictly business propositions being conducted under the amber lights. Supply and demand was clearly in supply and demand.

Bonnie was right on my wavelength. "Do you think Helen was turning tricks?" she asked.

"That's what I was just thinking. It's certainly possible."

"You know that saying, about the fruit not having far to fall?"

"You're thinking about the mother."

Bonnie shrugged. "I don't want to stereotype."

"I don't know why not. It's more useful than people like to admit. Helen Waggoner certainly didn't grow up behind a white picket fence. This place might be tame by comparison to some of her mother's job sites . . . but it's still got a nice veneer of sleaze happening. Maybe we should ask our lovely waitress."

Gail was returning with our drinks. She set them down on the table.

"No charge for the first ones. I took care of that." She smiled hugely, revealing quite a set of Chiclets.

Bonnie cleared her throat. "Listen, Gail. Would you mind if we asked you a few questions?"

"Sure. About what?"

"About Helen Waggoner."

Gail's pan-shaped face seemed to sag at the mention of the dead waitress's name. Her voice dropped. "Ain't that horrible?"

"Did you know Helen?" I asked.

Gail was hugging the tray with both arms now. "I'm pretty new here, actually. I've only been here a couple months. My uncle got me this job. He knows the owner. I live in Catonsville. So it's not too far to come in."

Bonnie pressed. "Helen?"

"I mainly work afternoons. Helen was on at night. They haven't replaced her yet, so they asked if any of us who work days could do some extra shifts. I'm going to college at night, but I told them I could do a couple. I could use the money."

I asked, "Do you like it here, Gail? Is it a good place to work?"

Gail glanced in the direction of the bar before leaning forward to answer. "Not really," she said in a loud whisper. "I don't fit in too good."

"What do you mean?"

She glanced quickly around the room again. "I just don't. It's different working nights. I don't think my uncle's ever been in here. I mean, at night. It's *different*."

"Were you here the other night, Gail?" Bonnie asked. "When Helen . . . on Helen's last night?"

"You know, I was here. I was subbing for Tracy. That's a friend of Helen's who works here too. She called in sick I think."

"What exactly did you see? Did you see anything suspicious?"

"I told all this to the police already. I didn't see anything. Nobody did." Gail shifted her weight and squinted in the direction of the bar. "Helen was down on the floor taking an order. Table six. Someone called her. On the phone. Ed took the call. Ed was the bartender that night. It wasn't even like five seconds and Helen threw down the phone and just ran right out the door. Didn't stop to put on her coat or nothing. And it was cold that night. That was the big storm." Gail gave Bonnie a knowing look. "You know that storm."

Bonnie offered a steel smile. "I know it."

"So nobody saw or heard what it was that made Helen go outside like that?" I asked. "She just took a call and off she went?"

"That's what happened."

I pressed. "Do you have any guesses at all, Gail? Did you remember seeing any strange customers? Someone who might have been harassing Helen?"

"No."

Bonnie jumped in. "Did Helen have anything going with any of her customers, Gail? Did you see anything like that? Maybe she rubbed one of these guys the wrong way?"

"I don't know if Helen was involved with anyone like that. Like I said, I mainly work days. It's . . . it's a lot different here in the days. You know? We get a lunch crowd and that's about it." She looked nervously over toward the bar. Her voice lowered. "This isn't a lunch crowd."

No, I thought. But they do have an appetite.

"Did Helen ever talk about her personal life?" Bonnie asked.

"Not with me. We didn't talk much, the couple times we were on the same shift. Though . . ." she trailed off.

"Though what?"

"Well . . . I do know she was talking about quitting."

"Quitting her job?" Bonnie gave me a look across the table.

"Yeah," Gail said. "I remember once I was here, about a month ago, when she *really* went off about it. She got all hot and was telling everyone she was going to quit. Said she didn't need this place anymore. Stuff like that. I remember, because she got into a big fight that night, with one of the customers. That was when she really started on about quitting."

Bonnie perked up. "What kind of fight?"

"You know. An argument."

"Do you have any idea what they were arguing about, Gail?"

Gail hugged the tray tighter against her breast. "Not word for word or nothing. But . . . I mean, I don't know exactly. I didn't hear them."

"Gail, was he trying to pick her up?" Bonnie asked. "Is that what they were arguing about?"

Gail remained tight-lipped. "I don't know."

I asked, "This guy, have you seen him in here before? Was he a regular?"

"The one she was arguing with? No. I've never seen him." She added, "But like I said, I mainly work days." She glanced nervously about the room. "It was kind of quick. They were talking. He was at a table. Suddenly Helen just slapped his glass off the table and yelled something at him. Then she slapped him and stormed off to the kitchen. The guy left. That was it. She didn't say anything about him. But later on she was going on about how she was going to quit and everything. That's when she kept saying she didn't need this place. Actually, she called it a dump."

Imagine.

I asked, "This man . . . he wasn't by any chance in here the night that Helen was murdered, was he? Do you remember seeing him?"

Gail shook her head. "I didn't see him. Look, I gotta get back to my other tables. I'm . . . it's a lot busier working nights than what I'm used to. I don't want to get fired. Can I get you folks anything else?"

I told her we were fine and Gail moved on to her other tables.

"Let's go," Bonnie said.

"You don't want your salad?"

"I'll live. Just leave enough to cover the bill and let's get out of here. This place gives me the creeps."

I pulled out a twenty and dropped it on the table. A large man with a ponytail and a ginger beard had peeled away from the bar. He was the size of a small truck. He stepped over to the electric piano and started flipping switches, then tapped a finger against the microphone that was mounted atop the keyboard. "Test. Test." A skinny woman wearing white bell-bottoms and a powder blue halter top appeared from the shadows and mounted the stool. She was about as wide as one of the guy's arms. She slid the guitar strap over her bony shoulders and got to work tuning the guitar. Her hair was straight and black and fell down to her waist. Her cheeks were sunken, though possibly this was simply the effect of the shadows thrown by her oversize nose. She gave her head a toss, letting the hair fan out over the neck of her guitar. She wasn't Cher, but she was working on it.

"Don't you want to stay for the show?" I asked Bonnie.

"I'd rather stick pins in my eyes."

As we skidded back our chairs, the keyboardist hit the first chords of "Let It Be." The woman on the stool leaned into her microphone. Bonnie was halfway to the door before the singer began crooning about times of trouble and what she does when she finds herself there. I spotted Gail at the service end of the bar. She was bobbing her head up and down as another of the waitresses appeared to be delivering a lecture to her. Gail took her gum out of her mouth and tossed it in the trash.

I added another twenty to the first one and left.

CHAPTER
6

I stood at the base of one of the small hills in Greenmount Cemetery and listened to Pops explaining to me why we might not be able to bury Helen Waggoner the next day. After three days of gunmetal gray, sunshine had finally broken out; like an egg being cracked in the sky, it dripped bright and yellow from one horizon to the next. But even with old Mr. Sun back on the scene, it was still brutally cold. We were in a frigid lockdown. And that was the problem.

"Maybe if I had some dynamite I could make a dent, you know? 'Cept I don't figure that'd go over real good with some people." Pops let his gloved hands drop against his sides. "I can't remember ever having to dig a hole in ground this cold. It's like permafrost, you know what I mean? I took a pickax to it myself before you got here and the damn thing bounced right off and nearly went right into my forehead. I don't think you got insurance for that kind of thing, kid."

I had a gruesome image of Pops lying dead on the ground with a pickax sticking out of his head and his blood soaking into the snow. "Insurance isn't the point, Pops," I said. "I wouldn't want to see you die in the line of duty."

"You're a real gentlemen, kid."

The cemetery's backhoe had thrown a rod and Pops's backup, his pneumatic drill, was also on the fritz. Pops's two assistant gravediggers were working on the hard earth with blowtorches. But you can only hope to soften up the topsoil with these; you're sure as hell not going to burn away a hole six feet deep and seven feet long.

"I'm telling you, kid, this is a grave that just doesn't want to be dug. I've never seen anything like this."

I looked up into the sky. Large, shredded clouds were moving slowly along under a beautifully toned blue bowl. Despite the dazzling light, I knew that this was not the sort of sunshine that would provide any real help with the thawing.

One of Pops's workers lit a cigarette off the flame of his blowtorch, then pinched off the fuel and came over to where Pops and I were ruminating.

"For shit," he announced. The guy had a scraggly beard and mustache, both of which were caked with ice. His hair was greasy and long, tied off in a loose ponytail that poked out from his wool watch cap like a raccoon's tail. He took a long pull on his cigarette. Practically burned it down to half. His hard eyes looked from Pops to me and back to Pops. He might have been daring us to tell him to get back to work on the frozen ground.

Pops looked to me. "Good men, bad tools. I'm sorry, kid. We can't dig your hole. Not in this weather." Bonnie was forecasting no let up in the temperature. And this time it looked like she was getting it right. It wasn't even cracking the teens.

"I'll work on the generator," Pops said. "We'll get the blanket back on her. And I'll see what the hell's up with my drill. You can forget the backhoe right now though. I'm sorry."

I told him not to sweat it and to just do what he could. Luckily, Billie and I had nobody else back at the funeral home waiting for burial. Only Helen Waggoner.

"Looks like we have a guest for an extra day," I told Billie when I returned from the cemetery. "I'll have to call the sister and tell her." I was at my desk, rubbing my hands together in an attempt to hurry along the hot pinpricks of thawing. Billie was standing in the doorway.

"You don't have to call her. She's here."

"She's here?"

Billie grimaced. "She brought a photograph."

I returned her grimace. Like identical twins, Billie and I had just shared an entire conversation without saying a word. Photographs. Relatives of the dead just *love* photographs.

Billie went to fetch Vickie Waggoner from upstairs, where she was waiting along with her nephew. We were beginning to double as day care on this one. I wondered whether this woman didn't have any better place to take the kid than a funeral home. Especially a funeral home that has his own mother lying dead in the basement. Am I nuts or do people not think things through?

As Vickie Waggoner stepped into my office I rose from my chair. The move seemed to throw her for just an instant, as if maybe I was rising to tell her to get the hell out, or to leap across my desk and go for her throat. I opted not to shake her hand—chilled fingers on an undertaker can't feel all that pleasant—and indicated the small armchair next to the window.

"Please. Have a seat."

She did one of those moves, running her palms down over her fanny to flatten her skirt out, then sat down and crossed her legs. I dropped into my chair and balled my fists together, an automatic habit when I'm talking to the bereaved. I've been trying for years to break it.

"So how are you doing today, Miss Waggoner?" I pulled

my hands apart and picked up a shake-shake paperweight from my desk. It had a little plastic crab in it, wielding a mallet, a vengeful smile and with the words MY TURN printed atop its shell. "A little better, I hope?"

Vickie Waggoner seemed to weigh my question before answering. "I'm not exactly sure how I am," she said. "Confused, I guess. None of this is seeming real. I'm sorry."

"Nothing to apologize for."

She gave me a blank look. Like an actor who has gone up on their lines. I decided to get the hard part out of the way up front. I set the shake-shake back down on the desk and explained to her the problems we were having trying to get the grave dug for her sister. I rattled off the situation with the backhoe and the rest. I reminded her that it's rare for Baltimore to get such a series of excruciatingly frozen days. She crossed her legs again as I prattled.

"We might have to put off the burial for a day. I'm very sorry. You've been through enough already, I know. It's our job to make this part as painless as possible for you. I'm afraid it's not shaking out that way."

The woman's gaze traveled around my office. There's nothing terribly exciting to see. I have a framed print of a Magritte on the wall opposite where she was sitting, but that's pretty much it. No bangles, no baubles. No coffin catalogs lying around. I was trying not to notice the physical similarity between Vickie Waggoner and her sister, but I was failing in my efforts. I had just worked on Helen, so the dead woman and I had a bit of history now. I had massaged Helen Waggoner's cheeks with my thumbs. I had spent some time on her lips. I had run a brush through her black hair. This is the part of my job that sends some people screaming out of the room, I know. But that's what I do.

Vickie Waggoner recrossed her legs and settled her gaze on me. "I want to apologize for yesterday. I sort of unloaded on you. All that stuff about my mother, I mean. I'm sorry. I don't know where that came from."

"There's nothing to apologize for. You needed to talk."

"I'm sure you have better things to do with your time than to hear about some stranger's mother who was a two-bit stripper."

I pointed out that she hadn't precisely branded her mother a stripper. "The word you used was dancer."

"You know what I meant."

"They don't do much ballet down on Baltimore Street."

"Exactly."

Our conversation bumped suddenly off the road. We sat there in our chairs looking at each other for about ten seconds. It was Vickie who broke the silence.

"I'm doing it again," she said.

"Doing what?"

"Dragging my mother into the room. I really don't know why I can't get her out of my head."

"Your sister has just been taken away from you. It's natural that you'd want to turn to your mother."

"And she's not there, right?" She gave a mirthless laugh. "Well, that fits."

A drunk driver must have been at the wheel of our conversation, because it veered across the road and for the second time in less than a minute went straight into another ditch. Vickie Waggoner was tensing up. Her green eyes looked at me pleadingly. My turn.

I asked, "How is the little boy taking all of this?" Not exactly a cheery icebreaker. But something.

"Bo? Oh, he doesn't get it," she said. "He's too young. I tried telling him that his mommy is in heaven, and he asked if we could go there and visit her. Now, every time we leave my house, Bo asks, 'Are we going to heaven?' " She let out a large sigh. "I'm afraid he's starting to think that your funeral home is heaven."

"That'll twist him up."

"I know. I . . . to be honest, I don't know what kind of a stand-in mother I'm going to be for him."

I considered telling her how I had been raised by my aunt after my parents died. It can be done. Done well. I let it pass.

"I don't really know him," Vickie was saying. "Helen and I . . . We haven't had much to do with each other for a number of years now."

"I had kind of gathered that."

"She and my mother . . . they were cut from the same cloth. You know what I mean?"

"You don't have to explain."

Apparently she did. Her gaze rested on my Magritte as she spoke. Mine settled on her. Simple enough.

"I guess . . . I don't know. I guess my mother tried, but she never knew what to do with either of us. She was a very self-absorbed person. She and Helen fought like cats and dogs, but you know what? They understood each other. I mean I'd actually get jealous sometimes when the two of them started in on each other. That's crazy, isn't it? But I would. They cared enough to rip each others' throats out. I think . . . in a way, I think that was how Helen demanded love. She insisted that our mother pay attention to her, even if it was just to scream at her."

"And you?"

"Me? I was the one who didn't cause any trouble. I was the well-behaved one. But I was the freak. In that family, anyway. And meanwhile, Helen was well on her way to being so much like our mother it's scary. If she . . . if this hadn't happened, she would have been the mother of *two* fatherless children. Just like Mama." She looked at me. "Did you know Helen was pregnant?"

"It was in the coroner's report."

Vickie let her hands rise and drop onto her lap. "Oh God.

What am I going to do about Bo? I don't know anything about
raising children."

"You've got to give it some time," said Mr. Platitude. "You
shouldn't expect to be up to speed so soon. What about the
father?"

Vickie took a slow take on my question. "The father."

"The boy's father."

"Oh. Him." Vickie shrugged her shoulders. "Like I said the
other day, there's not much to say. Helen hooked up with a
loser. She actually made the mistake of counting on the guy
for awhile. I guess you could say she learned that from our
mother. Making the mistake of counting on losers, I mean.
They were both tough women, but they were soft in the center. This guy Helen got caught up with . . . all he did was drag
her through the sewer. You've got to understand. Helen and I
grew up around men like that. Losers and letdowns. Men have
always been a temporary thing with the Waggoner women."
She floated a weak smile. "It's our legacy."

I let that one pass. "You said that Helen never knew who
her own father was, right?"

"That's right. I didn't know who mine was either." This
time the smile was a little braver. "There was a game we used
to play when we were kids, where we'd pretend that different
men in the neighborhood were our fathers. *My* father is the
man in the grocery store who keeps winking at Mom. *My* father is the man who drives the M-6 bus. *Mine* is the ice cream
man. It was a game, but it was also longing. That's obvious
enough. For awhile, Helen was convinced that she had actually figured out who her true father was. It wasn't a game this
time."

Vickie shifted in her chair so that she was looking out the
window. The sunlight split her face in two. She continued,
"Our mother was seeing a guy at the time. He bartended at
one of the clubs where she worked. He was sort of rugged look-

ing, a pretty good-looking guy. Especially to a twelve-year-old, which is how old Helen was at the time. This one was hanging on longer than most of them and Helen got herself convinced that it was because he was her real daddy and that he wanted to be with his family." Her gaze followed after something out the window. I couldn't see what it was. "He came over one night. This guy. When our mother was working. He had the night off I guess. He knew she wouldn't be there. He tried to force himself on Helen. Who knows, maybe he was picking up on her daddy vibes, and he took it the wrong way."

"That's no excuse."

"No. I'm not excusing him. Anyway, our mother had already given both of us the talk about how to defend ourselves if we ever got into trouble. Especially that kind of trouble. Helen was a tough little scrapper. I happened to come home just a few minutes after she had kicked him and he was still on the floor, doubled over. Helen was fighting mad. She was standing over him screaming at him. *You're not my daddy! You're not my daddy!* She waited until the guy got himself out of there before she burst into tears. Oh my God, she just turned to water in my arms. I think that's probably the closest we ever were. In fact, I know it was."

Vickie stared off at the memory. My phone rang. I immediately hit a button that flipped the call to my answering machine. It was Bonnie. I turned the volume down.

"I'm sorry," I said. "Go on."

"Well. That was the end of the game, that's for sure. Helen refused to tell our mother about what had happened, and she made me promise not to tell either. Of course, the guy dumped our mother right after that. She was pretty upset. That's when she and Helen really started in on their fighting with each other. They were at each other's throats all the time. It was fire and gasoline, I swear. But like I said, they were basically the same person. Underneath it all, Helen wanted so much for that damn woman to love her. That's probably why she fought so hard."

Vickie broke off her story and looked over again at the Magritte.

"What is that?" she asked.

"It's a Magritte."

It was Magritte's *Fiddle*. A woman seated on a verandah by the shore of a lake with a violin bow in her hand and a fish tucked under her chin. It was a gift from Julia. Vickie squinted at it, as if maybe that would make more sense of it. I could have told her. It wouldn't.

She turned back to me.

"I brought you something."

She unsnapped her purse and reached in and pulled out a photograph. She leaned forward and slid it onto the desk. I picked it up. The photograph was, of course, of Helen Waggoner. It was of Helen and her son, Bo. It appeared to have been a recent photograph, for the boy looked pretty much as when I met him the previous day. The two had their faces pressed together. Helen was giving her son a big bear hug. This was when I was able to make my assessment. The dead waitress had beautiful eyes. Large, chocolate and lovely.

"It was just taken in October," Vickie said. "Bo's third birthday."

The pair in the photograph looked like the happiest, healthiest, most wholesome pair of people on the planet. The photograph had been taken outside. There was something about it that seemed familiar to me. Then I saw what it was. In the background was a large, slanted pane of glass reflecting the green of trees as well as something that I couldn't exactly make out, something brown and white.

"Did you take this?"

"Me? No. I found it in Bo's room when I was packing his things for him to come over to my place."

"This was taken at the zoo."

"It was? How do you know that?"

"Here. Look."

She rose partway out of her chair to lean over the desk for a look. "In the background, see? That's the new visitors center. I was out there just the other day for its opening. That's an antelope, I think, in the reflection."

Vickie dropped back into her chair and crossed her arms over her chest. The sun was angling in through the window behind her, slicing a golden streak diagonally across her lap. A partial corona hovered about her hair.

"It's a good picture of my sister," she said simply.

I agreed it was. But what was I supposed to do with it? I suppose this was how Vickie Waggoner wanted to remember her sister, despite everything. Smiling and happy on a beautiful autumn day with her son. What I had down in the basement was a ravaged wreck, halfway gutted and stitched back up with a crude Frankenstein scar. I couldn't work the magic that would return Helen Waggoner to the pretty, smiling woman in the photograph. I had done what I could. But my best shot could never be good enough.

Vickie Waggoner was crying softly. I hadn't even heard her start.

"My sister deserves better than this," she said in a small voice. "This is so unfair. She . . . to live the kind of life she was living, and then end up like this. My stupid, stupid sister. She deserves to be alive. She . . ."

The floodgates opened. The woman hunched over in my small armchair and brought her hands to her face and wept with abandon. About time, I'd say. My guess is that she had been holding it all in. Maybe for the sake of the boy. That's no good. I let her have her cry, sliding a box of Kleenex to the corner of the desk. It would have been rude of me to just sit there and look at her so I picked up the photograph and studied it again. I agreed with Vickie Waggoner. This woman didn't deserve to die. She was all of twenty-five. She had this little boy and another child on the way. She was carving out her place in the world. Helen Waggoner looked out at me from that photograph with a large, happy, going-to-live-forever smile, a smile she would never smile again. Not in this life anyway. Now she was simply a ruined creature in the dark basement directly below us.

Heavy stomping sounded from overhead, followed by laughter and a high-pitched squeal. I knew what Billie was up to. Her old Bride of Frankenstein routine. She probably had Bo cornered and was tickling him unmercifully. I looked back down at the photograph. Somebody out there was responsible for making an orphan of this little boy. His mother would never again hear her son's high-pitched squealing or his laughter. She would never again be there when he cried. All that was already over.

It was totally unacceptable.

"I'd like to help you find out who did this."

I wasn't even certain that I had spoken out loud until Vickie looked up from her tears and blinked her red-rimmed eyes at me. A mixture of uncertainty and grief. And a bruised look from the running makeup.

"I don't really know what I can do. But . . . but I want to help. Is that okay with you?"

That's when I learned that Vickie Waggoner also had a beautiful smile. Just like her sister's. It was the first time that she'd shown it to me.

The tears on my cheeks weren't mine. They were Vickie's. They got there when she wrapped me in a grateful hug as she was leaving my office.

"Is that ink?" Billie asked, coming up to me at the front

door. Vickie and Bo were making their way carefully down the frozen sidewalk. Holding hands. I dabbed at my cheek. A smear of black came off on my fingers.

"It's mascara."

Billie glanced out the door as I was closing it. "Oh. I see."

"It's not what you think," I said.

Billie clucked. "I'm not worrying about what *I* think."

. . . .

. . . .

. . . .

. . . .

. . . .

. . . .

. . . .

. . . .

CHAPTER

7

A waterpipe under the street in front of the Oyster had cracked and ruptured from the cold. The flow had been shut off, but not before a large ice sculpture had formed on the edge of the street and up on the sidewalk. Depending on who you listened to—and from what angle you viewed the ice—the frozen mass resembled a large hawk in flight, a castle, Abraham Lincoln's profile, or a pair of obese copulating angels. Baltimore Gas & Electric had ringed the tabula rasa with plastic tape, which only served to make the frozen chunk even more of an attraction. By the time I saw it, someone had already placed a Christmas wreath on one of the jagged points.

"Ain't that shit?" Sally said to me as she pulled the door open wide. I had an armload of logs. I carried them into the bar and over to the far wall and dumped them atop the pile next to the small fireplace. I made three more trips to my car to fetch the rest of the wood. A mother was crouched down next to her son, who was staring at the ice hemorrhage with pie-pan eyes. Someone else was snapping its picture. Two teenage girls were approaching, giggling. One carried a string of gold tinsel.

Sally whipped up some hot chocolate while I got a fire started for her. I used some empty liquor cartons for kindling and soon had a roasty toasty going. We pulled up a pair of chairs and gave the flames a good look. I've always held that if music itself could get up and dance, it would make these sorts of moves. Sally had poured a taste of rum into our hot chocolates. It was an atrocious addition. But the bite was nice. After a few minutes, there was a low rumble from outside. I turned my head just in time to see several pounds of snow falling from the roof past the bar's window.

"There's my signal," I said. "Time to go."

"Good talking with you, Hitchcock," she said. "Thanks for the wood."

I rounded the corner to find my good friend John Kruk reading the riot act to a group of sullen-faced policemen out on the street. The first piece of hard evidence in the murder of Helen Waggoner had showed up. It was on Anne Street, one block over from the funeral home. Actually it didn't show up, it had been there all along. It was a car. A white Pontiac Firebird. I recalled Alcatraz sniffing around the car during one of his romps. I had assumed he was looking for love in all the wrong places. I hadn't realized he was sleuthing.

The car had been parked illegally, directly in front of a fire hydrant. Because of the mild anarchy brought on by the recent storm, it had taken several days before a patrol car had noted the violation and run a routine check of the car's plates. That was when it was discovered that the car had been reported stolen several days before, the same day that Helen was murdered. And that's when the gears started rolling.

Helen had been shot in the front seat of the Pontiac. Traces of her blood were recovered from the front seat. A pair of bullet holes were located, one in the floorboard and one in the door. Helen's fingerprints were all over the door handle and the window.

Kruk was ballistic. His officers should have spotted the car the night Helen's body was dumped off. The entire area should have been canvassed. In fact, it *had* been canvassed. Sloppily, it now appeared. The miserable icy, slushy, snowy, windy, bitter, crappy weather of that evening would no doubt be floated as an excuse. Kruk would no doubt give less than two seconds to such an excuse. The stolen white Pontiac Firebird, illegally parked, containing the murder victim's blood and fingerprints on the seat, door handles and passenger window had "lousy police work" written all over it.

I stood on the corner and watched the police going over the inside and outside of the Pontiac trying to pick up additional clues. Kruk ordered two of his men to practically crawl on their hands and knees from the car all the way around the block to the front door of Sewell & Sons. It wasn't too likely that whoever brought Helen down here bothered to drag her body all that way. More likely she had been dumped off, and then the car had been pulled around the corner and abandoned there. The inch-by-inch assignment carried the whiff of penance.

"You are a vengeful god," I told Kruk.

He ignored the compliment.

"I'm disgusted. We should have discovered this car that night."

"I don't know. White car in a snowstorm. I think your men could make a decent case."

"I'm not in the mood for you right now, Mr. Sewell."

I didn't bother asking if he ever was. Instead I asked, "So the car was stolen?"

"It was called in around noon the day of the murder. Taken right off the street in Federal Hill. Guy was having lunch at Sissons. Comes out, car's gone."

"So what do you make of that?"

Kruk shrugged. "The murder was probably planned. The killer picked up the car with the intention of getting Helen Waggoner into it. You can bet we won't pull the killer's prints off the car."

Kruk was watching his two foot soldiers as they made their way s-l-o-w-l-y up the block. If a person can look both pissed and pleased at the same time, Kruk did. I noticed, not for the first time, that the short detective was underdressed for the extreme temperatures. No scarf, no gloves, only a flimsy overcoat. It didn't seem to bother him. Maybe it was all the bad precinct coffee that coursed through his veins. Internal insulation.

"So, if it was preplanned does that count out crime of passion?"

Kruk lit a cigarette and pocketed the match. "It rules out an argument that just got out of hand. That will mean something when it gets to trial. It doesn't get me any closer to the killer."

"So the car doesn't help you, does it?"

Kruk shook his hammy head. "Not really. No."

I let the disgruntled detective go about his business. He ducked under the yellow crime-scene tape that had been stretched around the car and knocked a few more heads together. The two officers he had dispatched to cover the turf between the Pontiac and the funeral home reported back to him. They had found nothing. Kruk hadn't really expected that they would, though I heard him chewing the men out anyway. "A *fucking dog found more evidence than you did!*" I'd have to remember to congratulate my celebrated pooch.

The scene was a bust. The tow truck Kruk had called in arrived to take the car away. The Pontiac was winched up onto a flatbed truck and secured with chains. As the truck moved down the street, it let out a huge backfire.

I met with Bonnie at Alonso's Bar on Coldspring Lane. Alonso's is a dark, toasty bar just across the expressway from Television Hill. People from the station have been hanging out here since the time of Jesus. The outside of the building is comprised of glass bricks and a heavy wooden door with a porthole window. There is a small package liquor section in the front, a long horseshoe bar right past that and a half dozen booths in the rear, off the open end of the horseshoe. The rest rooms are beyond the booths, and beyond them is the kitchen. Moscow is about eleven thousand miles past that. If we want to go that far.

Bonnie was at a booth. As expected. Jay Adams was there with her. Not such a nice surprise. The Sunpapers reporter gave me a smirking smile as I squeezed in next to my honey bunch. Bonnie and I didn't kiss or otherwise show any outward signs that we were sharing the same sheets. Bonnie is rigid on this; she doesn't want her personal life on display for gawkers. She reached over with her hand under the table and goosed me. That's fine. Better than a peck on the cheek anytime.

"Jay is reporting on the Waggoner case," Bonnie said to me.

"I know. We've spoken."

Adams grinned out of one side of his mouth. "As I recall, you didn't have a lot to say when we spoke."

"Nope," I answered. "I didn't."

"Well?"

"Well?"

"Do you have any more to say now?"

I shrugged. "You know what I know. Probably more at this point." Of course, this wasn't the case and I knew it. I knew about the white Pontiac. I decided to hold on to that tidbit for the time being.

Bonnie spoke up, "Jay thinks that you know more than you're telling, Hitch. That's why he called me."

"Why didn't he just call me?" I turned to the man himself. "Why didn't you just call me?" I added, "Were you afraid I wouldn't ask you out to lunch?"

"Hitch, I asked Jay to join us. He can help," Bonnie said.

"Bonnie told me about your visit out to the airport last night," Adams said to me.

"Well, I know how to show a girl a good time."

"I'm glad to hear it."

"And I'm glad to report it." I couldn't keep the irritation out of my voice. Then again, I wasn't trying too hard. Bonnie was glaring at me. She wasn't used to seeing me in a pissing contest like this. Frankly neither was I. The fine-boned reporter was having an immediate and unpleasant effect on me. And he knew it. And he was enjoying it.

"I thought maybe we could pool our efforts," Adams said blandly, pretending to ignore my snit. The reporter's almond-shaped eyes flicked for a nano-instant from me to Bonnie. I didn't much care for the flick. "I tried to talk to the sister. She wouldn't talk to me. But you've talked with her, right? She's given you some information? Some background?"

The pompous little prick.

"You tried to *interview* a woman whose sister has just been murdered? Christ, don't you guys at least have some sort of forty-eight hour rule?"

"You spoke with her."

"I didn't *question* her. I'm handling her sister's funeral arrangements. It's customary to talk with members of the family when one is arranging a funeral. I was doing my job."

"So was I."

"I didn't badger the poor woman."

"Neither did I."

"Good!"

Adams lifted his glass—it looked like iced tea—and took a tiny sip. Bonnie was looking confused and displeased. I was feeling a sudden onslaught of claustrophobia. I don't like booths. I like barstools.

"What else did the sister tell you?" Adams asked as he set his glass back down. Delicately. "Besides the fact that the mother was a slut."

Bonnie gasped. "I didn't say that, Hitch. Jay, I didn't say that."

"It's okay." I patted her hand. To Adams I said, "Vickie Waggoner spoke to me in confidence. In case you don't know what that is, let me explain. It means that it wasn't her intention that I run to our intrepid Sunpapers reporter and recite our conversation."

Adams brushed a nonexistent piece of lint from his sleeve. "Off the record then."

"Out of the question."

"What are you protecting, Hitch?"

"I'm protecting someone's privacy, Jay. And don't call me Hitch."

"What do I call you?" he asked. The smirk was back on his face. If it ever truly left.

I ignored his question. "The police are investigating the murder. I know Detective Kruk. He's good. He'll figure it out."

"I know Kruk too. It would be nice for Bonnie if she beat him to it."

"For Bonnie. So you're really just being a pal here, aren't you."

"That's right."

"Well, Jay old buddy, I know how to say bullshit in six languages, but English will do."

"So you don't believe me."

"Your insight frightens me."

And so goes a standoff.

I decided not to stick around for lunch. I told them that I had business to attend to. Bonnie's big blues were filled with apology as she told me that she was going to stay put and talk a bit more with Adams. The lithe reporter insisted on shaking my hand as I got up to leave. His hand felt like the fish in my Magritte.

The bright sunshine was a welcome relief after the Alonso's catacombs. Since I was in the area, I drove over to Homeland, which is a nearby section of town where the sufferers of higher tax brackets brave it out in their eight and nine hundred thousand dollar homes. It's a neighborhood of large trees and nice lawns. The houses are primarily stone, many of them fronted with Tudor-styled patches of stucco. Neighborhood planning came to Baltimore early (one of the nation's first official shopping centers is in nearby Roland Park) and provided a few gems, Homeland among them. I drove down Springlake Way and parked between a Mercedes and a BMW. My Chevy Nothing stood out like a sore.

Among the aesthetic visions of the long-ago planners of Homeland was their decision for Springlake to split at Tunbridge Road and have the single lanes border a bucolic little park for the next several blocks. The reason I went there—to be honest—was because I'm a sucker for a winter wonderland and this little park, when it is covered with snow, is downright Currier & Ives. There are three linked ponds, each with strategically strewn boulders along their shores. I sat on one of the boulders and watched as a couple dozen skaters wobbled and raced and twirled and fell about the ice. Here and there were parents who had wrapped their toddlers up in so much goose down that the kids looked like little Michelin men. There was a teenage couple on the ice sliding a Frisbee back and forth to each other with brooms. A big sister was trying to teach her little sister how to skate. A boy was playing fetch with his dog. There was a snowball battle under way. A snowman was being built. Norman Rockwell would weep.

I sat on my boulder and took in the scene. Opposite me, on a rock of their own, sat an elderly couple, identically pink-faced and wearing matching plaid hunters caps. They had a Thermos of something steamy—coffee or maybe hot choco-late—and only one cup, the plastic lid from the Thermos, from which they were sharing. They were seated under a branch made heavy with snow. The occasional gust of wind was bringing shavings of snow down onto them.

After soaking up the blissful scene for a time, I pawed through my pocket and found the photograph that Vickie Waggoner had given me. Helen smiled up at me. What were the words that Vickie had used to describe her sister? A *scrapper*. I thought about my visit to Sinbad's the night before. I tried to picture Helen still alive, working a shift at the lounge. I tried to picture her laughing with her customers. Or gently telling some drunken widget salesman to get his hammy paws off her. Or maybe not so gently, come to think of it. I knew I shouldn't go romanticizing the dead. This happy snapshot notwithstanding, I gathered from Vickie's portrait of her sister that Helen hadn't at all suffered fools gladly. Was this partly why she was killed? Was it possible that Helen simply told the wrong person in the wrong way to stuff it? People kill for a lot less these days, it seems.

"Mr. Sewell? Is that you?"

I looked left and right. A person in a parka stood about ten feet away. I couldn't be certain if this was who had called my name. The parka's hood was up and completely obstructing whoever was in there. A voice—the same one—came from within the fur-lined periscope.

"It's Mr. Sewell, isn't it? Ann Kingman." The hood came down. It was the wife of the doctor we had just buried a few days before. I got up off my rock and pulled off my glove to shake her hand. Her glove, actually.

"Well, you're certainly the last person I would have expected to see here," she said.

"Mrs. Kingman. Yes, fancy meeting you here."

"Well I live here," she said.

"Oh. I didn't know."

"So what brings you here?"

"I was just in the neighborhood. I remembered this little place from a couple of winters ago. It's nice."

"Yes it is." She didn't say it with much enthusiasm. She was wearing one of those wide thermal elastics around her head. The word "BRUNDAGE" was printed on it. It looked a little like a bandage.

"How are you managing? If I may ask."

She looked out over the frozen ponds and took a moment. "I want to apologize for my behavior the other night. I was more upset than I was letting on."

"You don't have to apologize."

"I'm afraid I treated you like the hired help. I'm not always so bitchy. Honestly."

I started to point out to her that I *was* the hired help. I had a check made out to me for a nice tidy sum to prove it.

"Trust me, Mrs. Kingman, I've had some pretty loopy behavior go on at wakes and funerals. You were fine."

She looked out again at the frozen ponds. "It's funny. It's not altogether registering that Richard is dead so much as that he is simply not there. Does that make any sense?"

"I understand that."

"I mean, I'm very aware of his *not* being there. He's not in the sunroom reading the paper. He's not on the phone with the hospital. He's not off in his workroom in the basement. But . . . my memory of him being in all those places is still fresh. It's as if he's *almost* there."

She paused again and watched as the teenage couple put down their brooms and linked arms. A snowball zinged in an arc in front of us. "I'll tell you what it's like. Every time I walk into a room, it's as if Richard has just stepped out of it. As if I've just missed him. It actually gets me very angry. But dead?" She made a face. "What's that?"

Perhaps an undertaker is expected to have some sort of answer to that question. But I don't have one. No matter, the doctor's widow wasn't really expecting one. This is the listening portion of my job.

"I do want to thank you again for all your help, Mr. Sewell. You and your aunt handled everything very smoothly."

"I'm glad you were satisfied," I said. "And it's Hitch."

"Well. Thank you. And it's Ann."

This time she took off *her* glove and we shook for a second time. The widow held my fingers a fraction longer than necessary. Her expression was frank and a little too scrutable for my liking.

"I guess I'm still in shock over the death of my husband. But I just don't feel anything."

"That can be a symptom of shock right there."

"Perhaps." She withdrew her hand and tucked it back into her glove. "Richard and I were very easy and familiar with each other. But I don't really think we were very good friends anymore. A long time ago, maybe. But . . ." she trailed off and looked over at the elderly couple with the Thermos. When she looked back at me, her eyes had gone hard. She was about to say more, but just then a snowball ripped out of nowhere and grazed her just behind the ear.

"*Sorry!*"

A group of boys off near the street were aiming at street

signs and lampposts. They weren't aiming at us. I brushed some of the snow from Mrs. Kingman's hair.

"You okay?"

"Oh, I'll live."

The snowball seemed to have taken the spirit completely out of her. She gave me a disappointed look. "Well, it was nice to see you again, Mr. Sewell."

"Hitch."

"Fine." She batted some stray strands of hair from her face. "I hope you enjoy our pleasant little neighborhood." I could taste her bitterness in my mouth.

"I will. Thank you, Ann."

She looked over at the skaters on the ice. A spidering of crow's-feet were spread out in small fan-shapes from the corner of her eyes. She was slipping now, and I think she knew it. Not on the ice. In her life.

She sighed. "Richard loved the snow. He would have been out here skating with all of them. I would have been back at the house, putting together a warm lunch for everyone." She looked up at me. "You wouldn't care for a cup of coffee, would you?"

I shook my head. "I don't think so, Ann. But thanks."

She started to say something, then changed her mind. She turned and headed back to her house. Where someone was always leaving a room the moment before she stepped into it.

CHAPTER
8

I was starving.

When I got back to the neighborhood, I popped into Julia's gallery to see if maybe she wanted to join me for lunch. Even if she wasn't hungry she'd still be pretty to look at while I chowed down. Julia likes being looked at; she'd have no problem with that.

There were several people milling about the gallery. They seemed to be confused by what they were seeing. I asked Chinese Sue, who was perched on her stool behind the counter, if the genius was in. Sue was reading a book about hydrogen. She gave me her patented blank look and raised a single finger. Upstairs.

Julia was creating. As I reached the top of the spiral staircase I found myself looking at a perfectly chiseled fellow, perfectly naked, seated atop a sheet-covered box. Julia's hammock had been moved aside; the chiseled fellow was directly beneath the skylight, ablaze in the heatless white light. Julia stood some twenty feet away, behind her easel. She was wearing her silk bathrobe. Her hair was wet and finger-combed back off her face. The nonservice end of her paintbrush was tapping against her perfect teeth as she considered the hunk of golden flesh sitting on the box across the room.

"Hitch!"

I stepped past the mute model and over to my sexy exy. Julia lowered the paintbrush and gave me a peck on the cheek.

I looked at the canvas. It was entirely blank except for one small flesh-colored swab smack-dab in the middle. I glanced over at the model. Yes, she'd captured his swab perfectly.

"What do you think?"

"Are you going to force me to say 'minimalism'?"

Julia tapped the paintbrush against her teeth again. Her pupils were dilated. She looked as happy as a clam.

"I'm savoring," she whispered.

"How long have you been working on this?"

"This?" She looked over at her golden hunk. "Or that?" I reached out and took a pinch of Julia's wet hair between my fingers. Then a pinch of her robe.

"*That* I think I can figure out. Would you like me to come back later?"

"No. That's okay. This *is* later. Besides, the whole point of savoring is not to rush." She called over to her model. "Nils, sweetie. That'll be all for today. Thank you so much. I'll give you a call at the embassy when I need you again."

I turned my back on the fellow as he stood up and started to get dressed.

"Embassy?"

"Danish. Down in D.C. Nils is some sort of liaison. God knows. I don't understand politics. I met him at an affair there last month."

"An affair?"

"Function."

Nils was dressed. Julia introduced us. The Dane's grip was

rock-solid. He was probably all of twenty-two. A lock of golden hair fell perfectly just above his right eye.

"I'll call the embassy," Julia said again, forming her words largely. She turned to me. "He speaks about ten words of English. He just came over. He's from Elsinor. That's where Hamlet was from. He's somebody or other's son."

I noted that we're all somebody's son. Nils stepped over to the brass pole that runs from Julia's studio—which is also where she lives—down to the gallery. Julia's place used to be a fire station. It burned down. She renovated. She kept the pole. If she could have, she'd have kept the firemen.

Nils took hold of the pole and said, "Hello," and dropped out of sight. Julia turned briskly to me. All refreshed.

"Life is beautiful, isn't it?"

We supped at the Cup. The Admiral's Cup. It turned out Julia was ravenous.

"I can't remember the last time I ate." Julia was licking the ice of her margarita off the slender pink straw. She saw the expression on my face and stuck her tongue out at me. "Stop it."

"Did I say anything?"

"Volumes."

They don't serve margaritas at the Admiral's Cup. They do across the street, at the Admiral Fell Inn, which is a fancier place. It had taken Julia all of three seconds to convince the bartender there to give her a margarita to go. It was probably something in the way she promised to bring the empty glass back later (". . . when you're not so busy . . .") that clinched it. I hope I'm not giving the wrong impression of my ex-wife. I don't think I am.

Julia asked for two orders of fish and chips. I had a turkey club and a bottle of beer. The Admiral's Cup is right on the water, a stone's throw from the Screaming Oyster just up the pier. Great turkey clubs. Superb bottles of beer. Just a happy-making place all around.

"I don't remember if I told you, but I liked your zoo paintings the other day. Very clever stuff."

"Thank you, Hitch. I'll probably have to go out there every now and then to make sure they're rotating them. I actually did put thought into that, you know. It's not just a gimmick. It's supposed to correspond with the zoo as an active place where the animals mill around and blah, blah, blah." She rolled her eyes. "Of course, I'd really rather just stay home and paint Danish weenies."

"Yes, but you've got to pay the bills."

"You're so right. Speaking of which, how're things in the death business, dear Mr. Ghoul? Any more luscious bodies piling up on your doorstep?"

I told her no, just the one.

"Are there any new clues about who might have killed your little waitress? Have the police got any suspects?"

I told her that I didn't know. "I don't think so though. I'd think Kruk would give me a call if he had it wrapped up."

"Kruk. He's the one with dead eyes?"

"You mean he doesn't look you up and down like every other male on the planet."

"That's what I just said."

I started to tell Julia about my visit to Sinbad's Cave. But at the mention of Bonnie's name, Julia rolled her eyes.

"I would ask what it is that you see in that girl—except I know."

"Don't be jealous. It causes frown lines."

"Pooh. I'm going to be jealous of a weather girl? On top of which, Hitch, she's a *terrible* weather girl. My God, Albatross could do a better job predicting the weather."

"Alcatraz. And you know it's Alcatraz."

"I prefer Albatross, what can I say. You got that mournful

sad-faced creature right after you and I divorced. A deep and painfully obvious psychological statement, if you ask me."

"Which I didn't."

"Furthermore, you name your new postmarriage companion after a notorious prison. You tell me. I don't think I'm too far off the mark."

"Julia, I got him when I was out in San Francisco on a trip. You know this. I was taking a sightseeing tour of Alcatraz Island and for some reason this silly dog was *on* the island. He hopped onto the tour boat and bounded over and jumped up on me. He nearly knocked me over. It was love at first sight."

"Whatever."

"Julia, I found him *on* Alcatraz. I really didn't dig too terribly deep into my psyche to come up with the name."

She finished off her margarita. "Still."

I love that. *Still.* Women can defoliate an entirely succinct explanation with just one word. I suppose men can too, but we don't do it nearly as well. Julia was giggling behind her drink. She knows how "*still*" infuriates me.

"There's that face." She broke into laughter. "I love that face!"

"Try this one." I contorted, but I pretty much shot a blank. She had me and she knew it. Julia batted her eyes at the waiter and got him to run across the street and fetch her another drink.

"You could charm the pants off a fish," I observed.

"That's a good thing?"

I dragged the giddy lady back to the subject.

"So look. I was telling you. This place where Helen Waggoner worked? It was practically dripping in semen."

Julia pointed a French fry at me. "I *can* be disgusted. Just so you know."

I gave her a quick description of Sinbad's Cave. She got the picture.

"Primarily businessmen, right? They're staying at some airport hotel? Half hour from the city? They've seen everything on HBO. They want to unwind. They check out the local lounge. Lo and behold . . . women! Hitch, it's not exactly a new idea. Strangers have been copulating with strangers for centuries."

"I'm aware of this."

"So do you think it might have been some psycho traveling salesman who killed your waitress?"

"It doesn't really fit. A nutcase would have killed her on the spot and left her there . . . wherever that was. She was lured outside by a phone call. And then driven back into the city. Besides, someone stole a car to do this."

"And her sister has no guesses at all?"

"The two were basically strangers."

"Did she know that her sister was turning tricks out at the airport?"

"Well, technically speaking, I don't know that either."

Julia shrugged. "Assume the worst. Especially where sex is involved. You can always amend it later." Julia hunkered down to her fish and chips. Her drink arrived. I had stalled on my turkey club. I set my elbows on the table and was stabbing at the remains of my sandwich with one of the little plastic swords, over and over. Julia looked up from her feast.

"Is it dead yet?"

"Huh?"

"Your sandwich. It stopped gobbling ten minutes ago."

I jabbed the plastic sword into the coleslaw.

"Sword in the slaw," Julia observed, reaching over and pulling it out. "I'm queen." When I didn't react to her joke, she frowned. "What's wrong, Hitch?"

"I'm just thinking about these damn people. Here you've got a woman who was a stripper plus who knows what else. She has a couple of kids. No father for either of them. And now, right in her footsteps, there's a daughter who was more than likely hustling herself out at the airport."

"So what does the other one do for a living? The way you're talking, I'm ready to hear you say she's a porn star. Damn Hitch, it's nothing but sex, sex, sex with you, isn't it."

"I don't know what Vickie does for a living," I said.

"That's her name? Vickie?"

"Vickie Waggoner."

Julia had just started to tuck a French fry into her mouth. She froze.

"*Vickie Wagner* is her name?"

I corrected her pronunciation. "Waggoner. There's sort of an extra half syllable."

Julia's eyes had gone wide. "Christ. I know who Victoria Wagner is, Hitch. I guess it could be 'Waggoner.' But *I* know who she is. I *do* know what she does for a living."

"You do?"

Julia was holding the fry like it was a very limp pointer. "Uh-huh. Victoria Wagner. Jesus Christ, Hitch. She *is* a porn star."

The waiter cleared our table. I ordered a second bottle of beer. The waiter told me that they were all out of the kind I had just had. I told him—calmly—that I really didn't care a whole hell of a lot *what* kind of beer it was, I simply wanted a bottle to hold on to. He brought me one. I thanked him. He left. I counted to ten. Well . . . to five.

"*What?!*"

"Victoria Wagner," Julia said calmly.

"Waggoner!"

"Whatever. Dirty movies, Hitch. I kid you not. As God is my witness."

I reached over and took a sip of Julia's drink. "Okay, give it to me. Plainly and simply, if you can. First off, it's not that peculiar a name. And maybe not even the same name. It could just be a coincidence. What does your Victoria Waggoner, or *Wagner*, look like?"

"Hitch, she's not *my* Victoria Wagner. I just—"

"Eyes."

"I don't know. Who looks at eyes?"

"Hair."

"At the time I'm talking about, extremely blond. Fresh from the bottle."

"Vickie Waggoner is a brunette."

"Come on, Hitch, some women change their hair color as often as they change their minds."

"So this Victoria Wagner of yours. Does she have a pronounced widow's peak? A distinct vee?"

"Hitch, I don't know about widow's peaks. Come on. I'm supposed to notice these things?"

"You're an artist."

"I didn't paint the damn girl."

"Okay, okay. But essentially you've told me nothing."

"Fine. Don't get upset with me. You told me the name, I told you I know the name."

"You told me a little more than that. Okay. Let's hear the rest of it."

Julia took a long sip of her drink. She poked at her hair and got herself comfortable in her seat. She knew the foreplay was killing me.

"Ready?"

"Please. Squirm and primp as long as you want. I've got all day."

"Okay. So. Do you remember this guy who was following me around for awhile, right after you and I divorced?"

I started counting off on my fingers. "Jeff, Raoul, Clay, Rick—"

"Funny. His name was Terry. Terry Haden."

"Mr. Flak Jacket? The filmmaker? Sure, I remember that guy."

"Right. The few times you ran into him you kept asking, 'Where's the war?' You thought you were being so clever."

"No I didn't. I knew I was being obnoxious."

"Look, no argument from me. Terry Haden was a jerk," Julia said. "Though he did sort of have that rugged thing going. But he also had that hustler vibe. One of those guys who has a dozen things popping at once. On the move, on the make.

I recalled a guy who looked like a cross between Che Guervara in that poster and Al Pacino in *Serpico*. Lots of nervous energy. Never stopped moving. Like a shark. I had no memory of anything he actually ever said, only that he never stopped talking.

Julia continued. "Anyway, do you remember how I met him? The Maryland Institute was having me back for a show?" She laughed. "I like that, 'having me back.' All I ever did was sneak in and finagle supplies and some studio space. I never paid tuition."

"But then you went on to become such a big shot."

"Exactly. So now they air kiss my fanny whenever they get a chance."

"Cute."

"So you remember this? I was teaching a master class, I juried the senior show. All that stuff? I was hanging out again at the Mount Royal Tavern holding out my hem for the kids to kiss."

"Sure, I remember. You were in profound denial over our marriage dissolving and so you threw yourself into this distraction in a desperate attempt to keep yourself one step ahead of the dogs of depression."

"Oh yes, definitely. I could barely function. So anyway, I met Terry Haden while I was doing my MIA thing. He'd drop into the Mount Royal Tavern on a regular basis in that guerilla filmaker getup of his, trolling for girls in berets. I think it took him all of a minute after meeting me before he was going on about being a big-shot filmmaker. A real Von Stroheim in his own mind. He had done some work on a few of the early John Waters films, and he made sure he told me all about that and about everything else he ever did. It wasn't terribly long before he was suggesting we go back to his place so he could show me his lenses."

"You know, pumpkin, I don't really need to hear all the details. Compelling as I'm sure they are—"

"No. I already told you. I threw this fish back without a second thought. Self-absorbed photographers in flak jackets don't exactly top my list. Besides, like I said, there was something creepy about him. He was pretty insistent for awhile there, once he realized that I was big cheese.

"You mean he was after your panties *and* your fame?"

"I was just starting to get worried that this guy might turn out to be a stalker, but then he cooled off. Guys like Haden don't really have much patience. Once he saw that his hustle really wasn't going to work on me, he had plenty of easier fish in the barrel he could shoot at."

"Victoria?"

"Not yet. What happened was, Haden started showing up at the Institute. He announced to everyone who would listen that he was shooting a movie. Correction. An 'art' film. Quote unquote. Now, here's Terry Haden's idea of what makes a film an art film. Are you ready?"

I took a firm grip on the edge of the table. Julia leaned forward.

"You put art into it."

"Excuse me?"

"That's right. Literally. Art. Sculptures. Ceramic pots. You name it." She laughed. "The guy was literally auditioning *art works* at the Institute! Can you believe it? What a joke it was. He'd come around with a clipboard and a couple of Polaroid cameras hanging off his neck like some war correspondent and stalk around the place taking snapshots of different pieces, then he'd jot down the artist's name and phone number and all the rest. He took pictures of the artists themselves too. See, if you *really* want an art film, you also fill the thing up with real, live bonafide *artists*."

"Tell me this is all a joke."

"Of course it's a joke. And most of the kids at the Institute were smart enough to laugh the guy off. But there are always enough insecure wanna-bes who can get caught up in this kind of nonsense. You know how it is. Here's this guy who tells them he's worked on a couple John Waters films, and now he's trolling around looking not only to put them in a movie, but their *art* as well. Maybe he's the next Waters, right? Or Barry Levinson. Local boy makes good. Hollywood calling. Big bags of money and all that? To some of these kids it was actually enticing. Terry Haden brought his scam to the right place, and he knew it. I'm sure you can imagine the rap. It's all guerrilla filmmaking. Independent. No professional actors. All part of the rawness and honesty. Just real people."

"Freebies."

"Exactly. I mean, it was ridiculous. He wasn't even showing anybody a damn script. He was making it up as he went along. But you know, technically, that's how these art house train wrecks happen in the first place. You set up your camera and hope that the muses will show up and save your ass. When they don't, you edit like crazy then slap on a bunch of Phillip Glass."

The waiter came over to check on us. We each pulled our drinks protectively to our chests. Can anybody guess that we've known each other for years? I tapped my watch.

"Julia, are we inching closer to the point? I've got plans for Memorial Day."

"Funny. I'm getting to it. I just wanted to give you some background."

"Fine. Can we move on to the foreground, *s'il vous plaît?*"

"*Oui oui, mon petit fromage.*" She finished off her drink

and dropped the empty glass into her purse. "So. Anyway.
Haden took one more shot at me. He tried to convince me to
let him put some of my paintings in his so-called film. It was
pathetically clear that he just wanted to exploit my good
name. I turned him down. I told him that my agent would in-
sist on a contract, a fee for each painting that he used, a per-
centage of the box office, all that."

"You don't have an agent."

"I know. It didn't matter. At the first mention of pay, he
dropped the idea. In fact, he backed off from me completely. I
guess it got through to him that I was on to his game. Haden
wasn't making any goddamn art film. That was all a pretense. I
mean, who knows, maybe it started out that way. A way to get
himself snaking around the Institute. But basically that was the
lure. What he was looking for was freewheeling artsy kids
who'd be willing to toss off their clothes and have a nice little
orgy while Senior Von Stroheim rolled the camera."

"Great way to meet chicks."

"Exactly. The art house hustler. Some of these kids were
like ten years younger than him. And it worked. I'm telling
you, Hitch, I really don't know what it is about guys with cameras. Some of the unlikeliest women will fling off their knick-
ers at the drop of a lens cap. It's perverse. Anyway, this is where
Victoria Wagner comes in. Or *Waggoner*, as you put it."

"So soon?"

"She was one of the models they used for the life drawing
class. She was clearly new at it. Couldn't have been more than
nineteen. I had seen her posing. She couldn't sit still for very
long. She really couldn't hold a pose. But she must have figured it was an easy way to pick up some cash. Her body was a
knockout, no question about it. She wasn't one of those big
bucket, small breasted types they seem to prefer in life drawing. There's a big push to steer clear of the conventional hourglass figure. All about so-called realism. It's so silly. Well, this

woman—this girl—was voluptuous. Seemed real enough to me." Julia paused and unfurled one of her deliberately taunting smiles. "Is *your* Vickie voluptuous?"

"The word might apply."

"Well Terry Haden certainly picked up on it. I guess he must have spotted her during one of his reconnaissance visits."

"So what you're telling me is that Mr. Flak Jacket Von Stroheim got this Victoria Wagner to act in his silly movie, along with the boys and girls of the Maryland Institute of Art. Is that the chase you're refusing to cut to?"

"You really don't like my foreplay, do you?"

"I thought I did. I'm reconsidering."

"You're the one who started me down memory lane."

"Please. Hit the gas, lady."

"Okay, okay. Yes. Haden put her in his silly movie. Not only that, he starred her in his silly movie. He became fixated on her. He fashioned the whole damn thing around 'his discovery.' I remember he actually used those words. Hitch, I'm telling you, it was amateur hour. Victoria Wagner basically became Terry Haden's muse. Actually, she became more than that. They became lovers. They moved in together."

"It just gets uglier and uglier, doesn't it."

"Actually, it does. But here's the perverse thing, though. Haden was right. I mean, he didn't just shove her in front of the camera so that he could sleep with her. She really *was* the real deal. In a sense anyway. She certainly left those MIA beatniks in the dust. With that cheap blond hair and that body, she did have a sort of trashy Marilyn Monroe thing going on. The camera drank her up. It loved her. Haden even paid her, for Christ's sake. That tells you something right there. This wasn't just another silly art student anxious to hop into a project. This was a paid model. A working girl."

"But you said Victoria Wagner was, and I quote, a porn star. All you're really telling me is that this huckster shot her in a naughty movie. One step up from a student film, from the sound of it."

"You're right. And Haden didn't even finish it. He closed up shop halfway through. He knew he had a silly pretentious flop on his hands. A bunch of so-so paintings and a bunch of sub–so-so actors. But he had his big discovery. His star. Those two were as thick as thieves, Hitch. Right from the start. You could see it. She wasn't being exploited. It was the March of the Opportunists. You know those cartoons where the big, bad wolf looks at the little pigs and all he sees is a full course ham dinner on a plate? Well, that's how those two looked at each other, as far as I could tell. They were each other's meal ticket."

Julia prattled on a while more, recounting how, after Haden pulled the plug on his pretentious art house master-piece, he opened shop as a maker of cheesy skin flicks. It was a real life case of *Porn Is Born* with Victoria Waggoner standing in for Esther Blodgett. As I listened to her though, I refused to believe that Haden's Vickie and "my" Vickie were one and the same. It just wasn't adding up. Granted, people who make their living in the sex trade don't exactly walk around during daylight hours wearing a sandwich board advertising the fact . . . but still. I simply couldn't match the woman who had sat in my office earlier that same day crying her eyes out with the platinum-blond fleshpot thespian that Julia was describ-ing. It was like trying to force together two magnets of opposite polarities. The two women kept leaping apart the moment they even began to get close. It just didn't work.

"It's a different woman," I said, interrupting Julia's story. "It doesn't add up."

Julia stopped talking. She ran both hands through her short hair.

"But you don't know that, Hitch. In fact it *does* add up. Take a look at it. Mom and the girls. The stripper, the hooker and the porn queen. There's a pretty good argument there for nature *and* nurture."

"How is it that you know all of this, anyway? I mean, once Haden bagged his stupid project and moved on, you certainly had nothing more to do with him. Right?"

"Haven't laid eyes on him since."

"So how is it you know so much about the career of so-called Victoria Wagner? Has *People* magazine started putting out a low-life edition I haven't heard about?"

"I get around."

"It doesn't matter anyway. I'm convinced that we're not talking about the same person."

"Does yours have a tattoo?"

I shrugged. "Tattoo? I don't know. I didn't notice one."

"Mine does. A butterfly tattoo."

"Where exactly is this identifiable mark on this question-able screen queen of yours?"

Julia's slender index finger came forward, then swung around and settled lightly on her left breast. "Right here. A small one."

"I see."

"Small tattoo that is."

"That's what I figured."

"I don't suppose you've seen the left breast of your dead waitress's sister?"

"Nor the right one."

"Shame."

"But you saw both," I said. Julia nodded her head up and down. "In one of her movies?" She shook her head side to side.

"Your little friend has got a pretty active résumé, Mr. Sewell. Several years ago I was entertaining a group of Swedes who were in from Washington. They'd heard of The Block. I tried to tell them this wasn't no Bourbon Street, but they insisted on going. We ended up at this place called The Kitten

Club. Well, who do you think comes strutting onto the stage? I have to say, she wasn't quite as voluptuous as I had remembered. And the blond had grown out. But I recognized her."

"Victoria Wagner."

"In the flesh. I've got to tell you Hitch, the woman couldn't dance to save herself. Terry Haden might have had something going there on the tiny screen, but this girl wasn't exactly setting the place on fire. My Swedes were not impressed. She just looked tired. Depleted would be a better word. I don't know if it was booze or pills or what, but the light had definitely gone out. My little finger can be more seductive." She waggled the digit in question. I didn't doubt it.

"Was she still with Haden?"

"I don't know. I didn't see him. Unless maybe he was face-down on the bar. And I certainly didn't talk to her. It was sad. This kid was barely legal and was already burning out."

"This is when you saw the butterfly?"

"Yes. Right there on the breast. She didn't have that back when she was modeling. I suppose she picked it up for her films. Or maybe for the act. Believe me, it was the only thing up there with any life."

I called for the check. I insisted on paying. "You've been very entertaining, Miss Finney. As always."

We left the warm restaurant. Our faces turned immediately to ice. Julia swore.

"When the hell is this cold snap going to end? Has your little girlfriend found a crystal ball that works yet?"

"Don't kill the messenger."

She lifted her large purse. Her teeth were chattering. "I have to return this glass."

I left Julia sashaying through the door of the Admiral Fell Inn and headed straight for the funeral home. Billie met me at the front door. She was on her way out. She told me that

Vickie Waggoner had called about an hour before asking about cremation.

"Cremation?"

"She was wondering if that wouldn't just be the easiest thing to do at this point," Billie said. "What with our problem getting the grave dug."

"What did you tell her?"

"I told her not to make a rash decision. The last thing she'd want would be to have regrets later. I told her you would talk to her about it."

I studied my aunt's expression. Such as it was. She added, "This is your funeral, not mine."

I went inside and went directly down to the basement. Helen was right where I'd left her. Naturally. I pulled the sheet down to her waist. Between the bullet wound and the medical examiner's knifeplay, her body was pretty hacked up. But now that I knew what I was looking at, the little blue-and-red bruise I had noticed on the woman's left breast didn't look so much like a bruise to me anymore. It looked like what it was: the wing of a butterfly tattoo.

Helen was Vickie. Or Vickie was Helen.

Or I was Genghis Khan.

Somebody was lying.

I needed to take my thoughts out for a walk. I brought the King of All Things Laconic along with me. Alcatraz and I zigzagged through the hood, encountering very few others out on the street. Apparently these five-degree days weren't the rage. The usual smell of baking bread from the H&S Bakery was absent as we rounded the corner to Bond Street. Whether they weren't baking or the cold simply failed to carry the smells, I wasn't sure. I stopped at a market on the corner and picked up a ten pound sack of potatoes, then Alcatraz and I made our way on down the street. Bond runs into Thames, which dead-ends at an abandoned pier. I'm always a little surprised to see that the city hasn't put up a fence and a sign to warn people away from the pier—which is crumbling—or simply torn the thing down altogether. Whatever planks aren't rotting straight away are kicked out by neighborhood kids or removed by the local street population, who take them over to the ruins of a brick building that occupies a small dirt patch right next to the pier. Smoke was curling up from the ruined building. As Alcatraz and I swung around to the harbor side I could see a bonfire on what used to be the ground floor and a half dozen or so men standing around warming themselves. I recognized one of them as the ponytailed gravedigger from the cemetery. He jerked his head in a nod to me as I picked my way over the bricks to the fire. A few of the others shuffled their feet. Somebody grunted. Without anyone actually seeming to move, a place opened up for me and my dog to get next to their bonfire. Several large planks of wood were crossed in an X at the center of the blaze. These were from the pier; they were too rotten and slime-covered to actually catch fire, but they served to center the pile of more flammable debris and scraps that the men had piled up. The heat coming off the fire was a joy. The guy with the ponytail picked up a brick and tossed it into the flames sending a flurry of cinders kicking up and spiraling swiftly into the air. Someone tossed on another brick. Same thing. Another man kicked a cardboard box into the fire. The box caught immediately. It curled into itself, went black as a shadow and was gone. A wet plank whistled as it burned. The men stood silently and watched.

That's entertainment.

Alcatraz made his rounds. The men broke their frozen poses to give the insistent hound the scratching and rubbing he so whorishly demanded. I dumped the sack of potatoes onto the ground. There were a few grunts of gratitude as the bag was pulled open and potatoes affixed onto whatever was handy, large splinters of wood, a skinny metal pipe . . . whatever. To a person standing off a ways, say by the rotting pier, it might have looked like a bizarre marshmallow roast. But it was a potato roast. I didn't join in. I had money in my pocket and a place to go home to; I wasn't going to insult these guys by hanging around in the freezing cold and sharing their potatoes with them. Although I'm sure nobody would have said anything if I did. One of the guys pulled something out of his pocket—I couldn't see what it was—and offered it to Alcatraz, who greedily gobbled it up. The timbers shifted in the fire and a huge spray of sparks leaped into the air. If these men had been boys, there might have been an "Ooooh . . . Ahhhh." But they gave no such reaction, simply tilted their heads and watched as the sparks turned black against the gray sky and then vanished before having really gotten too far. I gathered up my hound dog and headed back toward home.

I had two messages on my answering machine, both from Bonnie. *Do you hate me because I'm beautiful or because I stayed for lunch with Jay Adams? I apologize if I was an ass. Watch me at six.*

The second message was the more terse of the two. *You knew about that damn car already, didn't you? I know you did. Are you really going to be a shit about this?*

It was hot dog night at the Sewell household. Boiled to the precise moment of splitting, then removed from the heat, served on a bed of white bread and drowned in an insouciant puree of ketchup. A real palate pleaser. For the Canis familiaris, dry crunchy bits, allegedly chicken flavored. And my plate to lick clean. A five-star experience all around.

I watched the six o'clock news. Mimi Wigg, the pint-size news anchor with ten pounds of hair, had her serious face on as she led off with a story about the execution-style killings of a lawyer and his wife in the Mount Vernon section of the city. The police had no motive yet for the killing, but they were investigating a possible connection to one of the lawyer's former clients. Mimi threw it over to a reporter on the scene who offered no new information except that neighbors were shocked and that the lawyer and his wife were being described as "just regular people." I'm sorry, but this isn't news. I spotted a familiar yellow-haired detective in the background, chewing out a uniformed cop. No surprise to me that

the reporter on the scene had been unable to get Detective
Kruk to say anything on camera. The reporter threw it back to
Mimi in the studio, who thanked him with a well-honed
solemnity and then burst into giggles and goo as she turned to
other news.

"In Owings Mills today, a happy ending for six senior citizens and the amusement park they call home. The city has decided that—"

I hit the mute button so that Alcatraz and I could sup in silence. It was a little too silent, so I invited Eliane Elias to play
the piano for us while we ate. *The Three Americas*. The beautiful Brazilian chanteuse delivered up the goods. Alcatraz likes
her too. He abandoned his crunchy chicken-flavored bits and
curled up right next to one of the speakers.

Bonnie came on after sports. I turned the sound back on.
She looked—as always—pert, perky, scrumptious, honest. As
Bonnie talked about what was going on "in other parts of the
country," my mind finally squared off for a look at what Julia
had told me at the Admiral's Cup. Allowing her story about
Terry Haden and "Victoria Wagner" to simmer quietly in a
far corner of my brain had done little to give me any real insight. I had to assume that, despite the name, the woman who
Haden had put in his dirty movies and who Julia and her
Swedes had seen up on the stage of The Kitten Club was Helen Waggoner, not her sister. The butterfly tattoo would seem
to cinch it. How likely was it that *both* sisters had the exact
same tattoo of a butterfly on their left breast? Maybe if they
had been closer with each other, I could see it. Teenagers
running off one afternoon to get tattooed. But by Vickie Waggoner's account the two sisters were oil and water; it was un-
likely that they had shared such a peculiar bonding
experience. No. The woman laid out down in the basement
at the funeral home had to be the person Julia was referring
to. I couldn't come up with any explanation for her having

called herself by her sister's name, but as for the rest of it, the modeling, the bleached hair, the sliding into the world of flesh peddling . . . That all had to be the dead waitress. Mama's girl.

Questions rained down. What about Vickie? How much of her sister's past did she know? Any? All of it? Was she aware of the appropriation of her own name? Or was Vickie Waggoner really as much out of the loop as she was suggesting? Did I have a pocketful of information here that was all news to her? If so, was it something I really ought to share with her? And what about Sinbad's Cave? Did she know about the sorts of things that went on out there? And was any of this really any of my business in the first place? A lot of questions. And each one was spawning a whole new set. An exponential experience. What I needed were some answers.

I poured myself some bourbon and let it wash through my system.

Of course, the bourbon didn't clarify a damn thing. But it simulated clarity pretty well, and that's sometimes good enough for the short term. It all kept coming back to my needing to have a talk with Vickie Waggoner. The woman had to have the answers to at least some of these questions.

I almost missed Bonnie's little message to me. She had just finished with the five-day forecast. *Freezing. Freezing. Freezing. Slightly less freezing. Freezing.* She turned to Mimi Wigg and slapped her little pointer against her palm.

"Looks like a record-breaking week without a hitch, Mimi. Well. One hitch, I suppose."

She threw a deadpan at the camera. It landed right in my lap.

"Did you get my message?" Bonnie asked an hour later as she came bounding up the steps.

"The conflicting ones on the phone?"

"My nice one. On TV. 'One hitch.' That was for you."

"I got it."

She draped her coat over a chair.

"I'm sorry about this afternoon. I didn't know you'd react so strongly about Jay." She reached down and removed her shoes.

"It's just chemistry," I told her. "That plus I think he's a smarmy, puffed up, self-important weasel who will use anybody he feels like using to further his career. Besides which he wants to get under your skirt. Or in this case, dress."

Bonnie had just stepped out of that selfsame dress. She held it aloft. "He'll be disappointed. Nobody's home." Her arms were twisting behind her back as she stepped over to me. She was unfastening her straps.

"I don't have a lot of time. I have to be back at the station. Would you unzip me?"

"Unzip you? You're already naked."

"I know. Would you please . . . unzip me, Hitch. I've had sort of a lousy day."

"Oh . . . unzip you."

"That's what I said."

I love euphemistic women. We hopped into the sack and unzipped each other. It was very fun, if very brief.

"I have to get back," Bonnie said.

"What for? Can't Mimi Wigg just tell us that it's cold outside and that it's going to stay that way for a couple days?"

"I have to do it."

"Call the station. Have them say you ran out on assignment."

"Can't. They sell advertising around my spot. I have to be there in the flesh."

"You're here in the flesh."

"I'm sorry."

"So am I."

"I promise I'll come right back. You don't have to move. Stay right here."

"And do what?"

Bonnie got out of bed. "Pine for me." She put her clothes back on as swiftly as she had taken them off. She stepped over to my side of the bed and backed up to me.

"Zip me?"

"As you wish." I zipped her zipper and gave her a smack on the fanny. "Zip me. Unzip me. You're a demanding little tramp, aren't you?"

She leaned down and gave me a kiss on the forehead. "I'm not a tramp. I'm just a healthy girl." She grabbed her coat. Alcatraz trotted in. Bonnie snapped her fingers.

"Here boy. Up. Keep him company while I'm gone."

Alcatraz stepped up onto the bed and collapsed at my side. All wrinkles and paws.

"It's not the same," I said.

Bonnie was laughing as she went out the door. "I hope not."

Here's the formula: Men are dogs. I am a man. Therefore I am a dog. (It doesn't work backward, by the way. In that regard, it's like evolution. Alcatraz, for example, remains a dog.)

After the eleven o'clock news, Bonnie had come back over for a warm winter's nap. She didn't seem aware the next morning that she was waking up next to a dog. Two-legged version. If she had been able to access my subconscious at any point during the night for a front row ticket to the evening's presentation of Hitchcock's Dreams, she might have known. It had been a Waggoner sister extravaganza. Bottle blondes. Hourglass figures. Butterfly tattoos *all* over the place. There were lights, there were cameras, there was action. There was even someone I took to be Gypsy Rose Lee—another of Baltimore's favorites—standing in for Ruth Waggoner. She was standing in an alley behind a brick building, holding open a stage door while several dozen versions of her daughters, dressed in glitter and veils and showing lots of leg, went dashing through the door into the building. *Everything's Comin' Up Waggoner.*

I hustled Bonnie on out of there. No coffee. No sweets. No

waffles. Nada. Nil. Zilch. I conjured a dentist's appointment I didn't really have and told Bonnie I would catch up with her later. It wasn't a terribly happy Bonnie who pulled on her coat and gave my front door an Olympian slam. The moment she was gone I was on the phone. I got Vickie Waggoner's phone number from information and dialed it. She answered on the third ring. I reached into my bag of lame excuses and pulled out a tattered veteran.

"I've got some papers for you to sign. I'm sorry, I forgot to give them to you yesterday."

She wanted to know if it could wait. "I don't think I can get a sitter for Bo," she said. "And I really don't want to take him over to the funeral home again."

I suggested that I could swing by her place. I invented an appointment at Hopkins University—which was near where she lived. I told her that I was going to be in her neighborhood.

"By the way, Billie told me that you called yesterday to ask about cremation. We can go over that as well."

She agreed to my stopping by. Though not with much enthusiasm. Alcatraz eyed me accusingly as I abluted with vigor.

Vickie Waggoner lived near Memorial Stadium, former home of the Baltimore Orioles, the Baltimore Colts and, for a short period until they got their new home, the Baltimore Ravens. Do you get the impression that professional sports teams couldn't wait to leave the place? It might look that way, but actually that's not at all the case. The Orioles and the Colts made Memorial Stadium their home for over four decades collectively before moving on. Each enjoyed a great number of heydays in the grand old horseshoe. The Colts only vacated Memorial Stadium because of the dictates of an imperious and tradition-snubbing owner who ordered the team in 1984 to pack their stuff into moving vans and sneak out of town.

Which they did, at three in the morning, bound for—it still hurts—Indianapolis. Local news cameras captured the predawn flight for posterity and eternal derision. To old-time football fans in Baltimore, the shadowy tape of the Mayflower moving vans pulling out of the training facility near Reisterstown is as indelibly etched on their brain pan as the Zapruder film.

The Orioles, on the other hand, mastered a graceful and emotional exit from Memorial Stadium in 1991 in order to move downtown near the harbor into one of the crown jewels of modern American baseball: Orioles Park at Camden Yards. A packed stadium watched on huge video screens as the Memorial Stadium home plate was dug up and whisked to the new facility downtown for a ceremonial planting at its new home. As for the football affront, the city eventually played tit for tat by venturing out to the Midwest to snatch up somebody else's football team (Cleveland's), rename it the Baltimore Ravens and bring it back to town with the promise of erecting a similar jewel right behind Orioles Park. During construction, Memorial Stadium had been dusted off so that the Ravens could move in temporarily, allowing Charm City sports fans the chance to undo the untimely silence that had befallen the venerable house and to pack the joint once more with roars and cheers and boos. Say what you will about the fickle infidelities of sports teams and their owners, Memorial Stadium refuses to roll over and die.

The stadium is located smack-dab in the middle of a working class neighborhood of brick row houses. The narrow streets shoot off from the stadium like wheel spokes. I found a parking space right in front of Vickie Waggoner's building.

"There's somebody here," Vickie whispered to me as she pulled open the door. It sounded halfway between an apology and a warning. She was wearing a brown plaid skirt, gray V-necked sweater, with pills, and a tired expression. Or worried.

Both, I decided. And it wasn't from her fanciful rompings in my dreams. What she didn't look like was a porn star and a stripper. Current or former. Her hair was pulled back off her face and bunched into a large, plastic clip—the same sort of coiff Helen had sported the night she was dumped at my doorstep. I took an extra hard look into her eyes. My mind reading technique. It hasn't worked yet.

Vickie's living room was tidy and unexceptional. More Ethan Allen than Ikea. Secondhand Ethan Allen. The sofa, the chairs, the throw rug, the coffee table . . . not a virgin in the bunch. The room felt a little musty. The painting on the wall above the sofa was large and lousy, a light-drenched depiction of a mountain, a glen, a river, a pine forest, a deer. The kind of thing you'd pick up at one of those so-called Starving Artist's Sales for $59.99. Cranking out garbage like this, it's no wonder the guys were starving. I once watched a fellow on television paint one of these. It took him all of thirty minutes. If he hadn't been yakking so much he'd have knocked the damn thing out in about half that time. I scanned quickly for any photographs. I saw none. There were no detectable personal touches. This could have been anybody's living room.

An archway led into the dining room. A man was seated at the table, along with Bo, who was interacting energetically with a bowl of cereal. Milk and cereal bits all around the boy's mouth made him look like he was wearing clown makeup. The man looked up as Vickie and I came in from the living room. It took me a few seconds to place the face. He was no longer sporting a full beard, though he appeared to be several days into a patchy new one. His hair was short and bristly, prematurely spiked with gray. The man's eyes were not as intense as the last time I had seen them. The fires had been dimmed; the whites had gone milky. In fact they looked half asleep.

Terry Haden no longer reminded me of Al Pacino in *Serpico*.
He reminded me more of Al Pacino in *The Godfather Part III*.

Haden didn't recognize me. He barely even acknowledged
my presence. I thrust out my hand, which he stared at for a
moment before taking it. He surprised me with a steel grip. I
led off the festivities.

"Hitchcock Sewell."

He murmured, "Terry Haden."

Apparently my uncommon moniker didn't register either.
Granted, we had only met a few times, but I would have
thought that between my name and my needling him about
his flak jacket, I might have landed a place in his recollection.
Haden wasn't wearing a flak jacket now. He looked thinner
than I remembered him. Aside from the hair ionizing into
gray, the rest of his rugged good looks had gone somewhat sal-
low. He was smoking a cigarette—it was burning in an over-
flowing ashtray on the table—which I thought was a cheesy
thing to do around a three-year-old eating his breakfast. Haden
released my hand and picked up the cigarette and took a drag.
He squinted at me through the smoke.

"Funny name."

"It's short for Terrence, isn't it?" I said.

"I meant yours." He gave me a not very pleasant smile.

"I know you did."

He took another pull on his cigarette and studied me as if I
were some sort of surrealistic sculpture. I gathered that he was
zonked on something. I smelled no liquor, there were no
glasses on the table, no bottle. Whatever it was it probably
came in pill form. Or powder. Haden seemed content to simply stare at me. Maybe he was actually asleep with his eyes
open. Maybe I was appearing to him as if in a dull dream.
Vickie stepped up next to me.

"I'm going to take Bo in for a bath." She reached for the boy.

Haden snapped out of his reverie, waving her off. "Leave him. He's fine." He turned to Bo, who was attempting to push his cereal bowl around the table using his spoon. "You're okay, aren't you?"

The cereal bowl was taking an uncharted turn, toward the edge of the table. Haden grabbed the bowl and dragged it out of the youngster's reach. He picked up a cloth toy—a large yellow clown with an ink-stained arm—set it down in front of the boy, then looked back up at Vickie. "He's fine."

"You really shouldn't smoke around the kid," I remarked.

"Well, yes sir." Haden made a show of jabbing out his cigarette. Then he made a show of his empty hands. Then he made a show of his ugly teeth. It was all a slow motion show. I decided to speed things up. I reached over and snatched up the butt-filled ashtray, took it into the kitchen, emptied it into the trash can, ran the ashtray under the tap to clean it out, then filled it with as much water as it would hold—maybe a quarter inch—and returned to the living room. I set the ashtray back down on the table, carefully, so as not to spill the water.

Haden glared at the ashtray. "What's that? I can't fucking use that. My cigarette'll get wet."

I tapped my finger against the tip of my nose. "Yeah, I'd heard somewhere that Einstein had a roommate."

There was nothing slow about the way Haden jumped to his feet. He was about five inches shorter than me, but he did his best to get in my face.

"Who the fuck are you anyway?"

"We just met," I said blithely. "Don't you remember? One of us had a funny name?"

"Screw you."

Vickie reached for Haden's arm. "Don't—"

Haden whipped around and caught her by the wrist. "Don't *what*?" He was twisting her wrist backward. I immediately reached out and clamped my hands over both of the man's ears and jerked his head so that he was looking straight at me. The limit of my suffering fools is when they start hurting other people. *"Don't be an asshole,"* I mouthed. Though, because I had Haden's ears blocked, he couldn't tell that I hadn't actually spoken. He looked confused, which was what I wanted. I jerked my hands, giving him a little taste of whiplash, and he let go of Vickie's wrist. Immediately I released his ears, keeping my hands up where he could see them. "Can we cool off here?" I asked. I didn't really intend it to be an actual question. Haden glared at me.

"You big guys always think you're tough."

I corrected him. "We always think we're big."

"Yeah," he muttered. He looked over at Bo, who had set down his spoon to watch the big people shove each other around. The three-year-old didn't seem at all bothered by it. "That's Bo," Haden said, as if I had just walked in the door.

"I know. We've met."

Haden's gaze lingered on the boy before he turned back to me. He was smiling that ugly smile again. Again I didn't like it.

"He's mine."

Haden and I retired to the living room while Vickie took the boy off for his bath. I was guessing that she was probably just looking for an excuse to get Bo away from Haden. A creep like this could carve a nasty impression into an impressionable little mind. It was clear to me that Vickie didn't want to say a whole lot to me in front of Terry Haden. Her eyes had warned me off from pursuing the issue of his being the boy's father. In the living room, Haden made a big deal of offering me a cigarette before he shook one out for himself. He gave me a patronizing sneer.

"Is it okay with you if I smoke in here?"

"It's a free country."

Haden sniffed at that. "Used to be."

He had taken a seat on the sofa, directly underneath the starving artist's painting of mountain bliss. The smoke from his cigarette curled right up past the deer.

"So what's this about Helen's funeral? You're the undertaker, right?"

"All your mortuary needs."

"What? You make house calls?" He laughed at his own joke. And he laughed alone.

"We've been having trouble getting the grave dug in this weather," I explained. "Murphy's Law, you know. Everything we'd normally use seems to be broken."

"That Murphy is a pain in the ass."

"He's good at what he does."

"So, why don't you burn her?"

Oh, the charm just oozed from this guy. You just wanted to run up to him and hug him. "In fact that's what I'm here to discuss with Miss Waggoner," I said. "By the way, we call it cremation."

"I know what you call it." He leaned back and draped his arms out along the back of the sofa. "I think *Miss Waggoner* just wants it over with. I think you can go ahead. I mean, with the cremation."

"I need her to tell me. She's the next of kin."

Haden took a long pull on his cigarette as he crossed his legs. He was attempting to affect a worldliness of sorts, and it wasn't working. I was seeing very few traces of the rakish young hustling filmmaker of only a few years back. Haden's budding Von Stroheim aura seemed to have abandoned him. I suppose veering off into pornography—not to mention uppers, downers and whatever else he was into (or was into him)—can do that.

"I'm the boy's father," Haden said. "Helen and me. Bo.

He's our kid." He picked something off his tongue. Tobacco, probably. I hope. "So I'm next of kin, too."

I corrected him. "Well in fact you're not. Your son is, but you're not."

"What do you mean? I just told you."

"Were you and Helen married at the time of her death?"

Haden let out a little snort. "What do you mean 'time of her death?' You mean like, two days ago?"

"Were you ever married to Helen?"

"Hell no. But that's her fault. Stubborn goddamn woman. The moment she finds out she's knocked up she shows me the door. Hardheaded bitch. Helen turned into a real pain in the ass, I'll tell you."

He swore again as he savored the memory. Apparently nobody had covered the concept of not speaking ill of the dead with the gentleman on the couch. He took another long pull on his cigarette.

"Bitch."

I'd heard him the first time. "So I take it that you two were madly in love."

Haden squinted at me. "What's that supposed to mean?"

Christ, what *was* this guy on? "Love. It's a term of endearment? Affection? I'm sure you've heard of it. It was invented by Cole Porter? It means never having to say you're sorry? Rhymes with June and moon?"

"What is . . . ? Is this supposed to be some kind of a joke?"

"Skip it."

"You're a pretty fucked up guy, aren't you?" Haden said.

It was too easy a straight line to even bother with. I simply shrugged.

"Anyway, what's love got to do with it?" Haden grumbled, stealing a line from Tina Turner. This spawned an image of Ike. Which—given this guy's exploitation of Helen Waggoner—maybe wasn't such an irrelevant image.

"Skip it," I said again. "I'm just accustomed to the idea of people being a little upset when someone close to them has been murdered, that's all."

"Helen was shot, man. That's fucked up. You think I'm some kind of hard-ass? Just because she was killed doesn't mean I suddenly got all these fond memories of her, that's all. I mean, we were cool for awhile there, okay? But pain in the ass is pain in the ass. Can't change that, man."

"Nobody's asking you to, Terry."

"I'm here, aren't I? I mean, I heard that Helen was killed and here I fucking am." He slapped a hand against his chest. "I don't have to be here."

I was tempted to ask him if he'd let me hold his Mr. Congeniality Award sometime. Instead I asked, "How did you hear about Helen's being killed?"

"What do you think? I can read. I saw it in the paper. Dead fucking waitress. There was her name."

I decided to go fish. "So Vickie didn't call you to tell you? I mean, as Bo's father?"

Haden's expression screwed up. "Her?"

"Yes. Her."

An ugly grin stretched across his face. "She's all right, isn't she."

I ignored his appraisal. "Did Vickie know that you were Bo's father?" I realized that Vickie had skirted that same question the day before in my office. Or maybe she didn't skirt it; but she didn't answer it. Neither did Haden now. He stubbed out his cigarette, his gaze wandering to the window.

"Helen, man . . . She was a piece of work. Maybe we should have stayed together, you know. I don't know. Even a pain in the ass the way she was, she was something else. I mean, when she really had it." He fell back on the couch and looked up at the ceiling. "Fucking Helen . . . Just like her mother."

This brought me to attention. "Her mother? What about her mother?"

Haden steadied his gaze at me. His pupils were doing side-strokes. "What about her? Ruth Waggoner. Now there was a fucking pistol, man. That woman was something in her day."

"Just how far back do you go with this family?" I asked.

Haden was looking at me as if I had sprouted a gourd. "You were a teenager once, weren't you? Didn't you ever go down to The Block? You know, use a fake ID and get in to see a show?"

"I never needed a fake ID," I said, unable to keep my own smarmy smile off my face. I stretched my legs out, just in case he forgot how much taller than him I was. If this guy wanted to talk about pain-in-the-ass, I can get in my licks.

My efforts sailed right past him. "Well, if you missed Ruth Waggoner, man, you missed the real deal. She could've gone places, you know, except by the time she came up they were already closing down the fucking Block. It's shit now. I hate that place. Ruth could've been another Blaze Starr. You know Blaze Starr, right?"

Sure. The Two O'clock Club. Stripper, proprietor and philanderer of southern governors. The last big thing on The Block. She has long since hung up her strings and retired to the family home in West Virginia.

"Of course I do," I said.

"Well, Ruth had some of that shit going. Most of these girls you see now, man, they're idiots. They're just pretending. It's all fucking coo coo coo and wrap themselves around the goddamn pole. Big deal. Ruth was for real. She gave you your money's worth."

I needed to straighten out the scenario. "So . . . when you met Helen you already knew that her mother was Ruth Waggoner? Your childhood idol?"

"Hey, what's your fucking problem, man?"

"I just asked a question."

"No, I didn't know who the hell she was. I just met her. I flipped when I found out though. I couldn't believe my luck."

Interesting way to put it. "But Ruth wasn't still . . . she wasn't still dancing by then, was she?" I asked. "She must have retired already."

Haden chuckled at that. "She pulled her clothes off for a living. You want to call that dancing, go ahead. She was a working girl, man." Haden pulled out another cigarette, then forgot to light it. It remained in his fingers.

"No man, when I met her she was beat. Saddest fucking thing I've ever seen. Here's this woman who did a real number on me when I was a kid, you know? I mean, Ruth Waggoner. A kid'll take a woman like that home in his dreams in a fucking heartbeat. I hook up with her daughter and so I go and meet her . . . and she's a wreck."

"The years took their toll, did they?"

"The hell with the years. The booze took its toll. The pills took their toll, man. And then the cancer on top of it all. She was a mess. All that good stuff she used to strut around on that stage, man. . . . I told Helen flat out. I told her look at your mother. I told her she better make sure she didn't end up like that. Fucking Helen never listened to anybody though. A goddamned kid. She was already pill crazy. I mean, you know, there's nothing wrong with a little pick-me-up, but keep a handle on it for Christ's sake. I mean, Jesus . . ."

He trailed off. He looked down at the cigarette in his hand like he didn't know how it got there. Then he looked over at me the same way. I got the feeling that whatever it was he was on had suddenly clicked into its next phase. Whatever handle he had on the situation looked like it had just dropped off. He had the gaze of a goat. Just then, Vickie stepped into the room. She stopped just inside the archway, looking at the two of us as if we were at a dance and she was deciding which was going to be the lucky one.

"I put Bo down for a nap," she announced.

"We were just talking about your mother," Haden said, snapping back to life. "The one and fucking only."

Vickie stiffened. "What about her?"

"I was just going down memory lane. Back to the good old days."

"That's what some people might call them."

"Don't you know it's not right to speak bad of the dead? Your mother made a lot of people happy in her day. What the hell's wrong with that?"

"Nothing's wrong with that," Vickie said in a tight voice. "So did Helen. They made the world a happier place."

"Goddamn right."

"They just didn't stick around to enjoy it themselves."

Vickie spat this last comment directly at the man on the couch. I saw the color flare up in her cheeks. Haden didn't seem to notice.

"Yeah, what do you want to do about Helen anyway?" he asked. "You want to cremate her? This guy's got to do something with her. He can't just keep her on ice until spring."

I got to my feet. "I'm pretty sure we can get a grave dug by tomorrow," I said to Vickie. I hadn't spoken with Pops again, but I knew he would be doing everything in his power. "It's your call. If you want cremation, I'll arrange it for you."

Haden snorted. "You're next of kin. You and Bo. I'm just the fucking father. You see how much that counts."

Vickie was looking extremely uncomfortable. And I didn't think it was *my* presence that had her rattled. "Do I have to decide right now?"

"Not this minute, no," I said. "Even if Pops . . . even if they've started on the grave, it's fine. Nobody's going to force you into anything you don't want." I half-directed this last bit in Haden's direction. If he caught the inference, he didn't show it. He was leaning forward on his knees, cracking his knuckles. His head was bobbing ever so slightly.

"I'll call you later then," Vickie stammered. "Is . . . is that all right?"

Haden mouthed off from the couch. "What's that mean? The guy's come all the way out here. He's here. What do you have to call him for? Can't you just make up your mind?"

"It's okay," I said. "Of course you can call me."

Haden fell back on the couch, exasperated. Vickie trained her dark green eyes on me. The mind reading trick. "I'm sorry you had to come all the way out here."

"No problem." I held a moment, then started for the door. Vickie followed me. "Didn't you say something on the phone about some papers you had for me?"

I pulled the door open. "They can wait."

Haden remained on the sofa. He was shaking another cigarette out of his pack. Apparently he had forgotten about the other one. It was on the couch, next to him. I couldn't say anything to Vickie without his hearing me. I wanted to ask her if everything was okay. This guy didn't look like he was planning to go anywhere in a hurry.

"Thank you," Vickie said. "I *will* call you."

Her eyes were flashing like silent sirens as she closed the door.

CHAPTER
12

Kruk had no time for me.

"I can give you one minute, Mr. Sewell. I've got bodies dropping out of the sky."

There was a sense of controlled frenzy at police headquarters. Everyone in the homicide section was either on the phone or dashing off.

"It's the lawyer," Kruk explained. "Prominent lawyer and wife gunned down as they were about to leave for Tio Pepes to celebrate their anniversary. Do you have any information about who might have done it?"

"Me? Of course not. I came down to—"

"Then you're down to thirty seconds. The mayor wants an arrest in this case yesterday."

"It's about Helen Waggoner," I said. I could tell that I was already losing him. A young woman hurried over and handed him a piece of paper. Kruk glanced at it, crumpled it and dropped it onto the floor.

"What about Helen Waggoner? Do you know who killed her?"

"You want me to do all your work for you today, don't you, Detective."

"Answer."

"No, I don't know. But I think you might want to take a look at the boy's father. His name is—"

"Terry Haden," Kruk cut me off again. "We're not unaware of him, Mr. Sewell. I've got a man running him down. But right now, fact of life? A highly connected lawyer and his wife. Execution style. Dead waitress. You can do the math."

"You're dropping the investigation?"

"Of course not. I just told you, I've got a man looking into Terry Haden's whereabouts the night of the murder."

"That's it? One cop?"

"You bring Helen Waggoner's killer in here, and I'll personally arrest him."

"What's with all this 'me, me, me' today? Do I get my ranger badge if I bring the killer in?"

Kruk sighed. "It's a question of manpower. We're doing what we can about the Waggoner killing. Unfortunately, the rest of the killers in our fair city decided not to wait until we were finished with that one. Time marches on. Bodies pile up. You know how it goes." He consulted his watch. "Do you know what it says, Mr. Sewell?"

"Tick, tick, tick?"

"It says bye-bye."

A phone on a desk next to us had been ringing. Kruk snatched up the receiver. "Kruk." He listened intently. Then he scrambled the papers that were on top of the desk until he came up with a pen. "Go on." He slid into the chair.

I was history here.

The police were putting Helen Waggoner's murder on the back burner. But at least they had a tag on Terry Haden. I had no proof on the guy, I simply didn't like him. If Haden did turn out to be Helen's killer, it seemed likely to me that he would trip up sooner rather than later.

But with the mayor climbing down their necks to come up with the killer—or killers—of the lawyer and his wife, the police might not exactly be hounding Terry Haden for an instant confession about the murder of Helen Waggoner. At least, that seemed to be the message that Kruk was flashing.

I took a left on Eutaw, passing a block from the Arts Tower. You get a clear shot of its clock face from a block away. The Arts Tower building is an exact replica of the Palazzo Vecchio in Florence. The city uses it now to house its office of cultural affairs. It used to house the offices of the Bromo-Seltzer Company. A replica of the famous, blue Bromo bottle once rose some thirty feet above the tower's turrets. It came down decades ago. The clock face doesn't read 1, 2, 3. . . . Instead, B-R-O-M-O-S-E-L-T-Z-E-R is spelled out in Roman-style lettering where the numbers would be.

When I looked up at the clock, it was E minutes past B.

I was halfway to the airport, puttering along in the slow lane, not paying as much attention to my driving as I probably should have been, when—for lack of a better word—a sensation suddenly descended on me. *I am going to find Helen Waggoner's killer.* This is a little difficult to describe. It filled the entire car. It was a knowing. Forget Bonnie, forget Vickie, forget anything wholly logical. Forget the fact that the dead woman was dumped on my doorstep. These were the tangibles. But this wave that swept through me transcended the tangibles. I really can't explain it much past that. I was suddenly infused with a clear and indisputable understanding that this was—for the moment anyway—my destiny. It sounds silly, I know. But I was going to figure out who killed Helen Waggoner. It was as simple as that. And with this thought came a sensation that some sort of residue that had been settling over everything the past several days had suddenly been wiped away. The sunlight was brighter. The painted lines on the road surface were sharper, clipping by in perfect unison. The other cars as well, the houses along the hillside overlooking the parkway, the trees flashing by, even my fingernails on the steering wheel . . . everything had an extra *crispness*, a clarity and perfect outline that hadn't been there just five minutes before. The same could be said of my mind. It was bizarre. Murders, muggings, rapes, wars, terrorist bombings, natural disasters up the wazoo, rampant infidelities, cronyism, corporate tax cheats, starvation, mass suicides, random acts of violence, cancer, AIDS, the heartbreak of psoriasis . . . all of it was still running full throttle all over the world, nonstop; twenty-four/seven, as they're now saying. The planet was one big marble of wretchedness. And as for me, I wasn't exactly being lifted aloft by Disney bluebirds either. I was wheeling down the Baltimore-Washington Parkway in my unexciting car on the fourth record-breaking freezing cold day in a row, tuning in to what seemed to be the preexisting fact that I was going to be tracking down a cold-blooded murderer. Should this really have been a happy-making moment? Or maybe not happy-making. *Vivid*-making? There was no way in hell I could argue that all was right with the world. Yet for about five minutes there, right before I took the airport exit, I experienced a clarity and an apparent understanding of God's big, bad beautiful plan that was downright embarrassing to me — once it was over. I was glad that nobody had been in the car with me. Lord knows what sort of nonsense I might have spouted.

It passed. By the time I pulled up in front of Sinbad's Cave — even uglier in the daylight — the world was back to its general state of random disarray. I turned off the engine and sat there a minute seeing if I could pick up the scent of any gas fumes that might have been leaking up from the tank. I couldn't smell a thing. Okay then, that's it. Apparently I had had a religious experience.

Funny, I would have thought maybe they lasted a little longer than that.

There are no windows in Sinbad's Cave. Inside the place, eternal night reigns. The joint looked exactly as it had three nights before, with the exception that right now it was basically abandoned. There were less than a dozen customers scattered about at the tables, quietly eating their lunch. No loud laughter. No leggy women. Nobody piling up glasses in a pyramid. . . . Dullsville. The sign said to seat myself, so I did. A waitress shuffled over and started to take my order, then recognized me. She pointed her pencil at me.

"You."

I shot back with a finger-pistol. "You."

It was Gail. She looked so much more in context running the lunch bunch. The chubby waitress glanced about. "Where's Bonnie Nash? Told my mother when I got home the other night, and she got all over me for not getting an autograph. She coming to meet you?"

"I'm afraid not. It's just me today."

Gail did nothing to hide her disappointment. "Shoot. Say, you guys married or anything?"

"We're just friends."

Gail snapped her gum. "Uh-huh." She poised the pencil over her order pad. "So what can I get you?"

I ordered a turkey club, split pea soup and a Cobb salad. Thirty-four years old and I wasn't even sure what a Cobb salad was. I'd always figured it was something they named after Ty Cobb.

"Cup or bowl on the soup?"

"A cup'll be fine."

"And to drink?" She made a conspiratorial face. "Can I get you a Wild Turkey?"

"It's a little early for that," I said. I glanced around the room. In here it could be any time you wanted it to be. "A cup of coffee'll be fine."

Gail scribbled down my order. "Oh. Thanks for the tip the other night. You went a little overboard though, don't you think?"

"Forget it."

"Forty dollars for two drinks? Are you kidding? I was a hero. You made my night." She added, "They don't really expect me to pull in big tips."

"Well, I guess we showed them."

She went off to put in my order. Rather, to put in the last order that Helen Waggoner had taken. Of course, I hadn't expected a bolt of lightning to hit me just for ordering the same thing that Helen's final customer had ordered, but I had to start somewhere. Gail came back with my coffee.

"We didn't get you in any trouble the other night by the way, did we?" I asked.

"No. Why?"

"No reason. Listen, Gail. Something you said the other night. About Helen Waggoner."

"What's that?"

"You said she really got into it with one of her customers a month or so ago. You said they were yelling at each other. Are you positive it was a customer?"

"What do you mean?"

"Could it have been an argument between two people who already knew each other?"

"You mean like a friend?"

I was thinking of Haden, of course. "Friend" isn't exactly how I would have characterized the creep. "Something like that. Think back. Was there anything specific that Helen said to this guy that you can remember?"

Gail whirled her gears. Nothing was coming out.

"What about the man? What did he look like?"

Gail put the effort of remembering into her face; she tried hard. But she came up blank again.

"I'm sorry. It's dark in here, you know. And the guy was off at one of the back tables. There's not much light back there. I really don't remember what he looked like. Just another customer is what I was thinking. You know, a businessman, coming over here to . . . you know, to get lucky."

I let it drop.

"You said that Helen had been making noises about quitting. Do you think she meant it, or was she just blowing off steam?"

Gail poked her pencil into her steel-wool hair, where it disappeared completely. "I don't know. I think she sort of meant it."

"What makes you think that?"

"Well, it wasn't just that time, that night she argued with that customer. The other night . . . the night she was killed and all. I mean, it was like it was on her mind or something. She kept saying, 'I don't need this place anymore. Forget this dump.' You know. Like that. Over and over."

"Like she didn't need the work anymore?"

This woman had been two months pregnant and on her own. I had to think that she needed all the money she could get. That just ain't quittin' time.

"Kind of. I don't know. Like I said, Helen had a temper. Maybe it was like you said, just her way of blowing off steam. I really didn't know her. But it sounded real to me. You really ought to talk to someone like Tracy. She'd know a lot better than me."

"Tracy?"

"That's who I was subbing for the other night. Tracy is . . . was a friend of Helen's. You know? Sometimes she'd baby-sit for Helen's boy. Stuff like that. She'd know better than me."

"Tracy. Does she have a last name?"

Gail looked at me like I was a two-headed rabbit. "Yeah. Who doesn't?"

Cher, for one. Madonna. Roseanne. The Amazing Kreskin . . .

"And that would be?"

"Tracy Atkins."

"Do you know how I might get ahold of her? I mean, other than here?" It was occurring to me that I would probably be wise not to become known as the guy who snoops around Sinbad's asking questions.

Gail was shaking her head. "No. But you can ask the bartender. Ed would know."

"Is that Ed?" I asked. The guy behind the bar was about forty. Receding hair, shoe polish black, combed back with a liberal dose of greasy kid's stuff, as the commercials used to say. He was wearing a black vest over a red shirt, and a black tie. He could not have looked more bored.

"That's him," Gail said. "He's the manager here. He's the one who hired me."

I remember Gail telling me how she landed this job. "Is that the guy who your uncle knows?"

Gail shook her head. "No. Uncle Lenny knows one of the owners. It's like a company or something that owns this place. You know, a bunch of people."

"A partnership?"

She shrugged. "I don't know. I guess. Something like that."

Gail brought me my food about ten minutes later. A Cobb salad is a plate of spicy chicken chunks, blue cheese, avocado and tomato on a bed of greens, doused with bacon-buttermilk dressing. Now I know.

"You need anything else?"

"This looks fine. Thanks." Gail lingered. "What?" I asked.

She was holding her tray up against her breast. I guessed that as a child, little Gail had probably been the security-blanket type. Possibly there was even a one-eyed teddy bear in her past. The love of her life.

"Something else about Helen," she said, lowering her voice.

"What's that, Gail?"

"Please don't tell anyone I said this."

I zippered my lips and threw away the key. This satisfied the waitress. Gail leaned closer. "I don't know this for sure. But I got the feeling Helen was fooling around."

Somebody should have scolded Uncle Lenny for dropping such a lamb into this den of wolves. The chubby waitress was probably the only one in this tawdry joint who *wasn't* fooling around.

"I got the feeling she was fooling around with Gary," Gail said.

"Gary."

"He's the guy on the keyboard. He was here the other night."

"The big guy. With the lovely sidekick."

"That's Gloria. They're together."

"Together. You mean as a duo."

"I mean they're a couple. They live together and everything."

"I see what you're saying. You think Helen might have been nosing in on—"

"Gloria. Uh-huh."

"Interesting."

"But I'm not sure. I mean I kind of think something like that was going on. But I don't know. Please don't say I said anything. I could be all wrong about it."

I reprised the lip-zipping move. "Thank you, Gail." Before she headed off I asked her, "So what are you studying, Gail?"

She beamed. "Computers. I'm gonna be a geek. I can't wait."

My soup was salty. My Cobb salad was unlike any Cobb salad I had ever had before. The turkey club was dry. I ate half, left half, then went over to the bar. Ed the bartender made half an effort to look eager.

"What'll it be."

"I'm looking for Tracy," I said to him. "Is she working tonight?"

"Who's asking?"

Um . . . how many choices do we have here? "Is she?"

"Why do you want to know about one of my workers?"

"I just said, I'm looking for her."

"Yeah? And?"

"Have you heard of Guaranteed Mutual Life Insurance?"

He said that he hadn't. Which would only make sense. I had just made it up.

"Well that's who I work for," I said. "I've got some questions I need settled before we move forward with a claim on a Helen Waggoner. She was employed here."

"Tell me something I don't know."

"I need to speak with Miss Atkins about the claimant." I wondered if I sounded as stupid to him as I did to me.

"The claimant is dead. You gonna throw money down a hole?"

"There is a son and there is a sister."

"So what do you need from Tracy?"

"I'm afraid that's confidential," I said.

The bartender shrugged with his eyebrows, then stepped

over to the service end of the bar and consulted a sheet of paper that was tacked next to a calendar. He came back over to me.

"She's off tonight."

"Have you got a number where I can reach her?"

"We don't give that out." His tone suggested that this was hardly the first time he had stated this policy.

"Can you make an exception?"

"Why would I want to do that?" Ed leaned forward on the bar. "Are you and me cousins or something?"

"I told you. I'm with Guaranteed Mutual."

"You got a card?"

"They're being printed." I winced. Ed was working up a knowing chuckle, the way some people work up a cough.

As I headed back up the parkway toward the city, I tried to remember where the nearest cash machine was downtown. A quick calculation of my two visits to Sinbad's Cave suggested they were doing something right. Forty dollars for two drinks and some information the other night. Ten today for lunch. Plus another forty. The going rate for phone numbers these days. Or so I was learning.

CHAPTER
13

"We're all set."

Pops clapped his gloved hands together. I was kicked back at my desk, my feet up on a mess of papers next to the telephone. Three tries so far to reach Tracy Atkins. No answer.

"We got the backhoe going again," Pops said. "It took some real slamming before we finally got the dirt to start breaking up." He chuckled. "Made enough noise to wake the dead."

"Gee, and after all the time and effort I went through to get them all settled in."

"Nothing I can do about it, kid. That's life."

Pops was still chuckling over his little joke as Aunt Billie walked in. Pops pawed his ratty cap off his head.

"Good afternoon, Mr. Bellamy," Billie said sweetly.

"Yes ma'am. How are you today, Mrs. Sewell?"

"Delightful. Thank you for asking. Have you brought us good news?"

Pops told Billie what he had just told me, that his crew was digging Helen Waggoner's grave at this very minute. He didn't reprise any of his jokes. Pops has always tried to impress Billie with his professionalism.

"I got to get back and supervise," he said, letting his voice drop down an octave. Or trying. Pops has had a crush on Aunt Billie ever since I've known him. At the moment, his ratty cap was feeling the brunt of his tortured affections. The old man was twisting it in his hands like it was a wet towel he was wringing out. Billie stepped aside to make way for him to pass. I noticed that she didn't leave *that* much room. The old guy had to scrabble sideways like a crab in order to get out the door.

"You fan that poor man's flames," I said to Billie as she plopped down in my small armchair. "You're such a tease."

"He's terribly deferential, isn't he?"

I brought my feet down off my desk. "Billie, he carries a torch for you. Pops thinks you're the cat's meow and pajamas all rolled into one."

"Silly."

"Seriously. He thinks you're top drawer. The living end. The bee's knees. The cream in his—"

"Now stop it. Arthur Bellamy has been digging graves for us for twenty years. If he's been thinking I'm the bee's knees all this time, I'm sorry for him."

"Don't you ever get lonely?" I asked.

"Don't you ever mind your own business?"

"Oh, come on. Pops is a sweet old guy. Who knows, he might even surprise you."

"Hitchcock, I'd rather not have any major surprises at this stage in my life. Besides, Arthur Bellamy is really not my type."

"I've never quite ever figured out what is your type," I said. "I mean after Uncle Stu. You're not going to find another one of him."

She laughed at the memory. "Lord, my family could never understand what I saw in Stuart. I don't suppose a lot of people did. I've told you of course what Father said when he heard I was heading off to Baltimore to become an undertaker's wife."

Of course, she had. But she wanted to say it again.

" *'Baltimore!'* " Billie looked up at the ceiling and laughed softly.

"Oh, Stuart was certainly a sourpuss. But he loved me. I was the one single thing that your uncle never ever complained about. I was 'it' in his eyes. He told me that once, Hitchcock. He told me that in his estimation I was the only good damn thing this earth ever produced." Billie brought her fingers to her face. "Goodness, you're going to make me cry."

"Go right ahead. Everybody who sits in that chair seems to be crying these days."

Billie cocked an eyebrow. "You wouldn't be referring to a certain Miss Waggoner now, would you?"

"I would."

Billie clucked. "It really is such a shame. First the mother and then the poor girl's only sister. And now she has that little boy to raise all on her own."

"Actually, the father has showed up. I just met him this morning."

I explained to Billie how I had dropped by Vickie Waggoner's house to discuss the possibility of cremating her sister. I trotted out my lie about needing to swing by Hopkins anyway, just to keep my aunt's eyebrows in their hangar. I skipped the part about Bo's father appearing to be high on drugs or that he had been involved in pornography with the poor little boy's mother, as well as possibly encouraging her to take up her mother's tarnished profession. Or for that matter, that he used to get off on watching the little boy's grandmother take off her clothes down on The Block back when he was a pimply teen. Certain things you just steer away from your dear old auntie. I did, however, describe Terry Haden as "a bonafide creep."

"Do you think he could be the one who murdered Helen?" Billie asked.

"Well, he's certainly not what you would describe as a model citizen."

"Model citizens shoot people too," Billie reminded me. "They simply lose their model status when they do it."

Just then the phone rang. Mine doesn't have a name. Billie shooed me away and took the call herself.

"Sewell & Sons, how may we help you. . . . Yes it is. . . . Uh-huh . . . Uh-huh . . . Well, in fact he . . . Yes, everything's fine now. Yes. We can go ahead if you'd like. . . . Uh-huh . . . Yes, dear, of course. That's fine. We'll take care of everything. Let's say ten o'clock? Will ten be okay with you. . . . Fine. Okay. We'll see you tomorrow then. Good-bye, dear."

She hung up the phone.

"That was Miss Waggoner," she announced. "We have a funeral."

The wind picked up Vickie Waggoner's hair as she stood at the edge of her sister's grave the following morning throwing roses down onto the casket, one at a time. One of the roses got picked up by the wind. It skittered over the tarp-covered pile of dirt beside the grave and blew up against Terry Haden's leg. The pornographer leaned down and grabbed it then stepped over to the grave and held the rose out to Vickie. She hesitated, then took it from him. She snapped the flower from its stem and crumpled it. The ruby flakes scattered and vanished. Vickie considered the thorny stem in her hand, then let it drop into the grave.

This is what we call a depressing funeral.

The only decent thing about the day was the sky. A battalion of large, cotton-candy clouds were bundled in a perfect line, like something out of a van Gogh, beautiful and dwarfing. Other than that, the small gathering at the gravesite of Helen Waggoner was a pitiful exercise of futile grief. There were less than a dozen mourners, besides Terry Haden and Vickie. Exclude myself, Bonnie, Jay Adams and a very uncomfortable-looking fat man sent over by Detective Kruk, and Helen Waggoner's farewell entourage could have squeezed into a minivan.

Vickie looked over at me, letting me know that as far as she was concerned we were through here. I gave the signal to Tony Marino, who had been standing some twenty feet off from the main action. God bless the lovesick Italian, he was braving the shriveling temperatures in his kilt and full regalia. He seemed impervious to the cold, though he must have been completely sheathed in goose bumps. At my signal, Tony hugged his bagpipes to his chest and proceeded to squeeze out his first-rate rendition of "Amazing Grace." Several of the mourners, a few waitress buddies of Helen's I recognized from Sinbad's godawful Cave, stepped forward and tossed some flowers into the grave. Everyone stood a moment and listened to the mournful sound of the bagpipes, then they started making their way back to their cars. I stepped over to the fat policeman.

"See any killers?"

"Who's that guy?" He pointed at Jay Adams.

"Suspicious looking, isn't he? I think you should arrest him on principal."

"He looks familiar."

"It's those John Dillinger eyes," I said. "That Al Capone complexion."

The fat man gave me a queer look. "What are you talking about?"

"Skip it." I added, "But I'd put a tail on him, just in case."

Vickie and Terry Haden hadn't left the graveside. Vickie looked up as I approached.

"Thank you for the bagpipes."

"Don't mention it. It's something we throw in now and again."

"It was very moving."

Haden snorted. "Big production number." Then he headed off toward the cars.

"Awfully sweet fellow, isn't he?" I said.

"Helen really knew how to pick them."

"Is everything okay? I can't say you looked exactly comfortable yesterday."

"I'm fine. I just didn't expect him, that's all. I grew up around men like Terry Haden, I'll be okay. He's just another loser." Vickie looked down at her sister's coffin. "He used her. It's the same old story. But I guess she used him too. I don't really know. Some people just suck off each other, it's all they can do. That's their version of love." She looked up at me. If I expected a sad face to go along with her wistful musings, I was mistaken. Her eyes were clear and frank; her lips were drawn back in something approaching a smirk.

"Growing up, I used to beat myself up for not being more like my sister. Can you imagine anything more stupid? Look where it got her."

"I'd like to talk with you some more, about Helen," I said. "Not now, of course. Sometime later."

"You think Terry Haden had something to do with it, don't you?"

"What do you think?"

"I'm beginning to think he actually loved her. That sounds strange, I know, but I think it's true. He's been babbling on and on about her since he showed up."

"What about Bo? Has he said anything about taking his son back?"

"He hasn't. And . . . I don't really know what I'm going to do if he does."

I had my opinion on that one, but I decided to keep it to myself for the moment. Vickie glanced over in the direction of the cars. Haden was playing James Dean, leaning against his Impala, smoking a cigarette. A few cars away was someone I didn't want to let leave before we'd had a chance to talk.

"He's got that don't-give-a-damn act going," Vickie continued. "But he's not doing such a great job of it. He seems pretty confused to me."

"Drugs and a life of general depravity can do that too, you know. So could killing someone. For that matter, especially someone you love. That might leave a person a tad confused, don't you think?"

"Can I ask you a question? Why are you doing this? Why are you trying to figure out who killed Helen?"

I didn't have a ready answer for her. I guess I wasn't sure myself. It wasn't really for Bonnie, although I suppose it had been at first. And Helen . . . I never knew Helen. Bo, perhaps. I just couldn't say.

"I don't know," I said.

Vickie placed her hand lightly on my arm. "Thank you, whatever it is."

I looked over at Haden again. "You should be careful around this guy."

Vickie cocked her head. "If Terry killed Helen because he loved her, then I'm perfectly safe, aren't I? He doesn't love me."

I was dying to get an explanation of Helen's apparent appropriation of Vickie's name. Deciding to use a fake name when you're making skin flicks is one thing. Or even regular flicks. Look at John Wayne. Or rather, Marion Morrison. But choosing the name of your own sibling is another thing altogether. I still didn't even know if Vickie was aware of her sister's peculiar paean. And the dead woman's fresh gravesite certainly wasn't the appropriate place to bring up the matter.

Vickie loosened a chunk of frozen dirt with her shoe. She nudged it into the grave. Her shoulders rose and then fell.

"I guess that's it." She winced a smile. "Sort of anticlimactic, isn't it."

"Funerals often are," said sagely old Sewell.

"I meant her life."

She moved off toward the cars. Pops and his crew were lingering some thirty feet away, next to a mausoleum. I gave the old man the nod. Bonnie and Jay Adams were standing next to the hearse, shooting the breeze. Sam, our driver, was behind the wheel—staying warm—rocking his big head to whatever rap trap was running through his Discman. Sam is a bouncer at several clubs and bars around town, as well as being on call to squire our coffins around. He's a good kid. As big as a wall. As kind as a pussycat. Smile that'll blind you.

Five or six cars down, the person who I didn't want to get away was fishing for her car keys. I made a signal to Bonnie to hang tight and I hurried over to an old MG convertible. A classic model, not in the best of shape; several patches of rust, a recently replaced fender with a not so well-matched paint job, some curls on the convertible roof. But still, pretty snappy. A redheaded woman was about to get in.

"Hold up," I said. She did. "You're Tracy Atkins, right?"

She was in her early twenties. Chinless. Lipless. Round face. Nothing to bark about. A big tug of ginger hair. She was wearing a down parka. A patch of duct tape on one of the elbows was peeling back.

"Yes."

"I'm Hitchcock Sewell."

"You're the underticker." She had a hillbilly accent.

"That's right. You worked with Helen at the restaurant, right? You were friends, weren't you?"

"I'm hair, rat?"

"Excuse me?"

"Said, hair I am."

"Of course. Look, I was wondering . . . I'd like to talk with you."

"'Bout what?"

"About Helen."

"What'd you wanna know?"

"Well, a little more than we can cover standing in the freezing cold. Can we go somewhere?"

The woman's eyes narrowed. "You pick up girls at funerals a lot?"

"I'm not picking you up."

"You really just want to talk 'bout Helen?"

"That's right." That's rat.

She gave me a quick once-over. "Okay. When?"

"How about now? Are you free?"

Her lips pulled back in a not very appealing smile. "Sure. Why not. Where'd you want to go? You gotta place?"

"Can you hang tight for just a minute?"

I hurried over to the hearse.

"Who's the redhead?" Bonnie asked, tight-lipped. She was still unhappy with the unceremonious hustling out the door the day before.

"A coworker of Helen Waggoner. Her name is Tracy Atkins. She might know something about Helen that could help us. I'm going to go talk with her."

"Do you want me to go with you?" Bonnie asked. She asked it in a way that signaled loud and clear that she already knew the answer.

"I think she'll open up to me more if it's just one-on-one." I regretted every single word the instant they left my lips.

"Call me later," Bonnie said coldly. "If you want."

"Of course."

Jay Adams—Mr. Smug—appeared to be enjoying this. I

wanted to stick a pin in him, but I let it go. No point in digging
my hole any deeper. I left them and went back to the MG.
Tracy rolled down the window. I noticed a FOR SALE sign on
the floor behind her seat.

"Are you selling your car?" I asked.

She was pulling on a cigarette. "Nah. Just got it. Why don't
you follow me?"

"Well, I came in the hearse."

Tracy twisted her neck to look over at the hearse. "I been in
one of those," she said. She looked back at me. "A boy I knew
in Morgantown. Guy could party. Git in."

I wanted to say good-bye to Vickie Waggoner. But she and
Terry Haden were already getting into a car. Two cars down,
Bonnie and Jay Adams were getting into his. I was climbing
into the MG. Something about the pieces on this game board
was feeling all wrong to me.

"You paying?"

Tracy Atkins shot through the cemetery gates and turned
right on Greenmount. She beat the yellow at North Avenue
and took a hard right, still in second, then slipped it into third
and slammed down on the accelerator. The little car held the
road beautifully. I just hoped the driver could hold the little car.

"For lunch?"

"What do you think?"

"Sure. I'm paying."

Tracy floated the gearshift into fourth and sunk into her
seat. She sliced the car smoothly around a Jeep that was
merely doing the speed limit. In no time we were at the
Mount Royal Avenue entrance to the expressway. "Hold on."

The entrance ramp to the expressway is one long right
turn. Three quarters of a complete circle. She took it at about
fifty.

• • •

If I were going to milk someone for an expensive lunch I'm not sure what I would choose. Maybe Peerce's Plantation out in the county. Or Marconis downtown. Or even Tio Pepes, the intended destination of the recently slaughtered lawyer and his wife. I'd want waiters who discuss the menu items as if they're eager to sit down and join you, maybe even a chef who pops in from the kitchen to pretend that his entire equilibrium depends on your favorable take on his blend of herbs and spices.

Tracy had different ideas. She back-flipped for Phillips Crab House, a local chain restaurant located in one of the Harborplace Pavilions. Baltimore is a city brimming with crab snobs, and I readily admit, I'm one of them. Of course half of the enjoyment of eating hard-shell crabs is the doing of it in hot weather, at a picnic table covered with newspapers, an Orioles game on the radio and a cooler of cheap beer on ice. The other half is decent-sized crabs that are practically pregnant with backfin. But the dead of winter is not exactly crab season on the East Coast. The winter crabs at Phillips were expensive and disappointing. They were shipped in from the Gulf. Like the restaurant itself, the little fellows were cold and half empty.

"Where's the meat?" Tracy asked after about ten minutes of cracking and poking and blamming away with the wooden mallet. The crabs had barely enough meat in them to pack a tooth.

"It's not really the right time of year."

"But this is Phillips." Apparently the popular crab eatery was expected to have some extra pull with the Lords of Crustacea. Tracy was starting to wield her wooden mallet with more frustration than precision. She snagged our waiter to lodge her complaint.

"There's nothing but shells and shit in these crabs. Look at 'em. A person could starve to death trying to eat these things. You got any bigger ones?"

"Those are the bigger ones, ma'am." The waiter was a high school kid. Light-years away from a fawning professional.

"Well, they stink." Tracy shot a look across the mountain of dead crabs. "You want any more?"

"How about you get us some crab cakes," I said to our waiter.

After he had shuffled off, Tracy made an elaborate job of cleaning off her hands with a wet napkin. She looked like a cat giving itself a bath. "We shoulda gone someplace good, like the Sheraton," she announced. She softened up once our crab cakes arrived. "That's more like it." She smothered her plate with tartar sauce.

"You're not originally from Baltimore, are you?" I asked.

She shoved a forkful of crabmeat into her mouth. "West Virginia. Wheeling. How'd ya know?"

"Lucky guess."

The next ten minutes were spent in an autobiographical overview of the life and times of the woman from Wheeling. I listened with half an ear. There seemed to be a trailer, some boyfriends, a father, some beer and—no surprise—fast cars. As her story finally pulled into Baltimore I perked up, though a five-minute side trip about a man who done her wrong and what Tracy did to set things right held things up a bit longer. Finally Tracy arrived at Sinbad's Cave and the subject of her murdered friend.

"I really liked Helen. I'm pissed someone kilt her."

"Were you and Helen close?"

"Oh. Sure. I mean. Pretty close. I liked her. She had a lot of spunk." Tracy pointed her fork at me. "I like spunk. She didn't take shit from nobody."

"Nobody like who?"

"Nobody like anybody. You been out to Sinbad's right?"

"Yes."

"Then you seen it. Guys come in there think every woman in the place is a piece of candy. How many times a night you think I tell a guy drinks don't come with extras, you know? I mean, I'm polite and all. I'm not an idiot. I work for tips."

"But Helen wasn't always so polite?"

"Oh sure. She worked for tips too. You gotta please the damn customer. But you get tired. You know what my mother used to say to me? Food goes to a man's stomach but liquor goes to his hands. She got that right, didn't she."

"Tracy, can I ask you a blunt question?"

Tracy set her fork down and gave her red mane a little toss. "Shoot."

"Did Helen sleep with the customers? I mean, that happens there sometimes, doesn't it?"

She snorted. "More like sometimes it don't. You born yesterday? Tips only go so far. Ever try to make ends meet waiting tables?"

"I missed that one."

"Well, it ain't easy, trust me. You probably make good money yourself, burying people and all, but not everyone can do that. These businessmen? Now *they* got money to burn. They got time to kill." Her eyes narrowed. "And they got a hotel room, too. Already paid for. You want me to spell it out for you?"

"I'm only trying to get an idea of who might have killed Helen."

Tracy's eyes went wide. She was mushing her crabcakes, before eating them. "You think one of the customers mighta done it?"

"Well, that's what I'm trying to figure out. What do you think?

"I dunno. I guess it's possible. Fruitcakes come in all sizes, don't they?"

"Did Helen have any regulars? That you can think of?"

"Helen had that kid. She was a good mother to that kid. She wouldn't just go off sleeping around and leave the kid with a baby-sitter all night. I'm not saying she didn't need the extra cash. But she was a good mother to that boy. You seen him? Cute little thing."

"So Helen didn't have any regulars."

"I didn't say that." She shoveled another forkful of crab into her mouth. "Truth is, I don't know for sure. It's none of my business."

I had the feeling that the gal from Wheeling was protecting her dead colleague, though from what I wasn't sure. Maybe she was just being careful not to speak ill of the dead. It just seemed to me that Tracy was the type to make her business anything she damn well pleased.

"Helen had an argument with someone at the bar," I said. "This was about a month ago. Were you there?"

Tracy wiped her nose with the back of her hand. A little dab of crab remained on her cheek. "Helen had plenty of arguments with people. I told you, men just think they can paw you half to death. She was a tough girl when she had to be. She wouldn't put up with a lot of crap if she wasn't in the mood. Simple as that."

I tried out a different angle. "Did Terry Haden ever come in to the restaurant?"

"Who's Terry Haden?"

I put my fork down. "I thought you said you were friends with Helen. Terry Haden. He was at the funeral just now. He's Bo's father."

"That's news to me."

"You mean Helen never talked to you about her son's father?"

"I don't pry. I told you, her business is her business."

She was lying. Her face was practically twitching with the

effort of keeping it as expressionless as she could. Why she would lie about something like that was a matter I'd have to think about later. Tracy's eyes went wide as saucers as I reached across the table and dabbed the crab off her cheek. I buried it in my napkin.

"Well . . . that guy at the funeral, the one standing next to Helen's sister. Do you ever remember seeing him at Sinbad's?"

Tracy gave it some thought. At least that's what it looked like she was doing. She might have been noodling over Fermat's Last Theorem for all I could tell.

"Could'a. I don't pay attention to faces. I can't say I remember seeing him there. But he could'a been. Helen and I didn't always work together." She took another biteful of crab. She shook her fork at me while she chewed. "I tell you what, though. 'Bout regulars? Helen *was* seeing someone. I mean, someone she was involved with."

"Are you talking about Gary?"

Tracy made a face. "Gary? Oh hell, Gary doesn't count. Gary'll sleep with anything's got two legs."

"But he's involved with whatshername, right? The singer? Don't they live together?"

"Gloria. Yeah. Now you know why he's so desperate to sleep around." She cracked up at her own joke. There was an unappealing little snort that went along with her laughter.

"I take it you don't think a whole lot of Gloria."

"I try not to. She's uppity. She sings like crap and she don't even know it. Listen to her talk you think her and Gary are about one inch away from being superstars. All I can say is she's got the attitude part down, anyway. Somebody ought to tell her that a little talent wouldn't hurt either."

"So was Helen sleeping with Gary?"

Tracy shrugged. "She might have given him a toss. He's not so bad looking, really. Big guy, too." Her eyes sparkled at me across the table. "Like you."

"Gary's got a good twenty or thirty pounds on me."

"Yeah, but you're tall, like him. You're not a squirrel. A girl gets tired of squirrels, you know?"

I didn't. And I didn't want to.

"Were Gary and Gloria playing at the restaurant the night Helen was killed?"

Tracy pointed her fork at me again. "You know you oughtta be a detective. They sure as hell weren't there, come to think of it. They were off that night. You think Gloria mighta kilt Helen? Damn."

"What do you think?"

"Sure. I could see that string bean taking a shot at Helen. I really don't know what the hell it is Gary sees in her anyway."

"Help me out here, Tracy. When you said just now that Helen was seeing someone, you weren't referring to Gary, right? If she was sleeping with him, that was just . . ."

" 'Cause it was fun," Tracy said flatly. And with that, I had a pretty good red-haired idea who *else* had taken the time to sneak around behind the back of a certain string bean singer.

"So you're saying Gary wasn't Helen's regular guy."

"Not a chance."

"So who was?"

"I don't know."

It was coming to me that I might not end up getting my crab cake's worth out of this woman. Though she was certainly getting her crab cake's worth out of me. These Sinbad's women apparently ran a pretty good hustle.

"How do you know she was seeing someone?" I asked, proud of myself for keeping my growing weariness out of my voice. "Did she tell you? Did you see her with someone?" Reading tea leaves? Come to you in a dream?

Tracy ticktocked her head. "Uh-uh. She never brought anybody to that place. Are you kidding? Sometime around, I can't remember exactly, sometime in the fall, I guess. All of a sudden, Helen's got this whole new attitude going on. Suddenly she's buying new clothes, and she's getting new things. New car. Stuff for the kid. I mean, suddenly it's like she's won the lottery or something."

"What was it?"

"She wouldn't say. I asked her right out, you got a rich boyfriend or something? But she was all mysterious about it. I mean, Helen sure didn't go out and rob a bank or anything. It was a guy. But she was clammed up about it."

"And you never saw her with someone at Sinbad's who you thought might have been this guy."

"No way. Whoever he was, she was keeping him clear of that place. I don't blame her either. She was talking about getting a new apartment. She was talking all the time about quitting. But she was still real closemouthed about it all. All I knew was something was happening there. And she was happy." Tracy shook her head sadly. "It's a bitch, isn't it? Nobody'd kill her when she was struggling. They gotta wait til she's happy."

I called for the bill. I paid with cash. For no particular reason—maybe because I was dining with a waitress—I left a large tip. Tracy stared at the money as I tucked it partway under the place mat.

"Christ. All he did was serve you some lousy food."

I walked her across the street to the parking lot. At the car, she pulled open the driver's side door. It caught a little. "They're supposed to fix that," she muttered. She got in. Her fingers snaked around the steering wheel. She looked up at me.

"You want to go somewhere or something? I got the whole afternoon off."

I pulled out my trusty lie. "I've got a dentist appointment. The office is just over on Eutaw.

She made a face. "I hate dentists. I knew one in Wheeling.

Drank like a skunk. He thought he was a real Romeo. So you know, what if you canceled?"

"It took me five months to get this appointment."

"Maybe some other time, huh?"

"Sure."

"I'm serious. Call me sometime." She leveled me with a look. "I know you got my number. Ed told me."

She turned the key, gave me a wave and fishtailed out of the parking lot. I hurried back across the street and phoned a cab. If it was possible, the temperature seemed to be dropping even more. While I waited for the cab I popped into a Harborplace shop that sold only scarves. I spent way too much money on a silk scarf that was mauve and peach and red and green and gold and blue and yellow. I had the saleslady gift wrap it for me in red and gold cellophane, then ran outside and hailed my good man.

I left a message for Bonnie that I would catch up with her after the six o'clock news. I added that my lunch with the redhead had been about as much fun as poking sticks in my eyes. Still, I was glad that I had the scarf as a peace offering.

Despite the frigid temperatures, I was sitting on an overturned wooden barrel alongside the tugboat pier, sifting through the information I had gathered from Tracy Atkins. Alcatraz was busy hiding his love notes everywhere. I had the photograph of Helen and Bo with me and was once more in a staring contest with the dead woman. The eyes. Those chocolate brown eyes. They nearly spoke. But the message kept being swept off by the wind before it could reach me. Was Helen laughing and smiling at the person who would be murdering her in three months time? Was that it? Was the killer right there, just behind the camera? That close? Maybe with a nuclear magnifying glass of some sort I would have been able to see the person's face reflected in Helen's happy lamps.

A large seagull landed on a mailbox a few feet away, tucking its wings up under its breast with a shudder, as if it were hugging itself to keep warm. Alcatraz bounded over. He planted his oversized feet in a wide stance and gave the gull a piece of his mind. The large bird snickered back at him. I hoped I wouldn't have to intervene. Alcatraz could well get his ass kicked. Seagulls fight dirty. And they have a perpetual height advantage. I pulled off one of my gloves and threw it at the bird. It hit him squarely on the side and fell to the ground. I took off my other glove and tried it again. This time the bird turned its snooty head and screeched at me to buzz off, or noises to that effect. I considered pulling off a shoe and seeing if I could dislodge the ruffian with a well-placed Rockport. But I didn't.

"Come on, Alcatraz. We don't need him."

I slipped off the barrel and retrieved my gloves. The bird's wings deployed and off it glided to the end of the pier, where it struck a picture-postcard pose atop a wooden piling. Alcatraz found my bare hand and washed it for me. I dried it among his wrinkles and we headed off to the Oyster.

I knew what I had to do next. But it would require my getting ahold of Vickie Waggoner. The woman had just buried her sister a few hours ago. For all the strong front Vickie had shown at the funeral, I also recalled her torrent of tears when she had allowed herself to break down in my office the other day. This really was not the time. It would have to wait.

The impromptu ice sculpture from the water main break looked like a keeper. Besides the wreath and the tinsel, someone had chipped several small notches into the ice and hooked a few tree ornaments onto it along with about a dozen candy canes, strategically placed. There were also some canned goods at the base of the thing. Green beans. Sauerkraut. A few cans of soup. I pulled out a ten-dollar bill and tucked it under the can of green beans.

Sally was off Christmas shopping with Julia. Frank was there—Sally's hubby—holding down the fort. To watch the two of us you might think that my former father-in-law and I don't get along. The fact is, my former father-in-law and the *world* don't get along. Frank is a sourpuss. How in the world such a creature had anything to do with the conception of someone like Julia is beyond reason and genetics.

Frank knows what I drink, but he makes me ask him for it. He uncapped the bottle of Wild Turkey with an irritation and fatigue that seemed to know no bounds. The only way to escape Frank's vortex is to attack it head on.

"Beautiful weather we're having, isn't it?" I sang out, sliding my glass away from his bony fingers. Frank wiped his hands relentlessly on a dish towel as if he were trying to strip off his fingerprints.

"Have you seen the stuff your daughter did for the zoo?" I asked, in peppy overdrive. "It's very clever stuff, Frank. You'd really flip." I threw back the contents of my glass.

I'd grow a tree out of my ear before this man ever came even close to flipping. Frank sucked his lower lip partway in. His moist eyes showed only half-life. Just then, Alcatraz made his move, going back on his rear legs and bringing his front paws up onto the bar. His bony head and floppy ears came up to my shoulders.

"How about a drink for my friend here?" I said to Frank. I wasn't sure who had the better poker face, the bartender or the hound. I got Frank to put a bowl of water on the bar, and I ordered a second shot of Turkey. Can't let the pooch drink alone. It was a little after three. The afternoon could slide away very easily if I didn't watch out. Frank poured me the shot and wandered off. I toasted the man in the mirror behind the bar. And the dog. They looked familiar. Vaguely.

An hour or so—and a few toasts—later, they looked only vague. That is, the man did. The dog had returned all fours to the floor and was sleeping at my feet. I had the photograph of Helen out on the bar. This time the eyes seemed to be scolding me. A warm bar. A warm bloodstream full of bourbon. Not really a serious care in the world. Ready to jump into action as soon as the next person dies. Thinking impure thoughts about the dead woman's sister. It really does take just the slightest of tweaking to become a bastard sometimes. It can happen before you know it.

I asked Frank for the phone. He brought it over to me, along with my fourth shot. Or maybe it was my fifth. I had sort of counted on Alcatraz to keep track for me. I called information and got Vickie Waggoner's number. I dialed it. At the Oyster you really *dial* it. I almost hung up, but Vickie answered on the seventh ring.

"I'm sorry to bother you," I said. "This is Hitchcock."

"Oh. Hello. That's all right." She sounded a little stiff. I shouldn't have called.

"It's not very professional of me."

"I told you, it's all right." Now she sounded annoyed. I looked past the bar at my reflection in the mirror. I wasn't looking all that professional either. Frank was making no effort to conceal the fact that he was listening to my end of the conversation. Were it not that his eyes always maintain a mild condemnation, I'd say he was disapproving of my call.

"I wanted to ask you about Helen," I said. "Do you have any idea who her obstetrician might have been?"

"Her obstetrician? Not at all. Why?"

"That friend of hers at the funeral. The redhead. I had lunch with her. She told me that she's pretty sure that Helen was seeing some guy who didn't mind spending his money on her. It occurred to me that if he happened to also be the guy who got Helen pregnant, maybe he's been footing the baby doctor bills."

There was silence for several seconds on the other end of the line.

"That's very smart," Vickie said.

"Thank you."

"But I have no idea who her obstetrician might have been."

"Maybe there's a bill or something like that, a phone number, lying around her apartment."

"I don't know. The police have been all over Helen's apartment."

"Did they mention anything?"

"Not to me. Not about anything like that anyway."

"I'm just trying to kick start some ideas here. I really shouldn't have called you today. I'm sorry. I—"

Just then I heard a voice in the background. I heard what I guessed was Vickie muffling the phone. I heard her—dimly— say, "It's the police." Then she spoke back into the phone, overarticulating her words. "Is there anything else, officer?"

"Haden's there, isn't he?"

"Yes, officer," she said artificially.

"Are you okay? Is there some sort of problem?"

There was a pause. "That's quite possible. Yes."

"I'll be right there."

"Yes. Thank you."

I let my sleeping dog lie. Somewhere between the Oyster and my car—at a full-tilt run—I sobered up. Or maybe not. The fuzzy bits left me. But there was still a slightly angular skew to things as I skidded to a stop twenty minutes later in front of Vickie's house. The skew grew even sharper when I saw a yellow cloth clown with an ink-stained arm lying face-down on the sidewalk leading from the front door. At the curb, where the sidewalk ended, was an available parking spot.

I had a sinking feeling that it hadn't been there for long.

Vickie's front door had been left unlocked and I let myself in. I discovered nothing in the house that might help me figure anything out. I guess I hadn't expected anything so helpful as a note sitting on the kitchen table. *The pillhead and I are out for a drive. We'll be back by dinnertime.* I felt a little guilty wandering through the place. I had no business there. And I couldn't imagine what I thought I was looking for. Vickie had converted what appeared to be a study—a desk with a computer, gray filing cabinet, bookshelf—into a bedroom for Bo. The half-sized sofa was folded out into a single bed. Kids' toys and books were tossed all around. Back downstairs I sat down in the same chair where Haden had been sitting the first time I came over. I could see the wall phone in the kitchen from where I was sitting. I imagined Vickie on the phone: *Yes, officer. That's quite possible. Yes.* I imagined her hanging up the phone and turning to Haden with a little shrug. And in less than a minute the creep is hustling her out the front door, the kid scooped under his arm.

Before I left I phoned police headquarters and left a message for Kruk. There was nothing else I could think of to do.

Mimi Wigg was bantering with the sports guy, Brett Brown. She was cooing with congenial envy about Brown's upcoming trip to Florida to cover Super Bowl week.

"Bring back a tan for me," Mimi chirped.

"You betcha, Mimi."

The cameraman standing next to me made a gagging gesture.

"And watch out for those cheerleaders," Mimi warned.

"Hey. You got it. I *will* be watching out for them."

The two floor cameras slid noiselessly forward toward the sports desk. Mimi Wigg, out of the picture, leaned back in her chair and gave the chattering jock the finger for a full ten seconds. When it was clear she wasn't going to throw him, she quit. Bonnie was tiptoeing over to me, careful not to step on any cables.

"I'm mad at you," she whispered, then put her tongue halfway down my throat. What fresh madness was this? She pulled back just as I started to respond. "My makeup."

She pressed up against me in the partial darkness. "You smell like a distillery," she whispered, then made her way back over the cables to her weather corner. Brett Brown was still gassing about the Super Bowl. Mimi Wigg was getting a perspiration pat down from the makeup man. She was a very tiny woman—less an hourglass figure than perhaps an egg timer—with a very large head of hair and a severely pretty face. As with our football team, we nabbed her from Cleveland a number of years back. They must really hate us out there.

Brett Brown wrapped up his sports report with a high speed recitation of local high school basketball scores and threw it back to Mimi with one more dig about the cheerleaders in sunny Florida. She ignored the dig and swung in Bonnie's direction.

"Well, for the rest of us who aren't scampering off to follow the bouncing balls in Florida, what's in store for us, Bonnie? Any break in the temperature? It's like one big refrigerator out there!"

"Yes, it is, Mimi. But I'm afraid we'll just have to get used to it." Bonnie swiveled to look directly into the camera that had been sneaking up on her. "Folks, we're going to have to hunker down for a while longer, I'm afraid. Mother Nature has more of the same in store for us. And that's more record-breaking cold temperatures. The conditions right now . . ."

Just off camera, Brett Brown and Mimi Wigg were throwing daggers at each other. It was all silhouetted gestures and silent mouthing, as the lighting in their areas had been dimmed. It looked like a puppet show; especially with Mimi's big hair bobbing furiously. Bonnie appeared oblivious to the shelling as she stepped smartly over to her blue scrim and began pointing out high and low pressure areas that on viewers'

TVs would appear as locations on the various maps that were electronically burned onto the scrim. At the conclusion of her segment, Bonnie told Baltimore to keep bundling up, then threw it back to Mimi Wigg. The diminutive newslady was calm and smiling again under her three thousand watts.

"I guess Mother Nature must have a new winter coat that she's been dying to try out, huh?"

Off to the side, Brett Brown let out a snort. Mimi ignored him and went into her wrap-up. The news music came up. The moment the cameras were off, Mimi yanked the lavaliere mike from her collar and marched off the set.

"It's beautiful," Bonnie said. She wrapped the scarf around her neck and tucked it into her cleavage. "I love it, Hitch. Thank you." Kiss, kiss, kiss. Wampum saves the day.

I told Bonnie on the drive over to her place what I had learned from Tracy Atkins. I decided to forgo the details of how Julia had filled in some of the pertinent blanks for me. Instead, I simply attached Julia's brief history of Terry Haden and Helen's skin flick days to the redheaded waitress's account. I included the fact that Helen had followed in her mother's footsteps, dancing barefoot and all the rest down at The Kitten Club. This brought Bonnie pretty much up to speed. I told her of my phone call with Vickie that afternoon, and how it looked to me as if Haden had dragged her and the kid out of the house the moment she hung up the phone. I didn't mention that I had snooped through the house.

"She was pretending I was the police," I said.

"Do you figure that was so Haden wouldn't know she was talking to you specifically?"

"I don't know. I don't know why he'd care. I think it was more a matter of her calling for help. Or trying to scare Haden off."

"It looks like it worked."

"Only he took her with him."

"Hitch, you can't be sure about that. I mean, you don't know that she didn't agree to go with him."

"It didn't have that voluntary feeling to it."

"So you're saying that Haden thought Vickie was talking to the police and then he hightailed it out of there. Taking her and the boy along. Against their will."

"Yes."

"So the idea of the police spooked him?"

"Yes."

"So he's guilty."

"Of something, I'm sure. The guy is a sleaze. But did he kill Helen Waggoner?"

Bonnie steered her car through the gates of the Mount Washington Apartments. She cleared the gate on my side by an inch. "Well, from what you've said, Terry Haden tops my list. I don't know about you."

"I don't know. What about Helen's mysterious boyfriend? This guy with the deep pockets that Tracy was telling me about."

"What about him?"

"Well, you see the word 'mysterious' that's attached to him? Call me nuts, lady, but that provokes my interest."

Bonnie pulled into the slot in front of her building. "So, you need to figure out who he is." She turned off the car.

"I know. But the first thing now is to locate Haden."

"Why? He's my number one, not yours. You think it's somebody else."

"Still. He's got Vickie and the kid."

"Hitch, can I remind you of something? It's his kid. He's the father."

"I know that. But look. From what I can tell of the guy, he had nothing to do with that kid since the moment the boy was conceived. And now suddenly, what? He's back on the scene and he wants to play poppa? I don't buy it."

"Well, what if he did kill Helen? Maybe he at least feels guilty enough to want to take responsibility for the child of the mother he murdered."

"This guy didn't by any chance win a Heisman Trophy in college then go on to star in car rental commercials, did he?"

"You're funny," Bonnie said. "And I'm freezing." She pointed at the building in front of the car. "You're free to join me."

We quit the car and went inside. Bonnie's place is new and modern and clean. Hit one wall switch and the whole place lights up. Wall-to-wall carpet. Open kitchen with a large green counter. Matching navy sofa and armchair and a large pinewood wall unit that includes books, CDs, TV and VCR and numerous framed photographs of Bonnie through the ages: Bonnie on a tricycle; Bonnie on a diving board; Bonnie in braids posing with her father in front of a weather map; Bonnie in long straight hair, perched atop the shoulders of a lacrosse team. . . .

For the record, there were no photographs of me to be found in Bonnie's apartment. I hadn't expected any. Believe it or not though, Bonnie and I had actually discussed marriage the very first time we met. I was fifty-five sheets to the wind and had proposed to her nonstop for a solid hour. In several languages. Some of which I don't even speak. We were at John Stevens Pub. She was trying to play pool, and I was trying to get her to marry me. Bonnie politely refused me throughout the hour. But she must have seen something in this tall, dark and winsome drunk, for she eventually offered up a consolation prize for all my efforts. In the morning she had asked me if the marriage proposals still stood, but I told her no, they were like eclipses and the time had passed. "Why?" I wanted to know. "Have you reconsidered?" She told me that a guy like me could grow on a girl like her and I told her that she made me sound like a fungus and she told me that I was an awfully sexy fungus. People do talk funny right after sex, don't they? At breakfast we had discussed whether this was to be a one-night stand or if we were going to attempt to see if the two of us—as a unit—might have legs. I warned her that I was divorced, though not damaged by it, but that my inclinations were to let considerably more water pass under the bridge before I decided whether or not I wanted to jump back in. "What if the water simply rises up and comes over the bridge?" Bonnie had wanted to know. She looked so damn luscious with her perfect hair mussed up and her large blue eyes racooned with makeup. I told her that I'd wash off that bridge when I came to it, and that had pretty much concluded our serious conversation. We retired to the bedroom to strike up a silly one instead.

Bonnie threw down her purse, shrugged out of her coat and inched her new silk scarf from her cleavage with the moves of a stripper. I was powerless against the name *Ruth Waggoner* as it invaded my brain. Bonnie backed me up against the wall. We moved like a pair of Siamese twins into the bedroom, plucked away at our garments and then plucked away at each other atop Bonnie's goose down comforter. At one point Bonnie whispered huskily, "My makeup," but her cheek was tracking across my stomach at the time, so I paid no attention. Sometime later I came to rest with my face against her thigh. Her fingers were strolling through my hair. The comforter was bunched at the headboard and halfway off the bed. Somebody was purring. I think it was me.

"Shit!" My head jerked suddenly from Bonnie's drumstick.

"What?"

"What *is* Terry Haden doing back on the scene?"

Bonnie frowned down at me. "I love it when you talk sexy to me." She scooted up, dragging a portion of the comforter over her alabaster charms. "What do you mean?"

"Haden. Why didn't I think of it? He and Helen split up after she got pregnant. Right? Now, three, four years later, she's pregnant again, and look who's hanging around."

"Your point?"

"The point is, Haden is back on the scene."

Bonnie slid off the bed and stepped into the bathroom. She called out, "You're just repeating what we already know."

"No. Look at it." I swung my feet to the floor. My toes sunk into the plush. "Our suspect list has just been reduced by one. According to Tracy Atkins, some man shows up in Helen Waggoner's life, right? What. Four or five months ago. He gets her pregnant. Well, presumably it's him. He's throwing money around. Helen's buying things. She's talking about a new apartment. About quitting work. All this stuff."

Bonnie chimed in, "This is the mystery boyfriend we're talking about now, right?"

"Right. Except, when has this happened before? When did Helen Waggoner last get pregnant and quit what she was doing for a living? Who was the man in her life then?"

Bonnie popped her head out of the bathroom. She had a shower cap on. "I'm going to take a shower. I've got to get back to the station."

"Come on. Who was her guy?"

"Terry Haden. So?"

"Right! And now? Round two. Pregnant. Again. Quitting her job. *Again*. It's him again. Terry's back. I'm being stupid. There *is* no so-called mystery man. It's Terry Haden again! They were getting back together. Or trying to. It's so simple it's boring."

"I thought you said the new guy in her life was loaded. I didn't get the impression that Mr. Haden was exactly Rockefeller material."

"Who knows about that? He's a hustler. Up one day, down the next. He probably had a big wad of money from somewhere, and he schmoozed his old gal with it. Promised her the world. And won her back. At least for awhile. This guy is a play-fast, lose-fast kind of guy. For all we know the two of them burned right through whatever money Haden had and ended up right back where they started. I can see Haden waking up one morning and realizing that the party's over. Again. Helen's pregnant again, and she's counting on him to deliver the goods this time, like he's been promising. I sure as hell wouldn't put it past someone like Terry Haden to start looking for a way out."

"Isn't murder a little extreme?"

"Of course it's extreme. But people still do it. I'm telling you, it's him. Forget this psycho customer business or this moneybags mystery man. It's Gentleman Terry, I'm telling you. And this afternoon he gets a whiff that the police are swinging by Vickie's place . . . and he flies like the wind."

"Shower," Bonnie repeated. A moment later the water started running. I went into the kitchen, to the refrigerator, and drank directly from the orange juice carton. I kept the carton in my hand as I paced back and forth over the carpet trying to slot the pieces together. I realized that I had too few details to paint a complete picture. But the outline remained clear and, for the most part, made sense. Haden was the one. For reasons that I could only guess at, he had weaseled his way back into Helen's life. Maybe he had been working toward pulling her back into the smut business. Maybe he knew that whatever cash he had wasn't going to last, and he wanted to reprise his golden goose days with Helen. Then suddenly she's pregnant again, and the guy just can't believe his rotten luck. Maybe Helen had told him that very day that she was pregnant. And in a snit, he grabbed a car, drove out to the place where she worked, told her to get the hell in and shot her.

And now Haden was on the run. He had taken his son along, as well as the boy's aunt. But why? Why drag Vickie along? If Haden was running from the law, he could run a lot faster without a third person along. Especially a person who presumably didn't want to be there in the first place.

Presumably.

Bonnie found me naked, standing at the sliding glass door to her deck, holding the orange juice carton and staring out into the early twilight. Headlights from the Jones Falls Expressway blinkered through the trees.

"This is how I want to remember you," she said. When I turned around and held out the juice carton to her, a large smile grew on her face. "No. Like *this*."

CHAPTER
15

Terry Haden wasn't listed in the phone book. I checked, first thing the following morning. Even if he were, I doubted he was sitting at home watching game shows with Vickie and Bo, waiting for visitors. But I had to start somewhere. I had no doubt now but that Terry Haden's loose cannon had gone off the week before, aimed at his former-and-possibly-once-again lover, and that now he was on the run. I had to find him. Bonnie had tried to convince me before heading back to the station the night before that this was a job for Superman, or at least the Baltimore City Police, but I refused to be swayed. I gave her a full-frontal view of the legendary Sewell stubborn streak.

"I thought you were all hot to catch a killer. Why the cold feet now?"

"I still am," Bonnie said. "What I'm not so hot for is seeing him kill you."

"Why would you think he'd do a thing like that?"

"Let's see. Desperation? Fear? Nothing to lose? Anger? Shall I continue?"

"The man is out there with two hostages—"

"Oh, Hitch, you just don't know that."

"I'm taking an educated guess. Look, if I'm wrong, if Vickie and Bo went along with Haden simply to bask in his uncommonly charming glow, then the worst I do is embarrass myself for getting all worked up. If they're safe, I'm safe."

"But if they're not. . . ."

We argued a while longer. In a sense, of course, Bonnie was right. This really wasn't my business. I had phoned the police, and that should really have been the end of it. Even if I did manage to locate him, what next? Would I stand there with my hand out and tell the killer to hand over his weapon and come quietly? Presuming that Haden really did kill Helen, who he ostensibly cared about, how much leeway could I expect him to give me? Someone for whom he assuredly *didn't* have a soft spot? I might have been taller than the guy and have a longer reach . . . but a pistol can be a great equalizer. I certainly didn't relish the idea of being shipped off to my own aunt for her professional bon voyage treatment. The truth was, I had no idea whatsoever how I would proceed if I were to locate Haden. I've always had fairly decent improvisational skills. I just hoped like hell they would show up when I needed them.

After checking with Billie to see if anyone had died lately who needed burying—and being told no—I headed over to Baltimore Street. On the way there I passed by the Flag House, where Mary Pickersgill sewed the mammoth American flag back during the War of 1812. That's the flag that was hoisted over Fort McHenry during the British bombardment of Baltimore, inspiring Francis Scott Key to scribble down the words of what was to become our notoriously ungainly National Anthem. The Flag House also happens to be my own personal ground zero. That's where I was conceived many moons ago. After-hours. It's not a long story. Obviously, it's personal.

I continued on past the Flag House and parked my car near City Hall Plaza. I walked a block over to Baltimore Street. The defanging of The Block shows in especially stark relief in the daylight, where the neon signs of its few remaining dens of sin blink anemically onto the indifferent sidewalk. The few people passing along the frigid street were clearly not in search of The Block's cheap thrills; they were simply on their way to someplace else. It was too cold—as well as too early—for the hawkers to be seated on their stools outside the strip joints trying to draw in customers with their oily "Check it out, check it out, live girls, check it out. . . ."

Baltimore Street runs west to east. On Commerce Street, one of the smaller streets feeding into it, about halfway down the block, was a blacked out window in which hung a large pair of red neon eyes, vaguely catlike. Every ten seconds or so the neon in one of the eyes flickered with what was evidently supposed to simulate the action of the eye winking. I ask, who could resist? I crossed the street and ducked into The Kitten Club.

At least the place was warm. Very warm. I stepped through the black velvet curtain just inside the front door and was confronted by a small bar, exactly four customers and a naked woman standing on a small runway-style stage that ran along the back wall of the bar. The woman was plugging quarters into a wall-mounted jukebox as I came inside. Actually, she wasn't completely naked: She was wearing high heels and a string of glass beads around her hips, attached to which was a piece of shiny green material about the size and shape of a shirt pocket . . . something to keep her privates private. The rear wall was actually a mirror. Attached to it—not in neon, but in hard red plastic—was the same large pair of cat eyes as the ones outside the club. In addition, there were plastic whiskers, four on each side, which looked as much like overlong swizzle sticks as anything else.

The room was dark, black with an amber hue, with a cloud of smoke hanging at about knee level with the dancer. A four-foot strip of red tinsel along the bar pretty much topped off the holiday decorating. The frozen water main break outside the Oyster was more festive than this place. As I slid onto the near-est barstool, Led Zeppelin's "Stairway to Heaven" started up and the dancer began to sway side-to-side in a slow, bored fash-ion, lifting and landing a high heel every once and again as if she were going through the motions of stomping listlessly on a bug. Her arms made a halfhearted effort to sway with the mu-sic, but basically they just lifted and fell against her hips. The effect was far from stimulating. The woman had a decent enough figure, though in the piss-poor lighting of the place it was a little difficult to judge. She looked bored, only vaguely caught up in Jimmy Page's rambling, and completely oblivi-ous to the throng of four—now five—who sat at the bar at about ankle-level, looking up at her.

A woman behind the bar in a bikini and a Santa Claus cap came over to me. She flipped a napkin onto the bar. A black light under the bar turned her teeth milky blue when she smiled at me. It did the same to her skin. She had very large blue breasts. She was wearing a wig of long, straight pinkish hair that looked like cellophane. She was either gorgeous, or she was a man. I just couldn't tell.

"Gitcha something?"

I asked for a beer. National Premium. Support the home team.

"That'll be eight dollars." I gave her a ten. I neither ex-pected my two dollars change nor got it. The beer was warm. Up on the runway, the dancer had placed her palms against the mirrored wall now, just below the eyes of the cat, and was leaning forward, as if a cop was about to frisk her. Her pelvis was thrust out. She was giving a sort of slow-motion rabbit tail shake with her rear end. Her rhythm had nothing at all to do with the song, whose tempo was revving up even as the dancer's rear end rocked languidly. I laughed. I couldn't help myself. It just came out. I don't even know if the woman was aware of the effect; the way she had placed herself on the mirrored wall, the swizzle-stick whiskers appeared to be shooting out directly from her bobbing fanny. The effect was nowhere near as sexy as it was ridiculous. Basically, she was mooning her audience. That's what made me laugh out loud. The dancer threw me a mean look—her fanny still ticktocking like a swollen metronome—and with a slow motion move she pulled one hand from the mirror and gave herself a lazy slap on the haunch. It was either a giddyap move from her bag of tricks, or she was letting Mr. Laughter over there know that he could just kiss her big old bobbing bundle for all she cared. The look she shot me suggested the latter. So did the greeting she gave me when she came over to me after her number, pulling a transparent robe over her treasures.

"What the fuck's your problem, buster?"

Her stage name was Misty Dew. She gave me a hard look when she said it.

"Dew. You know? Like the stuff that's on the grass in the morning."

"There's another kind?"

She cinched her robe tighter. "Never mind."

"What's your real name?" I asked.

"None of your business. What's yours?"

"Frosty Morn. We must be related."

She ignored me. "You going to buy me a drink?"

"Are you going to leave if I don't?"

"That's how it works, cowboy."

I paid a king's ransom for something called a Slinger. Where I come from we call it ginger ale. Misty turned out to be a talker. She got onto a jag about the Ravens. She carried a mighty torch for Stoney Case, the Ravens's quarterback. She didn't think the offensive line was giving him enough protection, and she was worried for him.

"Look what happened to Vinny Testaverde," she said.

"What happened to him?"

"He left. God, *there* was a good-looking guy. Big hunky puppy."

Several times as she was speaking she reached a hand over and set it on my thigh. Each time I returned it to her. At one point she cut off her sports report to gripe, "You got a problem? I'm just being friendly."

"I'm spoken for," I said.

"Yeah? Real news flash. So, is she here?"

"She's outside waiting in the car," I said, just to get a reaction. I got one. Miss Dew started immediately to slide off the barstool. I grabbed her arm.

"Misty, hold on. I'm kidding."

She pulled free of my grip. She eyed me suspiciously, but remained on the stool. "Look, you don't have to do anything. If you just want to buy me drinks, that's okay too."

As if to show me how it's done, she finished off her Slinger. She raised her pinky and the blue-breasted bartender appeared. The woman (I had decided she was a she) looked a little like a space alien as she stepped toward us. A space alien in a beer commercial. I ordered another Slinger for my gal Misty and another beer for myself.

"So, you know what I do. What do you do?" Misty asked.

I've seen many a light go out of many an eye when I answer that question truthfully. Besides, this was certainly a place where you checked truth at the door.

"I'm an architect," I said.

"No shit. Buildings and stuff?"

"You know the big mall, down by the harbor?"

"No."

"I designed that. You know the Science Center?"

"Uh-huh."

"Mine."

"No kidding. The Science Center, huh?"

"Yep. Harborplace? Moi." A knowing leer was creeping onto her face.

"Aren't you kinda young for that?"

"How about the symphony hall?"

"You mean that thing that looks like someone sat on a birthday cake? You did that, huh?"

"Yep."

She chuckled into her drink. "Oh yeah, I almost forgot. I'm the governor of Maryland, by the way. I just let that other guy do all the work."

"Misty, dear. You mean you don't believe me?"

"Honey, I believe whatever you want me to believe. That's why these drinks cost what they do."

It occurred to me that I had better hurry up and take a stab at the reason I had come down to this lovely pit in the first place. I was on the verge of enjoying myself.

"Can I ask you a question, Misty?"

"Shoot." In the dark.

"Have you ever heard of a woman named Victoria Wagner? She used to work here a couple of years ago."

She played the name around in her mouth. "Victoria . . . Could be. What'd she go as?"

"Go as?"

"Her stage name. This place might look like a dump to you, but it's still a club, you know. All the girls have names." Her logic was safe with her.

"You mean like, Misty Dew," I said.

"Gee, and he's smart too."

"I don't know," I said. "I thought Victoria Wagner was her stage name."

"Doesn't sound like one. But anyway, I don't think I know her. When was she here?"

"I'm not exactly sure. Maybe three or four years ago?"

"Ancient history, hon. Sorry."

"What about Terry Haden? Does that name mean anything to you?"

Misty tugged on the thin belt of her robe. "Are you a cop?"

"I'm not a cop."

"These are cop questions. I know one thing for sure, you're not an architect."

"If I were a cop I'd come in here with a better set of lies."

"No, you wouldn't. You'd come in here bullshitting, just like you're doing."

Very shrewd, I had to give her that. "I'm looking for a friend of mine who might be in some sort of trouble," I added. "A woman."

"Naturally."

"This Haden character's involved. I'm trying to track him down. I think he hangs around The Block a lot. Or, at least he used to."

"Look, how do I know you're not a cop?"

"I guess you're going to have to trust me."

Misty gave me a slow once-over. I felt cheapened. Marginalized. Objectified. I'd get over it.

"One way I could find out if you're a cop," the dancer said.

"How's that?"

"You take out a credit card. Or cash. We take a booth over there in the back."

"You mean you'll search me?"

She grinned. "If you want to put it that way. What I mean is, if you're a cop, you can't go there. That's committing a crime to solve a crime, or whatever it is you're doing."

"You sound pretty well versed about all this. Are you studying to become a lawyer?"

"You got to know about more than just dancing in this job," she said. "So what do you say? You want to go where it's more comfortable?" A purr was coming into her voice. The Kitten Club kitten.

"I don't think so. But thanks. It's nothing personal."

She let out a laugh. "Hey, it's never personal here, all right?" She sipped on her drink. "I guess you can still be a cop then."

"Or just a shy fellow."

She gave me that up and down look again. "So you going to buy me another drink or are we all finished?"

"I guess we're finished."

To my surprise, a look of disappointment crossed her face. She asked me what time it was. I checked my watch.

"Just after eleven."

Miss Dew shifted on the stool, settling back in. "What the hell? Lunch crowd's coming soon. I got to dance again at noon. I'll talk to you." She signaled for another drink.

"Why don't I just give you the money up front? I hate to see you drowning yourself."

"Can't do it. You don't buy drinks you might not leave a tip." The cellophane blonde, firing ginger ale into Misty's glass, looked over at me, making an "Oh boy!" face.

"So this guy you're looking for."

"Terry Haden."

"Describe him. Names don't mean donkey down here. What's he look like? What does he do?"

I described Haden to the stripper. Apparently I did a good job. *Jerk. Flak jacket. Porn films.*

"I know him." Misty slapped her hand down on the tabletop. "Mr. Hollywood."

"Mr. Hollywood?"

"That's what we called him. Beard? Sort of good looking? Talk, talk, talk? Is that the one?"

"He doesn't have a beard anymore, but yeah, that sounds right."

"Hell yes. I never even paid attention to his name. When I first started here he was in and out all the time. He hit on me a couple of times. Yeah. The movies. He said he'd put me in one of his movies. Like hell he would. I'm getting out of this game one of these days. I sure as hell don't want some damn dirty movie chasing after me. Can't you just see that? Meet a nice guy and get engaged and everything, then this stupid smut movie shows up? I don't think so. So like, whatever happened to that guy? All of a sudden he just dropped out of sight. I'd forgotten all about him til you brought it up."

"Is there anyone here who might know something about him?" I asked.

"You get turnover in a place like this. Hell, I'm already a veteran, and I'm just going on two years." She thought a moment. "I guess you could talk to Popeye."

"Who's Popeye?"

"He owns this place. Popeye's like a hundred years old. He probably knows, I don't know . . . name someone really old."

"Mae West."

"Isn't she dead?"

"But she was old before she died," I pointed out.

"Well, okay. Popeye probably knew her. He knows everybody. He'd remember this guy you're talking about. For sure he'd remember the girl, if she worked here. He's got a steel flap memory."

I didn't bother to correct her. I got her point. "Where can I find Popeye? Is he here?"

"He doesn't come in this early. But I know where you can find him. You know a place called Martick's? It's a restaurant?"

"Sure. Over near the library."

Misty Dew told me that Popeye, the owner of The Kitten Club, took his lunch every day at Martick's.

"Don't dare tell him I told you," she said. "He'll fire me like that. Popeye is a nasty old bastard."

I promised to keep her name—or, rather, her stage name—out of it. I thanked her for her time and for the information. I pulled out a twenty and handed it to her.

"What's this for?"

"Oh, nothing. Let's say, for what might have been."

She cackled. "Twenty? Might not have been much, I'll tell you that."

On an impulse, I gave her one of my business cards. "If you happen to hear anything about Terry Haden, call me. Let's say the twenty is for that."

"That makes a little more sense," she muttered. She looked at the card. "*That's* your name?"

"You can still call me Frosty."

"What's this mean? Are you an undertaker? You bury people?" She looked up at me with a perplexed expression. Unconsciously, she drew her robe tighter. "You shouldn't tell girls what you do for a living. That's just a piece of advice." She looked back down at the card, then back at me. "God, and you're so good looking too. What a shame."

Martick's Restaurant is a windowless black room over on West Mulberry Street. There's no sign outside. You just have to know that the place is there and buzz a buzzer to be let inside. Morris Martick is one of the best French chefs in the city. He isn't French himself—he was born right in the same building that houses his restaurant—but his pâté can stop you in your tracks, it's that good. I like the whole ambiance of Martick's. I pop in a lot. It has that World War II blackout feeling to it; the sort of dark, speakeasy atmosphere that can take you far, far away from the world outside. Not to mention the snakeskin wallpaper and the full-size statue of the thick-ankled motherly woman holding a loaf of fresh-baked bread. My parents used to frequent the place. They were old buddies of Morris.

There was an ambulance and a police car parked on the street out in front of Martick's. I didn't take this as a good sign. It wasn't. An old man wearing a pair of bottle-bottom eyeglasses was being wheeled out of the restaurant on a stretcher. He wasn't being wheeled out with any sense of urgency. There was no need. Once you're dead, you're dead. Popeye had been shot right in the middle of his pâté. I saw Morris Martick standing at the open door, looking back into the restaurant. He looked pissed.

I was experiencing an eerie sense of déjà vu all over again. For the third time in exactly a week, I stood by and watched as Baltimore City police and detectives moved about within the confines of a yellow crime-scene tape, sifting for clues to a murder. Unlike the case with Helen Waggoner, Popeye's murder had plenty of eyewitnesses. And the witnesses had plenty of conflicting memories of what they had just seen. The killer was either tall or medium height, bulky except where he was thin. He wore either a blue watch cap, a black ski mask rolled up, an Orioles cap or simply had a nice, thick head of hair, black or brown. He held the gun in his left or right hand—or both—and he either shouted something just before he pulled the trigger or he never uttered a sound. About the only thing that the witnesses agreed on was that the killer hadn't escaped in a hot air balloon. Or if he had, no one had seen it . . . yet. He did, however, hop into a black, green or brown two- or four-door car with plates from several states and took off in two directions at once. If he cried *Hi-ho, Silver, away!* nobody was saying.

Detective Kruk seemed to take it all in stride. I suppose if you were to pull your hair out in this game every time you came up against contradictory eyewitness testimony, you'd be as bald as Mr. Clean before your first year on the job was out. Kruk apparently had an internal meter that told him which portions of which statements from which witnesses to take as the more credible. It's a definite talent.

Kruk spent a lot of his time talking to Morris Martick. The restaurateur was wearing his trademark Charlie Brown sweater and an impatient look on his sad beagle face. I overheard him telling Kruk that Popeye came in for lunch every day of the week and that he sat at the same table and ordered the same meal, the pâté, a spinach salad and two Scotch and sodas. The strip joint owner had apparently just been served his meal when the gunman of many sizes and hats buzzed the buzzer and, on being let inside by Martick himself, stalked directly over to the table where the old man was sitting and took dead aim. He fired four times, three of the bullets entering Popeye's chest. The fourth bullet hit the old man in the foot. On this point—if on no other point—all of the eyewitnesses concurred that the gunman had very specifically lowered the gun after the first three shots and had taken aim at Popeye's right foot. Basically he blew the old man's big toe right off. I could see one of the detectives holding up a plastic evidence bag and turning it left and right. Inside was what was left of the shoe.

"Interesting."

I turned around. Jay Adams was standing there. The slender reporter acknowledged me with a slow nod. He was wearing all the trappings of his profession: a fedora *and* a long overcoat. I half expected to see the word PRESS on a piece of stiff paper tucked into his hat band.

"What brings you here?" he asked me.

I rejected my first two responses ("The pâté" and "A taxi") and settled on: "I was just in the neighborhood."

"You're becoming a regular Jessica Fletcher, aren't you?" Adams said. "The bodies are dropping like flies. It might not be so safe being around you."

"You could always leave," I suggested.

"Got to earn a living."

Adams went off to troll about the perimeter of the crime scene, asking questions and jotting down his Pulitzer prize–winning observations in his notebook. Kruk finished with Morris and moved on to a discussion with another of his detectives. As he ducked under the yellow tape, he caught my gaze and signaled me to hang tight. I went over to Morris and asked him what were the chances I could get a drink. "We're closed," he grumbled.

"Okay," I said. Then I asked him again what were the chances I could get a drink.

He grumbled again, "No mixing."

"Bourbon on the rocks." Morris gave me a sneer. "What?" I said. "Adding ice is mixing?"

Okay, okay, so a long-standing customer had been shot dead at the very beginning of the lunch crunch. The restaurateur was in a bad mood. I told Morris straight up was fine. He told me it sure as hell was, and he went inside to fetch me a glass.

Kruk had finished with his fellow detective and came over to me just as Morris was bringing me my medicine.

"Kind of early in the day, isn't it, Mr. Sewell?"

"My internal clock is different from yours," I said. "I can re-set it to be any time I wish."

"Are you going to make me ask the obvious question, Mr. Sewell?"

"You'd like to know what I'm doing here."

"Give the man a beer."

I pulled my whiskey to my chest. "Don't try to pull a fast one, Detective."

I explained to Kruk what I was doing at Martick's. He listened without interrupting as I told him about my phone call to Vickie Waggoner the day before and about her making as if I was the police. I told him how I drove over to her place to find the front door open, one of Bo's toys on the sidewalk and not a soul in sight. He knew vaguely of this, from the message I had left for him when I called the station. I explained to him how I had gone down to The Block this morning to see if I could scare up a clue as to where Terry Haden might be holing up and that a woman wearing three ounces of clothing had aimed me toward Martick's for a chat with Popeye.

I concluded, "As you can see, somebody ruined my plans."

One of Kruk's eyebrows went up the pole. "You're not suggesting that the old man was gunned down for the sole purpose of keeping him from talking with you, are you?"

"I should be so important, Detective. Of course not. I have no idea why the guy was shot. I'm just saying it was a matter of very bad timing."

"For him or for you?"

"Well, I'm still standing."

It was only then that my whiskers twitched and I glanced over my shoulder. Jay Adams was leaning against a nearby lamppost, making no effort at all to pretend that he wasn't listening. He had heard my entire story. In case I wasn't aware that he had, he gave the brim of his fedora a little tug and smiled a salamander smile at me. I turned back to Kruk.

"Isn't that man loitering? Can't you toss him in the hoosegow?"

"Come over here." Kruk led me over to his unmarked car. Adams didn't tag along. Kruk hitched his thumbs under his belt and let his eyes scan the rooftops of the nearby buildings, as if looking for a sniper. I set my drink on the roof of the car.

"So, you believe that Terry Haden is the one who murdered Helen Waggoner, is that it?"

I told him yes, this was exactly what I believed.

"And you base your suspicions on what?"

"Strong hunch," I said. "A new man was definitely in Helen's life. She was spending money she hadn't earned."

"So you assume."

"She was pregnant. That usually signifies a man has been somewhere on the scene."

"Go on."

"Well, as I see it, she and Haden got back together. I don't think it was a sudden attack of fatherhood on Haden's part. I've met the guy. I think that Haden and Helen got back together, and they partied like it was 1999. But I think Haden's intention all along was to get Helen back under his wing. To get his cash cow churning again. But just like before, she ups and gets pregnant and decides that she's going to keep this one too. I think that Haden went ballistic when Helen told him she was pregnant. I know for a fact, because he told me, that Helen could frustrate the hell out of him. I mean, *really* frustrate. I think he killed her. That's my theory."

"Nice theory," Kruk said.

"Thank you."

"Except it doesn't float."

"What do you mean it doesn't float?"

"You know how Haden makes his living, right?"

"A little of this, a little of that. Very little of it legal, I understand."

"Exactly. He's a hustler. A supplier. Drugs. Escort services. You name it. He's a one-man warehouse of illicit goods. We've had Mr. Haden downtown for coffee on a number of occasions."

"And he dabbles in the film arts as well."

"Real Oscar material, I can tell you. *Debbie Does Dundalk.*"

"You're kidding, right?"

Kruk shook his head. "Not on company time I'm not. That's for real. Terry Haden's got his fingers in all sorts of dirty pies. To be honest with you though, he's strictly small-time. He's a hophead. If the guy would make a serious effort to get off his little pills, he might actually amount to something I could worry about. But he's a small fish. I really don't see him as murderer material."

"But why would he hightail it the moment he thought the police were on the way?"

"He wouldn't need a reason. A hophead like Haden, his own shadow can spook him."

"I don't know. I like my theory more than I like your conclusion."

Kruk let out a sigh. "Your theory pretty much hinges on Haden and Helen Waggoner's getting back together, right? Her getting pregnant by him again and all the rest of it?"

"Right."

"Well, I hate to ruin your fun, but our friend Haden just got back last month from a ten-month vacation up in Jessup, compliments of the Maryland taxpayers."

"He was in jail?"

"Yes sir. Locked up like a sardine."

"You're kidding."

"You keep saying that. No, I'm perfectly serious. He's been rehabilitating for the past year. You see what that does to your theory."

"Haden couldn't have been the new guy in Helen's life."

"Exactly. And he didn't have any conjugal visits, I can tell you that much."

And you can't do this thing through the mail. Not yet anyway. "Damn."

"You sound disappointed."

I was. If Haden had been locked up in prison the past ten months, then Kruk was correct, my theory couldn't float.

"But then, why would Haden run off if he thought the police were on the way?" I asked. "I mean, you had already questioned him about Helen's murder. If he was innocent, why skedaddle?"

"Did Haden appear to be high to you when you saw him?"

"He was jumpy. Down one minute, very up the next. Yeah, I suspected he was riding some sort of train."

"There it is. That's a parole violation right there. Haden couldn't risk a by-the-book cop dropping in on Vickie Waggoner and deciding to crack his ass for parole violation. He'd have gone right back to Jessup. Not a place you really want to be."

"What was he in prison for anyway?"

"That little film I just mentioned? *Debbie Does Dundalk*?"

"So you really didn't just make that up."

"It's legit." He corrected himself, "It's for real."

"What about it?"

"Little Debbie wasn't old enough to vote. And old Lady Justice doesn't like that."

"*Child* porn?" I hadn't thought that my estimation of Helen's former boyfriend could have gone much lower, but it was practically spelunking at this point.

"Teen," Kruk corrected me. "Of course, Haden swore that she lied to him about her age. Blah, blah, blah. Who knows, maybe she did. But he cast her as a baby-sitter in his little epic. The girl had sweet sixteen written all over her."

I thought about Helen. She couldn't have been more than nineteen when Haden had gotten ahold of her.

"So, okay, that shoots Haden being the father of Helen's next kid. But still, only a month after the guy gets let out of prison and bang, Helen gets killed? Did Haden have an alibi for the night of the murder?"

"He gave us one."

"Did it check out?"

"He claims he was with Debbie."

"*Dundalk* Debbie?" Kruk nodded in the affirmative. "Is that kosher? I'd think that's a parole breaker right there."

"She's eighteen now. She can legally make whatever bad judgments she'd like."

"Still. It sounds like a weak alibi. What did Haden say they were doing?"

"He said they were at the movies."

"I think Debbie needs to get out more," I said.

We were interrupted by another detective, who came over to confer with Kruk. They moved off to where I couldn't hear them. I didn't even see Jay Adams until he was right in front of me. The reporter was smiling that salamander smile at me again. Damn, I wish the guy would just come out and show his dislike for me. It would make things a lot easier.

"Intriguing, isn't it?" he said.

"What's intriguing?"

"The foot."

"What foot? What are you talking about?" A gnat. That's what the man was. He was a gnat.

"The old man. Popeye. Three shots to the chest, one to the foot."

"Maybe the killer didn't want the old guy running after him."

"I think the three to the chest took care of that. So you really don't know, do you?"

"Know what?" The aggravation in my voice didn't faze him. It never does faze the ones who're prompting it. That's what is so aggravating.

The olive-skinned snake had a pencil in his hand. Right in front of my eyes he put the eraser end to the brim of his hat and pushed the fedora an inch or so up his forehead.

"The lawyer, you know the one who was killed the other day? In Mount Vernon? Along with his wife."

"The one everybody's quivering about. What about him?"

"I guess you don't read the papers."

"I would if I liked the writing." Blanks. I was shooting blanks at this guy. All he did was grin even wider.

"Same MO," Adams said. "Bang, bang, bang, point-blank into the chest. And then one more. In the foot. Same deal with the wife. It's the shooter's signature."

"You're saying that the person who just killed this old guy is the same person who killed the lawyer and his wife?"

"He left his signature. Look."

I looked over to where Kruk and his colleague were standing. The other detective was holding up the plastic evidence bag—the one containing the blown-apart shoe—turning it left and right. The two detectives looked as if they were hoping the shoe would suddenly speak.

"So who kills a high-powered lawyer and his wife and then goes after the owner of a two-bit strip joint?" Adams asked. I presumed the question was rhetorical. In the sky overhead, the cotton-candy clouds were breaking off into a half dozen tufts. Each tuft swirled into the perfect—if fuzzy—shape of a question mark.

I hadn't a good goddamn clue.

When I got back to the neighborhood, I headed over to Julia's place. Chinese Sue was reading an Action Comic at the register. One of her antennae twitched as I came in the door. She didn't look up, but she knew it was me. The gallery had only a few customers. Strictly window-shoppers. Nobody appeared to be on the verge of actually buying anything. Julia's stuff is fun to look at. Mostly she does skewed reality, people eating beach-ball sandwiches, pigeons enjoying afternoon tea, that sort of thing. For a king's ransom Julia will do your portrait. For twice that much she'll even do it straight. Though in my view that would be your loss. There is a CEO of one of the hotshot brokerage firms in Baltimore who proudly displays in the firm's swanky reception area the portrait he commissioned from Julia a number of years ago. The likeness is dead-on. Unsmiling. Vaguely menacing. Why Julia chose to seat him in a red Radio flyer and dressed like a monk is something else altogether. The CEO flipped for it. And paid through the nose.

"Boss lady in?" I asked Chinese Sue. A pale, slender finger

rose above the comic book, pointing toward the heavens. "Nice nails, Sue." Her talons were a nausea of color.

Julia was lounging in a silk robe on a wicker settee, languidly turning the pages of a travel magazine.

"It must be the reading hour around here," I observed as I came up the spiral stairs. "You got any Hardy Boys handy?"

Julia looked up slowly from her magazine. "I wish."

I plopped down on the hammock. "Planning a trip?"

She set the magazine aside. "Possibly. I was thinking about a cup of coffee in Corfu. How does that sound?"

"Alliterative."

"Besides that."

"You could always go for a touch of tea in Tanzania."

"Yes, Hitch. And a bottle of booze on the Bowery. We could do this for hours."

"What's wrong?" I asked. "You're in a mood."

"I am. I'm feeling wistful. Somewhere between wistful and deep blue funk."

Julia sighed and swung her feet to the floor. Her toenails were painted the same as Chinese Sue's claws. The girls must have been out prowling together. She picked up a fluted glass from the floor. It was tomato red. Literally.

"Do you want a Bloody? The fixings are on the woodblock."

I mixed myself a Bloody Mary and refreshed Julia's while I was at it. She sighed like Gloria Swanson when I handed it to her.

"I need some adventure."

I retreated to the hammock. "I see."

"It's probably just the weather. And the holidays. I'm just not in a home and hearth mood. I need sunshine. A cool breeze and a hot stranger. Lord, I'd even forgo the stranger."

"We *are* wistful, aren't we? Why don't you lie in your hammock and turn on a sunlamp and a fan and get hammered. Take a trip and never leave the farm?"

"What about the hot stranger?"

"You just said you'd forgo that."

"I'm a big liar." She took a long sip of her drink. "What about you, Hitch? Does Corfu appeal to your sense of oh-what-the-hell?"

"I've been to Corfu," I reminded her.

"Oh yes. The summer of love. They've written songs about it. The Vespa. The retsina. The girl from Scarsdale."

"Mmmmmm . . ."

"She gave you a black eye, if I recall."

"It was a misunderstanding."

"Black eyes usually are."

"We made up—"

"I know, I know. In the glorious olive groves. Squirming atop the summer harvest. You two must have smelled like squid."

"Is that what you think black olives smell like?"

"I haven't touched one ever since you told me that story."

"Julia, that's the closest you've ever come to sounding prudish."

She raised her glass. "Well, there you have it." We sipped and fell into silence. Julia was studying the rim of her glass. I was flipping through my mental snapshots of the girl from Scarsdale. It's a nice collection. She's married now. Lives in Manhattan. Has a couple of kids. And is still very pretty. I get a holiday snapshot every winter.

Julia set her glass down and languidly ripped a page from her magazine. She folded it into a paper airplane and tossed it in my direction. It nosedived into the mesh of the hammock.

"So, what's the latest on your dead waitress?" she asked. "Or, actually, on the sister. Was I right? Victoria Wagner? Queen of the sleazy screen?"

"No. It's the murdered woman who had the telltale tattoo. The butterfly. Just as you said."

"Then she used her sister's name."

"Looks that way."

"That's twisted. Why do you suppose she did that?"

"I don't know."

"You didn't ask the sister?"

"She's disappeared."

"As in . . . disappeared?"

For the second time in an hour, I rattled off the pertinent details of my amateur sleuthing. Julia rolled her eyes as I described how Haden had been sent to prison for his little *Dundalk* Lolita action. She tried to slow me down for a more detailed accounting of my journey to The Kitten Club.

"Was she pretty, this Miss Dew?" Julia cocked an eyebrow. "And don't tell me, 'She'll do.'"

"Me? You must have the wrong guy."

"You're the right guy all right. So tell me already. Was your stripper a looker?"

"She was the stripper," I said. "I was the looker."

Julia gave herself a head slap. "See! God, Hitch, it's like a sickness with you, I swear."

"Look, do you want to hear the rest of this, or do you want to just park it at the strip club?"

"Is that a snit I detect?"

"I don't know what it is. Maybe. Helen Waggoner was dumped off at my place a week ago, and I'm nowhere nearer figuring out who killed her. All that's really happened is that her son and her sister have disappeared, but it doesn't seem now that it's Helen's murderer who they disappeared with. On top of it all, someone's running around Baltimore shooting people in the foot."

It was this last bit of my rant that got Julia interested enough to hear the rest of my tale. As I concluded, she was rubbing her own foot. Whether consciously or not, I couldn't tell.

I picked up the paper airplane and smoothed out its nose.

"So that's about it. Kruk doesn't think Terry Haden killed Helen and neither do I anymore. Granted, his alibi isn't the best one in the world. But even so, Haden as the killer is just making less and less sense. He just got out of prison a month ago. But I'm missing the logic of his getting out and then immediately tracking Helen down and killing her."

"Oh, I see. You're looking for a logical reason for murder."

"You know what I mean. Twisted logic. But logic. Something. Why would he come out of prison and shoot Helen Waggoner? I don't see it. Haden is shaking out as a no-account piece of sleaze, but he's losing his grip as our best murder suspect."

"You know who I think it is?" Julia said, plunging into her Bloody M.

"You've been thinking about this?"

"Not really. But I'm a quick study."

"Who do you think?"

"I think it's the sister."

"Vickie?"

"Yes. I think it's her."

"Based on what?"

Julia fluttered her hand in the air. "Based on nothing. It's strictly a hunch. You've said that she and her sister didn't get along. Maybe they got into a fight."

I reminded Julia about the Pontiac Firebird and Kruk's theory that the murder was premeditated. "I don't think Vickie Waggoner would be running around stealing cars so that she could murder her sister."

Julia sniffed. "You're looking for logic again. I'm simply choosing the most provocative suspect. Women are always the most provocative suspect." She dipped a finger into her drink and dabbed the sides of her neck. "Maybe *I* did it. I'm a woman."

I crumpled the plane in my hand. "I'd noticed that. A

pretty arch one." I got off the hammock and went over to where Julia was sitting.

"I've got to go." I leaned over and gave her a kiss on the forehead.

"I'm down here," Julia grumbled. She tilted her head and looked up at me. Her wicked eyes were soft and a little doughy from the vodka. Her lips were plump and red, already slightly parted. "You don't have to go running off."

"I've still got to find Terry Haden."

"Why?"

"Haden has attached himself to Vickie Waggoner and I don't know why. Maybe it really is the boy. Whatever it is, I don't like it. I don't trust him. I don't think she's safe around him."

Julia leaned back against the wicker. Her long fingers ran absently along the silk lapel of her robe. "Hitch, are you about to show poor judgment again?"

"What are you talking about?"

"It might not be my place to remind you that it's not your place to run off saving damsels in distress. Especially ones who, if I understand correctly, haven't even called out for help. You've made this mistake once already, if you recall."

I grumbled. "Of course I recall. This is different."

Julia's big Bloody Mary eyes blinked out in code: W-H-Y?

"It just is," I said. I wondered if it sounded as lame to her as it did to me.

"Oh, then, by all means." She waved her hand dismissively. I stepped over to the fireman's pole. As I grabbed hold of it I looked back over at Julia, still draped on her wicker settee. She was worth a painting herself.

"You could stay."

"I've got to go."

Her chin floated in my direction. "You do know what you're missing."

• • •

I moved a large stack of papers from one side of my desk over to the other and then back again. I did this maybe three times. By the time I was finished, and the papers were back where they had started, the pile was half its original size. That's how we laugh our time away in the merry old land of Oz.

The phone rang.

"Sewell and Sons."

"What in the goddamn hell is going on?"

It was Bonnie, my sweet. She had heard about the snuffing out of Popeye the strip club owner and about the apparent connection between his murder and that of Mr. and Mrs. Lawyer (Michael and Sheila Fenwick; they've gone unnamed long enough now). I didn't even bother to ask how it was that she had learned of my being on the scene just moments after all the fun. I know snakes; I know how they slither.

"Same old same old," I answered her, my gaze coming to rest on my Magritte. "People are going way too far out of their way not to talk with me. First Haden, now good old Popeye."

"I'll talk with you."

We agreed to meet at the Belvedere Hotel, in the John Eager Howard Room. The Belvedere is a gem of a building over on Chase Street that was nearly demolished in the early seventies to make room for nothing that anybody can even recall anymore. The John Eager Howard Room is a mouthful that translates into: bar. It is woody and stuffy and plushy and comfortable. Its walls are decorated with portraits of the highbrows and blue bloods who came over from England in days of yore to escape persecution for their religious and social beliefs and who subsequently set up aristocracies and pecking orders of their very own here at the gaping mouth of the Chesapeake Bay. I got there before Bonnie. The bar was filled. I took a table, parking myself in front of Lord Somebody-or-other. A waiter came over and I ordered an ice water. I gazed at Lord Something-or-other as I waited for my water. He won the staring contest.

Bonnie came into the John Eager Howard Room looking good enough to eat. Legs, hair, breasts, eyes, skin, attitude, the wiggle in her walk, the giggle in her talk . . . the whole package. The old walruses and young sharks at the bar all thought so too. I stood up from my table as she crossed the room. I wanted everyone to see me. I even tracked slowly along the bar, making eye contact where I could. She's mine, you drooling fishbones. Hands off. I'm not exactly sure what had gotten into me. Another few seconds and I might have thrown my head back and started to crow.

Bonnie was pleased that I had stood up. She loves good manners.

"What's wrong with your eyes?" she asked suspiciously. "You're looking kind of demonic."

"I'm just in a weird mood," I said, sitting back down. "I was throwing back beers at eleven this morning in a strip club with a woman who was wearing little more than a filament, then the guy I was going to talk with over lunch was filled full of lead moments before I got there." I picked up my glass of ice water. "You know. One of those days."

"Crime fighting."

"I wouldn't say I'm fighting crime. I'm chasing. The crimes happen." I smiled across the table at her. "So. How's the weather?"

"It's out there, Hitch. Every goddamn where you look."

My Bonnie lass was becoming more beautiful to me before my very eyes. I was beginning to calculate how much a room at the Belvedere would set me back when she suddenly lowered the boom.

"Hitch, I think we should stop seeing each other."

"*What?*"

She lowered her eyes—the coward—and started fiddling with the place mat. I brought my elbows onto the table and leaned forward.

"What did you just say?"

Bonnie stammered. "I just think . . . I don't know . . . I . . . We're not . . . I mean . . ." She looked up at me, gave a large sigh. "It's hard."

"What's hard? Finishing a sentence?"

"Don't be angry with me," she snapped.

"I'm not, yet," I said. "Right now you've got me at the confused point. But give me a minute. You go ahead and make a lousy case and I'll move on to anger."

"No, you're angry now. I can tell. I can hear it in your voice."

"Well what gives? Bonnie, according to my diary, boy and girl are getting along swimmingly. I thought I was the hunk of your dreams. What the hell is this all about? Is it Adams?"

"No."

"Then what? Speak."

"I . . . can't really explain it, Hitch."

"College try, little girl."

"*That's* it!" She literally jumped in her seat. A flash of red stormed across her cheeks. Several heads turned in our direction. Bonnie lowered her voice to a loud hiss.

"That's it, Hitch. You're patronizing, damn it. Listen to yourself. You pat me on the head like . . . like I'm Alcatraz or something. It's this good little girl shit. I don't think you even know you're doing it."

"I'm a chauvinist is what you're saying. Basically that's it, right?"

"Well, yes and no."

"Ah, the woman's definition of definitive."

"*See!*"

"I'm *kidding*." I held up a hand—time out—while I took a

sip of water. I needed the moment for a quick internal conference. I finished off three quarters of the glass. "I'm not perfect," I said, swirling the glass. The ice didn't tinkle; it clunked.

"I didn't say you were."

"No. Exactly. You said I wasn't. And you're giving *that* as your reason for why we should stop seeing each other."

"You're twisting my words."

"Then untwist them for me. Bonnie, we should be having an *argument*. You should tell me you're *annoyed* with the way I deal with you sometimes, and we should argue about it. Don't you think breaking things off is a little extreme?"

"You're trying to manipulate me now."

"Fight back! Manipulate *me*. You're a grown woman. Goddamn it, act like one!"

"Don't you fucking tell me what to do!" She made a small fist and rapped it against the table. Her beautiful nostrils flared.

"Good, good—"

"Stop that!"

"That's better—"

"STOP THAT!" Bonnie lunged suddenly across the table and landed a perfect slap right across my cheek. It was loud. It caught us both by surprise. It caught everyone in the room by surprise. No one breathed. Except Bonnie, whose breath was coming out in little machine-gun bursts. I watched her face, wondering if it would melt into embarrassment for having just created a public scene. But it didn't. Her lower lip quivered for just an instant, then she drew it in and secured it. Her eyes grew dark and a ripple went through her hamster cheeks.

By God, she slapped me again! Harder. *Much* harder. This time with a primal gusto. Rehabilitative. Cathartic. Whatever. The woman practically knocked my teeth out. Her perfect hair flew and wispy strands rose with the room's static electricity. We glowered at each other like gunfighters in the Wild West. We circled each other without ever leaving our chairs. Bonnie didn't back down. Not one iota. And good for her. She needed that. And apparently, so did I. I could feel the eyes of every person at the bar. Even Lord Something-or-other looked a little bit smug. Out of the corner of my eye, I detected a waitress, black slacks, oversize men's white shirt, tray in hand. She was frozen on the spot, too scared to move.

The room set me back a hundred and thirty-five dollars. Every penny worth it.

The newly invigorated couple made plans to find the bad guys. Terry Haden was now officially deposed from his brief reign as Helen Waggoner's mystery boyfriend. Haden had been cooling his heels in the state lockup in Jessup during the time that Helen had begun showing signs of making free with someone else's money. On the latter count, however, Bonnie advised that we ought to remain cautious. It was still possible that Helen had come into some money all on her own, and that was what had been prompting her to make noises about quitting the Sinbad's scene, getting a new place and all the rest of it. I conceded Bonnie her point without a second's hesitation. The postslap Bonnie Nash was my heroine. Every fiber of the woman was buzzing with newly charged juice.

We were still in our love shack at the Belvedere. Technically we had the place until eleven the next morning. Bonnie was fresh from the shower and was wrapped in one of the Belvedere's plush towels. We had already determined that we were going to abscond with a few of the towels, for Bonnie. The large burgundy **B** on her towel hit her on the left-side rump, like a brand. I was by the window, wrapped in a bedsheet, looking out at the mere mortals twelve flights down. The two of us looked like a couple of Greek urn ornaments noodling about in the wrong century.

"So we need to cover both possibilities," Bonnie said. "We need to learn if Helen was onto something that was bringing in some authentic bucks. And we need to learn if there really was a boyfriend in the shadows at all."

"Somebody got her pregnant," I reminded her. "Cash alone can't do that." Actually, these days it could. But I didn't bring that up.

"What's-his-name."

"Well, that's exactly the problem," I agreed. "What is his name?"

"No. What's *his* name? The big guy. The piano man. At Sinbad's."

"Oh, you're talking about Gary?"

"Didn't your waitress friend say that Helen and that guy had a thing going on?"

Did I detect a little edge in that phrase "your waitress friend," or was I just being paranoid? The answers are: yes.

"Tracy Atkins," I said. "She thought that Helen might have slept with Gary a few times. She didn't make it sound like she thought it was anything serious."

"She might not have known if it was serious. After all, isn't this the woman who can't even tell you if her close friend was actually seeing somebody?"

"You're right. Except, I don't know that Tracy Atkins was in the dark so much as that she's just not telling all that she knows. I know that she was lying to me about Haden, for example. Though I don't know why."

"But why would she lie about that if Haden had nothing to do with Helen's murder?"

"We don't think he had anything to do with it," I reminded her. "We only know that he's not the one who got her pregnant, and he wasn't the one who was spending his money on her."

"So the lying?"

"I don't know. She's protecting somebody."

"Maybe she's protecting herself."

"From what? You don't think *she* killed Helen, do you?"

"She wasn't at the restaurant that night."

"I don't see Tracy Atkins hot-wiring a car in Federal Hill so that she could have a nice cozy place to kill Helen Waggoner."

The moment I said this however, Tracy's MG flashed across my brain—over the speed limit. Tracy was clearly fond of the little rusted gem. In fact she had just gotten it back from the shop. If, for whatever reason, Tracy had in fact planned to shoot Helen, she certainly wouldn't have been foolish enough to do it in her little MG. And as for hot-wiring the Firebird . . . now that I thought about it, this didn't seem to be a talent that would necessarily be outside the woman's scope.

For the time being though, we would shelve the question of Tracy Atkins and her questionable memory lapses. Bonnie and I decided that we needed to have a chat with big Gary.

"How do you want to do this?" I asked. "According to Tracy Atkins, Gary is pretty much a howling wolf when it comes to women. Do you want to try the Mata Hari approach?"

"You mean seduce him?"

My cheek tingled. "No, no. Of course not. I was just thinking if you got him into a conversation you might be able to draw some information out of him."

"How do I do that, Hitch? Do I ask him if he got the dead girl pregnant? Or do I just go right to the point and ask him if he killed Helen?"

I turned from the window in my king-size toga, unfurling it like Dracula's cape as I stepped toward the bed.

"Let's sleep on it."

"We don't have time, Hitch."

"We'll keep our eyes open."

The future of lounge music lived together in a small clapboard house a few blocks behind the library in Towson. There was a run-down look about the place. Maybe it was the couch in the front yard, with the stuffing seeping from both arms. Or, maybe it was simply the several missing pickets from the porch railing, itself about as stable as something anchored in Jell-O. Or the screen on the front door, which had a nice curl to it. Maybe they were going for that Allman Brothers Band album-cover look. Trailer-trash-meets-rock-'n'-roll. The screen door rattled under my knuckles. Out of the corner of my eye I spotted the rim of a car tire off in the corner of the porch. Of course. Where else would you keep it?

A shadow moved within the house and the front door opened with a Watusi move.

"Hey."

A big paw came forward. Gary and I were about the same height, but he had me licked in the girth department. It would take two of me to make one of him. I took his hand to shake it expecting a viselike grip and was surprised by his gentle tug. I might have been shaking hands with a minister.

"Come in. It's cold outside." Damn, and I had been hoping for a nice sit-down on that groovy couch in the yard.

It was cold inside too. I followed Gary into the living room. I caught sight of our reflection in the large mirror on the facing wall, but I couldn't make out much on account of the fussiness of the beer logo that spread across the glass.

"You want something to drink? Beer? Water?"

I chose the latter.

"I can make hot chocolate," Gary added.

"Even better." Something boiled sounded safer.

I followed him into the kitchen. His ponytail hung down to the middle of his broad back. It was knotted off with a leather lace. He was wearing a green sweater, jeans and boots that looked like a pair of rocks.

"I've never met a detective before," Gary announced, putting a pot of water on the stove and kicking up the flame.

I didn't break it to Gary that he still had not met one. On the phone I had danced deftly around the point, introducing myself as an "investigator" who was working along with Vickie Waggoner on the matter of her sister's murder. This was the truth, in essence. If Gary wanted to attach the word "detective" to me, that was his prerogative. It was my prerogative not to correct him.

The kitchen was clean and messy at once. I dropped into a Naugahyde chair at a Formica table. It was warmer in the kitchen. I scooted up to the table. I trusted that my body language would transmit my desire to conduct our interview right here.

Bonnie and I had decided on a plan to get Gloria out of the house so I could talk turkey one-on-one with Gary. Bonnie and the string bean were at this very minute off at Angel's Grotto, about six blocks away. Gloria was under the impression that Bonnie Nash was interviewing her for a local-interest segment for the news, to be called "Baltimore Women in Song." I had listened to Bonnie's side of the conversation when she called Gloria from our room at the Belvedere to set up the interview. "We've done Billie Holiday, Rosa Ponselle, Ethel Ennis . . ." Right. And now we'd have you, babe. Bonnie and I had killed forty minutes before I made my call to Gary. Killed 'em good.

"So, how well did you know Helen Waggoner?" I asked. I figured I might as well get a sense of the big guy's hedge factor.

"Well, I fucked her a couple of times."

Ooookay . . . sounds like an impressively small hedge factor. Right. I went for the whole enchilada.

"Did you kill her?"

"Nope."

The water for the hot chocolate hadn't even come to a boil, and we were essentially done.

"Why should I believe you?" I asked.

"About fucking her?"

"The other."

"Why would I want to kill Helen? I liked Helen."

"Did your . . . Did Gloria know that you were seeing Helen?"

Gary pulled a couple of coffee mugs from a cabinet and blew into them.

"I wasn't seeing Helen. We fooled around a couple of times. That was it."

"At Sinbad's?"

"No, man. How would I do that with Gloria there? I mean, okay, we kind of gave each other the message there. Flirted and all. But, like we didn't sneak off into a corner or something. Well, you know. Except once. Twice. Sort of." Gary emptied several packets of hot chocolate dust into the cups. "Helen would pass her kid off to a neighbor, and we'd do it at her place." He picked the teapot off the stove and looked over at me. "I feel kind of weird telling you this, man. What difference does it make?"

None, so far as I could tell. Besides, I hadn't really asked him for details, I was just letting him talk. My job teaches me to listen. People will tell all sorts of things to a receptive ear.

"What kind of person was Helen?" I asked.

"Man, I'm not good at that kind of thing. I told you. She was a nice girl. She was sexy. I guess she was kind of lonely."

"What makes you say that?"

The big guy shrugged. He poured the hot water into the mugs and brought them over to the table. He sat down.

"It wasn't like she was horny, you know. I mean, the girls

who work at Sinbad's, they don't have a problem meeting guys who want to take them to bed or anything."

"You didn't . . . You didn't pay Helen to sleep with her, did you?"

"What do you think? I'm going to *pay* to get laid?"

"The customers do. At least, that's what I understand."

"That's the customers, man." He rapped a large hand against his chest. "I'm the entertainment. Helen and I were coworkers, you know? This was like an office romance. And it was only like ten or twelve times anyway. Gloria busted me and I stopped."

"How did she find out?"

"Hey, what difference does it make? Are you trying to find out who killed Helen or who fucked her?"

"Well, Gary, it might turn out to be someone who did both."

"Count me out, man. I fooled around with her, I got busted, I quit and that's aloha, man. I didn't kill Helen." He smiled across the table. "I'm a lover, man. Not a killer."

"You said Helen was lonely."

"Yeah. Sure. She's got that kid. She's got no man in her life. She's messing with those asshole businessmen to get a few extra bucks now and then. Doesn't that sound lonely to you?"

"So, she turned to you for some . . . some what? Companionship?"

Gravity fell over Gary. His face sagged, as if its puppet strings had just been cut.

"Man, I don't know. I guess so. I . . . I just figured she wanted to sleep with someone she knew for a change, okay? She probably didn't even know those assholes's names that she picked up at the bar. They probably gave her fake ones, I don't know."

He dipped into his hot chocolate. He ran the tip of his tongue over his mustache, which had sopped up half of his sip.

"Helen, man. She was fun. Real frisky, you know. And then like . . . I told you, she was lonely. She cried a couple of times when she was with me, right in the middle of everything. She tried not to, and it got her all pissed off that she did it."

"Did she love you?"

"Hell no, man, it wasn't like that. What kind of detective are you? Aren't you listening? I mean, she *liked* me. And we did it good together, you know what I mean. But I'm with Gloria. Helen knew that. I mess around, I admit it. Women find me sexy. I can't help it. I'm a big guy, man. I got a big appetite. Helen just . . . She needed to get out of that place is what the deal was. She needed a better life than all that. I mean, especially with the kid and everything. But it wasn't going to be with me. She never thought that. I guess those times she cried she just got upset because it must have felt like, you know, normal for a minute or two."

Having an affair with a sleep-about like Gary, who was committed to staying with his woman. *That* felt normal?

I pulled the photograph of Helen out of my pocket and tossed it across the table to him. I watched his expression as he picked it up and looked at it. I wouldn't say that his eyes moistened, but he gave the photograph a long, considered look. He was genuinely affected by it.

"It really sucks, doesn't it?"

"Did you take that picture, Gary?"

He handed it back to me. "Me? No way. I don't even own a camera."

"Do you have any idea who did?"

"Did what? Took that picture? How would I know that?"

"Did you know that Helen was pregnant?"

"Shit." His jaw dropped. His eyes took the hit. It was no act. He hadn't known. "Shit," he said again. "Pregnant? Oh, man. Oh, Jesus. Whose was it?"

"That's the sixty-four-thousand-dollar question. Is it possible that it was yours?"

Gary signaled for the photograph again. I handed it over to him. He looked at it hard again, as if maybe he could coax a few words out of the image.

"Man, I don't know. She was a big deal about protection and everything."

"Do you know if Helen was seeing someone else?"

"You mean like, on a regular basis?"

"Exactly."

"I don't know. After I got busted by Gloria, I didn't talk to her much. Gloria might be skinny and everything, man, but she's a powerhouse. Get on her wrong side and you're ruined. I do what I have to to keep from tangling with her."

Except sleeping around. That would be asking too much. The appetite and all.

I cupped my hands around my hot chocolate mug, brought it up to my lips and gently blew the steam over the rim. I was pretty much done here as far as I could tell. Unless the big guy across the table was an Oscar-caliber master of deception, I didn't see where he had killed Helen. An idea hit me.

"When was the last time you slept with Helen?"

"How long was she pregnant?"

I shook my head. "You first."

He set his mug down gently on the table and tugged on his beard. "I . . . I kind of lied to you a minute ago," he said. He sounded like a little kid confessing.

"About what?"

"About . . . after I got busted, I did stay away from Helen. That was last summer. Like, July."

"The last time you slept with Helen was July?" That would certainly take him out of the sweepstakes.

"Well . . . yeah. Except for one other time."

"One other time."

Gary suddenly had everywhere to look but at me. "She was all weird, man. I didn't know what was going on. I knew she was drunk when she called me. Or something. High on something, I don't know. She called me up here, at the house, which she had never done before. It was just a miracle that Gloria was out with a bunch of her friends. One of them was getting married. Helen said she had to see me right away. She wouldn't take no. I asked her if something was wrong, because she was sounding so weird, and she just laughed. But it wasn't a ha-ha laugh. She told me to meet her at the Charm Inn. That's right next to Sinbad's."

"I've seen it."

"She had a room. I went there. I mean, I had to, you know. She didn't want to say two words to me, man. She just threw me down on the bed and jumped on top of me." Gary shook his head in wonder at the memory. "She was a tiger, man. She'd never been like that. She actually scared me. It was a very fucked-up thing, I didn't like it. I mean, the sex was incredible. But I didn't like the scene. Helen wasn't Helen. She was angrier than I'd ever seen her, but she wouldn't say about what. I don't know what the hell she needed me for. Any of those traveling assholes at Sinbad's would have blown their top for a ride like she was giving. Except for that anger thing." He tugged on his beard some more. "Maybe, I don't know. Maybe that was why she wanted someone she knew. I guess you go turning weird like that with a stranger, the stranger might turn weird right back. Then you'd have a real problem."

Gary stopped and looked over at me. "Maybe that's what happened to Helen, huh? You think? Maybe she got weird like that with some stranger. And he came back and killed her. What the hell is that all about?"

"When was all this, Gary?"

"This thing? Like, a couple of months ago. October. Yeah, it was like right before Halloween."

"So, about two months ago."

"I guess."

"Can I ask you another question?"

"What the hell, man. You can write a book about me already."

"Did you use protection?"

Gary blinked. One for yes. Two for no. He blinked twice.

"Oh, shit, man. How many months was Helen pregnant?"

I was holding up two fingers.

We had our man, but we didn't have our killer. Before I left, I had asked Gary "for the record" if he had an alibi for the night that Helen was murdered.

"I told this to the police already," he said. He was still in shock about Helen having possibly been carrying his child when she was killed.

"I'm not the police. Tell me."

"I was fucking Tracy Atkins." He hadn't said it with pride. He added that Gloria had busted him on that one too. Rather, the police busted him, and she was sitting right next to him when they did.

"What's the secret of your relationship, Gary?" I asked as I stepped back out onto the porch. "Seems to me you're beating the odds."

"Gloria thinks we're going to be famous. She thinks it's just a matter of time."

"What do you think?"

Gary was staring out at the Allman Brothers Band album cover.

"I think we suck."

• • •

While I waited for Bonnie to conclude her ruse interview with Gloria—we had set a time to meet, and it was still forty minutes away—I popped into a bar on York Road for a quick shot of antifreeze. It turned out to be a sports bar. The place was loaded with golden-haired preppies all wearing baseball caps, mostly advertising various colleges. They were drinking and chanting and screaming at several television screens posted around the bar, each of which was tuned to a different sporting event. The guys were, for the most part, fit and athletic-looking and boyish. The women, who looked as if they could have been some of these guys's sisters, were trim, small-breasted and vigorously attractive, with killer teeth. Overall, a handsome, if not very expansive, gene pool.

I ordered two shots of Jack Daniel's and a beer. I poured one of the shots into the beer. A Jack-in-the-Box. A guy standing next to me wearing a TARHEELS cap watched me mixing the two brews.

"Does that work?" he asked.

"Works for me."

"All right! I'm trying that next!"

I was glad I could launch the boy on his Jack-in-the-Box career. A blond girl materialized at his side. Her cap read HOPKINS. Her sweatshirt read GOUCHER. Maybe Billie and I should be putting out sweatshirts and baseball caps, I thought. Tasteful, of course. An image floated into my mind. A coffin next to an open grave, along with the slogan: WE'LL TAKE IT FROM HERE.

The bar was insanely noisy. Even so, I was able to think. It's a simple matter of switching your head to a different frequency. The Jack helps. I considered my talk with Gary. Even while one issue appeared to have been resolved—Gary was very possibly the father of Helen's unborn child—there remained more questions than answers. High up on the list was the nagging question of whether or not there really was a so-called mystery boyfriend at all. Gary had failed to acknowledge knowing about one. And I didn't feel that he would have bothered to lie on that point. Of course, Tracy Atkins had been convinced that Helen was seeing someone and spending gobs of his cash. But Tracy had not only failed to provide definitive proof—such as a name, a conversation with Helen about the guy, or an actual sighting—her general credibility was sliding.

I took a long sip of my drink. Or was it possible . . . was it possible that I was simply being duped? I had to look at it. Tracy Atkins's alibi for the night that Helen was murdered was the guy who had gotten Helen pregnant. Gary's alibi was a woman who was willing to sleep with him and who was an easy liar to boot. Should this tidy arrangement have been setting off alarm bells in my head? And then there was still Gloria. "Out with her friends" Gary had said, referring to the night that Helen was killed.

A larger question grew right in front of me. What was I to make of Gary's story about the night that Helen went psycho on him? By his account of it, something pretty severe would seem to have happened to Helen sometime around the night she allegedly jumped the big guy's bones with such a combination of anger and desperation. Gary's account of the evening certainly sounded to me like that of a person who had snapped. And Gary was right when he wondered aloud about the danger of Helen behaving this way with a total stranger. I thought about the waitress, Gail, and her account of Helen's dustup at the bar a month before her murder. I had been tending to slap Terry Haden's face—or even the face of the mystery boyfriend—onto Helen's antagonist. But what if it really was a customer? What if Helen had gotten tangled up and gone nutso with some guy who had a few ballistic buttons of his own?

Bonnie was waiting for me at the Howard Johnson's about a mile up York Road.

"Do you know what the capital of North Dakota is?" she asked as I squeezed into the booth. She had a hand pressed flat against the paper place mat in front of me.

"It's pronounced 'peer,' " I said.

"Ha! That's the capital of *South* Dakota. The answer is Bismark. I tricked you. I knew you'd go for the weird answer."

"Proud of yourself, aren't you."

"Damn straight." She lifted her hand from the place mat. Yep. There it was. Pierre, South Dakota.

I ordered a coffee from the waitress. Bonnie and I both noted—grimly—the woman's name tag. HELLO. I'M HELEN.

"What did you learn?" Bonnie asked, inching forward in her seat.

"This, that and nothing," I said. I gave her the rundown of my talk with Gary. She listened as I gave my impressions. I told her that I believed him. Gary had crumbled so quickly on his one lie, that he had not been with Helen since the previous summer, that I really didn't think he had lied about any of the rest of his story. Certainly he had been forthcoming about Tracy Atkins. Bonnie agreed with me that Gary didn't sound like much of a suspect for Helen's murder. She also agreed with me that Tracy Atkins was no George Washington when it came to telling the truth.

"Maybe she and Helen were rivals for Gary," Bonnie offered. "I'm not saying that she killed Helen because of it. But maybe that's why she didn't mention it. Or why she's pretending to be such a close friend of Helen's."

"Gail told me that Tracy and Helen were friends."

"Gail is lagging behind things, Hitch. That girl doesn't really know what she knows."

"But Tracy Atkins does know more than she's saying. I can tell. I just don't know if we can pull it out of her."

Helen arrived with my coffee. I watched her as she returned to the counter. I tried to picture her taking a telephone call then rushing out into the parking lot. I glanced out the window to my left. No idling Firebird. No killer leaning sideways to push open the door.

"So, how about you?" I said, snapping out of it. "How was your 'Baltimore Woman in Song?'"

Bonnie shook her head. "That's one nasty viper, that woman. And remember, she was trying to impress me—I was getting her best behavior. She's convinced that she's the next big thing. She says this whole Sinbad's gig is just to keep her voice tuned. Apparently she and Gary have written a whole lot of original songs."

"Gosh, we should have stayed longer the other night."

"No. You didn't hear me. Apparently she and Gary have written a whole lot of original songs."

I stared out at the empty parking lot. "Shit. We have nothing." I took a sip of my coffee. It tasted like cardboard. "What have we got. Helen pissed somebody off. That's the bottom line. She pissed off somebody enough that they decided to kill her. Haden. Some guy she was sleeping with. Someone. Or maybe it really was our 'Baltimore Woman in Song.' I didn't push that with Gary. But I certainly got the impression that this is a gal who comes out swinging. What if Gloria learned about Gary getting Helen pregnant? You tell me, would a woman kill over something like that?"

Bonnie didn't think so. "The woman I just met? I doubt if she'd kill for love, if that's the actual question. Maybe if Helen's presence was threatening to break up the act. But it doesn't sound that way. According to you, the big oaf didn't even know she was carrying his child."

"No. It looks like Helen was resigned to doing this whole thing on her own. Just like Mama."

Bonnie squinted at me across the table. "A man did this, Hitch. Okay? Let's use sexism responsibly here. Some man killed Helen Waggoner. Some man she pissed off. The killer is from your planet mister, not mine."

Bonnie had to get back to the station. I needed to check in with Billie. Surely *somebody* new had died by now. *We'll Take It from Here.* Bonnie and I agreed to meet at the Belvedere between her two evening newscasts. Might as well get our money's worth.

"What's going on around here?" Billie wanted to know when I got back to the office. "Suddenly nobody is dying. What is this, *Death Takes a Holiday*? That phone hasn't rung once all day. Where are all the dead people?"

"Stubbornly holding on to life?"

"Bah! It's ridiculous. Maybe the phones aren't working."

Billie followed me into my office. I dropped into my chair and picked up the phone. "Dial tone," I announced.

"Try a call. Maybe the dial tone is the only thing that's working."

"Billie, it's possible that no—"

"Dial!"

Vickie Waggoner's phone number was scribbled on my blotter. I dialed it. I didn't expect there to be any answer. There wasn't. I let the phone ring. Four ringy-dingies. Five ringy-dingies. As I held the phone up so that Billie could hear the ringing, Billie was moving aside to let someone step into the room. It was Vickie Waggoner. I hung up the phone.

"I was just calling you," I said.

Her tired smile filled the room. "Here I am."

I understood everything. Within limits, of course.

The early-setting sun ignited the far wall. Its brassy light tracked steadily across Magritte's *Fiddle* as Vickie Waggoner, in the chair by the window, told me her story. Her head was outlined in a brilliant copper corona. On the wall across from her, just to the left of the Magritte, was her shadow. It moved whenever she moved.

As I had pretty much figured, Vickie told me that no sooner had she set down the receiver than Terry Haden had announced that he was getting the hell out of there.

"That was just fine with me," Vickie said. "In fact, that's what I had hoped he would do. That's why I pretended you were the police."

"You knew he'd scram if he thought the police were on their way?"

She nodded.

"How?"

"I don't know if you know this or not, but Terry Haden just got out of prison. He was in jail for child pornography."

"So I've learned."

"Well, you saw how he was at my place. The guy is a mess. He wants nothing at all to do with the police."

"So, you weren't thinking that he'd hightail it because he might have had something to do with Helen's murder?"

"I don't think he was involved in that at all."

"Do you have a reason to think that? Or is it instinct?"

"Instinct." She added, "That's my reason."

Vickie's hope that her little telephone deception had worked had been immediately doused when Haden announced that he was taking Bo with him.

"He wouldn't listen to reason. I tried to convince him that the boy needed to stay with me. His mother had just been buried that morning. I asked him where he was taking Bo. He didn't say. He had no clue. All he knew was that he was leaving immediately. He just grabbed Bo off the floor and ran out the door."

"And you followed."

"I couldn't let Bo go off with that man. I don't care if he's his father or not. What kind of an aunt would that make me? So, yes. I grabbed my purse and Bo's coat, and I took off after them."

"You left your place unlocked."

"I didn't even think."

"Where did he take you?"

"Atlantic City."

"Atlantic City? What for?"

Vickie sighed. She looked very tired. "Gambling? Casinos? Who knows why he went there? He didn't even know. It's not here, that's probably about it. On the way there he rambled on and on about winning all sorts of money and flying off somewhere. He kept asking me where I wanted to go. I told him, back to Baltimore. No, he kept saying. Where else? Anywhere in the world. I'll show you the world. That kind of thing. He was nuts. A couple of times he called me Helen. This guy just isn't right in the head."

I thought about asking her at this point if she was aware— and could explain—her sister's use of her name in her . . . professional capacity. But I didn't.

"So then what happened? You three went all the way to Atlantic City and then came back?"

"Haden got a motel room, about a mile or so away from the casinos and the boardwalk and all that. I don't know if you know Atlantic City. The moment you step away from the glitz, you're in a run-down, depressed little town that is essentially broke."

In the shadows of the corporate-fed casinos, where hundreds of thousands of dollars are changing hands, the city of Atlantic City is starving to death. I've been there. It's a whole new level of depressing.

"Haden tried to get me to go to bed with him. He didn't try very hard. I just held on to Bo and stared him down. His batteries were about out. Finally he just dropped onto one of the beds and went right out. Bo and I walked back into town and found the bus station. We got back into Baltimore a few hours ago."

"Where's the boy now?"

"I left him with my neighbors. He'll be fine. They're an older couple."

"Then you came here."

"Yes."

"Why?"

The woman's shoulders rose and fell in a large sigh.

"I don't know."

Funeral home: not a place to lift one's spirits.

Bar: just the place.

Or at least, the place to try.

Vickie looked about the dark interior of the Screaming Oyster Saloon like she was either intrigued with the barnacle feel of the place or like she was trying to figure her best escape route. I fetched two beers from Sally and steered Vickie toward one of the tables in the rear.

Vickie was exhausted from her Atlantic City odyssey and from her bus trip.

"I'd better drink this slowly." She took the glass from me after she sat down. "I'm likely to pass out." She took a small sip then set the glass down. "Thank you."

"Don't mention it."

"I don't mean for the beer. Thank you for . . . taking an interest in Helen." She closed her eyes for a moment, then opened them. "I can't begin to tell you how . . . the guilt that I've been feeling ever since I got the call that my sister had been murdered. This is silly. But at first . . . I thought that I was being indifferent to the news."

"How so?"

"Not really reacting. Not feeling it. I went ahead and collected Bo and took him back to my place and then waited to feel something."

I reminded her, "You felt something in my office that day. That was far from indifference."

"Yes. Well, it turns out not to be indifference at all that I've been feeling. I've been numb. I guess that's what has been protecting me from my guilt. It started last summer actually, when my mother was dying of cancer. I knew she was sick. I knew she was dying. I . . . I didn't go see her. A couple of times I started to, but I always made some excuse to myself each time and ended up not going. She was right up the street here. At Hopkins. Meanwhile there's Helen, who had fought and fought with the woman every step of the way . . . who was always yelling at her and telling her how much she hated her . . . and Helen was there for her. She was the one who visited her. Helen called me a couple of times to say that I ought to get on up there. But I didn't. In the end, it was Helen who ended up being the dutiful daughter. Not me."

I sipped my beer. I said nothing. She wanted my ear, not my opinions.

"You knew that my sister was a stripper for awhile?"

I nodded.

"And pornography? That's where she and Terry Haden hooked up."

"I know about that too."

"God, he was terrible to her. He got Helen all mixed up with drugs and with prostitution. I think he was also her pimp. This guy hates women, don't make any mistake about that. I mean, Helen was walking right in our mother's footsteps. Terry Haden was just another in a long line of sleazeballs like the ones who hung around our mother."

"Haden told me he was a big fan of your mother."

"The whole thing is sordid. He dragged Ruth Waggoner's daughter through the mud. Some tribute, huh?"

"I have to ask you a question," I said. The time seemed right to get this out of the way. "Your name."

"My name?"

"Helen used your name. When she was stripping and when she and Haden were making their movies. She called herself Victoria Wagner. Do you . . . You knew about this, right?"

Vickie had gone visibly stiff. "How did you hear about that?"

"A friend." I left it at that.

Vickie's plump lips drew back in a line. The way she was looking at me across the table I thought for a moment that she was either going to storm out of the bar or throw her beer in my face. Or both. Even in the bar's darkness, I could see the roiling in her pupils.

"I can explain that," she said at last.

"You don't have to. I just—"

"No." She held a hand up. "No. I want to. It's really not all that complicated, in fact." She brought her hands together in a fist on top of the table and stared down at them. One thumbnail was digging into the other. She took a deep breath. "I told you about the incident with one of my mother's boyfriends? The guy who tried to take advantage of Helen?"

"I remember. She kicked him."

"She sure did." A glimmer of a smile touched her lips, then was gone. "And I told you how Helen really became a handful for my mother from that point on? That this was when Helen started fighting with her tooth and nail and never obeying her and all the rest?"

"Yes."

"That's also when Helen and I started to drift apart. She—" Vickie unlocked her hands. She took a long look around the bar. She was determined to keep the tears from flowing this time. "Correction. Helen hated my guts after that incident. The part that I didn't tell you is that about a week after the incident, after the guy had dumped our mother . . . he saw to it that she was fired from the club where the two of them had been working. Not long after that, our mother got Helen and me up early one morning and the three of us got into a cab. We came down here in fact. Or near here. To the harbor. There were a group of men out on one of the piers, getting a boat ready. I don't even know what kind of boat it was. She had the two of us stand at the foot of the pier while she walked over to the men. She came back to us a few minutes later and one of the men was with her. I remember he was wearing these big, black rubber boots that came up over his knees, and a big loose sweater. He wasn't all that good-looking, though he had a nice enough smile. His skin was pretty bad and there was a big scar that ran along his head, right over his eyes. Our mother introduced us to him. She said his name was Mr. Donovan. She told him our names and he shook both of our hands and asked us how we were. None of it made any sense to me. The whole thing couldn't have taken more than two minutes. I remember he asked me what I wanted to be when I grew up. It seemed like a funny question and I didn't really have an answer. I don't even remember what I said. But I remembered that he didn't ask Helen the same question. In fact, he definitely paid more attention to me. I could feel that. And then he said good-bye and went back over to his boat and we got back in the cab. On the way back, our mother turned around in the front seat and said, in this totally fake voice, 'Victoria, Mr. Donovan is your father. He told me to tell you that it was very nice to meet you.' But she was looking straight at Helen when she said it."

Vickie fell silent. She lowered her chin. When she raised her head again, I was surprised to see how calm she looked.

"I never saw the man again. And to be honest, I don't even know if my mother was telling me the truth. But in a way, it didn't really matter. The whole thing had been to get back at Helen. It certainly wasn't for my benefit.

"That was it for me and my sister. Helen never forgave me for knowing who my father was. She hated me for it, and she hated our mother for it too. So did I. Our mother had pitted us against each other. After that, Helen became completely unmanageable. She picked up the wild burr. Boys. Booze. Drugs. All of it. Our mother couldn't even begin to control her. How could she? Her daughter was following in her footsteps. She had practically shoved Helen's nose in them. She'd taunt her. 'You're just like me. You're exactly like your fucking old lady.' That's what she said. It drove Helen nuts. Mainly because it was becoming so true. Meanwhile, I was the good daughter. Our mother rubbed that in too. She knew it dug deep. Everything Helen did that was bad or wrong or mean was thrown back in her face. 'Look at Victoria. Victoria would never do that. Why can't you be more like your sister?'"

She looked down at her hands again. "She ruined us as sisters. Helen was a wildcat. I almost think she followed in our mother's footsteps as much out of spite as anything, you know? 'You think I'm bad, I'll show you how bad I can be.' She was . . . Helen was arrested, for the first time, when she was fourteen. For prostitution. Solicitation, to be exact. She had no remorse about it at all. None. In fact, you'd have thought it was the proudest day of her life. And she made sure that she stuck the knife in as deep as she could. She had no identification on her when the police picked her up but she gave them her address and her phone number immediately. Then she gave them a fake name."

Vickie chased a lock of hair away from her face. Violently. She gave me a grim look across the table.

"She gave them my name."

I had missed my rendezvous with Bonnie. I failed even to call her up. She would have gone to the Belvedere and sat in the room, her anticipation turning steadily to anger before finally having to head back over to the station to smile her pretty smile for all of Baltimore and vicinity. I don't know what she was predicting for the five-day forecast, but I knew *my* forecast. Very hot water.

Vickie was drained. She left her glass of beer half empty— not half full—as we left the bar. Outside, she began to cry. I brought her into my chest and let her cry there. It was dark out now and about two degrees with the wind chill. I wrapped my long arms around her as much to try to keep her a little warm as to contain the rattling of her shoulders as she sobbed. Tony

Marino, the lovelorn Italian, crossed nearby on his way into the Oyster. He shared his sad face with me, misreading in every way possible what he thought he was seeing.

Vickie's sobbing finally started to subside. "I have to get back and pick up Bo," she said in a small voice.

"Of course."

She slid to my side, remaining under my arm as we made our way up Thames then took a left on Wolfe. The bitter wind vanished as soon as we rounded the corner.

Vickie's car was parked in front of the funeral home, half a block past my place. She drove a pale blue Honda Accord. I could see it from my window on the second floor, as I was messing with the blinds. Vickie pointed it out to me. She was warmer now. But she was still trembling. In the ambient light sifting in the window, her skin was a pale blue. Her eyes and her lips were black.

"I have to go," she said again. This time in a whisper.

"I know you do."

A half hour later, she did.

"Someone finally died!"

Billie was all bustling and fussy when I got over to the funeral home. The dead person about whom my aunt was so giddy was pretty standard, an elderly man who had suffered a heart attack while shoveling his front walk. Billie and I played a game of cribbage to see who would take the lead on this one. The events of the past twenty-four hours—especially those most recent—refused to leave my head and I fell behind in the game.

"Is it the cards, Hitchcock, or is it you?" Billie asked, pegging her way around the corner, well ahead of me. "You stink today."

Billie had gotten a fire going in her small fireplace and had introduced a pair of Baileys on ice into the room. Alcatraz lay at her slippered feet, his way of thanking her for the cold soup she had put in his bowl when we arrived. My dog is a soup nut. A light snowfall was underway outside, sifting down past Billie's lace curtains as a visual counterpoint to the Bach sonata playing over the radio. Overall, the room was toasty, with a single thread of chill meandering through from the window in the next room, cracked open an inch.

Bonnie wasn't returning my calls. I had left several messages first thing in the morning on the phone machine at her home and on her voice mail at the station. I apologized for missing our rendezvous at the Belvedere and for not calling to let her know that I wasn't going to be able to make it. "Something came up," I offered lamely.

I was playing cards like a blind man. I kept trying to bat away from my mind the image of Vickie Waggoner, blue as ice, warm as fire, soft as snow. The effort was certainly not being made any easier by the literal presence around me of those very elements. Vickie Waggoner was all over the room. So was Bonnie Nash. Well, if not all over the room, right at my shoulder. Picking out the lousy cards I was playing. If I didn't pull it together quickly, I'd be spending this lovely snowy afternoon down in the basement, draining blood from a corpse. Something not likely to do a whole lot of good for the mood I was already slipping into.

"Fifteen-two, fifteen-four, fifteen-six, a pair for eight, a run for eleven and the right jack is twelve." Aunt Billie moved her peg twelve spaces farther down the board. She glowed. "It was the best of times, it was the best of times."

I grumbled, "A pair."

Billie dealt. As I sorted painfully through another dead hand, Billie was already slapping down her crib. She cut the deck. An ace. "Yum. Does that ace help you at all?"

"No."

"That's too bad."

"Hold on, I'll get a pan for your tears."

I gained a few points on the run, but my hand was still flat. Billie's was only a little better. But her crib was downright festive. In my mind, I was already pulling on my rubber gloves. I was unfurling the tubes and laying them on the metal table.

Correction. In my mind, *Bonnie* was pulling on the gloves. The dead guy stretched out on the table? That was me.

I pulled it together. Billie detected something as I was shuffling the cards. A certain snap was back in my wrist. "Just what exactly are you thinking, young man?"

"I'm thinking we make our own luck, good or bad."

"What does that mean?"

"You'll see." I dealt the cards. I fanned mine out to have a look. The entire royal family was crowded into my hand. In duplicate. Billie cut the deck and turned up a five.

Ten minutes later, it was over. I reached across the board and tweaked my auntie's pink cheek.

"Have a good funeral."

Vickie met me at Helen's apartment. We didn't mention anything about the night before. We didn't touch, we didn't kiss. We glanced at each other like the two awkward strangers that we, in essence, were.

Helen's apartment was small and messy. How much of the mess was Helen's and how much was due to the Baltimore City Police Department's investigatorial toss-around, I couldn't say. Vickie had been here already herself, when she came over to gather up some of Bo's clothes and toys. She had told me earlier that it had been her first visit to her sister's home. This one would be her last.

We were looking for two things at Helen's apartment. At least, I was. I was hoping that we could determine the name of the obstetrician Helen had been seeing about her pregnancy. Even with the likelihood that Gary had been the one who got Helen pregnant, I was still clinging to the possibility that if Helen had been seeing someone else perhaps that person had gone ahead and footed the bills for her. If we could talk with Helen's doctor, we might get a clue as to the fellow's identity.

The idea seemed weaker now than it had when I first came up with it. But it still seemed worth the effort.

The other thing I was hoping to find was a photograph of Terry Haden. The slow fuse of logic had finally ignited as I was leaving Aunt Billie's after giving her my good cribbage whopping. If I could locate a photograph of Haden and show it to Gail out at Sinbad's Cave, I could either confirm or dismiss Haden as the person with whom Helen had been having her loud argument at the bar. That argument had been looming larger in my head lately. Whoever killed Helen Waggoner lured her out of the bar with a phone call. Chances were pretty good, I felt, that the killer had at some point been to Sinbad's. Whoever Helen had been arguing with on the night that Gail had described, a month before her murder, I liked him for the killer.

We came up with nothing. No photo. No indication as to who Helen had been seeing about her pregnancy. Vickie was able to gather up a few more of Bo's belongings, but the pulsing red X that was supposed to be resting atop the all-important clue failed to show itself. Vickie and I brushed shoulders several times as we moved about the small apartment. Nothing came of that action. At least, nothing that either of us cared to draw attention to. Naturally I can't speak for Vickie. I could only speculate as to what she was feeling about the previous evening when the two of us had gone bump in the night. All I could read in her expression with any certainty was that she honestly did not want to go into any of it right now. I could respect that, as a man and a coward and a pragmatist.

Outside Helen's apartment we stood awkwardly next to Vickie's car. The snowfall had stopped, leaving only a light dusting. Even chances for a white Christmas. Vickie Waggoner was looking anything but jolly.

"I guess that's that," she said. She pulled open the car door and tossed a bag of her nephew's clothes onto the front seat.

"We'll find out who killed your sister," I assured her. Though at this point my doubts were beginning to seriously outweigh my hopes. I wasn't at all certain what to do next, but I didn't want to let Vickie know that. Vickie got into the car and rolled down the window.

"I wonder if it's really so important," she said, fumbling with her keys.

"Of course it's important."

"But why? I mean, ultimately. Finding out who killed her isn't going to bring her back. And . . . let's be honest about this. How much contact did I really have with my sister these last couple of years? Practically none. I don't even know if it's fair for me to say that I miss her."

"You're being a little rough on yourself, don't you think?"

"Maybe I'm just wanting to find out who killed Helen so that I'll feel a little less guilty about having abandoned her."

"You didn't abandon your sister."

"But I could have tried to keep in contact. I could have tried to get over some of the garbage that our mother put between us."

"It's too easy after the fact to start moaning about what you might have done. Helen could just as easily have reached out to you, you know. That wasn't your responsibility alone. People do grow apart. It's not a new thing."

Vickie wasn't ready to be convinced. "Still. I feel guilty."

I crouched down so that we were face-to-face. "Look, even if it is a sense of guilt that's driving you to find out who did this to your sister, so what? It's not too often that guilt comes in as a good thing. Some bastard shot your sister. Whatever your reason is for wanting to find out who did it is good enough."

She turned the key and had some trouble getting the engine started. When it finally turned over a great cloud of oily blue smoke belched from the exhaust pipe. I straightened. Vickie winced apologetically as the cloud passed over me.

"Apparently there's a crack in the engine block," she explained. "The mechanic I took it to said the crack can't be welded. It's aluminum. I really need to get another car. I just can't afford it right now."

"What is it you do for a living, anyway?" I asked. I had been wanting to know this since she first walked into my office. "I mean, if I can ask. It's none of my business."

"I think you can ask," she said in a small voice. This was as close as either of us had come to acknowledging the previous evening. "I'm a schoolteacher. I teach fourth grade at Owings Mills Elementary."

"A schoolteacher?"

"You sound surprised."

"I suppose I am. Though I don't know why I should be. I don't know any other schoolteachers, maybe that's it."

"Hitch, I need to ask you something. What are you doing this for? Why are you trying to find Helen's killer?"

"Your sister was left off on my doorstep."

She wasn't convinced. "Is that really a compelling reason? It's Christmas. You must have better things to do with your time than running around looking for the killer of someone you never even knew."

"Well, you'd think so."

"Yes, I would."

We shared a moment of awkward silence. Across the street a couple of boys were piling up snowballs on the hood of a car. I smelled an ambush.

Vickie reached a hand out the window and touched my arm. "Whatever . . . thank you."

She started to say something, then thought better of it and stopped herself. She rolled her window closed and put the car into gear and pulled away. The blue plume chased her down the street and around the corner. So did a few snowballs. They didn't come close.

• • •

When I returned from the fruitless search of Helen Waggoner's apartment, there was a message waiting for me to swing by the police station at my earliest convenience. The message that *wasn't* waiting for me there was nearly as succinct. In its very absence. The unleft message was that I swing by hell at my earliest convenience and consider just staying there. I shoved the issue of Bonnie back into a corner of my brain and headed downtown.

Kruk was making better headway with his several murders than I was making with my one. Of course, he had the resources of the Baltimore City Police Department to assist him, along with twenty-some odd years of Charm City crime fighting to call on. I'm just an amiable undertaker with a sleepy hound dog. Most of my dead people arrive with the particulars of their demise already typed up on an accompanying death certificate.

The murder of Popeye, the strip club owner, by the same shooter who had shot Michael Fenwick and his wife, had given Kruk something to work with. Kruk assumed that there was some sort of "mopping up" going on. Both Popeye and Fenwick, Kruk determined, were killed for a related reason. Once Kruk located the connection, the dominoes would begin to fall, presumably ending up at the feet of the killer.

"This killer is definitely sending a message to someone. This bullet to the foot routine . . . that's intended to let someone know loud and clear that the killer is working off a list of some sort. First the lawyer, then this Popeye fellow."

"You think there'll be more?"

Kruk nodded emphatically. "It's possible that it was a very short list, but I'd bet my hat on it that there'll be more." There wasn't a topper in sight. It must have been out getting blocked and cleaned. Kruk went on, "So, I guess you're wondering why I've asked you to come down here."

"Let me guess. You want to know if I marched into Martick's yesterday, shot the old man in the heart and the foot, then circled the block, ditching the murder weapon in a trash can, and showed up twenty minutes later doing my best innocent bystander imitation."

Kruk raised his palms toward the ceiling. "And I was going to beat around the bush."

"If you've got a confession typed up for me to sign, you can probably go ahead and take the rest of the day off."

"Yeah, well, unfortunately it doesn't work that way. What I really want, Mr. Sewell, is to warn you off the Waggoner case. I've been too lenient with you already."

"Warn me off? What does that mean?"

"What part don't you understand? It's very simple. My job is to serve and protect. This is the protect part."

"I don't get it."

"You're snooping around, you're trying to dig up some information about Helen Waggoner. I can't stop you from doing that. Snooping is protected by the constitution. But your snooping around yesterday almost put you at the scene of a murder just before it happened. A half hour earlier and you might have been sitting at the table with that old man, harassing him—"

"Hey!"

"—about Terry Haden and Helen Waggoner or whatever it is you think you're doing. You could have been killed."

"Why? The guy was gunning for Popeye, not me."

"He was also probably just gunning for Michael Fenwick last week and not his wife. But look who's not around today to enjoy being a widow."

I started to protest but Kruk cut me off.

"Frankly I would have thought you might have learned something from the last time you stuck your nose into a murder investigation, Mr. Sewell. Unlike you, I'm paid by the city of Baltimore to be curious. And I'm trained in how to protect myself from the consequences of my curiosity. But you're stumbling around. You might well stumble onto Helen Waggoner's killer and only know it when he's aiming his gun at you. And you're a large target. I'm telling you right now, if I find myself investigating *your* murder anytime soon, I'm not going to be happy about it."

"Neither will I. But it's nice to know you care."

"You've got my message then. Stay away from The Kitten Club. Stay away from Terry Haden. Stay away from Sinbad's Cave."

"What happened to my constitutional right to snoop?"

Kruk let out a sigh. "These are police matters. If you have any information you would like to pass along to us, I would be happy to hear it."

"Will that be all?"

Kruk dismissed me with a backhanded wave. I stood up from my uncomfortable chair and started for the door. As I reached it, Kruk said, "Do I have your word?"

I stopped and faced him. He took in my expression in about two seconds. He growled. "I didn't think so."

A parking ticket was tucked under my windshield wiper when I returned to my car. I decided to leave the car where it was—get a little something for my investment—and flatfoot it up Calvert Street to the offices of the Sunpapers. I asked the receptionist to direct me to Jay Adams's desk ("Elevator, fourth floor, first left, second right, ask there.") and found myself in a large open room filled with cubicles and people lounging about and chatting with each other. Here and there was a person either hunched over a keyboard or aggressively engaged in a phone conversation, but for the most part the place seemed to be involved in a permanent coffee break.

I found Jay Adams at his desk. He was on the phone, at the keyboard *and* chatting with someone who was seated just inside his cubicle. Actually what I saw first as I approached were his visitor's legs, slender, brown, crossed at the knees, one foot wagging. Adams saw me coming. He wrapped up his phone call and slid his keyboard off to the side. Adams said something to his visitor, and the foot attached to the brown leg stopped wagging.

"What a pleasant surprise," Adams said—almost as if he meant it—as I reached his cubicle. I winced my fake smile.

"Yeah. How about that."

Adams's visitor was taking me in with a slow vertical scan, starting at my thighs, which were about eye-level. When she reached my face I had my hat-tipping smile ready.

"Hello, Constance."

"Well, hello, Hitchcock. How are you doing these days?"

I turned to Adams. "Now *this* is a surprise."

"A pleasant one, I hope," the reporter said, his slender fingers lacing seamlessly.

I didn't answer him, but turned back to the woman in the chair. Constance Bell. She was dressed in a stylish wool suit. Earth tones, blending perfectly with her copper-colored skin. Constance Bell always wore a lot of makeup and always wore it perfectly. Her ubiquitous silk scarf was in place around her neck (today, pale yellow) and the brass earrings dangling from her ears looked like a pair of miniature mobiles by Calder. Her hair was meticulously cornrowed and spun into an elaborate knot at the back of her slender neck. Constance has astonishing teeth—a dazzling white keyboard smile—but for some reason she has always been self-conscious about them and so she holds her lips sealed in a slight pucker, keeping her huge smile reigned in. The result is that the rest of her face positively ripples and glows. When her smile does manage to escape, when for example she bursts out laughing, it's as if a gust of wind has kicked up. You expect loose papers to blow onto the floor.

Constance was keeping her smile reined in. But her large chestnut eyes pulsed with her delight in seeing me.

"How's your aunt, Hitchcock?"

"Oh, Aunt Billie is as Aunt Billie as ever."

"That's good to hear. And Julia? Are you still in contact?"

"Yes, ma'am."

"She's made quite a name for herself. I saw on the television the other day where she did something recently for the zoo?"

"I was out there for the unveiling. It's very clever, really."

"I don't doubt that. How is she?"

"Near perfect. Still."

Constance started to smile, but instead marshaled her features into a somber expression. She searched my face, one eye at a time.

"You two were the strangest divorce I ever handled."

"Well, you handled it beautifully, Constance. We couldn't be happier. And Mexico was a blast." I turned to Adams, who was happily soaking all this in. "Constance handled my divorce."

"I wasn't aware that you had been married."

I turned back to Constance. "And he calls himself a reporter."

Constance turned to Adams. "So, you haven't met Hitchcock's ex-wife. Let me tell you, my boyfriend happened to be in my office once when Julia dropped by to sign some papers for the divorce. Lord, he was no good to me for about a week after that."

Despite herself, Constance let fly with a smile. I wouldn't swear to it, but I almost thought I saw the slight reporter at his desk take a tight grip of the arms of his chair. Constance shut down the smile as swiftly as she had launched it. The fact of the matter is, if Constance was even halfway telling the truth, her boyfriend was an idiot. Julia is Julia, sure. But the savvy lawyer sitting here did not exactly inspire yawns.

"I'm interrupting something," I said. Belatedly.

"Actually, we were just wrapping up here," Adams said. "Ms. Bell, I want to thank you for coming down here. If I think of any follow-up questions I'll give you a call."

Adams stood up and reached a tiny paw across the desk. Constance rose, accompanied by a whiff of something nutmeg, and shook the reporter's hand.

"When do you expect the piece to appear?"

"I can't say yet," Adams answered. "I would hope within a few days."

Constance released his fingers and turned to face me. She lay a hand on each of my arms.

"It was nice to see you again, Hitchcock. Call me sometime."

"I'm afraid I don't have any divorces pending," I said.

"That doesn't matter. Besides, I don't do divorces anymore. I'm with a new firm now. I catch all sorts of odd cases that the partners toss down. Here."

She produced a business card from her snazzy brown purse and handed it to me. "A fellow like you surely can't stay out of trouble forever." She snapped her purse shut. "Tell Julia hello for me, when you see her again."

I told her I would do that. As Constance headed for the elevator, I shifted my weight just slightly, enough to block Adams's view of the departing counselor.

"What can I do for you?" Adams asked. The sugar had left his voice.

"What was Constance Bell doing here?" I asked, simply to irritate. "You're not getting divorced from someone, are you?"

"Didn't you hear? She doesn't do divorces anymore. Ms. Bell worked with Michael Fenwick. Fenwick's that fellow who got shot the other day, along with his wife."

I glanced at the business card in my hand. "Stern and

Fenwick. There goes the partnership. Now it's just Stern and Nobody."

"No. It's his old man who is the partner. Michael Fenwick was the young turk. Up and coming. Until this, of course. I'm gathering some background for a profile piece. Ms. Bell was kind enough to drop in so that I could ask a few questions."

So, Constance Bell had worked with the murdered lawyer. What a teeny-tiny world. That's how Baltimore works. I asked Adams, "Did you ask her about poor old Popeye? Have you figured out the connection yet?"

"I ran the name by her. It didn't appear to register."

"You sound doubting."

"In the absence of proof, I keep an open mind. Is that doubting?"

"Sounds like a good policy," I answered.

"This is just between the two of us, of course, but I've been picking up some vibes that the late Mr. Fenwick might not have always played everything exactly by the book."

"A crooked lawyer? They actually exist?"

"There goes your faith in all that's good in the world, I know. I'm sorry to do that to you. And at Christmas no less."

"I'll survive," I said. "So then this Fenwick was involved in something shady with the good Mr. Popeye?"

"That's the logical starting point." Adams sat back in his chair. "So, now what is it I can do for you, Hitch? I'm going to go out on a limb and guess that this isn't just a social call."

"I did just happen to be in the neighborhood," I said. "But you're right. I'm here to find out how much you really care about helping Bonnie and me on the Waggoner case, and how much is just hot air and bullshit."

The reporter made a teepee of his fingers and placed the tip to his chin. "You know, I'm trying to figure out why it is you dislike me so much."

"I never said I disliked you."

"It must be your body language then."

"Maybe you're just paranoid."

"You think I'm after Bonnie Nash, don't you?"

"Aren't you?"

"She's an attractive woman."

"That's like saying the sun is a hot ball of gas."

"All I'm saying is that it's natural for someone like Bonnie Nash to attract attention."

"You're not saying anything. Half the horny male population of Baltimore slobbers over that woman at six and eleven. I'm asking about you in particular."

"Let me see if I can get this right. No comment?"

What was especially irritating about the slender reporter was that he didn't even allow his smugness to show on his face. He sat there at his desk looking perfectly pleasant. Despite myself, I had to admire that in the guy. Maybe he was just someone who enjoys busting other people's chops. I decided to uncock my pistol and get down to the reason I had stopped in. Besides, the question wasn't so much if he was chasing after Bonnie—the constitution allows that as well—but whether or not she was running away quite as fast as she could. And that was something for me to take up with Bonnie.

Or not.

"I'm trying to get a hold of a photograph of Terry Haden. I thought maybe the photo archives of the great and powerful Sunpapers might be able to cough one up for me."

Adams accepted the blunt transition. He dropped the irritating teepee. "Why don't you ask our friend, Kruk? I'm sure they've got a nice mug shot on file."

"Detective Kruk would prefer that I keep my nose out of other people's murders."

"I see."

"Bonnie thought maybe you would be able to help on this." This was a stretch of the actual truth. But an acceptable one. "That is, with a photograph of Haden."

"Why don't you just track him down and take one yourself?"

"Last seen, Terry Haden was facedown on a bed in an Atlantic City motel room, passed out. I thought maybe this would be easier."

"*Bonnie* thought so."

"Yes," I lied again. "Bonnie thought so."

I watched as Adams considered whether or not to continue busting my chops. He must have concluded that he had more important matters to stir.

"Give me ten minutes."

"Fifteen. What the hell."

Twenty minutes later a runner appeared in the cubicle, carrying a brown interoffice envelope. Adams unwound the twine and pulled an eight-by-ten photograph from the envelope, looked at it and handed it to me.

"Will this do?"

The photograph was of three men, seated together at a table. Two of the men, dressed in business suits, were leaning in toward each other, conferring. The third man was Terry Haden. His attention was elsewhere. He looked bored.

"Who are these other guys?" I asked.

"His lawyers. This was taken at Haden's arraignment a year and a half ago. For child pornography."

"He doesn't look terribly concerned."

Adams shrugged. "Will that do?"

"It's fine. Thanks."

I probably should have shaken his hand as I got up to leave, but I didn't. Luckily his phone rang just then. He picked it up. "Hold on," he said, and he held the phone against his chest. I was just stepping from the cubicle when Adams said, "By the way, if you're planning to take that picture out to the airport to see if that waitress, what's her name? Gail? If Gail can identify Haden, I can save you the trouble. She can't."

The snake was smiling. I wasn't. "You knew that's why I wanted the picture."

"Bonnie told me. About the waitress, I mean. And the argument she witnessed between Helen and someone. I went out there to Sinbad's this morning."

"Oh. And when did Bonnie tell you this?" I said evenly.

"Last night. I ran into her at Alonzo's. After the late news. She wasn't in a very good mood, I have to say. She appeared to be, well, a little pissed off about something."

"You don't say."

"You could see it in her eyes."

"So, you had that photograph all along?"

He nodded.

"Why'd you make me wait twenty minutes for it?"

Adams smiled. "You're such wonderful company."

A lesser man would have ripped the photograph in half and tossed the pieces onto his desk. I waited until I got outside. I dropped them into a trash can. Half a block away I thought better of it, and returned to fetch them. A bum was pawing through the can. I stood politely by and waited my turn.

CHAPTER
20

Pops and his crew were digging a grave for a man who had died with a snow shovel in his hands. I wouldn't put it past the Supreme Ironical Being to consider toppling old Pops in the very midst of his shoveling the dead man's grave. I decided to swing by the cemetery to check in on them. Outbreaks of irony come without warning.

Pops was fine. He was supervising. The young turks were carrying the load. All of their equipment seemed to be back in working order. The backhoe was belching oily blue smoke from its vertical exhaust pipe; it reminded me of Vickie's car. An idea came to me as I watched the blue plume dissipate into the air. I tucked the idea into my pocket for later.

Since I was there, I decided to do a short walkabout and see if I could sort out either the tangle of Helen Waggoner's murder, my own duplicitous dilemma in the romance and scurvy bastard department, or maybe touch lightly on the Meaning of Life and the question of what exists beyond the stars. I took the issues with me to the graves of my parents and my unborn little sister. They had no answers for me, but at least they served to distract me for a few minutes. Ugly Uncle Stu had seen to it that the three of them each received gravestones in relative height to one another, so that my father's was the tallest of the three stones, followed by mama mia's, and lastly the little aspirin tablet of my unborn sister. My parents had not prenamed the child that my mother had been carrying to the hospital that day. After allowing me to sit with the news of the accident for several hours, Aunt Billie had taken me for a long walk along the harbor, during which she had offered me the privilege of giving my unborn sister a name so that we could put it on the tiny headstone. She left me alone and I had wandered by myself out to the pier at the end of Thames Street. I sat there for hours as the sun fell gently below the horizon to my right and the soft blue dome of night began sliding into place overhead. The early summer stars appeared, led by a flickery blue chip of light low in the east sky, brighter than the rest. Jupiter. Or so my twelve-year-old brain decided. The planet Jupiter, flickering and pulsing with a look-at-me energy and urgency that none of the other stars in the sky were displaying. After a while longer I returned to the funeral home. A dozen or so neighbors and friends of my parents had already come together at the news of what had happened. They all fell silent as I came through the front door and stepped over to my aunt and uncle to announce that I had named my new and already lost sister. "Jupiter Sewell," I said. It was when I added, "I would have called her Joop" that the tears finally came. Buckets of them.

After leaving my family's gravesite I took my imponderables over the hill to the grave of Helen Waggoner. I crouched down, and since I was now in a maudlin mood, I rested my bare hand against the earth of her grave. I wasn't really thinking about Helen though. I was thinking about her sister. I had rested my hand atop Vickie's bare stomach much this same way the night before at my place, after our brief and surprising bout. I had kept it there until her breathing—erratic and catching—had returned to normal. Her skin was every bit as warm and moist as the earth under my hand now was brittle and frozen hard.

On the way back to my car I spotted a figure crouching down next to the fresh grave of Richard Kingman, the doctor we had buried the previous week. I thought at first that it was the doctor's widow. Recalling our conversation the other day at the little skating ponds in her neighborhood, I thought maybe the woman was finally confronting the fact that her husband wasn't simply leaving rooms as she entered them, but that he was in fact gone for good. I started for the grave, working up a bromide I'm sure, when the figure rose up from its crouch. It rose too tall to be Ann Kingman. It was her son. The name escaped me. He turned and saw me coming.

"Mr. Kingman," I said. "Hitchcock Sewell."

The young man was drawing a blank. Then he got it.

"The undertaker."

"I didn't mean to interrupt. I was just—"

He waved his hand. "No problem. I happened to be passing by and thought I'd check in on the old man." He glanced down at his father's grave, then back at me. He attempted a laugh. "He's still dead."

The junior Kingman's attempt at levity needed some work. His face was too drawn, his entire bearing having given in to gravity. I noted again that, except for the red hair and the glasses, he looked much more like his mother. He crossed his arms in a hug and shuddered. It was strictly for effect.

"Brrr. Can you believe this weather?"

"Yes, it's something." I glanced over at the headstone.

There was a fresh bouquet of flowers there. If the young Kingman were just "passing by" how fortuitous that he happened to have a clutch of flowers along with him.

"I'm sorry about your father," I said.

The young man seemed to weigh my words. "Thank you," he said. "So am I." He twisted his head to look down at the grave. "I guess it's an old story."

"Which one's that?"

"Fathers and sons. I mean, fathers and sons who never really connected." Kingman's shoe had found a wedge of loosened sod at the foot of his father's grave. He kept his eyes on it as he noodled it about.

"I guess I did my best to ignore him. Or just to stay away from him. I had the feeling that he didn't really like me."

"I doubt that was the case. You were his son."

"Sure. I'm his blood. You've got to love family, I guess. But you don't have to like them." He looked up at me. "I didn't like *him*."

There was nothing I could say to that, so I kept quiet. I felt sorry for the guy. He was tall, like his father, but slightly built, the lanky look of a basketball player.

The silence between us was threatening to become awkward. "I'm sorry," I said. "I get bombarded with names."

"Jeffrey."

"Of course. Hitch." We shook hands. A crow flew overhead. "How's your mother, Jeffrey? I happened to run into her the other day."

"She mentioned that. She's fine. She's a tough broad, you know?"

"I know that it's none of my business, but I don't get the feeling that she's as tough as she pretends to be."

"She's fine," Jeffrey said again.

"Well, tell her I send my regards."

"I'll do that."

I left the happy camper to his fond memories. For my part, I decided I had had just too much fun in the graveyard for one day. I got the cemetery into my rearview mirror just as quickly as I could.

I wanted to follow up on the idea I'd had while at Helen's gravesite, but I knew that there was another matter that needed my immediate attention. I drove over to Television Hill, parked in the visitors's lot and tripped not-so-merrily along the sidewalk into the station. Bonnie's silver sports car was parked in her slot. The weather lady was in.

I found Bonnie on the set. An architect was going over with her a set of plans he had drawn up for overhauling the weather corner. They do this every three or four years. Put a new face on the old map. Bonnie saw me standing off in the shadows. She held up two fingers to me. Two minutes. For a moment I thought she was going to be holding up just one. Her expression suggested it.

"New set?" I asked when she stepped over.

"Where the fuck were you yesterday?" she hissed. "I waited at the goddamn Belvedere for two hours."

"We have to talk," I said.

"No we don't, I have to yell! Have you heard of a *telephone*, Hitch? Or maybe Western Union? Or say it with fucking flowers? Where the hell were you?"

"I had an emergency," I said.

"Fine. And did it take you away from *all* forms of communication?"

Would the monster within me cough up a lie? Or would the Boy Scout speak? And make the moment a living hell.

"I couldn't call you. I was out on a boat." Oh my God. *Him.* The liar roared and beat his hairy paws against the inside of my chest.

"A boat?" Bonnie blinked. "What boat?"

"Tugboat. A red one."

"I don't give a damn what color it was, Hitch. Why didn't you call me before you went out on a goddamn tugboat? Why were you on a tugboat anyway?"

"Can we go somewhere?"

"Not until you give me a satisfying answer."

Her blood pressure was up. Her cheeks were crimson. I realized that having crossed her Rubicon the other day, Bonnie was not beyond another well-placed smack to my cheek if I gave her even half a reason. *Beast. Speak.*

"Do you know Joe Donofrio?" I asked. I already knew that she didn't. I had just made up the name.

"No." She made a two syllable word of it.

"Joe Donofrio. He used to . . . run one of the tugs. Years ago. Retired. He died. The other day. Shoveling snow." (Might as well toss one bit of half-truth into this sham.) "We had him cremated. His wish was that his ashes be spread in the harbor. That's where I was."

Bonnie's eyes narrowed. "You never mentioned anything about this."

"With everything that's been happening, it just slipped my mind. Besides, it's shoptalk. You don't want to hear about every corpse that walks through the door."

Bonnie softened. "I don't know, Hitch. The cremation of a tugboat captain and a burial at sea? That's sort of interesting. I mean, I could see a human interest story in that. If it has the right elements. Did he leave behind a widow? Maybe I could interview her."

"No widow," I said quickly. Too quickly. "No family at all. In fact, Joe was pretty much an old crank. He didn't have many friends. It was a pretty bleak event all around." The beast was pawing at my throat. It wanted to elaborate. It always wants to elaborate. That's why the beast is not your friend. I bit down on my tongue.

"I should have called you," I said. "I'm sorry. I got caught up."

Bonnie smirked. "I forgive you. Which means I own you." She slipped her arm through mine. "What's that noise?"

"My stomach." The beast lumbering back to its lair.

"Let's go eat."

"Honeybunch, whatever you say."

Bonnie and I parked it at Frazier's, a low-ceiling dive of exquisite repute in Hampden. We ordered the spaghetti special. Their garlic bread is a killer. I put away an entire loaf. Penance. And insurance against the temptation to run off and kiss the wrong girl again.

It is a known fact that the wronged woman becomes all the more beautiful, especially to the eye of the bastard who has foisted that status upon her. But not exclusively to him. Guilt can gild, so to speak, and certainly it was doing so at Frazier's. Bonnie glowed. Most everyone in the small restaurant recognized Bonnie Nash from TV. She even signed a few autographs while we waited for our spaghetti. Sometimes her celebrity bothers her, but tonight she positively shimmered at the fawning. I had ordered a half carafe of Frazier's lousy red wine—Bonnie was abstaining due to her need for clarity at the weather map in a few hours—and, when it seemed to empty too swiftly, I ordered the second half. As our waitress was making the switch, I noted, "Half empty, half full."

About midway through our spaghetti I told Bonnie my idea. I didn't bother to tell her that it had germinated from the cloud of oily smoke coming out of Pops' backhoe. "So here's the question," I said.

"Where is her car?"

"Whose car?"

"Helen Waggoner's. Where's her car?"

"I don't know. What are you saying?"

"She had to get back and forth from home to work. Right? There's no convenient bus that I know of that runs to the airport from Woodlawn. Plus she had a child to tote around and another one on the way. The woman had to be able to get around. Where is her car?"

Bonnie shrugged. "Who says she didn't have a car?"

"I didn't see one."

"Didn't see one where?"

I looked across the table at my lovely friend. No beast. I crawled out onto the limb all alone.

"Vickie Waggoner and I met at Helen's place this afternoon. We were looking for something that might tell us what obstetrician Helen was seeing."

Bonnie's voice carried no inflection. "You didn't mention this."

"No. I'm sorry."

"Sorry?"

"I just . . . There's so much going on."

"I see. Did you and Miss Vickie find what you were looking for?"

"It was a bust. But it occurred to me later, this thing about the car."

"Hitch, how important is it whether or not Helen Waggoner owned a car?"

"I don't know. It might not be important at all. But a car is a large thing to go missing."

"If it has."

"If it has."

Bonnie was looking just a tiny bit less like an angel by the time we finished our dinner and paid up and left. She was not sounding like one either. We were on the sidewalk out in front of the restaurant.

"I'm so fucking sick of my goddamn job. Hitch, we've *got* to figure out this murder. I *have* to bring in a scoop to the station, I just have to. I can't grow old spitting out the goddamn barometric pressure. And the fact is, I won't. The shelf life for a female television personality is pretty goddamn short."

"We'll come up with the killer." I sounded about as confident as I had when I'd said the same thing to Vickie earlier in the day. Which wasn't saying much. Bonnie must have been reading my mind.

"Who will? You and me? Or you and the sister?"

Before I even had time to form the thought, I blurted, "You told Jay Adams about Gail."

"What?"

"Going out to Sinbad's."

"Who told you that?"

"The Jaybird himself. I went to see him this afternoon."

"Well, so what if I did? Jay is a colleague. We share information."

Then she blushed. *She blushed!* Bonnie held her gaze on me, but I could tell that she wanted to turn away. Well son of a bitch.

"Are you sleeping with Jay Adams?" I asked.

Her answer was immediate. "I don't have to answer that. Are you sleeping with Vickie Waggoner?"

"I don't have to answer that."

Now neither of us dared turn away. But it was too damn cold—and ridiculous—to stand there on the sidewalk in front of Frazier's and have a staring contest. It was Bonnie who blinked first.

"I'll withdraw the question," she said.

"Good."

"Aren't you going to withdraw yours?"

"If you'd like."

"I'd like."

Cautiously, we holstered our weapons. But we were still circling.

"Maybe I'll come see you after I get off work," Bonnie said. She was using a testing-the-waters tone.

"Uh-huh. Maybe I'll be there."

"Maybe you'd better."

"Is that a warning?"

"Maybe it is."

The following morning, while Bonnie was taking a shower, I phoned Vickie Waggoner. Alcatraz sat on the floor in front of me giving me his disappointed look. Vickie wasn't in. I left the vaguest of messages—"I'll call you later"—and hung up. When Bonnie stepped into the room some minutes later, rubbing her hair with a towel, Alcatraz let out a pair of bubbly barks. It's a good thing Bonnie doesn't speak dog. My hound was telling on me. Anything to ingratiate.

I am the King of Breakfast. My general philosophy is to front-load your day with as much of the good stuff as you can manage so that if and when the day slips away from you later, at least you have something worthy to look back on. I bombarded Bonnie with a colossal fruit smoothy, orgasmically perfect coffee, Belgian waffles—which I understand are no more Belgian than French fries are French or English muffins are English—and Jones's little link sausages, plump and bursting. My array of jams included boysenberry, huckleberry and plum; my syrup was 101 percent pure maple from the Green Mountain State; and my plates were authentic Ming Dynasty wannabes from the Wal-Mart in Glen Burnie. Bonnie's eyes went wide as she stepped into the kitchen.

"Hitch. I'm not really hungry."

And that's why we have dogs. Bonnie took a cup of coffee and the corner of a Belgian waffle. Alcatraz pigged.

I put the pans and dishes and cups and the rest in the sink, filled it with hot water and left it. God forbid a bus runs you over and you wasted your final morning washing dishes you'd never again use.

Our pillow talk had included a plan of action for the day. After I showered and dressed I phoned the number on a cocktail napkin that I had left on my desk several days before. Bonnie was watching me closely as I arranged a rendezvous with the person on the other end of the line.

"You're a pretty smooth operator," she said after I hung up.

"You knew that already."

"It's different when you get to see it in action on somebody else."

I fetched my car keys. Bonnie was sliding into her coat. "I notice you didn't mention that you weren't coming alone."

"Sometimes it's better to catch people off guard."

"I guess we'll see."

We caught Tracy Atkins off guard. Luckily I hadn't been so "smooth" that the woman was waiting for me in a lace teddy. Still, her disappointment at seeing that I was accompanied by some blond chick registered immediately as she pulled open the door. It lasted only a second—the disappointment—and was quickly replaced with hostility.

"Who's she?"

"You don't recognize Bonnie Nash? From TV?"

"No." It was probably a lie.

"Can we come in?" I asked, smiling my biggest we're-all-happy-here-aren't-we smile.

"Why not."

Tracy lived in a dump. I felt immediately as if I were in a wing of the Gary and Gloria house. The wall-to-wall carpet was snot green and severely tufted. The walls were beige—or simply dirty—and unadorned. The furniture looked vaguely bacterial. Tracy had straightened up in anticipation of my arrival, if shoving loose junk into the corner can be called straightening up. She was wearing lime green shorts, a blue tank top and a fresh patina of makeup. I hadn't noticed in the crab house how full and loose her breasts were. I noticed now. Tracy had teased her fiery red hair into a feathery cascade. Her nails were freshly painted. As I perched lightly on the edge of the couch, I caught a glimpse of a flickering candle out of the corner of my eye. Through an open door. Next to a bed. I seriously doubted I'd have gotten out alive had I arrived solo. Bonnie alighted next to me. I hoped Miss Atkins didn't keep a shotgun handy. We were sitting ducks.

"We want to ask you a few questions about Helen," I said.

"You did that already." Tracy crossed her arms over her bouncy breasts and dropped into an armchair. A puff of silvery dust leaped from the cushions.

"I know. I'm just trying to get the clearest picture."

"How clear do you want? Someone killed Helen. You don't know who. I don't know who."

"Well, now, you see, that's not a very clear picture." I pulled the torn photograph of Terry Haden and his lawyers from my pocket and leaned across the coffee table to hand her the half showing Haden. "That's Terry Haden."

She glanced at the photograph. "Okay. So?"

"You do recognize him, right? That's Helen's ex-husband."

She looked at the photograph again. Or pretended to.

"If you say it is."

"Just how close to Helen were you?" Bonnie asked. I would have preferred that she let me do the talking. The redhead stiffened.

"Better than you, I guess."

"This guy in the picture, Tracy, did you ever see him at Sinbad's?" I asked. "Did you ever see him and Helen together?"

"No."

I pointed at the front door. "So, if he were to come walking through that door right now, would he recognize you?"

If she were lying I'd know it. As far as she knew I had Terry Haden cooling his heels right outside. She answered immediately.

"Nope."

I believed her. I stole a glance at Bonnie. She did too. Good . . . we had a liar telling the truth. Progress. I asked my next question. My real one. "Did you steal Helen's car?"

Tracy answered slowly, "What do you mean?"

Bonnie attempted to clear it up for her. "He means did you steal Helen Waggoner's car after she was killed?"

"You can just shut up, lady!" Tracy snapped. "I don't have to listen to any of your crap."

I leaned forward, partly blocking her view of Bonnie. I lowered my voice. "Then you listen to mine, lover girl. Withholding information from the police is a crime. And you've done it. Withholding it from me is just general state-of-the-art lying."

"Who says I'm lying?"

"Where'd you get that nifty, vintage MG of yours?"

"What about it?"

"I asked, where did you get it?"

"I bought it. What'd you think?"

"How much did you pay for it?" asked Bonnie.

Tracy turned a sneer on her. "How much did you pay for those earrings?" Bonnie instinctively raised a hand to one of her ears. "It's none of my business, is it?" Tracy continued. "Same thing with my car. How much I paid for it is none of your damn business."

"How about if you paid nothing for it, Tracy?" I suggested.

"What does that mean?"

"How about if someone bought that car for Helen, paid to have some of that recent bodywork done? How about if, after Helen was killed, a certain redheaded waitress . . . a 'good friend' of Helen's just happened to know where she kept her keys?"

"I didn't steal that car. That's my goddamn car!"

"Paid for with all that good tip money you make at Sinbad's?" Bonnie piped up. "Or should I say, next door to Sinbad's?"

I caught Tracy Atkins before she got her claws into Bonnie. She came right across the coffee table. I had her by the arms and I kept a firm grip on her as I guided her back to the armchair. Her nostrils were flaring.

"You're a goddamn son of a bitch aren't you?" she murmured. I released her arms and she fell back into the chair. She crossed her arms over her chest and glared up at me.

"I'm not looking to get you in trouble," I said simply. "I could care less if you took Helen's car. It won't do her any good now."

"Then what's this all about?"

"We're trying to find out who killed Helen. I need to find out just who it was that was showering her with stuff like clothes and a car. You can keep the damn car for all I care. But I want to know who actually paid for it. Who gave that car to Helen?"

"I don't know, and I don't care."

I turned to Bonnie. "Truth?"

She was nodding her head. "I think so."

Tracy sneered across the coffee table. "Well, thank you."

I turned back to her. "Where were you the night Helen was murdered?"

"With someone."

"Does that someone have a name?"

She glared at me. "You're a total prick, aren't you?"

"It's just a question."

"I was with Gary."

"That's your alibi?"

"I don't need an alibi! I didn't do anything."

"Except steal the car of a dead woman." She said nothing. She just glared. "Where are the keys to the car, Tracy?"

"You're not taking my car!"

"I didn't say I was. And it's not your car. Now where are the keys?"

She whined a bit more but eventually came up with the keys. I tossed them to Bonnie who scurried out the front door.

"Is that your girlfriend?" Tracy asked, making certain that I caught her disapproving tone.

"Look, I'm sorry I had to play the heavy with you. I want to find out who killed Helen. So level with me, do you know *anything* about this guy she was seeing? Anything at all."

"I don't have to tell you a goddamn thing."

"Tracy, I'm holding a stolen MG over your head. If you want, I can get heavy all over again. I can give a friend of mine down at the police station a call. Now, do you know something about this guy or not? I promise I'll just keep harassing you if I think you're holding out. I'm good at being a pain in the ass, believe me."

"I got that part."

"Good. So, is there anything you're forgetting to tell me that might help?"

"Well. Maybe just one thing."

"And that would be?"

Just then Bonnie came back in. In one hand she had the keys to the MG, which she tossed to me. In the other she was holding the FOR SALE sign that I had noticed the other day on the floor behind the driver's seat.

"It's got a phone number on it," Bonnie announced triumphantly. I turned back to Tracy, who was smiling her bad-teeth smile.

"Same thing," she said. "That phone number. That's what I know. That's where Helen got the car."

Then she stuck her tongue out at me.

"Sure man, I remember her. She was a real piece of ass." The guy was looking over at Bonnie, whose upper half was invisible, as it was poked into the driver's side window of a bottle-green Valiant. "That's the girl from TV, isn't it?"

"That's her."

The wolf was giving a lamb-chop look. "Cool."

The phone number from the FOR SALE sign on Tracy's— Helen's—MG had led us to this garage near the intersection of Joppa and Belair Roads. The guy's name was Johnny. He had told me on the phone that I couldn't miss the place, and he was right. Johnny and his wife, Shirley, ran a lawn ornament business out of their home. All your plaster deer, lawn elf, balsa windmill, pink flamingo, stone Madonna, fake water well, ceramic rabbit needs could be met at Johnny and Shirley's. The quarter acre out in front of their little ranch house was choked with the stuff. Maybe it was just the time of year, but the leisurely pace of this sort of business seemed to suit the couple's other interests, which for Johnny was the restoring of vintage automobiles in his garage, and for his wife it was the watching of the daytime talk shows. A rousing dustup between serial infideliacs could be heard through the open garage door, coming from the television set in the room just off the kitchen.

"That MG was a sweet car," Johnny said, his gaze not yet wandering too far from the rear end of the TV celebrity in his garage. "Piece of shit when I got it too."

"So you did what to it? Bodywork?"

"The whole thing. The engine needed a ton of work. Pretty much had to rebuild it. Then, you know, new brake pads, universal joint, new clutch. The real trick is finding the parts. You've got to go to a lot of junkyards and shit like that to dig up some of this stuff. Most of the parts on the new models don't fit the old ones."

Bonnie popped back out of the Valiant.

"Are you selling this one?" she asked.

"I've still got some more work to do to it," Johnny said. "That's a hell of a car. It's a '64. V-6. Push-button automatic. She can really cook."

I asked, "How much are you asking?"

"You interested?"

"I could find a way to be."

"What are you driving now?" Johnny asked.

"An old Chevy."

"How old?"

"Not old enough."

"You got a number? I can call you when its ready. I'm waiting for one more part, and then she's pretty much done. You can come back out and take a test drive."

I dug out one of my cards and handed it to him. I almost got away with it, but at the last minute he glanced at it.

"You bury people?"

"Only dead ones."

Bonnie rolled her eyes. She had only been with me several months but that was long enough to have heard *that* one more times than she could count. Johnny shook the card several times, as if he was drying it off.

"I'll call you."

We were way off the track. "Look, about this MG, Johnny. The woman who bought it. How did she see it in the first place, did she say?"

"I had that car running for about a week or so before I put the For Sale sign on it."

"Then what? You parked it out front with the sign?"

"No. Shirley doesn't like when I do that. A used car out in front of the business. She says it looks cheap."

Bonnie and I tied for the Poker Face Award. The lawn ornament impresario continued.

"I just drove it around about a week with the sign on it. I must've gotten like a dozen calls in no time. Those were great-looking cars, those old MGs. The best thing they done for the vintage car business is put out the pieces of crap they're selling now."

"So you said you drove it around about a week before you sold it. Was that mainly just around here?" We were nowhere near the airport or the neighborhood where Helen had lived. I was wondering how she would have seen the car in the first place.

"Pretty much, yeah. Here. Towson. Timonium. I took it out on the Harrisburg one time, to open her up. See how she did."

"How'd she do?"

"She did me a hundred-dollar speeding ticket, that's how."

"How fast were you going?" Bonnie asked.

Johnny smiled. "A hundred miles an hour. A dollar a mile. The trooper who pulled me over was asking about buying it too."

"Can I ask how much you sold it for?" I asked.

"What is this?" Johnny suddenly said. "Is someone in some sort of trouble?"

"No. But I—"

"Like did that chick hit someone with the car? Man, I'll kill her if she messed it up that quickly."

"That won't be necessary," Bonnie said softly.

Johnny was looking at us suspiciously now. "What is this? Is this about insurance or something? I'm telling you right now, that car was in excellent shape when it left here, man. Nobody'd better be trying to say I sold her a bum car, man. She had a mechanic check it out and everything before she bought it. He said it was fine."

"Look," I said. "It's not about the car, the car's fine. We're not trying to set you up for anything. We're interested in the woman who bought it, that's all. Was anyone with her when she came in to look at the car?"

"I wasn't here the first time she came by. She talked to my wife." He turned toward the open door. "HEY SHIRLEY!"

A chorus of boos were sounding from the television studio audience. A few seconds later, a large woman in a housecoat and a head full of curlers appeared at the open door. I would have guessed her to be Johnny's mother, not his wife.

"That woman came by to look at the MG. She have anyone with her?" Johnny asked.

The question seemed to annoy Johnny's wife.

"You gonna fix the flagpole?"

"Did she have anyone *with* her?" When Shirley continued to glare, Johnny pointed at Bonnie. "Do you know who this is?"

Shirley sucked on the question a few seconds. "I don't remember if she did or she didn't," she said, then turned around and retreated to her television. Johnny's gaze lingered on the open door.

"She remembers," he said. "That means no. She came by herself."

"But she was here more than once," I said. "You said that she brought a mechanic."

"Yeah. He went over the car from head to foot. Told me I did a great job on her."

"But no one else, huh? Like a boyfriend?"

"Nope."

"How did she pay for the car?" I asked.

"Cash. And lots of it. I told you I got a lot of calls about the car? Well, I had one guy all set to give me a couple hundred dollars more than I was asking for it. I was going to sell it to him. Then this woman you're talking about calls me up. I tell her it's sold. I tell her about the guy offering me more money. She says hold on. I can hear her talking to someone. Then she offers me five hundred more. Hey. Money's money. I said sure. She said she had to have a mechanic go over it first, but otherwise she was ready to go. Cash and carry, you know."

I glanced over at Bonnie. She was thinking the same thing. When Helen had asked Johnny to "hold on" she had consulted her First National Boyfriend, who must have given her the okay to outbid the other guy.

I thanked Johnny for his time. I had only one more question. So did Bonnie. Mine yielded me a piece of paper on which was scribbled the name of the mechanic Helen had brought along to go over the car, as well as the address of the place where he worked. Hunt Valley Motors, on York Road. Johnny was pretty sure that the guy owned the place.

The yield from Bonnie's question sat on her lap as we drove back into the city. She said that she bought it for Alcatraz, to put next to his food bowl.

"I don't know if I could eat with that thing staring at me," I said as I took the ramp onto the beltway.

"You don't think it's cute?"

I thought the little lawn elf looked like a pervert. Especially nestled there in Bonnie's lap.

"He'll grow on you," she said.

"I hope not."

Bonnie had to get back to the station. She didn't even come inside to deliver her gift in person. I rapped my hand against the roof of her car and away flew the chariot. I went inside and presented the lawn elf to Alcatraz. He sniffed it, then looked up at me as if to ask, *Do I pee on it?* I stuck it on the floor in the kitchen, next to his food bowl. He growled. Alcatraz almost never growls. I was relieved to see that he shared my taste. I took the elf into the bathroom and set him in a corner on the floor.

I had a message from Constance Bell on my phone machine. *Hitchcock, it was nice running into you. What do you say we get together? I've got tickets to the symphony for this Saturday. Would you like to be my date? Don't know if that's tempting or not. You've got my work number. Let me give you my home number.*

I scribbled the number down on the same piece of paper where I had scribbled down the name and number of Helen's mechanic. Yes, that was tempting. A shot of culture never hurt no one.

I took Alcatraz out for his walk. The Yuletide ice sculpture was taking on a life of its own. Alcatraz and I popped into the Oyster to get warm. Sally was manning the bar. She was wearing a flower-print muumuu.

"Aloha," I said, sliding onto a stool. "Don't you have the wrong season here? You're dressed for summer in the middle of Baltimore's new Ice Age."

"Damn straight. Why do you think I put this on? I'm pining, young man."

I thought of Sally's daughter, lounging on her wicker divan, dreaming of island getaways. I could see where she got it from.

"Why don't you and Julia hop on a plane and fly off somewhere warm and exotic? You could take your muumuu with you."

Sally set me up with a Turkey and put out a plate of Kahlúa for Alcatraz. For as many years as I can remember, there had been an old, weathered dinghy that hung from the ceiling over the bar. Regulars at the Oyster had become so accustomed to tossing their empties up into the dinghy—which is what eventually brought it down—that they still occasionally launch a lazy hook shot up, up, up . . . down, down, *crash*. Anyone who is an Oyster regular is used to it, though I suppose it looks damned peculiar to a newcomer. I take the time to explain all this only to give a context. As Sally was setting my drink down in front of me, an elfin old coot down at the end of the bar polished off his beer and instinctively gave the bottle a toss up over his head. It came down behind the bar, landing harmlessly on the black rubber runner on the floor. "Sorry," he muttered, raising a finger to ask for another beer. Sally popped a brew and delivered it. I took a sip of my Turkey. Perfect. Good bourbon moves through your body like warm electricity.

"So, have they learned anything yet about that gal who showed up on your doorstep?" Sally asked, sliding onto the stool that she keeps behind the bar.

"Nothing yet."

Sally was eyeing me closely. "You wouldn't be sticking your nose into that business, would you?"

"Why do you ask, barkeep?"

Sally's flowered muumuu rippled in a shrug. "I'm just remembering the last time you tried to help a pretty woman track down a killer." She glanced up at the dangling chains overhead. "You nearly got killed yourself."

I took another sip. "That was different."

"Of course it was. And you *didn't* get killed. It all worked out. I'm just thinking of your aunt. If Billie ends up burying you, I'll kill you."

"And you would be saying . . . ?"

"You know damn well what I'm saying, Hitchcock. Why are you running around trying to solve the murder of a total stranger?" She pointed her chin at Alcatraz, who had lapped up his Kahlúa and was still licking the plate. "He needs a father. If you run off and get yourself killed, he'll never speak to you again either."

"Sally, your arguments aren't terribly compelling."

"Don't give me that compelling garbage, young man. Can't you just be satisfied doing what you do? I would think you get your fill of death as it is. Look at my daughter. There's a person who knows how to make the most of her life. You don't see any dark streaks running through my little girl."

"Have you seen some of the stuff she paints?"

"Oh, she's just having fun. The point is, that girl grabs after life like there's no tomorrow."

I looked up from my drink. "There's a tomorrow?"

"You know you'd piss me off if I wasn't already on to you."

"That's why I love you, Sally."

"So, do I have the pleasure of your progressively drunken presence for the afternoon?"

I finished off my drink and slid the glass into her hand. "Sorry. I've got to go out and track down a killer. It's what I do between funerals."

"Have I told you you should get out more?"

"That's what I'm doing." I was reaching for my wallet. Sally waved me off.

"On the house. If that was your last drink, I'd hate to think you had to pay for it."

I leaned over the counter and planted a wet one on her cheek. "Thank you, muumuu."

Hunt Valley Motors is just north of the town of Timonium, on York Road. York Road is one of those roads that started life way back, as a bridal path, and hung in there over the centuries to become a multilane speedway connecting the city and points north. Car dealerships, mattress barns, shopping centers and fast-food joints line the boulevard now. The former firewall of Shawan Road, running perpendicular to York, was leaped a few decades ago; fields where Herefords once grazed are now being parceled into easy cheesy housing developments with names like Foxcroft, Horse Trail Homes and Cedar Pine (who in hell thought of that one?). With all the traffic on York Road, I had to wait a full five minutes in the left lane to take my turn into Hunt Valley Motors.

Hunt Valley Motors proved to be a relatively small though extremely efficient operation. Four lifts. Two mechanics in addition to the owner, the chief grease monkey. His was the name that Johnny the lawn ornament king and part-time restorer of old cars had scribbled down for me. Chris Cochran. I was directed by one of the mechanics to the lot behind the shop. The shop itself might have seemed small, but the number of cars parked out back waiting their turn was staggering. And not just car cars. Mercedes, BMWs, little Italian jobs, a couple of Jaguars . . . Nothing but foreigners. It was like an automotive Ellis Island for the rich. I found Cochran standing alongside a blue Mercedes, listening patiently as the car's owner—a blustery, red-faced man in a hat and a camel hair coat—went on and on about why *his* need to have his car worked on immediately superseded the need of those who happened to have brought their cars in earlier. Cochran was in work boots, greasy overalls and an insulated hunting jacket. He looked to be in his late thirties. Dirty blond hair. Dirty white skin. Dirty fingers puffing on a cigarette as he listened to the song and dance. I pegged the car owner as a doctor, a lawyer or a banker. Not exactly a brain sprain to come up with those options. Cochran was nodding his head, showing full empathy and understanding of the man's dilemma. I waited at a polite distance. When the man finally concluded his lecture, the mechanic nodded one more time, then said, "Friday."

The owner of the Mercedes bellowed, "Didn't you hear what I just said?"

Cochran nodded again. "Yes sir, I did."

"Well?"

"Friday."

"I should just take it somewhere else!"

The mechanic rubbed his jaw and looked down at the car. "Okay. If that's what you want to do."

"What I *want* is for you to do the work. And I want it done before Friday. Can't you help me out?"

"Will you buy me a third bay and help me hire an extra mechanic?"

"Don't be ridiculous."

Cochran took his last pull on his cigarette and flicked it away. "Friday then."

"Fine! Okay. *Friday.* By noon!"

"No problem," Cochran said. The man marched off to an Audi that was idling just outside the lot. A woman was behind the wheel. Cochran turned to me.

"If he'd asked nicely I could have had it for him by Thursday. What can I do for you?"

"I'd like to ask you about a car you looked at a few months ago."

"I look at a lot of cars."

"Of course. This one was an MG. An old one. You looked at it for a woman who was thinking of buying it. Up near Parkville?"

"Sure, I remember that car. The body was kind of banged up. But mechanically it was fine. The guy rebuilt the engine. He did a good job."

I pulled my photograph of Helen and Bo from my pocket and handed it to him. "Is that her?"

Cochran glanced at the picture. "That's her. What's up? Look, you want to go inside?"

"This shouldn't take long."

"Fine." He pulled out another cigarette and lit it.

"How did that woman get a hold of you?" I asked.

"What do you mean?"

"To check out the MG. You didn't know her from before or anything, did you?"

"I never saw her before."

"So, did she call you? Did she stop in?"

Cochran started to answer, then he paused. His face had taken on the same look of suspicion that Johnny's had.

"The car is fine," I said, to reassure him. "I'm not with an insurance company. I'm not with the police. It's nothing like that. The woman in the picture there is . . . missing. I'm just trying to find her. I'm a family friend."

"So where does the MG fit into this? Is this about that guy they bought it from? Did you see all that crap in the front yard?"

"Yeah, I did. It was kind of . . . hold on. They?"

"What?"

"You just said 'they bought it from.' Who else do you mean?"

Cochran shrugged. "Her boyfriend. That's what I was about to say. If she's missing, why don't you ask him?"

Boyfriend? "I, uh, I don't know how to get hold of him."

A light of understanding flashed in the mechanic's eyes. "Oh . . . I get it. *He's* the one you're looking for."

"Well . . . sure. I'd like to talk with him."

"So what's the deal here? Are you sure you're not a cop or something?"

"I told you. I'm a family friend."

"Yeah, but what family?"

"What do you mean, what family?"

Cochran flicked his cigarette away. "You see the kind of cars I work on? I get a pretty good clientele in here, you know?

Like that guy who was just here? The car-by-Friday guy? Hell, the guy could *buy* a new Mercedes by Friday. Cash. I deal with these guys all the time. They come in here with their trophy wives and their trophy girlfriends and try to throw their weight around. I don't even pay attention to it anymore. These guys trying to impress their women by bossing me around."

"Was this guy trying to impress her?"

"You mean the girl in the picture? Not really. Not like that."

"So, what are you saying?"

"I was just asking which family are you a friend of? I don't want to go getting anybody in trouble here."

"I'm not following you."

"He ran off with this girl, didn't he? That's why you're here asking these questions. Old rich guy and a young chick. I see this shit more times than you can think. Except she didn't really strike me as trophy material, if you get what I mean. Usually they're all this perfect hair and these clothes and the jewelry and everything. I mean even in the middle of the day they look like they're going out to some fancy dinner, and they might just be going out to buy dog food or something. But this girl in the picture. I'm not saying there was anything wrong with her. Looker. But . . . I just figured the guy was slumming, you know? No offense or anything. But they don't usually leave their wives for a girl like that. This girl here . . . she was just a regular girl, you know?"

"This old rich guy. He was married?"

"I saw a ring. He didn't even bother to hide it."

"And Helen. She had no ring?"

"Man, you do sound like the police."

"I'm not. Trust me."

"Look, just who am I getting into trouble here? None of this is my business, you know. A guy comes in here, tells me he's heard I'm a good mechanic. He says he's got 'a friend' who wants to buy this car she saw for sale somewhere. That's how he said it 'a friend.' That's like a big, flashing arrow, you know? 'My friend' wants you to take a look at this car she wants to buy, blah, blah, blah. I guess some people are smoother than others about that kind of thing. Not this guy."

"So, he was the one who paid you to check out the car?"

"Yeah. Paid me to go out there to Parkville and everything."

"Did he pay with a check? Or a credit card?"

"Cash. I told him a check would be fine. But he had a pocketful of cash. Look, I got to get back to the shop. You can see all the work I've got."

"Just one more thing," I said. "Can you describe this guy?"

He could. He did. He described him very well. Apparently the mechanic had a photographic memory. My scalp began to tingle as Cochran ran through the description. Height. Weight. Face. Hair. A completely illogical part of the whole situation suddenly made sense. Cochran's guess at the man's weight was within ten pounds of what my own guess had been. His guess at the man's age—if it was the same man I was now picturing—was right on the money.

I asked, "Look. How late do you stay open?"

"Five-thirty."

I checked my watch. It was after four. It would take me nearly an hour to drive home and back again. Maybe fifty minutes . . . plus ten to take the damn left turn off York Road.

"I'll be right back."

It took me an hour. I had a different photograph with me. Cochran was in the garage under one of the lifts when I returned. I shoved the photograph under his nose.

"Him?"

"Yep. That's him. So, what's the big deal here? Did he run off with her or what?"

"She's dead," I said. "She was murdered."

Cochran dropped the wrench he had been holding. "No shit. Oh, man . . . So what's up? Did this guy do it? Did he kill her?"

I was shaking my head. "He was already dead."

CHAPTER

22

I was one of Santa's helpers once, one of his elves. I know what a rotten gig it can be. My time came in the second grade. Having lost the popular vote to appear as the Big Guy Himself in the school's Christmas pageant, I was relegated to the role of the head elf. Head elf my ass. In the second grade especially, there's either the Big Guy Himself or there's nothing. I really thought I had a lock on the role too. Both of my parents were appearing regularly on local TV at the time as cohosts of various programs as well as doing a slew of commercials and voice-overs. My father was the official voice for Hamburger Junction. It was an extremely popular place with kids, that delivered your burgers to you on an electric train set that ran around the restaurant's oval counter. I figured I'd ride my parents' coattails right to the North Pole. But I lost out to a new kid in school. His parents had been missionaries in Korea. I had no idea where in the hell Korea even was or, for that matter, what a missionary was supposed to do. But the kid got the part—I've blocked his name from my memory—and I was named his second in command, his head elf. Brownie. That was what they named me. Based on the ridiculous costume they whipped up for me to wear. Brown tights and a little brown vest over a dyed brown T-shirt. It was humiliating. I begged my parents not to attend, but of course they did. My job onstage, besides feeding setup lines to the Big Guy Himself, was to fill in, with white paint, a presketched design along the front of a refrigerator box that had been cut in half and decorated to look like a gigantic jack-in-the-box. There was a coat hanger and cloth handle attached to one side of the box, and on the back of the box, the side not facing the audience, was a large hole that had been cut out. This was the way I was supposed to communicate with Beth Garrison, who was inside the box costumed to look about as much like a jack-in-the-box as I did an elf. The idea was that I would slip to the backside of the box and cue Beth that I was about to start cranking the coat hanger handle. She could see my arm turning, and, after several turns of the handle, she was supposed to *pop* out of the box and flop around as if she were attached to a spring. The son of the missionaries from Korea would then give off a hearty "ho, ho, ho," wag his finger at me and say, "Now, Brownie, this is no time to play. There's work to be done." It had been decided that we would go through this little routine three times during the run of the play. Two of the times were set, I had a cue that I was to listen for. The third time was at my discretion; though, of course, I was too young to understand what the word "discretion" actually meant.

On the big night, I was miserable. Not only was I in shock about the ridiculous getup I was being forced to wear in front of the entire auditorium, but just fifteen minutes prior to curtain I had gotten into a fight with Beth, my jack-in-the-box. Actually, I had kissed her. She had come out of the girls room—looking a little like a court jester, a little like a clown— just as I was getting a drink of water from the water fountain, and with no premeditation whatsoever I had stepped over to her and kissed her on her big, red polka-dot cheek. She shrieked—it was impossible for me to tell if it was a shriek of delight or dismay—and ran off. The next thing I knew, every single elf in the cast was aware that I had kissed Beth Garrison. The news spread like wildfire. They were all making puckery faces at me and giggling. I was convinced that the people in the audience had picked up on the scandal as well. *Hey, the elf in the brown tights? Have you heard? He just kissed the jack-in-the-box. Can you believe the gall?* I thought maybe they had mimeographed an announcement to include with the program. *Please Note: Brownie has just kissed the jack-in-the-box.* I was as mortified as a three-and-a-half-foot person can be mortified. Which is plenty, believe me.

The play began. A snowfall of confetti kicked things off, then jolly old St. Nick took the stage to an explosion of applause from the audience. I even spotted my own parents clapping. Traitors. I made a mental note to run away from home just as soon as I got out of the damn tights. I slapped a few strokes of paint onto the box. But my heart wasn't in it. My first cue to release the jack-in-the-box was five minutes off. But suddenly inspiration hit and I put down the paintbrush and moseyed around to the rear of the box. "I'm cranking," I informed the painted Jezebel inside. I saw the girl's look of confusion, but I paid it no heed. This was at my discretion. I took hold of the coat hanger handle and gave it a few cranks. Beth and I had decided on three as the number of cranks on which she would pop up out of the box and waggle like she was on a spring. I cranked: One-Two-*Three* . . . and up she popped. The son of the Korean missionaries was in the middle of some business with a broken toy halfway across the stage. But at the sight of the jack-in-the-box bobbing over there above its box— bobbing with verve, I might add—he dropped whatever he was saying and let out his hearty "ho, ho, ho," followed by his admonishment to me about a time to work and a time to play.

The fact that I had cued Beth five minutes early didn't throw him all that much. He found his place and continued on with his business about the broken toy. Several minutes later came the actual cue, and I cranked the handle again and again Beth came popping out. The son of the missionaries again chanted his "ho, ho, ho," and the admonishment was again delivered. And the play continued.

I can't say for certain how many more minutes went by. I recall working the paintbrush around the presketched design and then realizing suddenly that I was accidentally painting *outside* the design instead of *inside* the design. I was screwing up! If I continued on in this fashion, the design on the over-sized jack-in-the-box would look like shit. But what could I do? I had started wrong and simply had to commit to the course I was on. Frustrated over this screwup, I suddenly strode around to the back of the box and muttered, "Pop!" I cranked the handle three times and the first girl I had ever kissed came popping out of the box again. This time the missionaries' kid was thrown. He tried to go on with his lines, then decided he had better run through the "ho, ho, ho" and the time to work, time to play routine once again, just to be on the safe side. The look on his face was priceless. To me, anyway. The look on Beth's face was priceless as well. And that was it. I might not have been cast as the Big Guy Himself, but I had figured out a way to steal the focus for the rest of the night. I cranked that handle like there was no tomorrow. Willy-nilly. For some reason, the son of the missionaries never found the nerve to simply ignore the bobbing jack-in-the-box. Instead, each time she popped up he plowed on ahead with his "ho, ho, ho" and his increasingly tedious warning. Likewise, it never occurred to Beth to simply stop popping out of the box. I cranked that damn handle all night long, interrupting the flow of the play again and again. Every few minutes, it was "ho, ho, ho. Now, Brownie, this is no time to play. There's work to be done." The hell. That's what *he* thought. It had been decided to run the silly play without an intermission, so there was no opportunity for our director—our second grade teacher—to halt my shenanigans. It appeared to me that the crowd loved it. They were sure as hell laughing up a storm by the time the thing finally ended. I'm not so sure about the missionaries from Korea. But I know that my parents laughed like crazy the entire drive home. We swung by Hamburger Junction to celebrate my disruptive triumph. My father even stood up at the counter and gave a basso-profundo recitation of the Hamburger Junction commercial. It was a big hit with the other diners. Never once did my parents chide me for fouling up the Christmas play. For the brief time that I had them, they supported me in every single thing I did. No matter what way I ended up doing it.

The Christmas pageant at Vickie Waggoner's school was pretty tame by comparison. No class clown emerged to send the play reeling sideways. I found Vickie sitting in an aisle seat near the rear of the auditorium. She had Bo with her. He was on her lap. I managed to get her attention and signaled that I would wait for her in the back of the auditorium. I stationed myself against the rear wall. The kids onstage blurred as my attention wandered. I already knew how their little play ended.

What I didn't know—what I *still* didn't know—was exactly how Helen Waggoner's life had ended. I didn't know who shot her or why. What I did know was that the person she had been seeing, the mystery fellow who had been so generous with his wallet, wasn't the person who had killed her. Theory One: down the tubes. He couldn't be the killer. Richard Kingman had the best alibi in the house; he had been laid out in an Ambassador model coffin in Parlor One at Sewell & Sons Family Funeral Home at the same approximate time that Helen Waggoner was getting called out of Sinbad's Cave for her final few moments on Earth. The celebrated heart surgeon might have been having an affair with Helen Waggoner and buying her all sorts of goodies, but he sure as hell didn't kill her. Why in the world it hadn't occurred to me—or to Vickie for that matter—to question Bo about his birthday visit to the zoo I couldn't say. We see our own noses every day of our lives . . . but do we notice?

I had to wait a few minutes after the show while Vickie told the children what a wonderful job they had done. I passed the time in the hallway, marveling at some of the things that kids will come up with when you hand them a piece of paper and a paint kit. The walls were lined with the stuff of dreams and psychiatry. When Vickie finally emerged from the auditorium—Bo in tow—she spoke first.

"I have some information."

"So do I."

"Let's talk in here."

She led me into one of the classrooms. Say what you will about this old world of ours changing faster and faster these days, elementary school classrooms pretty much remain the same. Granted, there was a row of computers on a table along the far wall, but other than that technological intrusion, the room looked pretty much like the one in which I had learned my reading and writing when I was a young Hitch. Maps, the alphabet running in a banner atop the chalkboard, miniature desks, the whole thing. The windows at the rear of the classroom had been decorated for Christmas, with paper cutouts of all the Yuletide celebrities: Santa Claus, Rudolph the Red-Nose Reindeer, Frosty the Snowman and some cartoony figure I didn't recognize. There were paper snowflakes taped all over the windows as well. Bo tottered off to a corner filled with wooden animals.

"Is this your homeroom?" I asked Vickie.

She nodded. "My kingdom."

I leaned up against the front of Vickie's teacher's desk. She squeezed onto one of the miniature chairs.

"You first," she said.

"No. You."

"Okay." She shifted in her chair. Like a child about to deliver a speech. "I found out the name of the obstetrician Helen was seeing."

"You did? How?"

"Bo. He came to me last night saying something about glass."

"Glass?"

"Yes. I didn't know what he was talking about at first. He said he wanted his glass. And then he handed me this." She reached into her pocket and pulled out a prescription container. "Childproof lid," she said, twisting off the cap. She emptied the container onto the desk. It was glass. About a half dozen bits of colored glass.

"Apparently Helen and Bo ran across this stuff somewhere and he liked it. Obviously you wouldn't let a child play with something like this. Helen must have decided to keep them for him in this container. There's no way Bo could get the lid off. Bo had a big duffel bag filled with his toys. It must have been in there all along."

"And there's a doctor's name on the container?"

"Yes, there is."

She scooped the glass bits back into the container, twisted the cap back into place and tossed it to me. There it was, in the lower left-hand corner of the label.

"I checked it out," Vickie said. "I looked the name up in the book and called. He's definitely an obstetrician."

I looked up at her. "That's not all he is. Let's go."

I stood in the doorway while Vickie put Bo to bed. I've always been under the impression that kids are a terror to get to sleep. But Bo put up no fight at all. I wondered if this might be a result of good mothering on Helen's part, or whether it was simply a matter of temperament.

Vickie left the bedroom door cracked open.

"Sometimes he wakes up in the middle of the night." She added grimly, "He calls for his mama."

We went into the living room. Vickie sat on the couch, underneath the lousy, framed pastoral. I sat as far away as possible, in one of the plaid armchairs. Up until that moment, the fact of our intimate shenanigan two nights before had been effortlessly forgotten in lieu of the information I had uncovered. Suddenly the fact was back. We both felt it. Even so, with a little boy sleeping in the next room, I was certain that we would find a way to push it aside once more.

"What do you make of all this?" Vickie asked. "Are you positive that it was this Kingman that my sister was seeing?"

"The mechanic who looked over her car described the guy perfectly, then he identified him from a picture." I pulled the picture from my pocket. I stepped over to her and handed it to her, then retreated to the armchair. "It's an old photo," I said. "Something like fifteen years old. But he still pretty much looked like that."

"She was seeing an older man."

"An older man with money. Did Helen have a thing about older men? I mean, that you would know about?"

Vickie looked up from the photograph. "Let's put it this way. Helen came out of the gate early. I told you, remember, that she was picked up for solicitation when she was fourteen? When you start that young, practically everyone is an older man."

"So, this doesn't surprise you?"

Vickie sighed. "Is it a news flash? No. It's not." She looked back at the photograph. "I . . . I don't get it. You say this guy was a hotshot doctor from Hopkins. What was he doing with Helen?"

"I wouldn't go looking too hard for sense in a case like this. Maybe it was a midlife crisis for this guy. I didn't get the sense from his widow that the two were exactly setting each other's world on fire anymore."

Vickie set the photo aside. "But he didn't kill her."

"Impossible."

"But . . . her murder is connected to him somehow. She was dropped off in the middle of his wake for crying out loud. It's creepy."

"You've got that. Whoever killed your sister was certainly aware of the connection with Kingman. I don't understand why she was brought to his wake. But we know that Kingman is the connection."

We went over the situation as systematically as we could. Vickie determined that Helen could quite possibly have met Richard Kingman at Johns Hopkins Hospital. She reminded me that her mother had been in and out of Hopkins the previous summer for cancer treatments, and that Helen had visited quite a lot. The timing made sense. Or was at least plausible. Ruth Waggoner had died in mid-September. If we could assume that the person who had taken the photograph of Helen and Bo at the zoo was Richard Kingman, then this would place the two together roughly a month after Ruth's death. The zoo photograph had the date that it was taken burned into the lower right-hand corner: October 10. Bo's birthday.

There was a piece of timing that made no sense to me, though I decided not to bring it up to Vickie just then. I needed to think it through a little first. It was Gary's tale about Helen's bizarre behavior on the night that she had insisted on seeing him at the Charm Inn. Gary had said that his run-in with Helen had taken place near Halloween. Helen was seeing Richard Kingman by then. Was it something that had taken place between Kingman and Helen that set her off that night? It had to have been something substantial, going by Gary's description of Helen's behavior. She had acted out all over the poor guy.

Vickie was reading my mind. "The child Helen was carrying. That was Kingman's?"

I didn't know. But I knew who would.

"Can I borrow that prescription bottle?" I asked.

Vickie pulled the bottle from her pocket and placed it on the coffee table. I stepped over to take it. Just as I reached for it, Vickie leaned forward and brought her hand down on mine.

"You don't have to do this. We should take this to the police."

"I will. But I want to have a talk with the baby doctor first."

I let my hand linger a fraction longer. Then I slid the bottle from under her fingers and slipped it into my pocket. I straightened. Vickie's green eyes looked sad and tired. Her lips were slightly parted.

"Do you want to talk?" I said.

She blinked slowly. "About?"

"About the other night."

Vickie's glance flickered out of the room. "I'd better go check on Bo. Will you wait a moment?"

She got up from the couch and disappeared into the next room. I heard the faint squeak of the door as she looked in on her nephew. I was still standing in the middle of the living room. A large, large part of me was suggesting that I make a quiet and dignified exit this very minute, while Vickie was off with the boy. That would be, I suppose, the smart thing. Of course, a large, large part of me was also keeping me rooted right where I was. The not-so-smart thing. Or at least, the risky thing. I hate these moments. Decisions like this contain only one guarantee: regret. Either way you go, regret hops on your shoulder and takes a free ride. Deciding which form of regret you'd prefer to contend with has never struck me as a particularly worthwhile means of coming up with a decision.

Vickie came back into the room while my diplomats were still locked in their mad debate. She stopped just past the archway.

"How is he?" I asked.

"He's fast asleep."

"I'm going."

It was the right decision. Good man. Good Hitch. The high road. I could throw myself a victory parade in the morning. Maybe let the marching bands drown out the low throbbing hum of regret. Vickie walked me over to the door.

"Good night."

It really was the right decision. Leaving. But I had to cancel the parade. If it takes five full minutes to say "good night," and all you manage to say in all that time is "good night" . . . well, that's not exactly the high road we were talking about now, is it?

CHAPTER 23

I had just reached the street and was digging through my pocket for my keys when the lights from a pair of headlights swept over me. Rapidly. Three times.

I looked up to see a car swerving wildly but bearing down on me nonetheless. I had no more than two seconds to leap out of the way, though if the car happened to pitch in the same direction I leaped, I would be throwing myself right into its path. That thought ate up one of my two seconds. The headlights caught me again. In the remaining second I simply threw myself—unthinking—toward the middle of the street. My left leg was clipped by the careening car and I was spun around so that as I hit the pavement, I was facing the collision of the speeding car with my parked one.

The explosion of metal smashing metal ripped the air. Something large and hard—it proved to be a headlight—flew out of the explosion and caught me just above my right eye. One of the cars' horns went off, a ceaseless and immediately irritating pitch. I had landed hard on my chest, knocking the air completely out of me. I was taking empty gulps of the night air—like a fish out of water—before a fist of oxygen finally slammed its way down my throat and into my lungs. I rolled slowly onto my side. I would later realize that blood from the gash in my forehead was swimming down into my eyes, blurring the scene. Even so, I was able to make out a pair of legs struggling from the front seat of the criminal car—mine was no longer a car, but an accordion—and stagger over to me. Cowboy boots. I recall noting to myself, *Is that armadillo?* I was trying to find the oxygen to speak when the legs suddenly scissored awkwardly and one of the cowboy boots came flying at my head. That was the last thing I remembered.

"If you wake up, Hitchcock, I promise to perform acts of unspeakable depravity all over your achy-breaky body."

Before I opened my eyes, I allowed a few seconds to see what my imagination might make of this promise. Mistake. All I conjured was an awareness of the intense pain I was suffering. I doubt I could have borne the pressure of even one chaste kiss to the cheek, let alone the promised depravities my ex-wife was dangling in her attempt to lure me back to consciousness.

"Hell-o? Is anybody home?"

I opened my eyes. Julia had put on a surgical cap for the occasion. This was the first thing that told me I was in a hospital. The second thing was the tube running into my nose. Julia's eyes were large and dewy.

"How are you feeling, Ralph?"

Despite the pain it caused, I winced a smile. When I was a pup I had been knocked unconscious briefly by a baseball. For about five minutes after I came around, I had been convinced that my name was Ralph. Of course Julia would remember the incident. She had been the one who hit the line drive.

I croaked weakly, "Ralph?"

Julia's face relaxed. "Yes, dear. You're still just eight years old. Anything else you think you remember past that has all been a dream."

"You mean . . . we never got married?"

Julia put her fingers to her throat. "*Moi*? Please. I'm still a virgin."

That was too much for me to comprehend. Or even pretend to. I drifted back into unconsciousness.

When I woke again, Billie and Julia were sitting in chairs across the room, laughing and giggling over God knows what. Billie looked over and saw me stirring.

"The prodigal nephew returns." She stood up and came over to my bedside, as if on rollers.

"A fine thing, ruining a perfectly good car." She dropped the act and touched me lightly on the cheek. "Please, don't do this to your old auntie again. How are you feeling, Hitchcock?"

I answered truthfully, "Heavily sedated. Not ready to get up and dance."

"That can wait. The doctor says you were lucky."

"The doctor is full of shit," I murmured. "Lucky" would have been getting into my car and driving home to a warm, safe bed. Julia appeared at Billie's side. She had removed the surgical cap and was now simply beautiful without props.

"You have a concussion," she said, smiling sadly.

"My leg hurts." When neither of them responded immediately, I felt a rush of blood flood into my face. "Shit! I do still have a leg, don't I?"

"Yes, Hitch," said Julia. "It's just not as pretty as it used to be. That's where the car hit you."

"Is it broken?"

"Mangled, I think, is the medical term."

"And my head?"

I raised my hand to my face. For the first time since I had woken up, I realized that my head was bandaged. The cowboy boots swam into view. "Why the hell did that guy kick the shit out of *me*? Wasn't running me over and wrecking my car enough?"

"He was high," Julia said.

"I find that to be no excuse," I murmured, closing my eyes.

"You know it wasn't an accident."

My eyes popped back open.

"Hitch, it was Terry Haden. He's under arrest. All sorts of charges. Including aggravated assault."

"Aggravated . . . Jesus Christ, what the hell aggravated *him*?"

"The police are saying he was pretty hopped up. I gather that the two of you didn't exactly hit it off when you met?"

"Is that any reason to run a guy down and kick half his brains out?"

"You were coming from Victoria Waggoner's house."

"So?"

"So, maybe he was jealous."

"Of what?" Even the simple act of frowning set the hammers loose on my skull.

"Terry Haden's very messed up. I really don't think you can expect to find a fully rational explanation here."

"Where's Vickie?" I asked suddenly.

Billie answered, "She's right down the hall. In the waiting area."

"What time is it?"

"It's nearly three in the morning. Would you like to see her now, Hitchcock? She's been waiting for hours."

Julia answered for me. "Of course he would."

Julia and Billie shuffled out of the room. I glanced around, as much as my aching, bandaged head would allow. It wasn't a private room; there was a second bed, unoccupied. My shades were drawn, though I could see a crack of blackness at the bottom. A small, framed print of a dandelion was on the wall beside the door to the bathroom. Plastic curtains were bunched at the head of my bed. A machine to my left was making a low blipping noise. Next to it was a baggy of goo on a pole. I was enjoying an IV snack.

Vickie came into the room. I guess no one had prepared her. She flinched when she saw me, then came over and landed softly in the chair beside my bed. I know I looked horrible, but she wasn't looking too swell herself.

"I'm sorry," she whispered, which I shooed away.

"It's not your fault."

I realized suddenly how drowsy I was feeling again. My eyelids were starting to droop.

"You should sleep," she said. She took hold of my hand and squeezed my fingers. I wanted to stay awake, but I had no choice in the matter. I dozed off. At some point later I woke. Briefly. She was still there, still holding my fingers. Her head was down on the edge of my pillow, rising and falling in deep sleep. I turned my battered head and put my nose into her hair and drifted back to sleep. When I woke in the morning—for good—she was gone.

I was kept in the hospital the entire next day with a promise that I would be released the following morning, "pending additional findings." Julia teased me about that phrase. "They're going to discover just how maladjusted you are. They'll never let you go."

It was far from the best day of my life, but far from the worst either. I went for a series of tests and X rays. As Julia had told me, I hadn't broken any bones. But I had taken a nifty impression of Terry Haden's fender with my calf. Nothing that several dozen stitches running this way and that wouldn't fix up. I also took a few stitches to my face, though mainly the damage had been limited to a couple of kick-ass bruises. I was given a vision test, a hearing test, a memory test. . . . I passed them all. My head was declared as good as it was ever going to be. I met my doctor twice, once in the morning and once at the very end of the day. I suppose that surgery, or maybe a few sets of indoor tennis, took up the balance of his day. His degree of concern for my condition was so focused and complete that I decided it was completely staged. It was the gang who ran all the tests on me who actually seemed to care. In the late afternoon, after I had been cleared for release the following day, I convinced one of the orderlies to outfit me with a wheelchair so I could travel the highways and byways of the hospital rather than sit in my hydraulic bed staring at Oprah. Bonnie had called from the station to say that she would swing by around four to look in on me. I also got a call from Constance Bell, who had phoned me at the funeral home and had heard from Billie about my mishap.

"I guess we'll have to postpone our symphony date," Constance said to me.

"When was that again?"

"Tomorrow, Hitch. I don't think you'll—"

"No. Tomorrow should be fine. I'm being discharged in the morning. I could use a little thoughtless recreation. Honestly I'd love to go."

"If you're sure."

I assured her that I was. We agreed to meet at the symphony hall at seven. Constance asked me just what it was that had landed me in the hospital.

"Your aunt intimated that you've been sticking your nose into other people's business. Is that true?"

"Talk to my lawyer."

She laughed. "Don't be cute, Hitchcock. Seriously, are you in some sort of trouble? I mean, beside being in the hospital."

"I'll tell you about it tomorrow."

We hung up.

Before Bonnie arrived, I wheeled myself out into the hallway and stationed myself near the elevator. Each time the elevator doors opened, I lowered my head. When Bonnie arrived she came off the elevator and walked right past me. I followed, calling out "Boo!" when she reached my room and found nobody there.

"I take it you're feeling better," she said.

"Bored out of my gourd."

"From one day? Boy, you would make a lousy patient."

"Is that a bad thing?"

We went into the room and Bonnie shut the door. I hoped she didn't have any funny ideas. I wasn't feeling *that* great.

"Your pretty face is a mess," she said.

"The doctors assure me I'll be looking like Abe Lincoln in no time."

"Terry Haden is going back to jail. Parole violation."

"Trying to kill an undertaker?"

"The drugs they found in his system. And in his car." Bonnie stepped over to the window and dented the blinds to have a look outside. Nothing but a facing brick wall.

"There's no way that Haden's running you down had anything to do with the murder of Helen Waggoner, Hitch."

"That's a question or a statement?" I asked.

"Both, I guess."

I agreed. "As far as I'm concerned, Terry Haden is free to go off and serve jail time for any or all of the many crimes he has no doubt committed. But no, it doesn't look like the murder of Helen is one of them." I filled Bonnie in on one of the discoveries of the day before. Her wide eyes went even wider as I told her how I had discovered that it was Richard Kingman who Helen had been seeing.

"Son of a bitch."

"I'd say that's a fair assessment."

"Good Lord, Hitch, that's amazing. You know, you're getting good at this. We're going to have to buy you a magnifying glass and one of those droopy pipes."

"Elementary."

"So, have you told any of this to Kruk?"

"I've been a little preoccupied or perhaps you haven't noticed. I'll get to it."

"I think so. You should call him right now."

I wheeled myself over to the bedside table and poured myself a cup of ice water. I held the pitcher up to Bonnie. She shook her head.

"I don't see the hurry," I said. "Kruk has put Helen's murder on the back burner. It can keep."

"But Hitch, this is important. You've got to tell the police."

"Kingman isn't the killer. He can't be. He was already dead."

"That's not the point. He's the reason that Helen was dumped in your lap in the first place. This definitely advances the investigation."

"I thought you wanted to come up with the killer yourself," I reminded her. "Where's your scoop if we hand it off to Kruk at this point?"

"It's a crime, Hitch, withholding information."

"Murder is the bigger crime. Look, I've just suffered a massive head trauma. I'm supposed to be clearheaded enough to run to the police?"

"So, what are you saying?"

"What I'm saying is that we give ourselves . . . forty-eight hours. What can that hurt? If we can't cough up a killer by Christmas Eve, we give Kruk the news about Helen and Kingman. But if we do cough up the killer, you run to management with your scoop and the world becomes a better place. Is there any harm in that?"

Bonnie thought it over. "Okay. Sure. Why not. Forty-eight hours." She paused. "Hitch . . . I know you're going to throw a fit. But let's bring Jay in on this."

"Adams? Why?"

"Because it couldn't hurt, that's why. He has done this sort of thing before. He might come up with some ideas that you and I haven't thought of."

"I came up with Kingman," I reminded her.

"True."

"I'm the one who nearly got killed."

"Not related to the case. Not technically."

"I was going over 'the case' with Vickie Waggoner. I got run over by Helen's ex-boyfriend and pimp as I was leaving. I'll take a merit badge for that one, thank you."

"Okay. You're right. I'm sorry."

A merit badge was also due Vickie Waggoner—Bo, actually—for coming up with the name of Bonnie's obstetrician. But this was a piece of information I was holding onto for the time being.

"Okay," I said. "Hand it to Adams on a silver platter. Tell him about Kingman. But is it possible to keep the guy on a leash? He sandbagged me the other day you know, with that photograph, taking it out to Sinbad's."

"So what? He saved you the effort."

She was right. Why not call in a seasoned hound dog like Adams at this point? I was close to the killer. Maybe Adams could help me get even closer. Of course, Bonnie won either way. So long as both Adams and I reported back to her and let her have her scoop, she would come out of this better off than when she went in. I suspected that she and Jay Adams had already reached an agreement that she would be allowed to bring the identity of the murdered waitress's killer to the public first. Adams had plenty of notches in his belt already.

Bonnie kissed me gingerly on the unbruised portion of my face. She had to get off to work. After she left, I wheeled myself out to the nurses' station. I thought a little flirting might cheer me up. But my heart wasn't in it. I wheeled myself back into my room and slept for fourteen hours.

• • •

Billie sent Sam to fetch me from the hospital. He picked me up in the hearse. By hospital regulations I was wheeled out the front door in a wheelchair, then allowed to rise up under my own power like a man newly healed at a revival meeting. Sam had brought along a wooden cane that he had used some years back after breaking his ankle in a melee at one of his clubs. He helped me hobble into the passenger seat of the hearse and away we went. And yes, people stopped and stared.

I had Sam for the day. He could always use the cash, and I needed a driver. What was left of my Chevy Nothing—now less than nothing—was already off in a junkyard somewhere. I'd have to pick up a new set of wheels as soon as possible. Meanwhile, I had the hearse and the human wall to drive me around. A little hint about hearses: Turn on the headlights at intersections and you can cruise right through the red lights. Sam is especially good at this. We covered the distance between the hospital and Cathedral Street without stopping once. Sam pulled over to the curb and pulled out a book.

"What are you reading?" I asked.

"It's new." He showed me the cover. I didn't recognize the title.

"What's it about?"

"A guy and a girl. They get together."

"Oh, yes," I said, taking hold of my cane. "I think I heard something about that one."

Walking on the injured leg didn't kill me. It just hurt like hell.

"Do you have an appointment?" the receptionist asked me. She was behind a sliding glass window. She wore cat's-eye glasses and a permanent pucker and was flipping through a magazine of people wearing nothing but their underwear. She gave me a slow once-over. Probably imagining me in my Calvins. Or wondering about the cane.

"I think I'm pregnant," I said. I had intended it to sound like the joke it was, but between the cane and the banged-up face, I apparently needed to put more levity into my delivery. She frowned, and I bagged it.

"I don't have an appointment. Just give him this." I handed her the little prescription container. She took it from me as if it were a urine sample and disappeared through a door behind her. She reappeared almost immediately.

"The doctor will see you now."

"How about that," I said, and she buzzed me through the door next to her window. I hobbled into the office.

Daniel Kingman didn't rise to greet me. He remained in his chair, his hands out in front of him on the desk as if he were handcuffed. The prescription container sat just beyond his knuckles. The two-inch high container held the doctor's complete attention.

"Come in," he finally said, without looking up. I was already in. I dropped into the leather chair in front of the desk and hooked my cane on the arm. Richard Kingman's brother finally pulled his gaze from the little container and looked sadly across the desk at me. Of course, I remembered him from his brother's wake and funeral. I especially remembered his outlandishly blue eyes, the only part of him that really showed any spark. He looked even paler now than I remembered, but that might have had something to do with the overhead fluorescent lighting in his office. Then again, it might have had to do with the plastic prescription container sitting there on his desk.

"I wondered when someone would show up," he said finally. "I figured it would be the police."

"Nope. Just me."

He let out a large sigh. "I didn't kill her."

"Who did?"

"I don't know."

Well, so much for that. The doctor picked up the prescription bottle and looked at it. He lingered on the label. I lingered too.

"That wasn't so smart, I guess," he said at last.

"What wasn't?"

"Writing out a prescription. Paper trail." He tried out a smile, but it didn't work.

"What wasn't so smart about it? You just said you didn't kill Helen. So, why would you have thought about not leaving a paper trail?"

"My brother."

"What about your brother?"

"*He* wouldn't have wanted a paper trail."

"Maybe you'd better explain this to me."

The doctor sighed. "I suppose I owe an explanation to the police."

"Consider this a practice run."

Kingman leaned back in his chair. Despite his silver hair, there was a slightly boyish look to his face. Or possibly I simply imagined it from the expression he was wearing, which was that of a person who has most definitely been caught and who most definitely feels small and rotten about it.

"My brother . . ." he began. "He . . . I know it's not nice to speak ill of the dead. But Richard could be a real bastard sometimes. Most of the time actually. Even as a boy, he had a very forceful personality. Everyone knew that Richard would make a big success at whatever he chose to do. Which, of course, he did. Richard was one of the best heart men they've seen at Hopkins. He was terrifically gifted."

He paused and brought his fingers together, holding them up to his lips. He might almost have been praying.

"I won't bore you with all of the sibling rivalry silliness I had growing up as Richard's younger brother. It was there. That's all you really need to know. I became a doctor as well. Like Richard. Like our father in fact. But I became . . ." His fingers moved out like a pair of wings, indicating the various framed diplomas that were on the walls of the office. "I became an obstetrician. The baby doctor. I have a solid practice. Richard, of course, went into cardiac medicine, the so-called sexy stuff. I bring lives into the world. Richard saved them." He paused, and the slightest of smiles brushed his lips. "One thing though. I saved Richard."

"What do you mean, you saved him?"

"I saved him. I got him out of trouble. Numerous times."

"I'm sorry. I'm not following."

Kingman picked up the prescription bottle and rattled it. He made a curious face and twisted the cap off. "What's this?"

"Colored glass," I said. "Helen's son keeps colored glass in it."

"God forbid he swallow it."

"Childproof lid," I said.

"Of course."

"So you were saying, Doctor?"

Kingman set the prescription bottle back down. "Yes. I was saying. My brother. Richard had what is euphemistically called a roving eye."

I know this euphemism. It means he had a roving weenie. "He had affairs," I said. No big surprise. Affairs happen. Just ask anyone.

"I'm not sure I would even characterize them as affairs. Flings might be more like it. Affairs are something that a person might actually take seriously. They're also something that loved ones might actually worry about."

"And you are referring to his wife?"

"I am. Yes."

"She knew about his . . . flings?"

"Some of them, yes. She did. You see, Richard didn't always go to any great lengths to cover his tracks. The word you need to plug in here, Mr. Sewell, is 'arrogant.' My brother was extremely arrogant. You find this a lot with gifted people, these people who have been told since childhood how special they are. Richard always insisted that the world come to him. It's as simple as that. And he had the charisma to make it happen. As well as the power. On those occasions when he got a girl in trouble—" He smiled thinly. "I'm afraid I'm addicted to euphemisms. When Richard got a girl pregnant, a woman pregnant, he sent her to me. The family obstetrician."

"And euphemistically speaking, you took care of things?"

"My brother had his own personal abortionist handy whenever he bloody well needed it. That's how it was."

"You don't sound like you were too crazy about that arrangement."

"That would be one way of putting it."

I glanced about at the diplomas on the wall. "I know this is none of my business, but if it bothered you so much, why didn't you just say no? Why didn't you refuse to help him out? Tell him to get some other sap to do his dirty work."

"Sounds simple enough, I know. But . . . let's just say, I didn't. He had his sap, and his sap was me." The doctor paused again. "Brothers, Mr. Sewell. Rivals. And at the same time . . . Well, you don't need to hear a lot of analytical nonsense. As much as I hated myself for doing it for him, I did it. That's all. Let's just leave it at that."

"How often are we talking here, Doctor?"

"This is something I really do not want to discuss with you further. Richard was . . . I'll just say, prolific." He tilted back in his chair and crossed his arms. "Richard was what would probably be called these days a sexual predator. He preyed on women, usually women he felt were well beneath him. These weren't affairs of the heart, Mr. Sewell. They were . . . let me be blunt. For Richard, they were snack food."

"So there were a lot," I said.

He nodded gravely. "There were a lot."

The way the man was sitting there with his arms crossed so tightly, he looked as if he were wearing a straitjacket.

"So, then Helen," I said. "Just the latest in a long line?"

"No. Helen Waggoner was different. Yes, Richard sent her to me. But this time he wasn't asking me to bail him out. He wasn't asking for an abortion. This time was different. A first. Richard asked me to take the woman on as a patient."

Kingman loosened his grip on himself. He came forward in his chair and picked up the prescription bottle again.

"He said that he wanted me to look after her pregnancy, to give her the best treatment I could provide, and when the time came, deliver her baby. Naturally I was stunned. As far as I could tell, it meant only one thing. He was leaving Ann."

"Did he tell you that?"

"I guess I haven't made myself clear. Richard didn't share information with me. That wasn't how our relationship worked. There was no dialogue going on. Richard was always brusque, always curt. This was not a man who felt he had to explain himself to anyone."

"So, you were just speculating that he was leaving his wife for Helen."

"Yes."

"So then . . . what?"

He gave a shrug. "So, I took her on as a patient. Just as Richard requested. This prescription was nothing out of the ordinary. Prenatal vitamins. She was doing fine."

I didn't really want to hear any more. The doctor's melancholy was creeping along his desk in my direction. I wanted to get out of there before it took hold of me. But I had to hear it all.

"When Helen showed up murdered at your brother's wake, what did you think?"

"What did I think? I didn't know *what* to think. It surprised the hell out of me, I can tell you that. Good Lord. Mr. Sewell, I have no idea who killed that poor girl, and that's the honest truth. And I have no idea how she ended up at your funeral home. I was absolutely shocked."

"Logic says that somebody besides you knew about Helen and your brother."

"Yes. Logic would most definitely say that. But I don't know who it would be."

"You don't suppose your brother confessed his affair to his wife, do you? I mean, if he really was planning on leaving her, he would have had to come clean at some point."

Kingman sat with my question a moment. He looked completely knotted up inside. Despite the complete tawdriness of what he had agreed to do—act as his brother's convenient abortionist over the years—I couldn't help but feel a little sorry for the man. He seemed like a nice enough fellow. Only pathetically weak and spineless.

"Ann didn't know," he declared.

"How can you know that?"

"I just know."

"I don't mean to rough you up here, Dr. Kingman, but that wouldn't really hold as a one hundred percent lock. *How* do you know?"

"If Richard had told Ann that he was planning to leave her, she would have told me. Ann and I are close. In our own, separate ways, we've been victims of Richard. There's a certain bonding in that."

"Does she know about the arrangement you had with her husband?"

He directed his answer to the floor. "No."

I got to my feet. "Remind me never to bond with you, Doc-

tor." I picked up the prescription bottle and rattled it. Kingman looked up at me. He looked as if he were about to cry.

"So, why haven't you told all of this to the police?" I asked.
"I'm sure it occurred to you that they might find some of this a
little interesting."

"Of course they would. I was thinking . . . it was Ann, if you
really want to know. I simply didn't want to throw open the
whole sordid mess of Richard and his infidelities to the police.
You know how Baltimore is. It's a big small town."

"You must have known it would come out eventually."

"What can I tell you? Each day that has passed without the
connection being made was another good day as far as I was
concerned."

"So then this hasn't been such a good day."

"No. It hasn't. Though to be honest, I feel relieved. This
hasn't been such a pleasant experience, holding on to this information."

"You can't hold onto it anymore. You know that, don't you?"

"Of course." He rose suddenly and thrust out a hand. I took
it. I recalled his grip the night of his brother's wake. It had
been fishy. This one was firm. This one had something behind it.

"It'll all be for the better, in the end," I said. It sounded
like a silly platitude, but I believed what I was saying. As I
snared my cane, the baby doctor asked me what happened to
me. "I met a man I didn't like." I touched the cane to my
brow and left his office. I closed the door quietly behind me
and waited. I heard nothing at first. Then I heard the doctor's
voice. Muffled, because of the closed door, but clear enough
nonetheless to make out what he was saying. He was making a
phone call. The person he was calling had apparently been
the one who answered the phone. He said a name. That was
all I needed to hear.

• • •

Rockwell, Breughel, Currier & Ives were all still being well represented by the pastoral display of frolickers and skaters out on the frozen ponds in Ann Kingman's neighborhood. A few of the snow bunnies paused in their revelries to watch as a ruby hearse inched slowly along the road bordering the park. We weren't creeping along for effect. Sam and I were looking for house numbers.

"There it is."

The number we were seeking was half-hidden by the ivy on a small stone gate at the entrance to an uphill driveway. I told Sam to park out on the street rather than attempt the driveway, which looked icy. He parked the hearse and offered to help me up the terraced steps to the front door. I opted for pride and recklessness over safety. I took a firm grip on my cane.

"Read your book, Sam. I'll be fine."

Three days later—so it felt—I reached the summit. Like half the houses in Homeland, the Kingmans' digs were impressive, a stately Georgian brick number with a columned front step, kelly green shutters, a large bay window bulging from the bricks to the left of the front porch and an overall sense of money well thrown around. The door knocker was brass, in the shape of the head of a mallard. I took hold of the brass bill and . . . I guess I rapped its gullet against the door. A moment later, the door opened. A boy looking a little like the future king of England was standing there looking at me as if he was already weary with me. I tagged him for around thirteen. Since he was giving me the bold once-over, I did the same. On his feet were those rubber shoe-boots that look like encrusted mud. He was wearing brown corduroy pants, a cranberry turtleneck and an indolent expression far more rich and deep than even your standard thirteen-year-old's indolent mug. I couldn't decide whether to go down on one knee or take a roundhouse swat at his head with my cane. I saw him look past me and figured he was seeing the hearse parked out front. I was tempted to intone, "It is time. Prepare yourself." But I refrained. My sensitivity training kicked in. I had concluded that this was probably a Kingman grandson. Death jokes might not cut it just yet.

"Good afternoon, young man. Is the lady of the house available?"

"Huh?"

"Is your granny home?"

Before he could answer—and it looked like he was working up a zinger—a woman I recognized as Richard Kingman's daughter came into the hallway behind him.

"Mr. Sewell," she said. She stepped up to the boy and touched him on the shoulder. "Thank you, Marcus. Did you introduce yourself to Mr. Sewell?"

The boy offered me his paw and muttered a Swahili curse. Or maybe he introduced himself. "And this is Mr. Sewell," the woman said, when I failed to remember my one line.

"How do you do, Marcus," I said.

"Mom?"

"We're leaving in five minutes. Go find your coat."

The kid retreated on his mud-encrusted shoes, inexplicably leaving no trail. "Won't you come in?" his mother said, stepping backward. I stepped over the threshold. "Oh. Your leg. Are you all right?"

"I'm fine. Thank you. I had a little spat with an oncoming car." I offered her my hand. "I'm sorry. I . . ." I was making the international face for "Now-what-was-the-name-again?"

"Joan Bennett," she said.

"Yes. I'm sorry. The names pour in."

"I understand. Please, come in. Is my mother expecting

you?" She closed the door (the mallard clicked) and made a move for my coat.

"I don't think she is," I said.

"Well, she's upstairs. Marcus and I just dropped by to look in on her. We're on our way into Towson for some last minute Christmas shopping."

"I take a forty-four long," I said, handing her my coat. She blanked for a moment, then got the joke. The resemblance to her darling son rose as she winced a fake smile.

"How is your mother doing?" I asked.

"As good as can be expected." She turned from the hall closet. I recalled then the veritable torrent of tears that this woman had unleashed at her father's wake.

"How are *you*?" I asked.

She took a beat. "Same answer, I suppose. You must hear this so often that it's nothing but a cliché to you. But I can't believe my father is dead. It is still such a shock."

"Clichés are nothing but irrefutable truths. Of course it's still a shock. Your mother told me you were close to your father."

"Yes. We were very close. I suppose I was Daddy's little princess."

"Do you think I could see your mother?"

"Do you mind my asking what it is you need to see her about?"

"Just some details," I said.

"Details?"

"Paperwork."

"I don't mean to sound rude, Mr. Sewell, but haven't we concluded our business with you and your mother? I—"

"My aunt."

"I'm sorry. You and your aunt? My father has been buried. I happen to know that you and your aunt have been paid. My husband took care of all that. What else is there?"

"Little things," I said vaguely, hoping she wouldn't ask me what.

"Like what?"

"I'd really rather just go over it with your mother, if you don't mind."

I was trying to sound pleasant. And I suppose she was trying not to bristle. Neither of us was doing such a bang-up job.

"He was my father, Mr. Sewell," she reminded me. "A daughter is no less than a widow."

"I didn't mean to imply that. I apologize."

She suddenly softened. "I apologize as well. I'm sorry. I just . . . well nevermind. I just so wish that my father would suddenly come down those stairs and ask us what we're having. This house is dead without him." She reddened. "Bad choice of words."

"It happens. Look, Mrs. Bennett, I'm terribly sorry about all this. I should have phoned ahead, but I've just gotten out of the hospital. I'm a little off my game."

"I understand. Please. You can wait in the living room. I'll tell Mother you're here."

She showed me into the living room, then went upstairs to fetch her mother. The room was fussy with good furniture and hunting prints and a great stone fireplace, currently empty and black. The mantelpiece was lined with holiday cards. I spotted the ski-vacation photograph—framed—on the wall near the liquor cabinet. Joan Bennett's debutante photograph took center stage on a small round table that probably dated from the Revolutionary War. She looked like one half of a wedding cake couple, in a long white dress and a clutch of flowers in her gloved hands. On one of the end tables next to the couch, Jeffrey Kingman was represented by what I guessed was his high school yearbook picture. I'm sure if he could go back and jettison the tortoiseshell glasses and give up the early-Beatles haircut, he would. Memories are one thing. Pictures of them are another.

Ann Kingman came into the room. I hadn't even heard her approach. Her daughter gave me a wave from the hallway on her way out. Marcus had reappeared wearing a down parka. He didn't wave. Ann Kingman remained just inside the living room entrance, stock-still. She was clearly holding off our conversation until her daughter and grandson had vamoosed. They left. Ann Kingman came into the room and alighted on the couch. She looked older than when I had last seen her, all of a week and a half before. Her eyes looked harder. The lines around her mouth were a harsh set of parentheses. I sat down in the closest chair, which turned out to be an uncomfortable wooden rocker. Neither of us had yet spoken a word when the front door suddenly flew open and Joan Bennett roared into the house. She was completely red in the face.

"There's a goddamned hearse parked out front!"

I raised my hand. "That would be me."

"*What* is it doing there?"

"Idling?"

"This is *not* funny, Mr. Sewell. My father has not been dead two weeks, and you come out here in a *hearse*? Is this your idea of a joke?"

"My car was just totaled."

"I don't care! That is no excuse for—"

"Joan!" Ann Kingman spoke without bothering to turn around to look at her daughter. "Joan, I'm certain that Mr. Sewell did not intend any disrespect."

"But—"

"But nothing. We have business to attend to. If you would please—"

Her daughter made a huffy exit. The mallard banged loudly. A moment later we heard the twin *thmps* of Joan Bennett's car doors followed by the sound of the motor firing up. It wasn't until those muffled noises had receded and mother and son were on their way to Towson for some last minute Yuletide spending that Ann Kingman and I shifted in our separate seats and moved from a grim staredown to the matter at hand.

"You knew I was coming," I said. "Right?"

"I received a phone call. Daniel swore that he had convinced you I knew nothing about Richard's little fling."

"Daniel is a lot less convincing than he thinks. He was reaching for the phone even before I was out of his office."

"Let me guess. You listened through the door?"

"I didn't really have to. Except for the crucial detail of what precisely your husband had done to piss you off, your behavior . . . well, your temperament at your husband's wake and then again when I ran into you last week wasn't really doing much to hide the fact that *something* about your husband had you in a snit."

"You didn't think that I was merely angry with him for dying and leaving me alone?"

"No. Your daughter, maybe, I'd buy that from—"

"My daughter." I thought she was going to say more. But apparently she was satisfied with that.

"So, you knew about your husband and Helen Waggoner."

"Would you care for a drink?"

"No, thank you."

"Well, I'm going to have one. I hope that's okay with you."

"Allow me." I started to get out of the rocker, but I missed on the first pass.

"No, no, don't bother. Please." She rose from the couch and went over to the liquor cabinet. "Lord knows I've had to pour enough of my own drinks over the years." She made herself a Scotch and soda and brought it back to the couch. "You're making me drink alone."

"I'm not making you do anything."

"Don't get nasty with me, please. I'm not always so sweet."
I let that pass. She settled back on the couch and crossed her
legs. She cupped her drink glass in her hands and set them in
her lap. "You look like a truck ran you over."

"I think it was a Lexus."

"Is your leg going to be all right?"

"I won't win the swimsuit competition."

"Excuse me?"

"Never mind. Yes. The doctors say I should be fine in no
time." We paused. Sizing each other up. At least, that's how I
saw it. "I got run over as a direct result of trying to figure out
who killed Helen Waggoner," I said.

"I'm sorry to hear that."

"Yes."

"Are you looking for sympathy?"

"It's a bad habit of mine."

"I'm sorry you got run over." She took a sip of her drink. "I
mean that. I've been in a very cynical mood lately, but I mean
that. I am sorry for your injuries."

"So am I."

"So, why exactly are you here, Mr. Sewell? Is it to browbeat me?"

"I don't browbeat."

"But I'll bet you could if you wanted to."

"How did you find out that your husband was seeing Helen
Waggoner? Did he tell you?"

"He didn't have to. Richard is generally a more convincing
liar than his brother. I'm sorry. Was. Oftentimes, however, he
didn't even bother to try."

"Then he told you."

"Richard? No. His behavior made it clear that he was fooling around again. I know all the signs by heart. Richard's
schedule was always erratic. A doctor's wife learns to deal with
that or she's in big trouble from the start. But we also learn—

or at least I did—to distinguish professional erratic from recreational. I knew that Richard was off again on one of his manhood rejuvenations. He's been doing that off and on ever since we were married. What I didn't know—" She took a sip of her drink and lingered a moment, as if recalling a memory. "What I didn't know at first was that this time he was planning to leave me."

"Helen was pregnant."

She waved her free hand in the air. "Pregnant. What do you think, Richard turned into a saint if he got one of his silly girls pregnant? No. He just sent them over to Daniel and told his little brother to make the problem go away."

"Which he did. Even though he told me he hated himself for it more than he hated his brother."

"Well, that's one of Daniel's problems. He has always hated himself more than he hated his brother. Richard intimidated Daniel. Daniel always wished he could be more like his brother. He was envious of Richard. Envious of his house, his stature, his reputation. His wife." She paused. Possibly to give me a moment to linger on the thought. "What I mean is that Daniel hates himself for not being more of a son of a bitch like his brother. He hated that he never stood up to Richard. It was humiliating to him. Just once, he got the best of Richard. But even that fell short."

"And why was that?"

"Because Richard never even knew about it. Daniel pulled one over on his big brother and then he didn't even get to enjoy it. We call that, I believe, a hollow victory."

"What was it?"

"An affair. Only the participants ever knew about it. Daniel, of course . . ."

I leaned forward in the rocker, tipping a finger to point at her. She nodded.

"And me."

"I see." I let the rocker take me back.

The widow continued, "It was only for several months. Daniel and I both had our reasons. Separate reasons." She let out a small mirthless laugh. "None of which, I suppose, were satisfied. Are you certain you won't have a drink?"

I was certain. She seemed annoyed with me as she continued.

"I guess Daniel thought he was getting another one over on his brother. By telling me about Richard and this Helen girl. Telling me that she was keeping this baby, with Richard's blessings and all the rest. I don't know what it is about men Richard's age. It's such a cliché. I actually felt disappointed in him."

"Disappointed. That's a tame word."

"Well, I was. He's been tomcatting all his life. That's Richard. Big ego. Big appetite. It was usually some little tramp. Though not always. For God's sake, when I met Richard he was involved with someone else. *I* was the other woman. So, I'm not exactly a saint in all this myself. But for Richard to decide he was going to be a new father all over again. To take on this new girl and . . . What was he doing, pretending he could fool the clock? I simply expected better of him."

"So, why did you have Helen killed, Ann? Your husband had just died of a massive heart attack. I would have thought your sense of—" I stopped. The woman's expression had turned . . . ghastly. That's the only word to describe it. "What's wrong?"

She seemed to be having trouble getting air. Suddenly she let out a brittle cackle. "You *must* be joking! Oh, my goodness. Is *that* why you're here?" She threw her head back and lifted a toast to the ceiling. "God help us all." She looked back at me. "Oh, my . . . Mr. Sewell. *I* didn't have that poor girl killed. Please, tell me you're joking."

"Who did?" I knew I had turned completely red. I could feel the tingles in my cheeks. Unless she was a damned good

actress, Ann Kingman was telling the truth. "Who killed her?"
I asked again. "You do know, don't you?"

"Definitively? No. I don't have any signed confessions I can
hand to you."

"But you do have a damned good guess."

"So do you."

"Help me out. I just accused you."

"Do the math," she said softly. "Who knew about this girl?
Besides, of course, herself and Richard?"

"Apparently only you and—"

Suddenly I was thrown back in time. Not too far back, only
about five minutes. I leaned forward in the rocker again, this
time I tipped my finger to point off into the distance.

She nodded. "I haven't talked to Daniel about it. I refuse
to. I want to know nothing. The whole damn thing simply
makes me ill."

I got to my feet. I snatched up my cane. "Ill? Well, maybe
you should see a doctor, Mrs. Kingman. A person can get over
'ill.' The 'whole damn thing' made a young woman *dead*."

She set her glass down on the coffee table. She was totally
implacable. "You can't see a doctor for that now, can you?"

I left the house without answering.

CHAPTER 24

I should have gone directly to the police station, handed the whole ugly mess over to Kruk and then just gone back to the merry work of draining blood from cadavers and sticking them into the ground. If it turned out that Daniel Kingman was responsible for the murder of Helen Waggoner, then Kruk's warning to me had nearly come true. I did practically jump up and down waving my arms in the face of a killer. However, if Daniel Kingman killed Helen, he also had an accomplice, someone who was willing to drop off Helen's body at Richard Kingman's wake. I thought about this as Sam steered the hearse out of Homeland. If Kingman had an accomplice to drop off the body, it seemed to me a better than even chance that the spineless pediatrician had an accomplice to actually do the deed itself, to murder Helen Waggoner.

"The whole damn thing simply makes me ill."

I had Sam make a left turn onto Charles Street. *I* was getting ill. If Daniel Kingman truly was the man in the middle here, what did it all mean? I gazed out the window watching the bare trees pass by. I dreaded taking this information to

Vickie. What was I supposed to tell her? That her sister had been slaughtered by a peevish obstetrician as a final—and strictly symbolic—snub to a brother whose shadow he had never escaped? That was worth a death? My heart sank even further as I thought of Helen's body out there on the front steps, out in the snow. What was Kingman thinking when he decided to have Helen's body dumped off at his brother's wake? Was this some sort of latent reflex, displaying the proud kill to his brother's widow? I couldn't decide if I was horrified or incensed. Both, I decided. That's what was making *me* ill.

I didn't go to the police station. I didn't go to see Vickie and tell her what I had uncovered. I nearly went to see Julia, who has time-tested methods to make me drop out of the world for a few hours. But I didn't go see Julia either. And I didn't go to Bonnie. In fact, it seemed there were a lot of places I didn't go. I didn't even go to the Oyster, though my thirst was deep and profound. But the Oyster wouldn't do either.

Sam turned onto Coldspring Lane and headed over to the expressway. We passed by Alonso's. It was conceivable that Bonnie was in the bar this very minute, swapping shoptalk with her work chums. Or with Jay Adams. Despite a stoplight directly in front of the bar, Sam flipped on the high beams and the hearse slid right by without pausing.

Much like the last time I had been out there, Sinbad's Cave was pretty much dead in the afternoon. The seedy lounge was for night crawlers. All of three people were at the bar when I went in, and not too many more were scattered at several tables on the floor. The bartender—Ed—recognized me as the guy who had given him forty dollars to cough up Tracy Atkins's phone number.

"First one's on the house," he said to me, slapping down a

napkin and a tumbler of Turkey. I wasn't in the mood to play grateful. Fishing for a tip by giving away management's booze is not exactly putting yourself out there. I downed the drink in two pulls.

"Now that we've gotten that one out of the way, let's get a tab going."

My leg ached. The doctor had told me to start off slowly and to keep it elevated as much as possible the first couple of days. I wasn't doing a great job of following his instructions. I had been given some sort of pills to take if I found it difficult to sleep at night, or if the pain simply became too aggravating while I was awake. I wasn't to drive tractors or operate any other heavy machinery if I took the pills during the day. I hadn't taken any yet. I decided I would try the Wild Turkey cure first.

I didn't want to think about Bonnie and Vickie. Or Vickie and Bonnie. Or any other combination of the two. Closer to the surface than I cared to concede floated the growing sense that my time with the lovely Miss Nash was drawing to a close, and that my time with Vickie Waggoner had already concluded. I knew I could be wrong. Or I could try to do something to alter it. But I could also simply be right, and maybe there wasn't a goddamn thing I could do.

I pulled my bottle of painkillers from my pocket, opened it and poured the pills onto the bar. I pulled out Helen Waggoner's prescription bottle and emptied Bo's collection of colored glass alongside the pills. I added my two photographs to the little altar, the one of Helen and Bo at the zoo—taken, I now assumed, by Richard Kingman—as well as the Kingman family ski-trip photo. I noted that Jeffrey had ditched the tortoiseshells by the time the family traipsed off to Vail or Telluride or wherever they had gone. He had the wire rims already. He looked much more like he did now than in that goofy high school picture.

A third drink came along. It left before long, and another was forced to take its place. There was no mirror behind the bar at Sinbad's. That's smart for a place like this. Fantasy and imagination are three quarters of sex. Especially sex with a stranger. Slap a mirror up there so that a guy can see how pathetic he looks picking up a woman who can barely conceal her true indifference and you'll blow the whole game. It being the middle of the afternoon, I didn't have that problem. Nobody was hanging on my arm or popping gum next to my ear. I was grateful there was no mirror simply because I didn't want to see myself. I should have listened to Kruk. Finding Helen's killer wasn't making me feel good. Or whole. Or self-satisfied. Or powerful. Just the opposite. I see way too many dead people as it is in my line of work. But at least for the most part they die a better death than the one Helen Waggoner died. I suppose I should have been proud of myself for discovering the details of her murder. I wasn't. I didn't want to be the messenger of that kind of information. I had no choice now. The best I could do—short term—was to kill the messenger. Or more accurately, get him stink-ass drunk and put off the delivery a little longer. Smashed up leg, smashed up car, smashed up relationship . . . I was warming nicely to my pity party. I was smashed, or well on my way. Eyeing the electric piano in the corner, I swore to myself that if I were still on this barstool by the time Gary and Gloria came on to set the world on fire . . . well, I'd start ordering doubles simply to get it all over with. In fact, why wait? I beckoned Ed over to ask for another pair of nails in my coffin—ha, ha—but before I could ask he picked up one of the photographs from my little scrapbook.

"That's Helen," he said. I was gone enough at that point, it took me a moment to recall how it was that this guy would know who Helen was. Shit. That's right. She worked here. *Here.* This was the last place where Helen saw people she knew who weren't about to kill her. This guy, this bartender.

Ed. Ed had been here that night. A thought (amazing) occurred to me.

"Ed. That night that Helen was killed."

"Yeah? What about it?"

"Who took the phone call for her?"

"I did. Why?"

I took the picture from him. "What did the guy say? On the phone. The guy who called. For Helen." It felt like climbing steps in lead boots just to get a question out.

Ed shrugged. "He asked for Helen. What? You think he said is Helen there, send her outside so I can shoot her?"

"I'm just asking."

"Well, you know what champ? He didn't."

"Fuck, Ed, don't bust my chops. I just asked you a question." I guess the bartender saw his tip going down the tubes.

"Is that all?" he said.

Ed rubbed his pointy jaw. "I said she's working. We don't like these girls taking personal calls. This guy said it was about her kid."

"About Bo?"

"Sure. So I called her over."

"Did you happen to hear her end of the conversation?"

"Do you happen to think you're being nosy enough?" I rode that one out. He went on. "I didn't. She didn't talk long anyway. She just slammed the phone down and said something about the kid being sick and out she went."

"Bo was sick?"

"Look, I told all this to the police already. Don't go thinking you're Columbo or something."

"What did the police say about it?"

The bartender shrugged. "They figure whoever it was just said whatever he had to to get her running out of here. I guess a sick kid'll usually do it." Ed picked up the Kingman family photo.

"Who's this guy?"

"Big Pappy." I took a deep breath. "Helen was sleeping with him. He's the reason she got killed."

There, I had delivered the message. Well, practiced, at any rate.

"No. Not him. The other one. The squirrelly guy with the glasses."

"That's his son."

"I've seen him."

"Seen who?"

"The kid. He's been in here."

I struggled to get my own voice back. "In here? You're sure?"

"That's all I fucking do all day and night is stare at faces. This guy was in here. I'm positive. Like, I don't know, a month or so ago."

I tried to think, even though I had put a pretty good liquid barrier between me and my brain. But I tried. *Jeffrey* Kingman? At Sinbad's? *Think*. What did the younger Kingman do for a living? Did I know? Was it something that would have required business travel? Sinbad's Cave was too far from the airport for a person to drop in while waiting for a flight. They would have to be . . . No. The thought died before it took form. Jeffrey Kingman lived in Baltimore. Business travel or not, he wouldn't be kicking up his heels at Sinbad's low-life Cave. Not without a compelling reason. Ed was still looking at the photograph. He was also eyeing the pile of pills and colored glass.

"You're not going to swallow that shit all of a sudden, are you?"

I ignored the question. "You remember seeing this guy? You're absolutely positive it was him?"

"I remember." The bartender picked up the picture of Helen and Bo again. "That's him. He was in here fighting with Helen."

This time I didn't even speak. My face simply went slack. He went on, "Yeah, they were arguing up a fucking blue streak. Not at first, I mean. At first he was just sitting there in the back. Helen didn't pay him any attention. None that I saw anyway. Next thing I know they're off in some big deep conversation, then suddenly Helen's showing him how good she can swear. And how good she can hit."

This was the guy! This was the guy Gail had seen arguing with Helen! It didn't make any sense. But this was *him*. Jeffrey Kingman.

"I was about to toss the guy out, but he left on his own. He was all pissed off. Helen was a fucking witch the rest of the night."

"Did he come in again? Did you ever see the guy after that?"

"Nope. That was it."

"You're sure."

"Believe me, I'd have remembered. Like I need that kind of shit going on in here?"

"Did Helen ever say anything about him?"

"Not to me she didn't. I doubt to anyone else either. How well did you know Helen anyway?"

"Barely," I said. Not at all. Never met her alive. Embalmed her. Buried her.

"Well, if you worked with her you knew just to give the damn girl her space. You know what I'm saying? She could be sweet one minute and then she could take your head off. Whatever this guy said or did to her, that was none of my business. As far as i was concerned he was just another asshole, and Helen had just had enough of assholes for one night."

That was as far as Ed was concerned.

• • •

I stumbled out of Sinbad's Cave and crawled into the rear of the hearse. "Don't you want to sit up front?" Sam asked. The gentle bouncer was clearly concerned about the condition of his employer. "Just drive," I snarled, whacking my cane against the roof of the car. That's the last I remember. Sam told me the rest. Forty minutes later the hearse pulled up in front of Sewell & Sons and Sam came around back and pulled open the rear door. If any of the neighbors were watching out their windows and expecting to see a coffin being pulled out, they were disappointed. Sam reached into the hearse but what he dragged out was the undertaker who had been lullabyed to sleep by the gentle rocking of the car's chassis during the drive in from the airport, as well as by the bourbon that was currently taking up valuable space in his bloodstream.

Several hours later the ruby hearse pulled up in front of the Joseph Meyerhoff Symphony Hall and out stepped a freshly showered fellow in a tuxedo and overcoat, pale as death, gripping a wooden cane and smiling gamely at all the pretty people who had paused to gape on their way inside the hall. Constance Bell was among them. She wasn't even trying to keep her thousand gigawatt smile under wraps.

"Well, look what the hearse dragged in." Constance slipped her arm through mine. "Let me help you."

"Do I look that bad?"

"Honey, you look as handsome as an international spy who's been dropped off a cliff. Now come on."

Inside, we checked our coats and went directly to the bar. "Coffee," I murmured, "I need a serious tango with some caffeine."

"And what have we been celebrating?" Constance asked as we took our coffees back into the lobby. The burble of unintelligible conversation in the large curved room was—surprisingly—soothing.

"No celebration," I said. "More like mourning."

"Thus the hearse. I see. Nice touch."

Constance's dress was a long indigo number. A large, beaten brass ornament adorned her chest. I don't know what you call a necklace when it comes down like that, like a shield. Whatever you call it, this one was adorned with all sorts of garnets and must have weighed close to a pound. The lawyer's cornrowed coil contained a few specks of a reddish confetti. An aroma of vanilla and nutmeg seemed to be traveling with her as well.

We went inside when the chimes sounded and found our seats. The governor was in attendance, along with his wife. They were seated in one of the boxes, nearly over our heads. I waved my cane and got the First Lady's attention. She tugged on her husband's sleeve and pointed me out to him. They both waved.

Constance was impressed. "You know the governor?"

"Nah, not really. For a hundred bucks if you call in advance they'll set up the little waving routine for you."

Constance rolled her eyes. "Whenever you decide to finally give a straight answer to something, I hope you'll alert the press."

"I met the governor and his wife last year during the campaign. They dropped in for a funeral."

"That's better."

"I also helped to throw the election his way, but that's another story."

The lights dimmed before Constance could field that one, and the big band came out and cooked up some Bach, Brahms and Beethoven. It was a B-concert. I missed the name of the conductor, but he was a short little fellow, shaped roughly like a snowman, with a pink bald head bordered by long streams of thin white hair that jerked and danced as the man bounced around on his padded box. The band was hot, especially the strings. The soloist was a rope-armed Asian woman, who truly beat the hell out of her fiddle. She seemed intent on punishing the damn thing. The program said that she picked up her first violin when she was two. She was twenty-two now. This seemed to be a troubled relationship. By contrast, there was a guy on the xylophone who was having the time of his life. Happy as a clam. He literally lifted off the ground as he peppered away with his mallets. Love taps every single one.

At the intermission I took Constance over to meet the governor and his wife. I was already learning that if you play it right, you can use the fact that you're using a cane to your advantage, especially in a crowd. Constance and I plowed easily through the gathering sycophants and went directly up to Governor Davis and his wife, Beth. As I made the introductions, I noted that Beth Davis was still as bashful and unpretentious as when I had met the two, during her husband's spirited romp to Annapolis. The governor was his customarily charming self, with just the slightest touch of patronization in his great-to-see-you countenance, but overall he was a good guy. Politically he didn't seem to be sinking the Ship of State; that was a good thing. When he discovered that Constance was a lawyer, he beat me soundly on the arm.

"I hope our boy here isn't in some sort of trouble. He seems to have a nose for it." He indicated my cane. "What happened?"

"I fought the car, and the car won." I turned to Beth Davis. "I'll never play the piano again."

"A loss for the world of music," the governor said, laughing. He was looking at Constance. "That's a lovely necklace you're wearing, Miss Bell."

"Thank you, Governor."

"What firm did you say you were with?"

Constance named the firm. I watched the governor process the name in seconds. His expression darkened.

"Stern and Fenwick. Miss Bell, I'm so sorry about Mr. Fenwick. Tragic. Truly tragic." He turned to his wife. "You know the one I mean, Beth. That lawyer and his wife who were killed in their own home?" The First Couple shared such a sad look, you'd have thought they felt personally responsible.

"I'm very sorry," Beth Davis said to Constance. And she meant it. One hundred percent.

I wished the governor and his wife happy holidays. "The fruitcake is in the mail," I said to Beth Davis, just to watch her blush one more time. Constance and I made way for the others waiting, with decreasing patience, to get in some face time.

"Nice people," Constance said as we snagged another coffee for me. "Why are they in politics?"

I shrugged. "He wants to save the world, and she loves her husband. It's almost quaint."

As the second half of the program was about to begin, Constance asked, "So when do I get the sordid details of your accident?"

I answered, "It's nothing. Dead body on the doorstep. I've been trying to figure out how it got there. Seems to piss a few people off."

Constance leaned sideways and whispered, "I think I've got some answers for you."

I blurted, "You?"

Someone in the row behind hushed me. I turned to Constance, but she was holding a finger to her lips. As the lights dimmed, she let that damn smile escape.

I tapped my toe for fifty minutes, suffered through an insufferable encore of a Christmas music medley that was not nearly so cute as they must have thought it was. Then I used my cane to high advantage in order to get Constance and myself out of there.

"Where should we go?" Constance asked. I had released Sam for the evening. He had to bounce at one of his clubs. Constance had a car.

"You're looking too gorgeous just to stuff into the back of some smoky bar."

"The Belvedere is close by," she suggested.

Recent memories. Not all good. "Pass," I said.

We settled on Henry's Bookstore and Café on Charles Street. Books in the front, double-decker café in the back. Constance found a parking spot directly in front. There was a new Anne Tyler out in time for Christmas. An entire table had been devoted to it, she being a local girl and all. Constance stopped at the table and picked up a copy of the book. "No other writer alive passes the first-page test better than Anne Tyler." She turned to the first page and began to read aloud. When she reached the end of the page she snapped the book closed.

"Hey. At least finish the paragraph," I said.

"See what I mean? You want more. Every single time. Here. I'll buy this for you. Merry Christmas."

Constance paid for the book, then we took a table upstairs. It's a little more private up there, especially in the back. I asked for a big plate of calamari. Constance ordered a white wine. I was sick of coffee at that point. I asked about the available merlots. Our waiter launched into an assessment of the several choices. The words that are used to describe wines are almost always the same ones we use to describe personalities. This always gets me; I'm not choosing a friend, just a drink. I cut the waiter off. "Just pick one out for me, please. One that has a strong jaw." The fellow bowed slightly, and left.

"What's a strong jaw?" Constance asked. "I've never heard of that."

I hooked my cane on the edge of the table. "It's nothing. It's something Julia cooked up once just to have fun. Nine out of ten waiters will simply nod when you say it as if they know what the hell you're talking about."

Her white and my strong-jawed red arrived a minute later. We shared a holiday toast. I set my glass down and pointed a finger-pistol at Constance.

"Okay. Spill it."

Constance pursed her lips, then set her wineglass off to the side and leaned forward, setting her elbows on the table.

"This body on your doorstep you referred to. It was left there the night of the blizzard."

"It was."

"During a wake, as I understand it."

"Right again."

"You are familiar with the name Michael Fenwick?" Constance asked.

"Sure. He was your colleague. You work for his daddy's firm."

"Did you know that Richard Kingman retained our firm to handle his family's affairs?"

I told her that I didn't. Or hadn't.

"Apparently Michael was a family friend. A few months ago, Michael asked me to handle a change of will that Richard Kingman was requesting. I met with him. With Kingman. He came into the office."

"What were the changes?"

"Well of course I'm not legally allowed to reveal that sort of information. It's privileged."

"Of course. I suppose only under the threat of say, bodily danger or a deep red wine being tossed on your snappy clothes, you might be able to justify having spilled such privileged beans. Something like that?"

"Something like that."

"See this cane?"

"Richard Kingman wanted to add a beneficiary. This is what I thought you might find interesting."

"Let me guess. One Helen Waggoner."

Constance looked disappointed. "There goes my punch line. Yes. Helen Waggoner. How did you know?"

"Call it a lucky guess."

"Well then, what do you say you pick me some lottery numbers?"

I took up my glass and gave the wine a swirl. "So, Richard Kingman stuck Helen in his will. Our little Sinbad's waitress really did find herself a gravy train this time, didn't she. His goddamn will. Constance, I'm beginning to fear my eventual midlife crisis like crazy. This guy meets a pretty young waitress and decides that she is his new lease on life. He buys her a car. They get a baby going together. He carves out a spot for her in his will and everything. At least you can say the guy had no trouble with commitment. So then tell me, did he slice his wife out of the will? Was he *that* much of a prick?"

"Not at all. He didn't substantially alter the financial arrangements he had set up for Ann Kingman. He left those intact. He restructured from other parts of the will."

"What a good old romantic," I said bitterly. "Keeps a nest egg for his wife of thirty-five years. I wonder if he thought he was buying his way out of guilt."

"Who can say? But I thought you'd find this bit of news interesting."

"I do, Constance. I find it very interesting. It almost makes me believe in a vindictive God. Richard Kingman didn't live long enough to enjoy his new life with Helen Waggoner, and Helen didn't live long enough to cash in on her newly minted good fortune. This is a major argument for family values, don't you think?"

"It's a major argument for something fishy is what it is."

"Well, you're right. But there's nothing fishy about Kingman's death at least. His big magnanimous ticker blew up in the middle of surgery. That's just the way that the world goes round."

"I was thinking of Helen Waggoner. Come on, Hitch, think about it. The woman was killed within days of her lover's death and deposited on the door of his wake, for Christ's sake. What's that all about?"

The waiter returned with our calamari. He asked after my merlot. I told him its jaw was pretty firm, but that it had loose teeth. He walked away puzzled. I hope. The calamari was good. Sometimes it's like eating deep-fried rubber bands. This time it wasn't. Henry's did it right. I wolfed down a few squid and chased it with a splash of the dentally challenged merlot.

"I think I can tell you what that's all about. And I've certainly been trying to figure it out." I set my elbows up on the table and gave Constance the short version of what I had learned over the past several days. I told her about my figuring out in the first place that it was Richard Kingman with whom the waitress was having her affair, that it was Kingman who had purchased her sporty little car for her and who was financing her new wardrobe and preparing to locate a new apartment for her and all the rest. I told her how Kingman had directed his new gal to go see his brother, the baby doctor, to look after her pregnancy, and how Dr. Dan had immediately scurried off to Kingman's wife to tell tales out of school.

"Daniel Kingman loathed his brother and envied him at the same time. The closest he ever came to getting back at him was to have an affair with Kingman's wife. It lasted several months and then, I guess, simply petered out. Not exactly a rousing revenge."

"But killing his brother's lover *after* his brother is already dead . . . you think that's a worthwhile revenge?"

"Well, for me it wouldn't be, no. I like to stare into the eyes of the person I'm getting back at. I'm a gloater. But Daniel Kingman . . . He strikes me as preposterously spineless. He could never stand up to his brother. I mean, here's this guy, an obstetrician. A good solid practice. He has probably brought hundreds and hundreds of babies into the world. Thousands, I suppose. But every time his brother waltzes in and needs someone to take care of some woman he's knocked up, Daniel is ready to jump just as high as big brother says."

"So then what are you telling me, that after Richard Kingman dies, this Daniel Kingman orders a hit on Helen Waggoner? I'm not sure if I buy that. It sounds much more plausible to me that the wronged widow would be the one."

"She said she wasn't. And I believe her."

"Yeah, but you're a sucker."

"I won't take that personally."

She started to laugh, then held back. "You should."

I leaned back and folded my arms over my chest. "Now explain something to me. If you knew that Helen Waggoner had recently been added to Richard Kingman's will, why didn't you take that information to the police? Why am I hearing this from you now?"

"I didn't even hear the name Helen Waggoner in connection with Kingman's wake until a few hours ago."

"You can explain?"

Constance dabbed at the side of her mouth with a napkin before answering. "Of course I can. For starters I wasn't even in town the night this all happened. I was up in Boston. The storm locked me in for an extra day. I was stuck on the runway at Logan for four hours before they finally canceled my flight. In fact, when I got back to the office I swapped war stories with Michael about the blizzard. He told me how he had spun out in his car and flipped it onto its side."

"Where was this?"

"Down there along the Jones Falls. Near the Streetcar Museum?"

"Interesting. Was he hurt?"

"Enough to be taken over to Mercy Hospital. He said he was knocked out for a little bit. He had a slight concussion, and there was something about his elbow. Bone chip or something. But he was lucky. He said the emergency room at Mercy was a zoo. People were just flooding into the place. He was there for hours just waiting to get X-rayed."

"So then he didn't even make it to the wake."

"No. He didn't." Constance pointed her empty fork at me. "But what he did do, Hitchcock, was he pulled the Kingman will. Rather, he already had. I was out of town when Kingman died, so Michael handled things with the family. I mean, he probably would have in any case, given his connection with them."

"So what do you mean you only made the Helen Waggoner connection a few hours ago?"

"This is the thing. You have to remember, Michael and his wife were murdered just a few days after the Kingman funeral. I think you can understand how that took most of my attention for awhile. It's a horrible thing. Of course Michael's accounts had to be covered by others at the firm. Divvied up. I reinherited the Kingman estate, so to speak. It was only this evening that I took a look at them."

"This evening?"

"Hitchcock, despite what people might think, lawyers work hard for the money. Even though this is Saturday, I was working on some briefs at home and I realized that I needed to pick up a few other files from the office. So I swung by there on my way to symphony hall. I don't know what made me look at the Kingman file, but I did. And that's when I saw that the will Michael had pulled was the old one. It wasn't the one I had worked on with Kingman."

"The one that named Helen Waggoner as a beneficiary."

"Exactly. So I kept looking. It's standard practice for our paralegals to keep the files on our clients updated. The Kingman file included several newspaper articles concerning this peculiar event that had taken place the night of Kingman's wake. And there it was. Or rather, she was. Helen Waggoner."

Constance took a sip of her wine. I sat with the information while our waiter came by to check on us. He was a young guy. Wire-rim glasses. A thought came to me. As soon as he had taken off I asked Constance if she had ever met Jeffrey Kingman.

"No. Why?"

"Because he knew about this, too. Or at least some of it. He knew about his father's affair."

"He told you that?"

"Jeffrey? No. I found that out just today. I knew that Helen had had a fight about a month ago with some guy at the bar where she worked. One of the waitresses out there remembered. At first I thought maybe this was the guy who killed her. Maybe it was just a customer with a loose nut. Later on I figured it might have been Helen's lover, that he had come out to the bar and the two got into a lover's quarrel. But when I was out there at Sinbad's today, the bartender recognized Jeffrey Kingman from a picture I had with me. He remembered this was the guy who had gotten into it with Helen."

"So then what? Kingman's son knew about the affair and he was out at the bar to confront Helen?"

"That's my guess. Jeffrey Kingman apparently never got along with his father. He definitely sided with Mama. It makes sense to me that if he learned about the affair, he might go out there to stir things up."

"And how would he learn of the affair?"

"Well, Daniel Kingman knew. He passed the news on to Ann Kingman. What do you think? Mommy has sonny over for dinner and tells him that Daddy is screwing around again? I can buy that."

"Did you ask her if she told her son?"

"No. At the time I was out at the Kingman house I didn't know that Jeffrey was even in the picture. I didn't find that out until I went back out to Sinbad's glorious cave."

"So you've got two suspects, Hitch. Not just one. Kingman's brother and Kingman's son. And frankly, since I wasn't there to get the snow job you got, I'd say you actually have three."

"Ann Kingman."

"She doesn't sound like a milquetoast to me."

I held up my hand and waggled everything but my thumb. "Four," I said. Constance lifted an eyebrow. "Michael Fenwick. Fenwick was not in attendance at Kingman's wake."

"He was in a car crash."

"So you say. So he says. And if he really was at the emergency room at Mercy like he said, then fine." I curled down one finger.

"Why in the world would Michael Fenwick want to murder Helen Waggoner?"

I shrugged. "I don't know, Constance. I'm just turning over the cards here to see what we've got. You said that Fenwick was a family friend of the Kingmans. How so? Do you know the connection?"

"I think he went to college with the son."

"Jeffrey."

"I'm almost positive. I know that Hal Stern was very pleased when Michael brought the Kingman accounts over to the firm. I'm pretty sure I recall that it was a college connection."

I finished off my merlot. Constance was close behind. "Do you want another?" I asked.

"I don't think so. I'm getting tired. This is going to be a short evening for me. Is that all right?"

I told her it was fine with me. My day was already a week long. I signaled the waiter. While we waited for the bill, I asked, "Constance, can you do me a favor? It's a big one. If it's at all possible, can you make as if you didn't pick up the Kingman file today?"

"Well . . . I suppose I could. Though I don't see why I should. The police will certainly want to know what I've come across."

"Of course. And they will. But today's Saturday. No one would expect that you'd been into the office anyway. And tomorrow . . . can't this wait until Monday, Constance? What's the harm? Can you give me just two days?"

"I don't like this, Hitchcock."

"I'm not asking you to like it. I'm just asking if you'll do it."

"And you'll tell me why?"

I pawed through my ragged satchel of charm and dragged out the best imploring expression I could find. It probably wasn't my best, given my fatigue, but it was apparently sufficient.

"I shouldn't," Constance said darkly. She allowed the implication to echo: she would.

My list of suspects was contracting and expanding like an accordion. No sooner had I tossed out Haden, Gloria, Gary, the mystery boyfriend who turned out to have already been dead himself at the time of Helen's murder, and a non-existent irate psycho-customer at Sinbad's, and had narrowed it all down to Daniel Kingman, then the list expanded again to take in Ann Kingman and Jeffrey Kingman and now there was even Jeffrey's college chum, Michael Fenwick, to consider.

Constance dropped me off at my place and I took Alcatraz out for a much-delayed relief romp. We headed away from the harbor—our usual route—and went instead up the block a few doors, where I stood for a long time on the curb across the street from the funeral home—in front of St. Teresa's—and gazed at the front steps, trying to picture Michael Fenwick dragging Helen out of the car and up the several steps. But then what? Did he ditch the Pontiac, hop into his own car and hightail it several miles north where he "conveniently" lost control on the slippery street and flipped his car over? The section of roadway that Constance described is not heavily traveled, especially at night. It's possible that Fenwick could have fudged the time of his accident. He told Constance he had been knocked unconscious. If no one witnessed the spin out, Fenwick could have reported the incident having taken place a little earlier. Coupled with the time it took for Helen's body to be discovered on my front doorstep, the lawyer would have laid the groundwork for a fairly decent alibi, in the off-chance that one would have ever been required.

I went across the street and sat down on the cold top step. Alcatraz remained over by the church, mingling with the plaster farm animals near the manger. He looked as if he was trying to get them to come out and play. I tried to replay the scene again, from this new perspective. From ground zero. I imagined the Kingman wake going on inside. Ann, Jeffrey, Daniel . . . all of us moving about in our somber slow dance. I pictured the white Pontiac pulling to a stop right in front of me. The door opening . . .

Damn it. Michael Fenwick was the one I wanted to talk to. The one person I couldn't speak with. Alcatraz trotted across the street. "Thanks for nothing," I muttered. I didn't mean my dog. I was thinking about the guy who had so rudely seen to it that Michael Fenwick would be forever unavailable for comment. Just my luck. First Fenwick, then . . .

I was off like a shot.

• • •

Misty Dew was dancing to Lynyrd Skynyrd's "Freebird" when I entered the club. I paused just inside the velvet curtain to adjust to the low lights. The dancer's interpretation of the rock classic was both complex and primal all at once. "Freebird" is a very energetic song, once it gets rolling. One thing I noticed—and I had noticed this the last time I was here—the physically loquacious Ms. Dew was certainly feeling a different rhythm than the one suggested by the screaming guitars and slamming drums. She was swaying like a flower child at Woodstock, her showcase hips working a nifty figure-eight as she bumped and ground in front of the big whiskers on the mirrored wall. Misty was wearing pretty much the same ounce of costuming she had worn on my last visit. The trailing end of her string of glass beads were skipping and dancing about her hips like a little whip.

I slid onto a stool and immediately a hand reached out of the darkness and slid onto my crotch. Yes, nice to meet you too. The woman with the cellophane hair leaned in from the stool next to me. I got the picture. That was her hand. Her cellophane was a different hue tonight. Blue. She was pretty in a sexy, android sort of way.

"So you're not working behind the bar tonight?" I asked.

"Uh-uh. This side. You thirsty?"

"Actually I came in to see her." I indicated the free bird up on the stage.

"You can see her just fine from here, can't you?"

"Sure."

"But you can see me better." Her fingers started massaging.

"I believe I can feel you too," I said.

"What say you buy me a drink."

I removed her hand and set it onto the bar. "What say I don't much like the going price of flat ginger ale in this place."

"Are you going to be nasty? Is that it?"

"Will that cost extra?"

She gave me an ugly smile. "Usually does." She signaled the bartender to get us started. Uh-oh. Here goes the college tuition for my dog. I put a fistful of money on the bar and told the bartender—a mean looking bald guy in a muscle shirt— "Can you turn this into a couple of beers?" To the woman at my side I said, "I really did come in to see Misty. No offense."

The movement on my right was the sound of the woman with the cellophane hair quitting the barstool and heading for greener pastures. "I didn't catch your name," I said as she crossed behind me.

"Fuck off."

Hmmm. Catchy.

Lady Dew spotted me during her big toe-touching finale. This time she wasn't mooning her audience, she was facing us and mooning the mirrored wall behind us. In a sense, we still got the message. She was snaking her arms down in front of her, reaching for her toes, when she caught sight of me out of the corner of her eye. I waved; she winked. Some guy thrust a fistful of cash in her direction. She snatched it, leaned impossibly farther forward—I suspected a yoga regimen—and kissed the horny fool on the top of his head. Right. Great investment. The "Freebird" anthem finally wrapped up ("Woah, woah, woah, woah, whoaaaaa . . ."), and Misty quit the stage.

"Quite a number," I said to her a moment later as she alighted on the stool to my left. Her hands remained in plain sight. Such a lady. She was again wearing her transparent robe.

" 'Freebird,' " Misty said, in case I had been deaf during the past five minutes. "I'm trying different things."

"Have you considered Brahms?"

"What's he do?"

"A lot of strings. It's probably not on the jukebox though."

"Yeah, can you believe they make us use our own quarters? It's so humiliating."

I decided not to put Misty through my flat ginger ale routine. I needed to talk with her. I made the same offer that I had before, that I could simply give my cash directly to her rather than siphon it off to the cash register for that lousy swill.

"You promise to leave the bartender a tip anyway?" she asked.

"Scout's honor."

"Tell you what. Let's go to a booth."

I put a hand on her arm. "I just want to talk. I mean that."

"Look, what you do with your money is your business. I got to generate cash flow, all right? That's *my* business. If you keep it flowing, you can do whatever you want."

We retired to a scrungy booth. I made a mental note to take a dozen showers as soon as I got home. "Let me slide in next to you," Misty said. When I started to protest she said, "Come on, just let me. What are people going to think if they look over here and see me sitting across from you? Like we're having a conversation?"

"You're right. God forbid."

I slid over and Misty came down next to me. She led with her hips and pressed me against the wall.

"Are you comfortable?" I asked.

"Yeah. That's good. You?"

"Nifty."

"So, what do you want to talk about?" she asked. "Sports? Weather?"

"Popeye."

"Oh. Yeah. How about that, huh? Somebody shot him in the foot."

"Yeah, well they also shot him in the heart."

"Pretty good shooting, I'd say. It couldn't have been very big."

"So, I take it you're pretty devastated by all this, huh?"

"You mean him getting killed? Sure, that sucked. But I mean, nobody here really liked him much. Some old men are nice and fatherly and all that shit. But Popeye was a Grade A prick. He was just an old man with an old man attitude. He could care less for the dancers. He never even looked at us when we were up there dancing. An old man like that who can't even get interested in a stripper anymore? I don't know, I think I'd shoot myself if I got that way. That's half dead anyway."

"Well, it looks like someone decided to do the shooting for him."

"Yeah, isn't that something. You were on your way up there too. I remember. It was that same day, wasn't it?"

"Yes, it was."

"You weren't going over there to shoot him yourself, were you?"

"What makes you think that?"

"I don't think it, I'm just wondering."

"What? Do you think a bunch of us were starting to line up and whoever got there first won?"

"I don't know. You just all of a sudden were more interested in talking to him than you were to me. That's the part I remember."

"I didn't mean for you to take it personally. I was hoping that Popeye could give me some information."

"On that porn guy?"

"Terry Haden. Yes."

"I guess you didn't get any information, did you?"

"It doesn't matter. I've got something new I'm trying to figure out. That's why I wanted to talk to you."

She gave me a funny look. "You're not going to shoot *me* are you?"

"Misty, why in the world would I do that?"

"I don't know. It's a fucked-up world is all. You never know what anyone is going to do."

"Well, I'm not going to shoot you." Hell, I wasn't even going to touch her. Or ask *her* to touch *me*. Didn't the stripper know a saint when she was squeezed into a dark booth with one? "I want to know if you can give me some information."

She laughed. "Shoot."

"You're a card," I said. I set a handful of cash on the table. It disappeared in a heartbeat. "About two weeks ago, this would be a Wednesday night. Do you work on Wednesdays?"

"Every day but Sunday."

"So, you would have been working here that night. It wasn't this past Wednesday, but the one before that. The night of the big blizzard."

"Sure. I was here."

"Was Popeye here that night? Do you remember?"

"Popeye was here every night. Except for lunch, he spent all his time here. Nice life, huh?"

"So then he was here that night. Now here's what I want to ask you. Do you have any memory of a man coming in that night. A man in a suit."

"You have no idea how many suits we get in here."

I pulled a newspaper clipping from my pocket. The previous week's blizzard had snaffued the weekly recycling schedule. Piece of luck. I handed her the clipping.

"This guy. Do you recall seeing him in here?"

Misty took the newspaper clipping and squinted at it. There was just enough light seeping into the booth for pulling down zippers and groping in the dark, but not a hell of lot for looking at newspapers. But Misty seemed to have decent night vision. She held the clipping nearly to her nose, then handed it back to me.

"Maybe. I think so. Yes."

My heart—which had not even blipped an extra beat when I was groped by the android—jumped now.

"Misty. Which of those three answers is it? Maybe? You think so? Or yes?"

"Let me see it again."

She took the clipping from me again and again held it up to her nose. "Sure," she declared. "That's the guy."

"*The* guy? What do you mean, Misty? The guy what?"

"The guy who came in. It was one of those nights. Crazy night. Poor Popeye. I almost felt sorry for him. I mean, I really didn't like him, but still, he was getting jerked around all over the place that night."

"Jerked around. By this guy? Did this guy come in and jerk the old man around?"

"Well, wait. Hold on to your big horse. One thing at a time, okay? I was dancing. We weren't all that full yet. You know how it is. Like the last time you were here. A few guys at the bar, a couple tables. Not a real fast night. And in comes this guy."

"The man in the picture?"

"No. I told you, hang on. He was later. You got to listen. It was this other guy. I've seen him coming in and out of here a bunch of times. Kind of like that other guy you were asking about the last time. The porn jerk."

"Haden."

"Yeah. Like him. Coming around like he owned the place. This guy was kind of like that. Except he didn't hit up on us or anything. I mean, he wasn't trying to get us to star in porn flicks or anything. He had some sort of business with Popeye. He never paid any attention to us. I thought he was a creep. None of the girls like him. There's just something nasty about him. You know the type."

"Do you know his name?"

"We just call him Bob. I don't think that's his name. Someone just came up with that. You know, like a nickname. Bob. It's the same forward as backward."

"So, what was 'Bob' up to that night?"

"He was pissed off. That's why I remember it. He came

storming in here like he was ready to take someone's head off. Like I said, I was up on the stage, so I could see it pretty good. He went right over to Popeye, who's always over there at the corner of the bar, and he started yelling at him. I couldn't hear about what, because of the music. And it wasn't too long. He and Popeye went into the back office and shut the door. And you could still hear the guy yelling at him back in there. Even with the door closed and the music going. You could also hear something hitting the wall."

"Like maybe Popeye?"

"Like maybe him, yeah. The guy was definitely roughing the old man up."

"How long were they back there?"

"I don't know. Fifteen minutes? Maybe more. I don't wear a watch onstage."

I didn't bother to note that if she did it would be her biggest piece of clothing.

"So then what else, Misty? Did anything else happen?"

"Nah. The guy finally left. He practically knocked over a couple of customers on his way out. He was pissed off, I mean *really* pissed off. Popeye stayed in the back for awhile, and when he came out no one said a word to him about it. He had a cut on his chin. It looked like he was moving even slower than normal. But no one said a word. Hell, he doesn't care about us, what are we going to do, start caring about him?"

"So, what happened next?"

"What happened next was later on the same night this guy in the newspaper, this guy here, *he* came in. I don't know when it was. Maybe like a couple of hours later? I couldn't tell you for sure. It was a lot later. I was sitting at the bar. I had a customer. So, I was, you know, busy. But I saw Popeye's face when this guy came in. I'd seen him before, by the way. This guy you showed me in the picture. I'd seen a couple of times before, over in the corner, talking with Popeye about something or other. I just figured Popeye was mixed up in something illegal, you know. It's none of my business."

"Why would you think that?"

Misty took hold of my chin and ticktocked my head to look around the club. "Look around. A guy in a big-deal suit comes in to talk to Popeye? What do they have to talk about? The guy sure isn't Popeye's stockbroker, you know what I'm saying? I'm just guessing. Running this joint was probably about the most legal thing Popeye ever did. And I know for a fact he had to grease some palms here and there to keep us going. They can bust you for just about anything these days, you know?"

"Go on. What happened?"

"Well, Popeye saw this guy come in and I swear, if the old man knew how to look scared, that's how he looked. It was like he expected this guy to come over and rough him up too. But he didn't. I mean this guy with the suit, he's not a tough guy or anything. Besides, he had his arm in a sling. I remember that. How good can you beat up an old man when you got one arm in a sling, you know?"

"Good point."

"Well, he and Popeye go back into the office too. This time there isn't any roughhousing. And like a half hour later, out comes this guy, and he storms right out of the club too. It was funny. Both these guys going into the office and then storming out. I don't know what Popeye was telling them back there, but it wasn't making either of them too happy."

I wasn't sure of the specifics either. And I wasn't real certain that I would ever uncover them. Killers don't like to talk. And dead men can't. And if I was reading things correctly, that's what I was dealing with here. A killer and a dead man.

"How about something to remember me by?" Misty said as I motioned her to let me out of the booth. She slid out first and turned to face me. The light from the bar and the stage behind her filtered in through her transparent gown and outlined the dancer's body in an amber silhouette.

"I'll remember you." She didn't give me much room to pass as I squeezed out of the booth and stood up. She looked up at me and tapped a finger against my chest.

"I still got your card," she said. "If I die I'll call you."

It was too late to be calling on people unannounced. But there was nothing I could do about that. The clock was running. I was now holding on to way more information than I should. Kruk would want to know what I now knew. What I should have done when I left The Kitten Club was to walk down two blocks to police headquarters and leave Detective Kruk one hell of a message. An early Christmas gift.

That's not what I did. I found a pay phone and called Jimmy's Cabs. The dispatcher told me that she had a couple of cabs idling down at the harbor and that she'd send one up to me. Several minutes later a powder blue car pulled up to the curb. I got in.

"Homeland," I said to the driver. I gave him Ann Kingman's address.

It was too late to be calling on people unannounced, but there was nothing I could do about that. I'm aware that I'm repeating myself, but the thought occurred to me twice; once when I gave the cabby the address and again when he pulled up in front of the darkened house. We had passed midnight on the way over.

"Wait until you actually see me go inside," I instructed the cabby. "Then you can go." I gave him enough money to cover an extra ten minutes past what the meter was reading. I figured it could take that long to wake Ann Kingman and to convince her to let me inside for a little chat.

It took much less than ten minutes. Ann Kingman came to the door only a few minutes after I pummeled the mallard.

"Sorry to disturb you so late," I said.

"No you're not."

"Can I come in?"

She gave me a frank look. "Are you going to give me one good reason why I should? The last time you came in here you accused me of being a murderer."

"That won't happen again, I promise."

She wasn't convinced. "It's late. Why don't you—"

I slammed my hand against the door before she could shut it.

"It's me or the police, Ann."

"Don't threaten me, young man."

"Look, I'm about to collapse, okay?" I indicated my bum leg. "I wouldn't be in this condition if it weren't for your husband."

Despite herself, she smiled, albeit grimly. "Wasn't he a sweetheart?" She paused. "Oh what the hell."

She pulled the door open wide. I waved off the cabby. He flashed his headlights and pulled away. I followed Mrs. Kingman into the house. She was wearing a quilted bathrobe and slippers. But she didn't look like someone who had just been woken up.

"I've been up reading," she said to me as if she had intercepted my thoughts.

"Anything good?"

She was leading me into the living room. She stopped, her hand on a wall switch, and gave me a sour look. "You've come all the way out here in the middle of the night to hear a book review?"

She hit the wall switch and a row of track lighting over the fireplace lit up. She turned a knob and dimmed the lights.

"Can I get you anything to drink?" she asked, starting for

the liquor cabinet. A mirthless chuckle followed. "We've already done this once today, haven't we?"

"We have." Just to break up the pattern, I stepped over to the couch and sat down there. "I'll take a brandy if you have it," I said. I wanted something abrasive yet warm. Come to think of it, I often want something abrasive yet warm.

"I do," she said, and she pulled out a bottle and two small-globed glasses. "I'll join you." She poured out the drinks, brought mine over to me and retreated to the chair where I had sat earlier in the day. A day that was feeling to me about a week old at this point. I knew that when exhaustion finally hit me, it was going to hit hard. I could feel it beginning to creep up.

"Just to answer your question about the book I was reading, I can't even tell you if it is any good. I'm just using it to try to put me to sleep. I haven't slept well ever since Richard's funeral." She raised her glass in a toast. "I'm sure you understand." We both took a sip of our brandies. Mine could have stood to be a tad rougher. Mrs. Kingman's sent a flash of red across her face. She set the glass down on the table next to her and folded her hands on her lap.

"Daniel Kingman had nothing to do with Helen Waggoner's murder," I said.

"Daniel? Of course he didn't."

"You knew that already when I was here this morning, didn't you?"

She dipped her chin, almost imperceptibly.

"But you let me think he was responsible."

"If you recall, Mr. Sewell, you were pointing the finger at me and at Daniel. You don't know me too well. So, perhaps I should tell you. I am an extremely precise person. I had nothing to do with the murder of that girl. That's really all that I told you."

"You implied that it was Daniel Kingman," I said again.

"I don't happen to know for a fact that Daniel isn't responsible. Though I seriously doubt it. Daniel was very quick to run to me and warn me that Richard was fathering a child with this Helen woman and that I had better prepare myself for the likelihood that he was planning to leave me. But I never suspected Daniel of seeking such a nasty revenge. What would be the point, after all?"

"Exactly. Or should I say, precisely. What would be the point?"

I took another sip of my brandy. The fatigue that had been waiting in the wings all of this long, long day was indeed finally gearing up for its attack. I could feel the troops moving into place and taking up position.

"Let me ask you outright. Do you know who is responsible for the killing of Helen Waggoner?"

"Ultimately, Richard."

"I don't mean ultimately, and you know it."

"You're going to believe me if I answer?"

"Yes, I am. I've defended your credibility once already today."

"How chivalrous. You don't even know me."

"I realize that. And you can lie through your teeth to me and make it sound legit. I have no doubt about that. But if I didn't think I had at least a shot at hearing the truth from you I wouldn't have come all the way out here, would I?"

"Is that supposed to guilt me into telling you the truth? I could cover your cab fare and tell you to get the hell out of my home immediately. We don't have to be having this discussion."

"You didn't have to let me in in the first place."

"True."

"Besides, you can't sleep anyway. Why not chew the fat with your friendly neighborhood undertaker for awhile?"

"Why not indeed."

"So?"

Ann Kingman stood up from the chair and went over to a desk that stood in the corner. One of those antique desks whose angled front folds down to become the desktop. She brought the desktop into place and reached into a small cabinet drawer. I couldn't tell what she was fetching until she turned back around and returned to her chair and sat down. She set a small silver pistol on the table beside her, next to her brandy glass. She crossed her hands again onto her lap.

"So."

Even if I had wanted to act quickly, I couldn't have. The marshaled troops of fatigue had begun their march. Besides which, even at full speed the distance between the couch and the chair where Ann Kingman sat was too great. All I would have accomplished in lunging forward would be to give her a larger target. And the distance to the doorway was even greater. My back is large. Hard to miss at that range. The woman had me neatly pinned down. And we both knew it.

"That's not the gun that was used to kill Helen Waggoner," I said.

"No, it's not. At least . . . to be precise, to the best of my knowledge it's not."

"Trust me. It isn't."

"You say that with some sense of authority, Mr. Sewell."

"Helen Waggoner was killed by a professional. Or at the very least, a semiprofessional. I'm not very well versed in this, but I don't think professionals use popguns like that."

"You think this is a 'popgun?' I've fired this pistol, Mr. Sewell. There were a spate of break-ins several years ago, here and in Guilford. Richard bought this pistol for me. For my safety. He was, after all, out of the house quite a lot. I took lessons in how to shoot it."

"You aim it and pull the trigger. Right?"

"That's pretty much it."

"Are you expecting a break-in tonight, Mrs. Kingman?"

"Call me Ann."

"Whatever you say, lady. You're the one with the gun."

"I'm not expecting a break-in. However, a man I barely know *has* showed up at my door in the middle of the night demanding to be let in."

"You sound as if you're practicing your lines."

Her hand reached over to the table. She picked up her brandy glass. "I hope I'm not."

"Look. Ann. This is all getting too arch for me. You're not going to shoot me for no good reason, are you?"

"Now *you're* the one being precise. No. I'm not going to shoot you for no good reason. All you have to do is convince me that I have no good reason, and that will be that."

Several advancing snipers within me were squeezing off shots. The brandy had been a mistake. I felt as if my blood was being rapidly replaced with sludge. It might be hard to imagine a man yawning while a woman in the same room has a pistol sitting next to her. But I did.

"Who do *you* think killed that woman, Mr. Sewell?"

"A hired killer."

"And who do you think hired him?"

"Michael Fenwick."

"That's what I think too."

"And I think the same guy came around a few days later and killed Fenwick along with his wife, who had the great misfortune of being at his side at the time."

The woman nodded. "But you think even more than that, don't you?"

"Yes I do." That's when my increasingly sluggish brain finally guessed at the reason for Ann Kingman's having introduced a pistol into our little talk.

"What is it that you think?" she asked.

"You're a fiercely protective mother lion, aren't you, Ann?"

"The mistake was mine. I should never have told Jeffrey

about that girl. I mean, that she was pregnant. Or that Richard was going to leave me. That was my mistake.

"I never expected him to get so incensed. Yes, I *am* a fiercely protective mother lion, as you put it. And Jeffrey is a fiercely loyal son. Loyal to his mother anyway. Jeffrey has always been at war with his father. Richard could make himself very easy to hate. Trust me on that. Jeffrey was somewhat like his uncle in that regard. Except that Jeffrey has a lot more fire in him than Daniel. A lot more anger. I told him what Daniel had told me, and he went . . . well, berserk. I tried to rein him in but he was absolutely furious with his father. Jeffrey has known in the past about some of his father's little affairs. But it was the idea that Richard would actually leave me this time, that he would do that to me, throw it in my face, make such a public mess. That's what Jeffrey could not abide. I wouldn't tell him the name of the woman. I wasn't sure what he would do. But he got it out of his uncle easily enough. Jeffrey told me that he tracked the woman down and demanded that she abort that child and that she have nothing else whatever to do with his father. I gather she laughed in his face."

"In fact, she slapped his face."

Ann Kingman raised an eyebrow. "Is that so? Jeffrey didn't tell me that."

"Did he tell you that he planned to have her killed?" Ann said nothing. "I don't know about you, but that seems to me to be an awfully drastic reaction to a little slap."

"Please don't be cute, Mr. Sewell."

"So he did tell you."

"I have had no discussion with my son on the matter."

"Do you really expect me to believe that?"

"Frankly I don't care what you believe. It happens to be the truth."

"Tell me this much. When Helen appeared at your husband's wake, did you know who she was?"

"Believe me, I was as shocked as anyone else when that happened. I didn't know for a fact that this was the woman. I had never seen her. I had no idea what she looked like. But I did know her name: Helen. And there it was, on that damned little name tag of hers. It was disgusting. The whole damned thing is disgusting."

"But, of course, Jeffrey had seen her. He had gone out to the place where she worked and tried to strong-arm her for you. Are you trying to say that you didn't ask your son if this was the woman who your husband had been planning to leave you for?"

"I didn't have to. One look at Jeffrey's face and I knew."

"But you didn't *say* anything to him?"

"For one thing, Jeffrey wasn't in the car with us coming home. He was following in his own car. I rode with Joan and the children. Lord . . . *that* one started to get hysterical. Joan. I thought I was going to have to smack her. Her *children* are in the car, for god's sake, and she's shrieking, 'Who was that woman! What's going on here?' I think I told you, Joan was daddy's little girl."

"You did."

"Yes. Well, she didn't take too terribly kindly to this . . . *person* ruining her daddy's wake. I finally had to yell at her to shut her up. I told her that this woman had nothing to do with us and that was the end of it."

"She believed you?"

"She settled down. We agreed that the smart thing was to call our lawyer. Joan was concerned anyway when Michael hadn't made an appearance at Richard's wake. That surprised me as well. It turns out he was in some sort of accident on the way there. The roads were horrible, if you recall."

"So you phoned him?"

"Joan did on her cell phone. Michael was at Mercy Hospital. He got to the house not long after we did. Jeffrey was a mess by then. Michael had us all gather here, in the living room. Minus Joan's children, of course. He sat right where I'm sitting now. He said that the smartest and the safest thing to do at the moment was to remain completely silent on the matter of that woman. He made no implications. Michael was a smart young man. He simply said that we clearly had an un-usual situation here, and for the time being, as our lawyer and a concerned family friend, he insisted that we not discuss the matter, not even amongst each other. On that point he was adamant. He reminded us that there was the likelihood of a trial somewhere down the road. He said it quite plainly. 'You cannot testify to something that you did not hear.'"

"He was telling you that the persons responsible for Helen's murder were right in this room."

"Michael was setting the agenda. He implored us not to discuss the matter. And I took his counsel. As have the rest of my family. Believe that or not."

I was shaking my head. "Ann . . . You're asking me to be-lieve that because your lawyer told you to stick a gag order on this thing, that you didn't discuss it with your family?"

"I did discuss it with Daniel. Once. That's true."

"But not with *Jeffrey*? Not with your daughter?"

"Joan and I could not pass two words in a week and neither would be the sadder."

"But Jeffrey, Ann. No disrespect here, but this guy's a mama's boy. Right?"

"I told Jeffrey that I was going to obey Michael's request, and that I wanted him to do so as well."

"And the obedient boy clammed up."

"I would appreciate your not running down my son in my own house, Mr. Sewell."

"But you suspected him of being involved in Helen's mur-der. Come on now. This is ridiculous."

"Mr. Sewell." She sighed. "Of course I did. It took me a little while to put it together that Jeffrey must have requested Michael's help in finding someone who would . . . do that. It wasn't until Michael was killed that I figured that part out. I was in a bit of a daze right after the funeral." She picked up her brandy glass. "I deliberately put myself in one, if you must know. It's been easier that way."

"Sorry to be the one to sober you up."

"Don't be."

I wasn't touching any more of the woman's brandy tonight. The order had now been given, and the fatigue troops were firing away. Ann Kingman could see that I was struggling to stay alert.

"I've been worried about Jeffrey ever since Michael was murdered. I don't understand what's going on."

"Why haven't you just asked your son?"

"I have. I asked him to tell me what he knew about this girl's murder. He said he knew nothing."

"He lied to you."

"He's protecting me."

"Fiercely loyal little cub."

"Jeffrey's not a cub, Mr. Sewell."

"He's guilty of murder. I don't really care what you call him."

Ann Kingman picked up the pistol and bounced it in her palm, as if testing its weight.

"You weren't supposed to say that."

"*You're* loyal. But you're not stupid. You don't think the police are going to piece this together?"

"You came over in the middle of the night. Stinking of brandy." She smiled when she said that. "You've come around several times since the funeral. Neighbors spotted you out at the park just a few days ago. You were here earlier today. In your hearse. Don't think that didn't draw some attention. Perhaps I had a sense that you were stalking me for some reason? Then tonight you forced your way in. A woman has the right to defend herself."

"You've been reading too many cheap mysteries."

"I told you, I can't sleep."

Sleep. The very sound of the word was acting as a narcotic. Ann Kingman was growing blurry. Even the light that was catching the silver pistol, as she bounced the little gun in her hand, was blurring. I was dropping off. I suppose this might sound peculiar to some people. Not to me. I'm a person who regularly falls asleep in the dentist's chair. Maybe it's a denial response, who knows. Whatever the case, the full-scale assault was on, and the last thing I remember was blinking slowly and leadenly, the woman in front of me with the pistol fading out more and more with each slow blink . . . until finally . . . she was gone.

CHAPTER
25

The cushions on the Kingmans' couch had slipcovers on them, somewhat like envelopes with flaps, held in place with large plastic buttons. I awoke with my cheek pressed into one of these buttons. I was alone in the living room. It was daylight. A light snow was falling outside. I rolled to an upright position. I picked up the high school photo of Jeffrey Kingman from the nearby end table and squinted at the sliver of my reflection afforded by the gold frame. The plastic button had left a perfect impression of itself on my cheek. I tilted the frame to have a look at my morning hair and my whiskers. I was lovely to look at, no two ways around it.

The smell of freshly brewed coffee came into the room, followed by Ann Kingman. She was out of her robe now and was dressed in slacks and a sweater. There was no pistol in sight.

"Good morning." She sounded pleasant enough.

"You didn't shoot me."

"That's correct. Would you care for some coffee?"

The inside of my head felt as messed up and gone-to-hell as the outside looked. A hot cup of joe seemed like just the glue to start putting the pieces back together. I followed Ann King-man into the kitchen. It was large and clean and modern and had a little breakfast nook—an add-on—jutting out into the backyard. We took our coffee there, on a linoleum table, surrounded on three sides by ceiling to floor glass. The coffee traveled all the way to my toes. It was so good I could have kissed the chef, except that she had been holding a gun on me just several hours previous. I held the mug just under my chin and took in the steam.

"How are you feeling? You dropped off like a rock."

"I had a long day yesterday," I said. "I'm coming back to life. What time is it, anyway?"

"A little past ten."

I had no clue if I was supposed to be somewhere or not. My head wasn't up to speed yet for that sort of thing. I took another few sips of coffee and looked out at the snow coming down. It was a real snowfall, not just a passing flurry. It was sticking. I heard a little voice within me praying that Bonnie had called for snow in her last forecast. The poor woman needed a break. I was feeling very paternal toward Bonnie Nash. Which suggested to me that I was adjusting to the new distance that I gathered had started to grow between us. Sometimes you can just feel these things. I was feeling it.

"I've phoned Jeffrey," Ann Kingman said, interrupting my reverie. "I told him you were making some accusations and I needed him right away. He should be here any minute."

"Was that such a wise thing to do?"

"You said it yourself last night. If you've figured it out, the police can't be far behind. I want to stay out ahead of this thing."

I didn't quite like the sound of that. "What exactly does that mean?"

Ann Kingman was looking up at the snow falling and melting on the glass overhead. She aimed her answer in its direction. "I don't want my son to go to jail. It seems so . . . It serves no purpose."

"A woman was killed," I reminded her.

"Jeffrey didn't shoot her."

"He's responsible."

She quit her snowflakes and looked over at me. It wasn't a friendly look. "I said this to you already last night. Ultimately, Richard is responsible. He started this whole mess in the first place. Richard is now dead. So is Michael. And Sheila, poor girl. That's three deaths for one. What practical purpose does it serve to drag Jeffrey into this? Or to throw him in jail?"

"The law isn't about 'practical purposes,' " I said. "People who go around arranging murders are supposed to be hauled in for it."

"Please. My son doesn't 'go around arranging murders.' You can rest assured that he won't do something like this again."

"Am I supposed to tell that to Helen Waggoner's sister? The boy is sorry? His mother promises he won't do this sort of thing ever again?"

"I don't know a thing about any sister. It's none of my concern what you tell her so long as you leave Jeffrey's name out of it. Tell her that the man who arranged for her sister's murder is dead. That is the truth. What more does she want for crying out loud?"

I set down my mug and glared at her. "Mrs. Kingman. Ann. *Lady*. I don't like you very much."

"I'll survive your disdain, I'm sure."

She got up and took my mug over to the counter to freshen it. Impeccable hostess skills. Shabby values.

"Since you chose not to shoot me—for which, by the way, I am eternally grateful—what do you propose to do about me? I'm a blabbermouth, I'm telling you that right now."

"We'll talk about that once Jeffrey gets here. It's his decision ultimately, after all."

"Correction. It's mine."

"We'll wait."

We did. Call me crazy, but I just didn't see the Kingman clan deciding that the best course of action here was to follow one extremely ill-considered homicide with another. I felt safe enough. Besides, I was bushed.

It occurred to me that almost lost in all of this was the actual triggerman himself. I was nearly positive that it was the fellow Misty had described for me, the fellow she knew only as "Bob." It appeared that this Bob character had swung by The Kitten Club either right before or right after killing Helen and had kicked old Popeye around the office for one reason or another. Michael Fenwick had also hustled his way down to the strip joint at some point later that same evening and had similarly pitched a fit with the club owner. A good lawyer will fight for his client. A foolhardy—and overly loyal—one will go too far, fight too much. This appeared to be the cut of young Fenwick's cloth. As for the fear that Ann Kingman had stated about her son's safety, especially in light of Fenwick's murder, it dawned on me that she had little to worry about. My guess was that Jeffrey Kingman had several layers buffering him from the ubiquitous Bob. There was Michael Fenwick, and there was Popeye. Both dead now. Both unable to give out Jeffrey's name to the hired killer, presuming that he had even wanted it anyway. Which I had to doubt. I had a hunch that Popeye himself had never known the identity of the man who asked Fenwick to go out and hire a killer for him. Of course that did nothing to explain how it was that Bob decided to dump his cargo off on the front steps of my funeral home. I still had to work on that. But Jeffrey Kingman was—it would seem—practically in the clear. He could walk right past hit man Bob and neither of the two would even be aware of just how much blood they shared. I decided not to share this theory with Ann Kingman. If she thought her son was in danger of being knocked off by Bob, so be it. Let the woman shake.

A half hour passed, and Jeffrey didn't show. His mother's face could have passed for a clock. With each passing minute that her son didn't show, her expression darkened and the lines around her eyes and her mouth grew deeper. We fell out of conversation and sat waiting. The wind had picked up and shifted the snowfall into a slant. The snow was coming down harder now, the flakes larger and more wet. They were hitting the glass of the breakfast nook with the occasional *splat*, and breaking into icy bits which slid slowly down the glass. Ann Kingman was getting worried. Maybe her son wasn't as dutiful as she had thought. Maybe he had panicked. Maybe he was heading for the hills.

We both jumped when the phone rang. Ann jumped higher than I. It had been forty minutes since she had told me that Jeffrey would be here "any minute." She got to the phone before the second ring.

"Hello? . . . Yes it is."

I happened to glance out at the backyard before looking over at the counter where Ann Kingman was standing with the receiver to her ear. Two things hit me at exactly the same time. One was that the woman's skin had gone every bit as white as the snow that was covering her spacious backyard. The other thing that hit me was that she was holding the phone just the way that a person might who was holding a gun to their head and about to pull the trigger. It must have been her expression more than the actual pose that triggered the image. She was standing there in a silent scream. Eyes wide, mouth open, no sound coming out. I stood up. She turned her head, letting the arm holding the receiver drop to her waist.

"It's Jeffrey," she said to the large kitchen. "He's dead."

CHAPTER
26

I never actually saw what remained of the car that my parents had been driving on their way to the hospital when they met—squarely—with the unsuspecting beer truck at the intersection of Broadway and Eastern Avenue. Certainly I wasn't present when they were pulled from the wreckage and rushed up the street to Hopkins, where they were pronounced dead, dead and forevermore, dead. I was never given the choice. I had just been dropped off at Aunt Billie's and ugly Uncle Stu's after a family outing at the B&O Railroad Roundhouse Museum over on Eutaw Street. My mother had started cramping in the middle of a laughing fit that was brought on by a little prank she and I had just pulled inside one of the vintage trains in the huge roundhouse. Dropping me off on the way to the hospital had been a last minute decision so I could tell my aunt and uncle that the big moment had arrived. We were to hop in a cab and join up with my father at the hospital. Ugly Uncle Stu had already purchased a box of pink cigars and a box of blue ones. That was how I told them that my mother had gone into labor. I rushed up to their apartment and grabbed up the two boxes from the sideboard by the front door. "Guess what!" Later on, there were some who would try to placate me by telling me how lucky I had been not to have been in the car when it veered—for reasons no one who knew would live to explain—into the path of the oncoming beer truck. This little logistical tidbit was supposed to make me feel better, but, of course, it didn't even come close. I had a little logistical tidbit that I could throw right back at them. If my parents hadn't taken the time to drop me off in the first place, we'd have all been safely through the intersection of Broadway and Eastern a full five minutes before the fateful beer truck even appeared on the scene. Looked at through *that* lens, dropping me off to deliver the good news set the stage for the onset, just a few short minutes later, of the worst news of my life.

I stood next to the tow truck as the signal was given by the men down below the bridge to let her rip. Wooden blocks had been wedged in behind the rear tires of the truck but even so, the chassis rose up like a stretching cat as soon as the cable went taut. Extra time had been taken when the truck first arrived to clear away the snow and chip away the thin layer of ice that had formed on the roadway, all this to give the truck as much traction as possible. Still, the big truck slid several inches closer to the embankment as the cable tightened around its metal spool and began slowly cranking. Several men down below were working their way up the hill alongside the broken car. They couldn't exactly guide the thing—it weighed some several thousand pounds—but they each kept a gloved hand on the side of the car nonetheless, as if they were comforting a large animal being helped by Samaritans out of a ditch into which it had fallen. Like I said, the procedure was taking a while. Nobody was really in any great hurry. The car had skidded off the road, broke through the bridge's old stone guardrail and plunged into the Jones Falls tributary leading out from Lake Roland several hundred feet away. The person behind the wheel had been removed already and taken to the Greater Baltimore Medical Center, where he had been pronounced dead. His mother had been called. She had been waiting for her son, sharing coffee in her kitchen with, of all people, an undertaker. There are those, I'm sure, who would find that detail creepy. Frankly, I'm one of them.

Of course, it was considered an accident. The snow was fresh and wet. The road surface was pure ice. The county's salt trucks—ironically, housed less than a mile away from the scene of the accident—had not yet iced the Falls Road bridge. They usually get to it last, just before the trucks pull in to load up on more salt.

Nobody considered that the driver of the car might have been going too fast on purpose. Or that he might have suddenly jerked the steering wheel as he hit the crest of the bridge. The word "suicide" never entered the picture. Or rather, "self-homicide." If there was an explanation for the car going off the Falls Road bridge—other than the obvious assumption of snow and ice and tragic carelessness—no one lived to explain it.

After watching Jeffrey Kingman's car get dragged up the incline and loaded onto the flatbed of the tow truck, I returned home—after asking my cabby to swing by a bank machine; this taxi-taking lifestyle was killing me—and took a long, hot, painful shower. Billie phoned to tell me that Ann Kingman wanted us to handle the funeral of her son. It seemed awfully perverse to me until Billie added that Mrs. Kingman had said something to the effect of wanting some "continuity" and "closure" in the matter of laying to rest both her husband and her son. Billie said that Ann Kingman had instructed the hospital to contact Sewell & Sons to come pick up Jeffrey's body as soon as it was released. Billie had already contacted Sam. I told her that I really didn't want to handle this one. I murmured something about my injuries. Billie sensed something in my tone, I'm sure. She volunteered to handle the Kingman funeral. No cribbage on this one. I thanked her and hung up.

I phoned Bonnie at the station. I knew that she'd be at work. The weather slot gets shoved right to the top of the broadcast at the slightest hint of accumulation. The snow had not let up all morning and was now an official "weather emergency." After being put on hold for ten minutes, Bonnie came on to tell me that she really had no time to talk.

"It's Jeffrey Kingman," I blurted. "Now *he's* dead. His car went off a bridge."

"Hitch, I really can't talk right now. Have you looked out the window?"

"It's snowing," I said blandly.

"Damn right its snowing. And guess who called it *perfectly*? I've really got to run. I'm coordinating a thousand things at once."

"But, Bonnie, it's all coming out. Jeffrey Kingman hired someone to kill Helen. Someone went on a virtual killing spree afterward."

"Call Jay. He'll know what to do. He can coordinate. I've got to go." She hung up.

I did what she bid. I called Jay Adams at the Sunpapers. Why not? Adams was at his desk. I guess a couple of flakes of snow hadn't sent the reporter dashing off in a hundred directions at once. I was glad to see someone was showing some perspective.

"Jay? Hitchcock Sewell. Bonnie's all tied up with the blizzard of the century. I thought maybe you and I could take the opportunity to fight to the death. Plus, I've got some information for you."

"Where and when?"

"Do you know the Screaming Oyster Saloon?"

"I do."

"Meet me there . . . in an hour. Can you do that?"

"Do I bring my own weapons or are they being provided?"

As much as I didn't like the guy, I liked the question. "On the house," I said, and I hung up the phone.

The last call I needed to make was to Vickie Waggoner. With the big snowstorm, "paralyzing" the area, I was pretty certain that school would have been canceled, especially farther out in the county. I pictured Vickie sitting in her living room looking out at the snow coming down. I thought of Bo. Maybe she and the boy were outside playing; maybe she was showing her nephew how to build a snowman. Did she really need the phone to ring and have it be me bringing her snow day to a grinding halt with the details of just how purposeless and callow the decision to kill her sister had been? I couldn't even bring Helen's killer in front of her and say, "Him. He did it." I also couldn't present her with Jeffrey Kingman. The junior Kingman had either hit an ice patch as he was rushing in his car to see what his mother needed him for right away, or he had instinctively known that the game was up and had gone ahead and hit the gas as he reached the highest point of the Falls Road bridge. Nobody would ever know. Either way, Jeffrey Kingman was dead. But if I was guessing correctly about Vickie Waggoner, I doubted that she would be finding much solace in that fact.

I didn't call her. I picked up the phone three times, and three times I set it back down.

An hour later, just before I was about to leave to go meet up with Jay Adams, I finally picked up the phone and dialed. Vickie answered on the fifth or sixth ring. She was out of breath. I cringed inwardly when she said that she had been out back with Bo, building an igloo.

"You should hear him try to say 'igloo.' He's so cute."

"Igloo," I repeated. I couldn't think of a single thing to say. I shouldn't have called. I knew it immediately.

"Hitch, are you okay?"

"I'm fine."

"How are you feeling?" It took me a moment to realize that she was referring to my injuries. It came back to me, the image of Vickie seated at my hospital bedside, facedown, sharing a corner of my pillow, fast asleep. It seemed like centuries ago.

"I'm fine," I said again. "Much better. A little banged up, but . . . I'm fine."

There was a pause on the other end of the line. "You sound strange," she said.

"I've got some news."

"News?"

"About Helen. I have the whole story, Vickie. At least as much of it as I think we're ever going to know."

She didn't say a word for about twenty seconds, maybe longer. When she did speak, it was to Bo. Something about his boots. I think she had lowered the phone to speak to the boy.

"Hitch, I'd like to hear it," she said back into the phone.

"I'm about to run out to meet up with someone," I said. "I don't want to do this over the phone."

"Neither do I. I can come over."

"No. Don't do that. The snow and . . . you've got the kid. Don't go driving in this mess. Please."

"When will you be back?"

"I'm not sure. I'm meeting a guy right down the street. I'll call you when I get back in. How's that? I'll come out."

"Do that. But call first," she said. "And Hitch?"

"Yes."

"Never mind. I'll be here. Call me as soon as you get back."

We hung up. I got into my foul weather gear and went out

into the foul weather. I was in a foul mood as well. And I had no gear for that.

Jay Adams was already at the bar when I arrived. So was Julia. She was behind the bar. My spirits soared at the sight of my former bride. Adams, of course, couldn't keep his eyes off her, though he was doing his best to be discreet about it. Trying for a peripheral ogle. Most men just sit and stare. The reporter got a few points in my book simply for his efforts.

I hopped onto the stool next to him and jerked a thumb in Julia's direction.

"That one? I threw her back."

Adams took the opportunity to turn his head and give a full frontal stare to the lady behind the bar.

"You should seek professional help."

Julia came over to us, walking cowboy-style. She whipped her dishcloth at the counter in front of me.

"What up?"

"What's he drinking, Agnes?" I asked.

"Him?" Julia gave Jay Adams her slow-motion smile. "You can't touch what he's drinking, Mister. Tell you what. I'll give you some milk, and I'll put it in a dirty glass for you. How's that?"

I picked up Adams's glass and sniffed it.

"What *is* that?"

Adams answered, "Seltzer."

"And?"

"And ice."

Julia reacted as if a shiver had just gone down her spine. "Ice. On a day like this. You see? I tried to warn you what you were up against."

"Thank you, Gerty. How about a simple old-fashioned beer."

"If you say." She grabbed a glass and stuck it under a draught spout. "I prefer Agnes."

"I prefer Julia, but I don't want to give this guy any inside information. He's a professional snoop as it is."

Julia overpoured my beer and then sipped it down a half inch before setting it down in front of me. She got a beer foam mustache.

"We were married once," she explained to Adams, licking the foam away. "But correction. He didn't throw me back."

"It was mutual," I agreed.

Julia grinned her best grin. "Would you boys like any nuts?"

"Don't answer that," I said to Adams. "It's a trick question."

Julia sighed. "Ho-hum." Then she moved off down the bar to torture someone else.

"She's beautiful," Adams said.

"Even a blind man can see that." I took a sip of my beer. "Okay, let's get to it. You're the expert here. Or so Bonnie keeps telling me. I'm going to tell you what I've got, and then you can tell me what I've got. How's that sound?"

"Fire when ready."

I gave the reporter the entire enchilada. Some of it he knew already, due to his own sleuthing as well as Bonnie's periodic updates to him. But a lot of it was fresh, and he listened with the placid eagerness of a hungry person who waits patiently for all of the dishes to be set down on the table before commencing to gorge. I told him how a surly creep known to me only as "Bob" showed up in a foul mood at The Kitten Club the night of Helen Waggoner's murder and proceeded to use the club's owner as a punching bag. I told him how, sometime later, Michael Fenwick had also showed up at The Kitten Club in a highly agitated state. Clearly *something* had gone awry that evening. And whatever it was, Popeye was taking the brunt of it. The fact that both Popeye and Fenwick were murdered within the next week, both by the same gunman—almost certainly Mr. Bob—seemed to confirm that whatever it was that went awry, Bob wasn't going to stand for it. Locating Bob would be the only way of discovering what the problem had been. On that count, I told the reporter, I had no leads and no intention of looking for any. Kruk's warning that I stop making myself an easy target for a killer was finally taking hold. I was ready to cash in my chips.

I saved my last piece of information, well . . . for last, where it belonged. I told Adams about Jeffrey Kingman. I told him about the man's lifelong disdain for his father. I explained how the younger Kingman had pitched a fit when his mother confided to him the latest exploits of his father, and how Jeffrey had gone out to Sinbad's Cave to try and do a number on Helen Waggoner, to try to coerce her to abort the child she was carrying and to just disappear into the sunset.

"Clearly he didn't know Helen," I said. "I've gotten a pretty good portrait this past week. This is not a woman who would take kindly to this sort of crap. The *last* thing she would have done would have been to fold her tent and slink away."

I finished off my beer. The devilish angel behind the bar drifted over to see to our liquid needs.

"How about you?" she said to Adams. "Are you ready for a refill?"

He was, and Julia filled his glass from a nozzle. Her eyes traveled back and forth between Adams and myself as the glass filled.

"Is everyone having fun?" she asked.

"Where are Sally and Frank anyway?" I asked. "What puts you behind the bar?'

"Daddy hurt his back shoveling the snow. Sal has a cold. Daughter to the rescue. Will that be all, gentlemen?"

Adams picked up his glass, gave a terse nod to Julia and sipped. "You pull a mean seltzer."

Julia had him in her pocket. "Thank you, sir. Let me top

you." The reporter set his glass back on the counter. Julia fired two quick shots into it, taking it right to the very rim.

"You gentlemen need anything else, just call. I'll runneth over."

After she left, I asked Adams what was up with the seltzer. "Is it a no drinking on duty thing?"

"It's a no drinking period thing."

"You no like?"

"I love. I no stop."

"I see," I said. "I'm sorry."

He waved it off. "Forget it. Turns out I enjoy actually recalling whatever it was I was doing the night before. I'm fine with it now. Salut." He tapped his glass against mine.

"Tell me about you and Bonnie," I said.

He met me with a simple and unthreatening refusal in his almond-shaped eyes. "Finish your story."

I did. I drained half my beer and then finished off the story.

"Jeffrey Kingman and Michael Fenwick went to college together. Constance Bell told me. Old buddies. It was Jeffrey who connected Fenwick's firm with his father. That's the link. As I see it, Jeffrey Kingman's fuse lit after Helen slapped him in the bar and told him to mind his own goddamn business. Here was his father in the ultimate screw over of his mother and, for that matter, the rest of the family. Dumping Mom for this saucy waitress. I can't know it exactly, but my guess is that when Richard Kingman keeled over in the middle of the operating room, that spun it for Jeffrey. Michael Fenwick was his good friend. Fenwick must have told Jeffrey about the change in the will, about Kingman carving up the pie in a new way to include Helen Waggoner. I have no idea how Jeffrey talked Fenwick into it. The way I see it, he asked Fenwick, being a lawyer and all that good stuff, if he maybe knew how to get ahold of the kind of person who would take care of a little unseemly business in an unseemly fashion. For a nice nickel, of course."

"I'm sure. Maybe Fenwick was getting a piece of that action, who knows?"

"Have you learned anything about Fenwick in your snooping that suggests the guy maybe didn't always play it straight?"

"Reporting," Adams said.

"What about it?"

"That's what it's called. It's not 'snooping.' "

"Is that what I said?"

"It's what you're always saying. I'm a reporter. I ask questions. I investigate."

"That's different from snooping?"

"I like to think so."

I tapped his glass with mine. "Well, Merry Christmas, Jay. I'll give it to you. In your *investigation*, did Fenwick come up stinky?"

"Inconclusive, I'm afraid. People I talked with called him ambitious. Not all of them said it in a complimentary tone. I think Fenwick was fine with stepping on toes when he had to. I gather he was gung ho to prove himself to the old man."

"So, it works for you then? The idea that Fenwick might be the type to . . . overexert himself?"

"Do something illegal?"

I placed the tip of my finger on the tip of my nose. Adams chuckled into his seltzer.

"I guess part of the irony here," I said, "was that Jeffrey was angling some of his inheritance from the old man to pay for knocking off the old man's lover, who I'm sure Jeffrey considered at that point nothing more than a gold digger and not at all deserving any of his daddy's money."

"So Jeffrey talks to Fenwick? Fenwick has some sort of connection with kindly old Popeye, and the hit gets set up?"

"I can go with that."

"And Bob's little tantrum the night of Helen's murder?"

"Something pissed him off."

"Money," Adams said. "When it's not sex, it's always money."

"That's my guess too. Maybe Popeye was siphoning off too much as the middle man and he got caught. I can see both Bob and Fenwick getting a little riled about that. Whatever the case, the bodies fell. And this morning, another one fell."

Adams showed the patience of Buddha as I took another sip of my beer. It was for dramatic effect, of course, though the instant I did it I felt like a heel.

"Jeffrey Kingman," I said. I told him about Kingman's car going off the Falls Road bridge and into a gully earlier that morning. "Maybe this guy Bob did have a number on Jeffrey, and Jeffrey knew that he was a goner. Or maybe guilt finally caught up with him. Or maybe it really was just plain old ice and a slightly pissed off God."

I finished off the rest of my beer and—a slave to cheap theatrics—landed the empty glass heavily on the bar.

"The end."

Adams didn't say anything for a full minute. His eyes traveled languidly around the bar, almost as if he were looking for the source of a leak or trying to determine an alternate way to get out of the place besides the front door. But I could tell that he wasn't noticing a thing about the bar. Not really. He was letting the details of my story sift into place. He was poking them and prodding them, sending them out into the air like they were paper airplanes and seeing just how well they flew. I didn't interrupt. After about a minute—maybe even longer (time in a dark bar, in the daytime, behaves mysteriously)—he turned back to his seltzer, pursed his lips and began shaking his head.

"Nada."

That's all he said. One word. Nada. I know that word. That's Spanish for "You ain't got shit, Buster Brown."

I protested, "What do you mean *nada*? Just exactly which part of it is nada to you?"

"Don't be offended, Hitch. It's a good story. You've really done the work on this one."

"So, what don't you like about it?"

"Oh, I like it. I actually think you've nailed it. The problem is, you can't prove any of it. You have nothing concrete to take to the police. It's a great story, and possibly an accurate one. But that's all it is, a story. A maybe. A what-if. In a word, nada."

"Christ, Adams, you sure know how to deflate a guy."

"I'm sorry. You asked me down here to give me your assessment. I like your conclusions. But they don't get you anywhere. Unless this Bob character surfaces and fills in the blanks, or confirms enough of your account, it's all speculation."

He picked up his glass. "But really, what's the difference? If you're right about all of this, most of the bad guys are dead anyway."

"But Bonnie has no story," I said. I must have sounded even less convincing than I thought. Either that or the reporter on the barstool next to me had a very well-tuned ear.

"You don't care about that," he said flatly.

"Says who?"

"Look, Hitch. You and Bonnie are none of my business."

"Like you and her are none of mine?"

He took a beat, then cracked a crooked smile. "It's all fucked up, isn't it? What's going on here."

"Yes, it is."

"Is this where we fight each other to the death? I recall that was part of your invitation."

"I don't think so," I said to the slender reporter. "I'd slaughter you."

"Don't be so certain."

"You mean you'd kick my bum leg?"

"I'd do what I have to do."

"Well, look, I suggest we remain civilized about the whole thing. It's an imperfect world and that's never going to change. So, there must be a reason. Why don't we just keep it at 'it's all fucked up,' and let it go at that."

We clinked glasses and toasted all things fucked up. Of course, my glass was already empty. But I suppose that's fitting for such a toast. Julia caught my eye, but I waved her off. After the long day I had had previous, I needed a little more clarity in this one. I decided that I'd take the oath. At least until sundown. Maybe the seltzer-sipping reporter was inspiring me.

Adams and I left the bar together. The show outside was spectacular, the snow was still coming down in large lacy flakes. Soft, white humps had appeared where once there had been cars. The red tug in the harbor wore a frosty beard on its bow, frosty eyebrows on its windows and a frosty tuft on its exhaust stack. Adams said that he was parked over on Bond Street. I was going in the opposite direction. He headed off. I considered making a snowball and beaning him in the back with it, just to seal our newfound truce. But I decided against it. I still wasn't quite sure what I felt about Bonnie and me. I decided it was better to reserve the right to dislike this guy all over again. He vanished in the snow.

I went directly to the funeral home. Jeffrey Kingman's body had already been released by the hospital, and Sam had picked it up. It was down in the basement. Aunt Billie was standing in the front hallway when I came in the front door, talking with Daniel Kingman. Until they invent a better description than "hangdog" to describe the kind of look that was on the obstetrician's face, that one will have to do. The two turned toward me as I came in.

"Hitchcock, I believe you know Dr. Kingman."

"Yes, I do." I took the baby doctor's hand and shook it.

Gently. There was nothing there. "I'm very sorry about your nephew," I said. "This is certainly the last thing that your family needs."

The obstetrician was there to handle the arrangements. I asked after his sister-in-law. "How is Mrs. Kingman holding up?"

"Ann? I . . . I can't honestly say. She phoned me at the office and asked if I would handle this for her. She said she really didn't want to talk about it."

"Did she say anything else?" I asked. I had the man's dreary eyes directly in mine. If he were lying, I'd know.

"Anything else?"

"Never mind." The image of the little silver pistol suddenly popped into my head. "Someone should be with her," I said. "It doesn't matter if she says she wants to be left alone. Someone should be there. What about the daughter?"

"I spoke briefly with Joan before I came down here," Kingman said. "Naturally she is devastated. Jeffrey was such a fine young man."

This was the wrong setting for me to argue the point. I let it pass.

"Someone should be with Mrs. Kingman," I said again. "You should call the daughter again." He saw in my eye that I was deadly serious about this.

"I'll call her."

I left the two of them to their funeral plans. Billie told me that she had already informed Pops. He and his happy crew would be out at the cemetery already, digging a hole in the snow. I went into my office and plopped down in my chair. Tahiti was sounding good about now. Sky and sea a matching blue. Maybe there was some sort of New Year's package to paradise that I could dig up at the last minute. I looked over at the Magritte. A sailboat on a lake. Sunshine. Sounded just perfect. I realized that the person I was envisioning lounging on the bow in my perfect Magritte vacation was not Bonnie; it was

Vickie Waggoner. I guess that pretty much told it. Like the wind they come, like the wind they go. And just how the hell is a person expected to hold on to the wind for very long anyway?

I came out of the office when I saw Daniel Kingman in the hallway, preparing to leave. He got into his overcoat as if it was made of lead.

"Is everything set?" I asked.

"Everything is in place," Billie said. She turned to Kingman. "Thank you for coming down in this weather, Dr. Kingman. I know this isn't easy."

He muttered something, I couldn't make it out. As the three of us turned to the front door, as if by magic, it opened. In stepped a hooded figure. It was Vickie.

"Hi. I know you said to wait for your call, but I got antsy." She stomped her feet against the rubber mat that Billie had set out. "Hello, Mrs. Sewell."

"Hello, dear. How are you?"

Vickie threw me a dark glance, then aimed a smile at my aunt. "I'm fine. Thank you." She pulled the hood down off her head.

"Miss Waggoner, this is Dr. Kingman," Billie said, making the introductions. Vickie freed her hand from its glove and extended it. The doctor was frozen in place, staring at Vickie as if she had two heads.

"I'm sorry . . . I . . ." he stammered. "I missed the name?"

"Victoria Waggoner," Vickie said.

"It's very nice to meet you, Miss Waggoner." Kingman was not quite on automatic pilot, but he was close. Belatedly he took her hand and shook it. He moved over to the door.

"You'll give me a call if you need anything, Dr. Kingman," Billie said to him. "Anything at all."

"Thank you," Kingman muttered. He looked back once more at Vickie, who was getting out of her coat.

"It was nice to meet you, Miss Waggoner," he said again.

Vickie looked up. "Thank you."

The doctor left. Billie closed the door behind him.

"The poor man is distraught," she said.

Vickie looked from Billie to me. "That was him, wasn't it? That was Helen's doctor."

"Why don't you come into my office," I said, putting a hand on her shoulder and turning her to the left. "I'll catch you up on everything."

CHAPTER
27

The storm had reached blizzard conditions. It was falling frantically, as if it couldn't come down fast enough; at the same time it was being wind-whipped in all directions at once, creating a virtual whiteout. Across the street, the baby Jesus was completely covered over. The wise men were knee deep. A snowplow moved past, all but invisible except for its blinking amber lights and the large yellow scraper, good for a momentary redistribution of the snow at best. Clearing was out of the question. For all practical purposes, the plow's tire tracks never even existed.

Billie, Vickie and I sat in Billie's living room upstairs, watching the storm. Well, Billie and I were watching it. A fire was going in the small fireplace. True to my oath, I had declined my aunt's offer of hot rum cider and was working on a mug of hot chocolate. I had dashed out into the snow after my talk with Vickie and fetched Alcatraz. He was curled up now in front of the fireplace. Vickie was on the floor next to him, her thoughts lost in the flames, her hand buried in the hound's multiple folds. Billie sat in her rocking chair, sipping her cider. Any minute now, Robert Frost was going to step gently into the room, whispering, *"Whose woods these are, I think I know . . ."*

Vickie had listened almost completely without comment to my account of her sister's murder. Only a few times had she halted me to clarify a point, for the most part she had taken in the information with a blank mask on her face. She was still wearing that mask. Though as I stole glances at her on the floor there next to my pooch, I could see in the flame's light dancing about her face that the mask had become heavy. Somber and wounded. I had made the mistake of telling her that Jeffrey Kingman's body was downstairs in the basement waiting for Billie to come down and take up her needles and tubes. Kingman was stretched out on the very table where Vickie had last seen her sister's body. Now the man responsible for putting Helen there was there himself. But, as I had predicted, the news that Jeffrey Kingman was dead had given Vickie no real satisfaction. Her motivation for wanting to learn the circumstances of her sister's murder had never been revenge. She had simply wanted an explanation. Vickie sat on the floor next to Alcatraz and continued to stare into the flames. Her family was gone, beaten up by cancer and by uncaring men. After I had explained everything to her down in my office, Vickie had asked if she could use my phone to call her neighbors. The kindly old folks were — again — looking after Bo. She dialed the number and asked if Bo could be put on the line. I'm assuming that he could. I don't really know. Vickie's expression didn't change one iota. The placid mask was in place. But tears had suddenly filled her eyes and immediately overflowed, running down her cheeks. She sat and cried, finally managing to whisper a few words into the phone — I missed what they were — before hanging up.

Billie was putting off going to work on Jeffrey Kingman until Vickie was gone. This was beginning to present a dilemma, for the storm had reached the point where going out into it in a car had become increasingly unwise. Nobody was saying anything yet, but it was becoming ever evident that Vickie was not going to be driving home anytime soon. Billie signaled me to join her in the kitchen where she told me that she would suggest to Vickie that she stay over.

"I can put her up in your old room," Billie suggested.

"What about Kingman? You need to get to work on him."

"I know. I thought that maybe the two of you could go out for a walk."

"In *that*?" I pointed at the window.

"It's only snow."

"And wind gusts up to a million."

"Why don't you take her over to the gallery and show her some of Julia's paintings?"

"You have funny ideas, old lady."

Vickie wasn't in the living room when I came back out of the kitchen. I assumed she had popped into the bathroom. I heard the phone ringing in my office downstairs. By the time I got there, the machine had picked up. I played back the message. It was Jay Adams.

"Call me as soon as you get this. I've got some information."

I dropped into my chair and dialed the number that Adams had given.

"Hitch, you got it wrong," he said the moment I identified myself.

"What do you mean?"

"I mean you got it wrong. I've been doing some digging since I got back to the office. You got it wrong, Hitch. But you were close. Listen."

Adams told me what he had uncovered—all from his desk at the Sunpapers, using the phone, the Internet and the paper's extensive archives. It was my turn to sit and listen, though unlike Vickie Waggoner I didn't take it all in silence. A few

"What?'s" and "Holy shit!'s" later and I hung up the phone. At almost the exact same time, I heard a scream from the basement. It was Vickie. The sound of feet running on stairs followed. A few seconds later, Aunt Billie came rushing into my office.

"Oh, Hitchcock! Come! Hurry!"

Do the math. When visibility is down to around a foot and the length of the hood of the car that you're driving—in this case, a hearse—is around eight feet, that leaves a good seven feet of hood and tires and engine pretty much just hanging out there somewhere in front of you, out of sight. The headlights were doing me no good, simply reflecting back into my face off the fuzzy wall of snow that appeared to be moving along at exactly the same speed as the car. Which was slow. I was creeping along on faith, somewhere between twenty and thirty miles an hour on an expressway that welcomes sixty and tolerates seventy. At the speed I was traveling, the trip took me nearly an hour door-to-door, as opposed to the twenty minutes it would have taken normally. With great relief, I finally pulled to the curb and shut off the engine.

"Are you sure you want to do this?" I asked Vickie, who was seated next to me. I leaned over and opened up the glove compartment and took out the pair of sunglasses Sam always keeps there.

"Yes."

"No police?"

"That's for later. I don't want any third parties. Not for this."

If the family was surprised to see me, they didn't show it. Joan Bennett answered my knock and stepped aside to let me in. She threw a confused look at the woman in the sun-glasses, then held out her hand to introduce herself.

"I'm Joan Bennett."

The hand floated there, untaken.

Marcus Bennett was sitting on the steps leading upstairs, his chin was in his hands. He appeared to be pouting. Joan Bennett breezed by me and stopped at the foot of the stairs.

"Marcus, you remember Mr. Sewell from the other day? And this is . . ."

She was fishing for my companion's identity. Her hook remained empty. "My friend," was all I said. Joan Bennett's mouth pinched in a little, then she led us into the living room. My glance went immediately to the table where only thirty-some hours previous had set a little silver pistol. It was gone now.

Ann and Daniel Kingman were seated together on the couch. Joan's husband—I had no memory of his name—was in the chair beside the pistol-less table. He stood up as the three of us entered the room.

"Russell, this is Mr. Sewell. You remember him from Daddy's funeral." The woman didn't even attempt a third shot at cadging Vickie's name. I stepped over and shook hands with Russell Bennett. The man was roughly my age, though on a faster track to middle age. A receding hairline, some puffiness already around the too-tight Brooks Brothers shirt collar, the slight whiff of bay rum. He reminded me a little bit of one of those guys in the sports bar in Towson, now congenially going to seed.

Daniel Kingman had risen as well, though somewhat slower than his nephew-in-law. I turned to him and surprised everyone in the room I'm sure with the glare that I put on him, accompanied by the raised index finger and the unequivocal "or else" in the tone of my voice. "You keep quiet."

He lowered back to the sofa. His eyes were wet and plead-

ing. But if the obstetrician was cowed, his niece was another
story.

"What is this all about? You can't just storm in here and order my uncle around like that!"

I wasn't looking at her, I was looking at Ann Kingman, who
hadn't said a word since I—correction, since *we*—had come
into her home. Our eyes met for just an instant and then she
turned to her daughter. "Sit down, Joan," she snapped. "Or
stand, I don't care which. But keep quiet."

Joan Bennett crossed her arms and scowled at me as she
stepped across the room. For a moment I thought she was going for the desk. But she stopped at the windows, turned to
face the room and leaned back against the windowsill. The
floor was mine.

I took Vickie by the arm and led her over to a small chair
against the wall by the living room entrance. The sunglasses
masked her true expression. But I had a pretty good guess. I
turned back to the others.

"I apologize for barging in like this. I know full well what a
horrible time this is for the family."

No one spoke. And then the ham began to rise up in me, I
couldn't help it. But also, I didn't try to stop it. The alternative
was pure anger, and I really didn't want to start breaking
things. I stepped into the middle of the floor, and clasped my
hands behind my back like an old-fashioned schoolteacher in
an old-fashioned movie. God help me, I even rocked on my
heels.

"So. Who here would like to take responsibility for the
murder of Helen Waggoner?"

Silence. No show of hands. No big surprise there. I turned
to Russell Bennett.

"Would you care to take responsibility, Russ?"

The man gave me an understandably contorted look.
"What the hell are you talking about?"

"I'll take that as a no," I said. I whipped around to face the couple on the couch. Two more guilty-looking visages—one angry, one depleted—I could not imagine.

"Ann? May I still call you Ann?"

"That is completely up to you."

"Ann. When your brother-in-law came to you several months ago with his gossip about your husband's most recent . . . misadventure, what was your first reaction? Your first thought."

"I don't recall," she said flatly.

"Was it that you wanted to strangle your husband's neck? After all the years and all of your forbearance, and here he was planning to have a child with his new, young chippy? Didn't that make you want to tear his eyes out?"

"The thought did cross my mind."

"Or maybe even shoot him with that little pistol of yours?"

"I lied to you," she said, smiling grimly. "I've never shot that gun."

"Did you think about it then?"

"Don't be absurd."

"Well, how about the girlfriend then? What about her? Did it cross your mind to take out some revenge on her? You couldn't have been too thrilled about this little development in your husband's life, could you?"

"No, I wasn't."

"Helen Waggoner. Your brother-in-law did give you the name, am I right?"

"Yes, he did."

"And did you pass it on to your son?"

"Why don't you come to the point?"

"I plan to. I'm coming to it. Now, you and I know that Jeffrey tracked down Helen where she worked and tried to dissuade her from this whole business, don't we? What did he tell you after he got back?"

"Nothing, really. Jeffrey told me that he had had a big fight with her, and that he thought she was cheap trash through and through. I told him that that didn't surprise me in the slightest. If you knew Richard—"

"Mother!"

Joan Bennett pushed away from the windowsill, then immediately sank back onto it. I kept my focus on Ann Kingman.

"Let me just ask you right out, Ann. Did you have anything to do with Helen's murder?"

"What do you think?"

"I think you didn't."

She didn't thank me. I hadn't expected her to. I shifted my attention to Daniel Kingman.

"You told me in your office yesterday that your brother had been . . . the word you used was 'prolific.' You suggested that over the years he has sent quite a number of women to you to 'take care of.' Any idea how many women that would be?"

"I couldn't say."

"Is that because you don't remember, or because you don't want to."

"Do we have to go into this?"

"Fine. Do you remember a time fairly long ago? I don't know, I think we're going back twenty-some odd years? Twenty-five, twenty-six? Do you recall helping your brother out way back then? Do you know what I'm talking about here, Dr. Kingman?"

"Yes."

"Help me out then. Was this the first time your brother had come to you for this kind of help? Or was it just the first time since he had been married?"

"What difference does it make?"

"You're right. I guess it doesn't. So now, what did you do? Did you do your big brother's bidding like a good boy?"

"You don't have to be snide," Ann Kingman snapped. "Stop dragging this out. You have something to say, then say it."

"Did you?" I asked again.

The obstetrician's voice was barely above a whisper. "No."

"What happened?"

He looked around at the others in the room, as if one of them might be able to bail him out. But no one could. And he knew it. He let out a difficult sigh.

"The woman changed her mind," he said. "She wanted to keep the baby. She promised me that she would not bother Richard about it at all. The two of them were finished anyway. She was smart enough to know that. She was . . . she was a shrewd woman. You didn't know Richard, Mr. Sewell. My brother thought he was the noblest thing on Earth in even sending these women off to me to 'help them out.' As far as he was concerned he owed them nothing."

"But in this case?"

"She wanted to keep the baby. She made me promise not to tell him."

"Your little secret, eh? Something you could secretly hold over your brother?" He didn't respond. "So what happened?"

"She came to term, and she delivered a healthy baby. I delivered it for her."

Ann Kingman stiffened. This was news to her.

"And you never told your brother?"

"As you said, it was my little secret. My pathetic little secret. For what it was worth. No. I never mentioned it to Richard. Not until last summer."

"What happened last summer?"

Kingman made a silent appeal to the woman seated next to him, but she was refusing to look at him. Kingman spoke to his hands, "Richard ran into the child's mother. It was purely by chance. She was sick. She was in the hospital. At Hopkins. She had cancer."

"And what was the woman's name, Dr. Kingman."

He looked over at the woman in the sunglasses. Vickie remained stone still. The obstetrician sighed, then answered.

"Ruth Waggoner."

I asked, "What did your brother tell you?"

"He told me that he had come across this woman at Hopkins. He saw her name on the door of her room. At first he didn't go in and see her. But the next day he saw a young woman coming out of her room. It was . . . it was the young woman who got killed."

"Helen."

"Yes. Her."

"And what happened next?"

"Richard went in and spoke with the woman. With Ruth. He told her who he was. She was terribly ill. He could see that she was dying. He asked her who was the young woman who had just been in her room. She said it was her daughter. Helen. And then she told him . . . that she was his daughter too."

Were I to claim that the room fell so silent that we could hear the snow falling outside, I'd be exaggerating. But not by much. Nobody spoke or moved. And then Russell Bennett blurted out, "What the hell are you saying? Richard had an affair with his own *daughter*? Jesus Christ!"

Bennett's outburst loosened the room. Joan Bennett turned her back on the rest of us and stared out the window at the snow, one hand half covering her mouth. Ann Kingman's glower traveled calmly about the room, resting on the man on the couch next to her. Daniel Kingman withered under her glare. It was clear that he had never shared this secret with her. I well imagined that Kingman hadn't shared it with anyone. I stepped over to Vickie and touched her on the shoulder.

"Are you all right?"

She nodded, but didn't dare to speak. I turned back around and addressed Russell Bennett. The look of disgust was still on his face.

"Kingman didn't have an affair with Helen. That was what everyone assumed, of course, given his history. Your father-in-law was a slummer. According to what the good doctor here told me in his office, Richard Kingman went for women who he felt were well beneath him, who he could easily discard. What his own son referred to as 'pure trash.' If he got them into trouble, he sent them off to his brother."

Ann Kingman muttered something. I missed what it was, but it was obvious from the look on Daniel Kingman's face that he had heard it. Loud and clear.

I continued, "Something apparently struck a chord though when Richard ran back into Ruth Waggoner last summer. Who knows? Maybe it was actual pity, seeing the horrible way that her life was ending. Maybe the two talked out a lot of things, we'll never know. One thing does seem certain, it appears that the news that he had a daughter . . . another daughter . . . it appears that the news got to him. What was it he said to you about that, Dr. Kingman? Did your brother suddenly get sentimental after all these years? Was he glad to discover that he had a daughter he had never known about?"

The doctor looked up from his balled fist. His mouth opened. But he said nothing. I pressed, "Go on. Tell us. Did Richard rush to you and thank you profusely for what you did? Was he overjoyed that you had tricked him like that? That you had lied to him and then kept it from him all those years that he had another child out there somewhere?"

"Of course not," Kingman said softly.

"I'll bet 'of course not.' I'll bet the bastard pitched a bloody fit."

"Accurate," was all that the man on the couch could say.

"Okay then. So, did your brother contact Helen?" I asked. "Or did Ruth finally let her daughter in on this piece of information that she'd been holding back all these years?" I stole a glance at Vickie, who was remaining mute and stoic behind her sunglasses.

Kingman shook his head slowly. "I don't know."

"Well, whichever it was, they got in contact. However it shook down, the point is that Richard Kingman decided to take care of Helen. He became the ultimate sugar daddy. He bought her new clothes, things for her son, an old MG that she had seen on sale. It's amazing what guilt will do." I took a step toward the couch. "Isn't it, Doctor?"

For a fraction of a second, a look of anger flashed across Daniel Kingman's face. As quickly as it appeared, it vanished.

"You lied to me in your office yesterday. Richard didn't pretend to you that he was having an affair with Helen, did he? That's too perverse, even for Richard. When he brought her in to see you, you knew exactly who she was. You knew this wasn't his lover he was asking you to take care of. Why did you come up with the story that Richard was planning to run off with this woman? That's what you told Ann, isn't it? You pretended with me that you were 'protecting' Ann from this horrible truth. But the fact is, you came up with that horrible *lie* yourself and fed it to her. What I don't understand is why? What did you possibly think would happen? If Ann were to confront her husband about this 'affair,' the truth would surely come out, right? And along with it, so would your part in all of this. I don't get it."

All eyes in the room were on Daniel Kingman. Slowly he unballed his fists and looked up, searching for a sympathetic face. He didn't find any. He settled on me. I was the only one not staring daggers.

"Richard was getting away with it again. Like he always did," he said calmly. "After all those years of taking care of his 'problems,' now he had me hooked up in another one of his secrets. And this one he was actually thrilled about. I can't explain it, but once he adjusted to the fact, Richard was very happy about this new daughter. That doesn't mean he thanked me for what I had done. He was angry about that. And somehow . . . I don't know. Somehow my taking this girl on as a patient and having to keep this secret for him . . . It was all just becoming too much for me. I wanted to hurt him."

"Correction. You wanted Ann to hurt him," I said. "But why didn't you just tell Ann the truth about Helen? She would certainly have had plenty to blow up about hearing that her husband has had a love child all the years of the marriage."

Kingman locked his gaze on me. He didn't dare let himself look elsewhere. Especially not at the woman seated right next to him. "First she would have blown up at me."

This time I heard the word that escaped from Ann Kingman. "Pathetic." Daniel Kingman lowered his head and stared again at his hands. Then he brought them up to his face and began to weep into them. Hands that giveth and hands that taketh away.

Russell Bennett again broke the uncomfortable silence.

"So, come on now, what are you getting at with all of this? Are you saying that Dan killed that girl? That's completely ridiculous."

I ignored him and instead addressed Ann, "Are you aware that your husband made some changes in his will several months ago?"

"This is the first I've heard about it," she answered.

"So, the will that your lawyer produced after the funeral . . . it made no mention of Helen Waggoner?"

"Not a peep."

"And yet your husband did change his will. I happen to know this for a fact. He had been taking care of Helen and her son. He was planning to move them into a new apartment. He put Helen in the will. Just so that you know, he didn't alter any provisions concerning you. Those arrangements remained intact. What he did was to slice away a portion from his other

children, from Joan and from Jeffrey, so that he could give
something to Helen. That's only equitable, after all."

"Richard's will never mentioned that woman," Ann said
again.

"No. I'm sure you're right. It didn't. The will that you saw
didn't. It was the one that your husband had drawn up before
he even knew that Helen Waggoner existed."

"Then how—"

"Michael Fenwick," I said. "I'm sure that your husband
gave no indication to Fenwick at the time he requested some
changes in his will that he was going to be doing anything
drastic. That would be why Fenwick gave it over to Constance
Bell to handle. Once he reviewed it, however, and saw that
this Helen Waggoner person was cutting into Joan and Jeffrey's portion of the pie . . . Well, I guess a sense of loyalty to
the family moved in and . . . How do you want me to put this,
clouded his professional judgment."

"Meaning?"

"Meaning he put his foot into the shit, Ann. He started a
ball rolling that ended up getting Helen Waggoner killed.
That's what I mean."

"Michael was a good friend of the family," she said simply,
as if that fact alone forgave everything that transpired.

"A good friend of the family. I gather that he was," I said
icily. "Since high school, in fact. Michael Fenwick spent a lot
of time in this house when he was a teenager, didn't he? He
and Jeffrey attended St. Paul's together, am I right?"

Ann waved a hand lazily.

"Then Fenwick went on to the University of Virginia. That
is where he went, isn't it? UVA?"

"Correct."

"Didn't one of your children also attend Virginia, Ann?"

"I believe you know the answer to that question already,
Mr. Sewell."

"You're right. I do. I'm just looking for someone to volunteer a little goddamn information here, Ann. I know it looks like I'm having so much fun, but I'd be just as happy if we could end this."

"Then end it," she said curtly.

"Did Jeffrey attend Virginia?" I asked.

From behind me, still facing the window, Joan Bennett spoke up. "You know full well that he didn't." She turned to face the room. Her arms were as tightly crossed as if she were wearing a straitjacket. "Jeffrey went to Washington and Lee. *I* attended UVA."

"And you went to St. Paul's too? St. Paul's for Girls, I mean. That's the one down the hill from the Boys School, right? You dated Michael Fenwick in high school, didn't you? His picture even appears on your senior yearbook page." I hadn't seen this, but Jay Adams had seen it. He had seen a lot of other things too, during his deskside investigation. "The two of you decided to go to Charlottesville together. If I'm not mistaken, there was even a brief engagement? That one of you then broke off?"

Her head nodded almost imperceptibly.

"You're the one who got Michael's firm and your father together, aren't you, Joan? Constance Bell had that wrong. She told me she thought it had been Jeffrey. But Fenwick was much more your old chum than he was your brother's. And so, when he got this news about someone named Helen Waggoner nosing her way into your and Jeffrey's inheritance, he came running to you, didn't he? Not to Jeffrey. You didn't know who Helen Waggoner actually was any more than your mother did. I doubt she even shared with you her erroneous information that your father was mixed up with this young woman. Though I'm sure you were able to leap to that conclusion all on your own. I'm guessing you didn't like it much, yes? This woman coming in and stealing money from you and your children? Then suddenly, your father dies. What exactly happened Joan? Did you simply freak out? Or were you calculating about the whole thing? You got Michael Fenwick to pull the old will, the one that didn't mention Helen. And then what? Were you worried that whoever this Helen Waggoner was she was going to rise up and make a stink? Expose your father's extracurricular activities and demand her part of the pie? Was that what you were afraid would happen? I'd love to know just how much of it was you wanting more of your daddy's money and how much of it was you wanting to protect his reputation. Why don't you tell all the good people here just which it was?"

"Why don't you just go to hell?" she said calmly.

"Give me one more minute first. So, how did it work? Did you ask Fenwick outright to find someone who would"—I tipped my head in the direction of the couch—"take care of this little problem for you? Did he agree? I gather he was the type to go the extra mile, so to speak. Was it his idea, Joan, or yours? Did he tell you that he could dig around and come up with someone who would be willing to kill Helen so long as the price was right? And what was the price anyway? I'm dying to know."

She said nothing. She had her mother's steely reserve; I could feel it from all the way across the room. I glanced over at Vickie, who stood up from her chair and crossed over to me. I turned away from Joan Bennett and addressed my question to the entire room.

"Let me ask my question again. From earlier. Does anyone in this room want to take responsibility for the death of Helen Waggoner?"

Joan Bennett uncoiled her arms and stepped calmly over to where her husband was sitting. She made a small gesture that her husband read as her wanting a cigarette. He pulled a pack from his jacket pocket and handed one to her, along with a plastic lighter. Joan Bennett looked over at me as she was flicking the lighter.

"Sure. I'll take it."

That's when I gave Vickie the signal to remove her sunglasses. Russell Bennett was the first to see it, or at least he was the first to react. "Oh, my God!" Cool, calm, calculating Joan was a beat behind him. She hadn't even exhaled the first puff of her cigarette; her jaw literally dropped and the smoke curled over her teeth like dry ice.

"In that case," I said, taking hold of Vickie, who was shaking now, "you really ought to apologize to your sister."

A gasp came up from the couch. Ann Kingman.

"Oh, my God in heaven."

No pun intended, but Billie did a bang-up job with Jeffrey Kingman. Most of the injuries he had sustained from his accident—that's what it was, an accident—were internal, not counting, of course, the lower abdomen, where the steering column of his car had impaled him as the car tumbled down the icy embankment. His face had been left relatively unmarred, and Billie had been able to fashion it into the peaceful-sleep contour that is so soothing to the bereaved. Jeffrey's glasses had been snapped in two, a clean break on the bridge that Billie was able to repair with a teardrop of Super Glue. Billie hadn't had the chance to get around to repairing the eyeglasses until after Vickie and I left to go over to the Kingman house. When Vickie went down to the basement on her own—slipping quietly out of the apartment while Billie was puttering about in the kitchen—Jeffrey Kingman's glasses (in two pieces) were sitting on a shelf, along with his wristwatch, which had survived the crash and was still ticking. And so Vickie had been able to see, when she pulled the stiff sheet away from Kingman's face—the little star-shaped dot on the side of his nose, the small, bluish birthmark that was hidden from sight so long as Jeffrey Kingman was wearing his glasses. The small, oval nosepiece of his glasses came down right on top of the nearly insignificant blemish, just as the nosepiece of Sam's sunglasses came down over the very same blemish on the very same location on the side of Vickie's nose. That's what she saw when she went down to the basement. That's why she screamed.

It will forever remain anyone's guess as to what Ruth Waggoner had had in mind when she decided to identify Helen to Richard Kingman as his bastard daughter. Perhaps she was still out to jerk poor Helen around. Old habits die hard, after all. Perhaps seeing her brief lover of so many years ago, Ruth Waggoner suddenly seized the chance to jerk *him* around, letting the man know that there had been a child of his out there all these years but failing to tell him that this particular woman, Helen, wasn't really the one. Like I said, it will remain anyone's guess. I asked Vickie on the drive back to her house if she thought that perhaps her mother had, in fact, simply decided to give her daughter a break after all these years. To finally just give Helen a father, even if it was not her true one.

"Look how it almost worked out," I said. "Helen got the little princess treatment from Kingman, even if only for a few months. Maybe your mother was hoping it might work out like that. It's possible, isn't it? She knew she was dying. Maybe your mother had all the best intentions in the world."

Vickie tried to buy it, but she couldn't. "He was my father, not hers. It's like that game I told you about that Helen and I used to play. But she cheated. They both did. Helen didn't even know she was cheating. At least that's what we have to think. But who knows. Maybe she knew full well. She stole my name once, didn't she? Why not my father?"

Joan Bennett confessed. She told Kruk that Michael Fenwick had been informed by Popeye that if he could come up with fifty thousand, Popeye could arrange for Helen to be "taken care of." Fenwick had been leaning on Popeye concerning a number of violations at the club as part of an effort to coerce the old man into selling the place to a group of investors who were eager to get their hands on the property. The lawyer promised that the harassing would all go away if Popeye could come up with a person who didn't mind killing a total stranger in return for a nice chunk of change. Half up front, half on delivery. Popeye knew these kind of people. And apparently Popeye had taken his role of middleman seriously. He had arranged for this Bob character to kill Helen, promising him all of twenty thousand for the job. The other thirty thousand, Popeye planned to pocket for himself. But it all fell apart on the day of Richard Kingman's wake. Joan Bennett told Kruk that she had had a change of heart—a panic—and had asked Michael Fenwick to call off the hit. She said she figured she would meet with Helen in person and see if she couldn't buy the woman off. Joan figured that the twenty-five thousand was gone, but the rest of the money she would add to the pot in her attempt to get Helen to quietly go away. Her hope was that her father's lover—so she thought—might not know that she had been added to the doctor's will. But when Michael Fenwick contacted Popeye in an attempt to cancel the contract, the club owner had a difficult time tracking down the killer, who by that point had probably already picked up the Pontiac Firebird in Federal Hill and was on his way out to Sinbad's. Popeye left him several messages. By the time the hired gun retrieved them, Helen was already in the passenger seat next to him. Dead. This was when Bob came storming into The Kitten Club and threw Popeye all around the office. The guy insisted he get paid the balance of the money for the job. Popeye balked, saying it wasn't in his hands. With a little persuasion, he gave up Michael Fenwick's name to Bob. Fenwick had been on his way to the Kingman wake when his car slid on the ice down next to the Jones Falls. His wife had stayed home. According to Joan, Michael told her that Sheila had taken a phone call from someone who needed to get ahold of her husband right away. An emergency. She told the caller that Michael was at a wake at a funeral home in Fells Point. The caller must have been Bob. The disgruntled killer proceeded to Fells Point where he dropped off Helen's body on the front steps of Sewell & Sons Family Funeral Home. The message was clear. The job is done. Pay up. Or else.

Only, Fenwick wasn't even there. As he had told Constance, he was at Mercy Hospital waiting for X rays. Joan Bennett reached him on his cell phone and told him what had happened at her father's wake. Mercy Hospital, as it happens, is only a few blocks from Commerce Street and The Kitten Club.

Michael Fenwick had been able to tell Joan this much of the story. Kruk stitched the rest of the story together. Bob, he determined, had taken his issue directly to Fenwick's apartment in Mount Vernon a few days later. Dissatisfied with the response he received, he killed them both. The man must have learned the full amount of the intended payment and realized that Popeye was holding out on him. A few days later he walked into Martick's and put four bullets into the old man. That took care of anyone with a direct connection to Bob's involvement in Helen Waggoner's murder. Kruk concluded that Bob had no clue about Joan Bennett. If he had, the bulldog detective said to me when I went down to headquarters to receive my tongue-lashing, she'd be dead.

Joan Bennett was given the opportunity to attend her brother's funeral, in police custody. She declined the invitation. Maybe it was me she didn't want to see. If so, I'm glad for it. The only reason I would have preferred Joan Bennett to be present at Jeffrey's funeral would have been for the satisfaction of seeing her flanked by the authorities. If ever I have met a person in need of some serious humility, it was Richard Kingman's daughter, Joan. But like I say, she chose not to attend.

Ann Kingman, of course, was there. So was Jeffrey's uncle. The two didn't stand particularly close to one another. Old eagle-eyes Sewell spotted that right away. I found myself wondering about the obstetrician. I wondered if maybe Daniel Kingman felt that had he been more forceful all those years ago, he could have persuaded Ruth Waggoner to go ahead with the abortion. In that case, Vickie would have never been born. And Daniel Kingman might not be standing where he was standing that cold afternoon, at the fresh grave of his nephew. If that's what he believed, then he could certainly manage to make the argument that this entire mess had been *his* fault practically as much as it had been his brother's. It wasn't until after the funeral, when Billie and I were up in her living room talking the matter over that she offered an alternate possibility.

"Hitchcock, it is perfectly plausible that Daniel Kingman didn't simply fail to dissuade Ruth from deciding to go ahead and keep her baby. It is every bit as possible that, in fact, he was the one who talked her out of aborting the child. Think about it. Whether out of spite against his brother or not, the man is an obstetrician. His training is in bringing children into the world, not destroying them. He might have failed to tell Ann Kingman the truth for the simple reason that he had been the one who convinced Ruth Waggoner to keep his brother's child in the first place."

Billie made sense. She often does. Certainly it was something to think about. Every now and then, I still do.

Jeffrey Kingman's funeral took place on Christmas Eve. I met up with Bonnie later that evening at her place to swap gifts and to make it official that we had come to the end of the line. Bonnie cried a little at one point, but by the time we parted company she was laughing. According to her, the tears were not really because she was wanting us to try to keep working on things between us. She sniffed them back almost as soon as they had showed.

"It's mandatory. If we're not going to scream and shout at each other then one of us has to cry at least a little," she said. "I can't wait around all night for you to think of it. I've got to be at the station in an hour."

Before I left, I asked her what the next day's forecast was. She gave an oversize shrug.

"Sunny as hell. Highs in the nineties. How the fuck do I know?"

"There goes that mouth again."

She reached up and kissed me on the lips. "You're right. Here it goes."

She turned and left.

Julia had left a Christmas ditty on my phone machine.

> *God rest you merry Hitchcock man*
> *What tricks are up my sleeve?*
> *The gift I got you, ho, ho, ho,*
> *You really won't believe!*

She was right. I couldn't believe it. It arrived late that afternoon. As soon as I saw it, I ran outside without even bothering to put on a coat. Aunt Billie followed a few minutes later.

"It's nice having wealthy friends, isn't it. You do like it, don't you?"

"Are you kidding? But how did—"

"A man called here while you were in the hospital, asking

for you. He said that you had been interested. I mentioned it to Julia. She agreed with me. It was a call from heaven, considering what happened to your poor little car."

Johnny had polished up the bottle-green Valiant so that it looked like glass. A red ribbon was tied around the antenna. In the rear seat was another plaster elf. I tried to give it to Billie, but she'd have no part of it.

"Merry Christmas, Hitchcock."

I ran back inside to get my coat. There was a message from Vickie on my machine. She had just gotten back from Memorial Stadium where the Eye Bank of Maryland sells Christmas trees every year.

Bo helped pick it out. But he's not much help setting it up. I was wondering . . .

I brought my trusty assistant along for his first ride in the new old car. The valiant Valiant ran like a dream. Alcatraz turned out not to be much help with the tree, but he kept Bo occupied while the boy's aunt and I set up the tree and decked it out with colored lights. Vickie didn't have any ornaments, only the lights. I fetched the elf from the car and placed it beneath the tree. Bo plopped down next to the elf and let out a squeal of delight.

Vickie turned off the overhead. We kicked off our shoes and sat down on the couch together to admire our good work. Quite nice. Where the tree touched the ceiling, its shadow ran out in a triangle, fuzzed up with colored bits, red and green and yellow and blue. The shadow stretched to just over our heads. One of the lights on the tree was flickering; it was probably just loose. I started to get up to go fix it, but Vickie placed her hand on my arm.

"Leave it."

If you enjoyed *Hearse of a Different Color,* be sure to catch Tim Cockey's newest novel, *The Hearse Case Scenario,* coming in February 2002 from Hyperion.

Apparently I was the first person Shrimp Martin called after Lucy Taylor shot him. It was a Saturday afternoon. Early June. The sun was high and I was low. I had a wicked toothache and I had just gotten off the phone with a guy named Roger, who was taking my regular dentist's calls while my regular dentist was away at his vacation house in Jackson Hole, poor guy. Roger sounded gung-ho to see me. He was going to fit me in that afternoon, between a root canal and an extraction. Well, good for Roger. Me, I had no gung-ho at all, just the sore tooth. Just before we hung up, Roger had asked me quite earnestly how my gums were. I didn't know how to answer that question. I was still pondering it when the phone rang.

"Sewell and Sons."

The voice on the other end was raspy and hoarse. Like someone whispering and gargling with glass at the same time. "Who's this?" it rasped.

"Excuse me?"

The voice croaked again. "Who's . . . this?"

"You called me," I pointed out. "Sewell and Sons Family Funeral Home. Now. Your turn."

There was a pause. I leaned back even farther in my chair and recrossed my legs, which were up on my desk. Lately, that's where they had been spending a lot of their time. Up on my desk. Not a lot of people were dying these days. My aunt and I were suffering a beginning-of-summer drought. Currently we had only one customer on ice, down in the basement. Mrs. Rittenhouse, from around the corner. Shakespeare Street. Her next-of-kin was due by any minute to drop off a dress for the viewing. A fact that was about to make this phone call all the more interesting.

A hissing sound was coming over the phone, like air going out of a balloon. I asked again. "Who is this?"

"Sssssssss. . . . Shrimp Martin."

Shrimp Martin. Nightclub owner. Blatant self-promoter. Borderline sleaze. A legend in his own mind.

"Shrimp? This is Hitchcock Sewell. What's up? What's wrong with your voice?"

"Lucy," he croaked.

"Lucy?" My heart iced. Nine out of ten people who call me at work are calling to talk about a corpse.

"Lucy."

"Lucy. I got that part. What about Lucy?"

"She's . . . not . . . here."

I switched ears and glanced out the window. Sam and some kids from the neighborhood were hosing down the hearse. Actually, the kids appeared to be hosing down Sam. Who didn't appear to be minding much. Sam's just a big kid anyway. Two hundred and ninety pounds worth.

"Shrimp, why don't we start this whole conversation over? I'm not looking for Lucy. I didn't call you, okay? You called me. So what's up?"

Shrimp sighed again. He sounded irritated. "Who's this?"

Now *I* was getting irritated. "I told you. It's Hitchcock Sewell, Shrimp. What the hell is going on?"

"Lucy," Shrimp said again. "She's gone. She . . . left me. She—" He interrupted his own sentence with another groan. This one stretched out in sort of a singsong fashion, almost a humming. It sounded as if Shrimp was channeling a tone-deaf drunk. Which was the conclusion I was beginning to reach. Not that Shrimp was channeling, but that he was definitely coming to us from the Land of Liquor.

"What do you mean, she's gone?"

Aunt Billie had just stepped into my office. She was holding a rat by the tail, at arm's length. Presumably dead. If not, then faking it nicely.

"Who's gone?"

I palmed the mouthpiece. "Shrimp Martin says that Lucy Taylor has left him."

Billie sniffed. "Lucy Taylor has a brain." She leaned sideways and dropped the dead rat into my brass spittoon. I don't spit. I use it to keep the door propped open. And, apparently, for storing dead rats.

"Mrs. Rittenhouse is all done," Billie announced. "Pretty as a picture. I'm just waiting on her dress."

At that precise instant, the front door opened. I could see a pair of arms wrapped around a blue chiffon number. Well, I call it chiffon. I don't really know these things. It was blue. I made the "voilà" gesture (one-handed version) and Billie floated out to the lobby to do her thing. Shrimp was still gurgling into the phone.

"I'm sorry, Shrimp. I missed that. What were you saying?"

He sounded strained and defeated. "Lucy," he mumbled again. For a man who was refusing to come to a point, he was driving one home nonetheless.

"Yes. Lucy. You just said that she left you. When, Shrimp? When did Lucy leave you?" I was beginning to overenunciate, the way you do when you're trying to get through to a foreigner. Or a child.

"Half . . . hour."

"A half hour ago? Jesus, Shrimp, come on. A half hour isn't really an awfully long time."

Billie was coming back into the office. She showed the dead woman's next of kin—granddaughter—to the chair in front of my desk. The young woman plopped down into the chair, the blue dress bunched in her arms like a bag of groceries. I held up a hand to indicate that I'd be right with her. Shrimp finally got to his point.

"She shot . . . me."

"She what?" I don't even remember it happening, but my feet were suddenly on the floor and I was standing at my desk. The phone felt tiny in my hand, like it was a child's toy. My sore tooth exploded with pain. "What are you talking about?"

Shrimp wheezed, "Lucy . . ." I sank slowly back to my chair as Shrimp struggled to locate enough air to conclude his short sentence. ". . . shot me."

"When, Shrimp?" I said, cocking an eyebrow at my guest. I noticed that there was a smudge mark on her cheek, the ripening of a fresh bruise. "When did she shoot you?"

Shrimp's answer was depressingly deadpan. "Right before . . . she left."

There was a pause, then he added, "I think I've lost a lot of blood."

And the line went dead.

Bad sign.

"Shrimp? Shrimp, are you still there?" I did what they do in the movies. Rattled my finger up and down on the little jiggy-wazzits where you hang up the phone, then I hung up the phone. The young woman in front of me was shifting the dress in her lap. Her hand emerged from underneath it and she set something blue and ugly on my desk.

"How's he doing?" she asked.

I steepled my fingers and lighted my chin on the tippy top. Undertakers have a knack for being able to draw their faces into a blank. That's what I did. Then I reached down with my index finger and swiveled the barrel of the little pistol so that it wasn't aiming directly at me. We're also not idiots. Then I resteepled.

"Well Lucy, I wouldn't say he's sounding terribly chipper. If that's what you're asking."

CHAPTER 2

Lucy Taylor and I go way back. She's an old friend of mine and of my ex-wife, Julia. We were kids together. The three of us grew up within rock-throwing distance of each other down here in the Fell's Point section of Baltimore, which is where all three of us still live. I mean that literally by the way, the rock-throwing distance. When I was twelve and Lucy was nine I beaned her just above the right eye with a rock as she was stepping out the front door of her father's house on Shakespeare Street to take out the trash. I wasn't aiming at her specifically; I was having an especially bad day and was just throwing rocks indiscriminately at the world. Poor Lucy. It is so like her to have this sort of thing happen. Crazy girl was just born to fall into puddles. Anyway, when I beaned her she went down like a small sack of potatoes and I got her up the street to Hopkins as fast as I could. The doctors patched her up with a few stitches then gave me a lecture about how I might have blinded my little friend and should be more careful in the future and all the rest of it. Lucy didn't hold it against me. She knew I had been upset that day and she was completely understanding. But still. I felt terrible, of course, and I doted on Lucy for weeks afterward. I took her to the movies, I plied her with banana splits, I sneaked her down to the basement of my aunt and uncle's funeral home and let her see a dead body. (Let it never be said that I can't show a girl a good time.) I even badgered Julia to badger her parents to let me open a tab for Lucy at the Screaming Oyster Saloon; any old time she wanted, Lucy could go into the Oyster, saddle up to the bar and drink Coca-Colas to her little heart's content. Lucy Taylor loved her Coca-Colas, and in practically no time she was making the trip to the S.O.S. three and four times a day, sometimes more. She'd climb up on the barstool and plant her pointy elbows on the bar and pull nonstop on the twisty straw, then sing out for a refill. I didn't really have the cash to pay my tab, nor did I have the heart to suggest to Lucy that she maybe slow down a little. It seemed to make her so happy, knocking back free Cokes at the Oyster. I offered to Sally, Julia's mom, to do some chores around the place if that would help any, and Sally's response was to hang her large head—no doubt to hide the grin—and ask me only that I'd promise to come visit her and Frank and Julia once they got shipped off to the poorhouse.

One other thing. Julia swears to me that Lucy Taylor was always the way she is, which is something of a hard-luck Harriet. She says that Lucy came into this earth with her fall-in-a-puddle karma firmly in place, that it was already evident well before I cracked her in the head with a rock. As proof, Julia recalls Lucy at age seven, daydreaming so hard on Christmas day that she walked right off the end of the pier and into the harbor. Or a year later, when Lucy went chasing after a stray cat and ended up getting stuck in a drainage pipe and had to be set free with a pickax. And it's true, the general take around the neighborhood has always been that Lucy was a sweet and generous girl—indiscriminately kind (which is what leads a person like Lucy to a person like Shrimp Martin)—but that she was simply born with a card or two already plucked from her deck.

I'm a sucker for a gal in a uniform. This one's name tag identified her as Nancy. Nancy smiled as sweetly as an angel as she plunged a needle into my arm.

"It's very good of you to offer a blood donation, Mr. Sewell. We're in one of those low phases. People just aren't donating the way they used to." Nurse Nancy nibbled on her lower lip as she pulled back on the plunger, sucking the life force out of me. "O negative. We can always use O negative around here." She smiled up at me as she flicked free the knot on the elastic around my arm.

"All done. You might feel a little woozy for a while. We recommend that you don't drive until you've rested and had something to eat."

"Perhaps you'd care to join me," I said, rolling the sleeve of my muslin shirt back down over my elbow. "The Hopkins Deli makes these gargantuan sandwiches. Do you get breaks around here?"

She shook her head. "We don't leave the floor." She labeled the vials of my blood and stowed them in a small Styrofoam carrying case.

"I could get a sandwich and bring it back," I said.

"The sandwich you describe sounds too big to carry."

Big grin. "I'm a packhorse. I can manage it."

Small smile. "Thank you. But no thank you." She zinged open the curtain that had secluded us from the rest of the world. There it was, just as we'd left it. Cradling my blood, the nurse stepped away silently on her white rubber shoes.

Shrimp Martin was still in surgery. When I had arrived at the hospital I had been told by one of the EMS workers who brought him in that Shrimp had been found unconscious in his living room, lying on top of the phone. He had lost a lot of blood, as indeed he had hypothesized to me over the phone. I sensed a touch-and-go vibe. I could probably get away here with pretending that it was the news of how much blood Shrimp had lost that prompted me to offer a donation of my own. It wasn't. It was Nurse Nancy. The uniform. Something perversely sexy about all that starched white. She wore a blond bob and a shy smile and had seemed enthusiastic about taking me up on my offer that she go at me with a needle.

Soon after my blood donation, I got a report. Shrimp was stabilized. They were still working on him, but he was going to survive. He had taken a single bullet in his stomach. It apparently ripped sideways, right to left, and meddled with a few important organs before exiting directly through his left kidney. In all senses, the kidney was shot, and so the doctors were removing it. One of the emergency room surgeons had emerged from behind a pair of automatic doors—his green smock smeared with blood, his hands wrapped in prophylactic—to let me know about the kidney.

"We're going to perform an emergency nephrectomy," he said. He seemed to want to know where I stood on nephrectomies. I stood nowhere. "He'll live a normal life," he added. Apparently this guy didn't know Shrimp.

The doctor excused himself and went back into the operating room to nephrect. A uniformed policeman came off the elevator and beelined for the nurse's station. I beelined into the stairwell. I wasn't in the mood for chatting with the police. Not yet anyway. I pictured poor Lucy slumped in the chair in my office and the Papa Bear in me simply came out. I just wasn't ready to turn her over. Besides which, my tooth was pulsing with a disco beat by this time and I was feeling very cranky. Cops don't generally like cranky. So really, I was doing this for him, too. I went round and round and up and up and up, and came out on a quiet floor. I strolled to the end of the corridor and gazed out a window onto a gravel rooftop several stories below. Two guys in green overalls were smearing tar around some sort of vent, a bubble-shaped aluminum thing with fan blades. Two pigeons on a nearby exhaust chimney were watching them. A blimp was floating, off in the distance. Pimlico racetrack. I remembered. The Anniversary Stakes were today. Technically, I should have been finding a TV. I had a hundred bucks in the Screaming Oyster pool. A horse called Tango Wallop. I'm not really a horse guy. It was names from a hat. Simple bar betting. Tango Wallop's odds were middling to crappy, which was probably why I wasn't scaling tall mountains and fording great seas in search of a TV set.

Eventually I found my way back to the emergency room. The uniformed cop had left. Shame. It occurred to me that I should be hitting the phones, but I really wasn't sure who to call. I knew Shrimp had a sister. I had met her once down at the club. A big soft overweight girl who cornered me for three years one evening and melted both my ears on the subject of tarts and strudels and hot-cross buns. The Martin family, so I learned, has been running the extremely popular Mabel's Bakeries for several generations, ever since Great-granddaddy Martin opened the first shop down on Preston Street a century or so ago. As I recall the tale, Shrimp's refusal to follow in the footsteps of his father and his father's father's father had resulted in the sister now being groomed to take over the bread and pastry dynasty when the time came for Daddy to step down. Apparently there was bad blood between Shrimp and his father as a result of this bucking of tradition. The sister was clearly both fond of her brother and thrilled to be next in line to run the bakery dynasty. Standing there in the hospital I could conjure her face and her soft doughy presence, but I couldn't snag the name.

I found a phone out in the waiting area and called Billie to let her know that Shrimp was pulling through. I asked her if Lucy had shared with her yet her reasons for taking a shot at him.

"I can't get a peep out of her, Hitchcock. She's just sitting over in the corner staring out the window. I gave her some Coca-Cola and we put some ice on that cheek. She's looking like a very sad raccoon."

"Put her on the phone, will you?"

While I waited for Lucy to come on, I snagged a young doctor who was passing by and asked him what he'd recommend for a sore tooth. He recommended Tylenol. Just like they say on TV. Billie came back on the line and told me that Lucy didn't want to talk.

"Did you tell her that Shrimp is going to pull through?"

"Yes."

"What did she say to that?"

"Very little." Billie's voice lowered. "What about the police, Hitchcock? I believe they like to be told about these sorts of things."

"They know," I said. "A cop has already been here."

"What did you tell him?"

"Well . . . I didn't actually speak with him. I want to give Lucy a chance to snap out of it first. This is going to be rough on her. It's the least we can do."

"I suppose we can plead ignorance," Billie mused. "I mean, I *am* so tragically daft, after all."

"Loopy as a loon," I said.

"There you have it."

"As spacey as Sputnik."

"If you will."

"The queen of the senior moment. Voted most likely to—"

"Okay, young man, you've made your point."

We hung up. I called Roger and left a message with his answering service that an emergency had come up and I wouldn't be able to come in this afternoon after all. Shrimp was just then being wheeled out of surgery. The bloodied surgeon gave me the rundown. Shrimp had pulled through. He'd be in the hospital for a few days at the very least. Henceforth, he'd be filtering all of his toxins through his remaining kidney but the doctor assured me that this should pose no real problem. I returned to the waiting area and dropped into one of the molded plastic chairs. And slumped. The damn tooth was pulsing, more like Morse code now. The TV set in the corner by the ceiling was showing a red-haired chef waving her arms through volumes of smoke and crying out "I live to feed!" I was too lazy to go channeling for the Anniversary Stakes. Tango Wallop didn't stand a chance anyway; I could kiss that Franklin bye-bye. I picked up the only magazine on the glass table in front of me, but decided I wasn't really motivated to learn how to put the zing back in my marriage. A hundred and one ways. My marriage with Julia had lasted exactly one year. We had relocated the zing simply by bagging the marriage. I doubted the magazine was going to offer this sort of advice. I settled in and gazed up at the chef. For no reason that I was able to discern, she had donned a red clown's nose and was wielding her spatula like a microphone.

I tuned my thoughts back to Shrimp Martin. Shrimp, Shrimp, Shrimp . . . Hell, I didn't even know the guy's real name. Why in the world he would have called me instead of 911 was something that I had not yet worked out. It wasn't as if old Shrimpster and I were backslapping buddies. I had only met the guy several months previous, the night that Shrimp's and Lucy's orbits had first crossed. Julia and I had taken Lucy over to Shrimp's nightclub as part of Julia's campaign to help poor Lucy bounce back from her latest romantic misstep. A little music-soothes-the-soul therapy. As it happened, the tactic blew up in our faces when the club's torch singer had opened her set with "I'll Be Seeing You" and Lucy beat a tearful retreat to the women's room. "Old familiar place," Julia noted wryly. A few minutes later—still no Lucy—a bucket full of ice and champagne had arrived at our table, followed by an unctuous fellow in a white dinner jacket, bad skin and a foxin-the-henhouse smile. Shrimp Martin. I recognized him from his numerous suck-up poses with club patrons and local celebrities in the photographs that were tacked up on the walls just inside the club's front door. I had already noticed a chubby guy with a camera prowling about. Clearly, the night-club owner had Julia Finney in his sights. Aside from being ar-guably the sexiest woman on the Eastern seaboard, Julia is also a highly successful and celebrated painter. She's been hung all over the world. It was abundantly clear that Shrimp was a major hobnobber. While Shrimp jimmied elaborately with the champagne cork, Julia had preened and cooed and made such big can-you-believe-this-jerk eyes at me that I thought the lovely brown bulbs were going to fall right out of their sockets. Shrimp finally wrestled the cork from the bottle, losing half the bubbly over his wrist. It was just then that Fate had trotted forward, dressed up this time as Lucy Taylor. Eyes red and childlike from her bathroom crying jag, a big gooey smile grew on Lucy's face as she approached the table. "Cham-pagne? Oh, I *love* champagne!" And the smooth operato-holding the bottle hadn't missed a beat, grabbing hold of the empty chair and sliding it back from the table. "My compli-ments," he crooned as he tucked little Lucy into the table. And then he introduced himself. "I'm Shrimp Martin," he said, giving a slight bow. "*Mi casa es su casa.*" Lucy summarily beamed and blushed and handed over her tiny paw to the next mistake in her life. "Lucy Taylor," she chirped. "Nice *casa.*"

"Lean in folks!"

Flash! The chubby photographer captured the moment.

A phone freed up. I dug out another quarter. I had a date that night that I wasn't particularly looking forward to, but the prospect of trading it in for a hospital vigil seemed a worse bet. I really did need to get someone else to come down here and take over the Shrimp vigil. I called Julia's cell phone. I hate cell phones. Julia loves them. You tell me, was that marriage not doomed?

"Where are you?" I asked when Julia answered, which in the era of cell phones is the greeting that has replaced "Hello." Julia, it turned out, was way the hell out in the county. Our connection sounded aquatic.

"I'm at the Manor Tavern," she burbled.

"What are you doing way up there?" I asked.

"Eating ribs."

"Oh? Whose?"

"Ha ha. I needed to get out of the city, Hitch. It's too darned hot."

I scanned for a song lyric quip but found nothing. "How did you get out there, anyway?" Julia doesn't drive. Generally, she takes taxis. Or she is squired.

"His name is Tom," she said.

I nodded sagely. "His name is Tom."

"He is a gentleman and a scholar."

"He's a polite professor?"

"Telephone repairman."

"Oh. You're having problems with your phone?"

She giggled. It sounded more like a gurgle. "Not anymore."

"Jules, this still doesn't explain why you're out in the county."

"I told you, I wanted some fresh air. Tom was fixing my phone. He had his repair truck. He offered to take me for a drive. He's gorgeous, Hitch. Male. Blue jeans. Tool belt."

"Jules, listen. We've got a situation here. I'm at Union Memorial. Shrimp Martin has been shot and—"

"He's been *what*?"

"Shot. You know. Bullet? Entry wound? The—"

"Holy Jesus. How's Lucy? Does she know? Is she there?"

I took a deep breath. "Here's the thing. Lucy is the one who shot him."

I had to pull back from the phone. "*What*? Lucy *shot* him? Jesus Christ, Hitch! Where is she? Is she under arrest? Oh God . . . this is *so* Lucy."

"Slow down. She's with Billie right now," I said. "Everything's fine. We're going to pretend that we were too scattered to think about calling the police right away. Billie's keeping an eye on her. She's pretty much in shock, I think."

"Poor Lucy."

"Shrimp's going to live, by the way. I know that was your next question."

"Oh, Shrimp Martin is an idiot, Hitch. Someone was bound to shoot him sooner or later. So come on, tell me. What happened?"

"I really couldn't get anything out of Lucy. I have to guess it was some kind of accident. Here's the thing. Can you get your stud muffin to run you back into town? I need you to get over to Billie's. I think you're the person she needs to see."

"Of course. I'll come in right away."

"I also need to get someone to baby-sit Shrimp down here. I've got a date in a few hours."

"Date? It wouldn't be with that dancer, would it?"

"It would."

"Your enthusiasm is underwhelming."

I grumbled. "We'll go to a restaurant and she won't eat. We'll go to this big dance performance she has choreographed and I won't get it. Do you hear the theme of 'unfulfilling' running through this?"

"What about afterward? Have you two knocked knees yet?" Julia has been racking up euphemisms for sex for as long as she has been racking up sex itself. Ergo, she's got a ton of them.

I told her that I didn't know if "yet" was the right word. "Dead end" was pretty much written all over this one.

"Hitch, is there really any reason for you to even go on this date? Why don't you call her up and give her the perfectly ac-

ceptable excuse that you have been called to the hospital bedside of a friend in need?"

I had an answer to that. "A bad date is still preferable to a
night drinking cardboard coffee from a hospital vending machine. And Shrimp Martin hardly qualifies as my friend. So
look, do you have any idea how I might be able to get a hold of
Shrimp's sister?"

"The chubby girl?"

"Yes."

"God, she is more tedious than death."

"I'm not asking for someone to come entertain him. I just
want to get someone over here so that I can leave."

"Mary Ann."

"Mary Ann! That's right. Mary Ann Martin. Perfect. I'll
give Mary Ann a call and you get your big beautiful bucket
back to town and over to Billie's."

"Charming."

I hung up and dialed Information. With a little cajoling I
got the operator to work with me. There were seven "Martin,
M"s listed, and I was able to get them all on one request,
rather than the usual limit of two. The first four I called were
not Shrimp's sister. This was easy to determine. My opener
was "Hi, I'm looking for Shrimp's sister." Three of the four
simply hung up. The fourth was a man with an Eastern Euro-
pean accent who started griping to me about UFOs and what
they were doing to his dog. I struck gold on the fifth call.
Nearly gold.

"Hi, I'm looking for Shrimp's sister."

"This is Mary."

"Mary Ann?"

"Mary."

"Mary?"

"I live here, too. I'm Mary Ann's housemate."

"That must get confusing."

"Who is this?"

"This is Hitchcock Sewell," I said. "Is Mary Ann there? I need to speak with her."

"I'm afraid she's not."

"Do you expect her back soon?"

Mary said that she thought that Mary Ann would be back within the hour. "She went to a matinee of *My Fair Lady* at The Mechanic." That brought back memories. The Gypsy Players botched that little gem about four years ago. I was Higgins. My British accent stank. And I sang like a mule. Julia was Eliza. Of course, she was loverly. And an even worse ham than me. *The rine in Spine fools minely oon the pline.*

I told the woman on the phone that Mary Ann's brother was in intensive care at Union Memorial with a gunshot wound to the stomach, that he was going to be all right but that someone needed to get over to the hospital right away. Mary was duly impressed with my message.

"Shrimp's been shot? What happened?"

I lied. "I'm not sure. But I can't really stay here with him much longer. I've got to be somewhere in a few hours."

"Mary Ann has a cell phone. Maybe I should call her."

I pictured Henry Higgins in the middle of his silly "By jove I think she's got it!" number when out there in the dark a damn cell phone begins to chirp. By jove, *get it.*

"I wouldn't do that," I said.

"What about I come over? It's not that far. I'm just over near Lake Montebello. I can leave Mary Ann a message on the kitchen table."

It seemed an unnecessarily generous offer. I took her up on it. I told her where to meet me at the hospital.

"How will I recognize you?" she asked.

"I'm tall," I said. "Dark hair. I've got one of those little Superman curls that sort of falls—"

"Okay."

"How will I recognize you?" I asked.

"I'm short."

"That's it?"

"I'll be there in twenty minutes," she said. "I've just got to throw some clothes on."

Intriguing detail that it was, I let it pass. We hung up. I went back to the molded plastic chair to wait for Mary Ann's short friend Mary. I went ahead and glanced at the article about putting zing back in the marriage. Guess what? They suggest more frequent sex. Along with candles and wine and surprises. Big shock.

"You must be whatshisname."

A woman with a freckled face and short damp blond hair was standing directly in front of me. Her approach had been pure stealth. Slipped in under the cover of my daydreaming. I stood up. Her freckled nose leveled off around the latitude of my elbow. Pale blue eyes looked up at me. Mine are blue, too. Turns out these were the only two things we had in common.

"And you must be Mary." I offered my hand. Hers disappeared into mine. Like a whale swallowing a bonbon. "That was fast," I said. Though I had no real idea how much time had passed.

"Twenty minutes. As promised." She released my hand and ran hers through her damp hair, which was sun-streaked gold and short enough to get away with a finger-brushing. Her face was apple-shaped. If you can picture that in a good way. Farmer's daughter, with an urban edge. "You're lucky," she added. "I was just getting out of the shower when you called."

I wasn't sure why that made me lucky, but I let it pass. I placed Mary in her early twenties, fresh and well-scrubbed. Maybe it was the freckles, along with the pulsing peach tan. The remaining inventory supported this first impression. Simple white V-neck T-shirt, blue jean cutoffs and flip-flops. She was all of five feet tall if she was an inch, toned and glowing, a trim vertical package with well-carved little hips and intriguing breasts. I realize that I'm coming off like an auctioneer, but these are simply the facts. She looked beach-ready and very sure of herself. And as humorless as a stone.

She caught me staring. At least it seemed she did. She crossed her arms over her intriguing breasts and frowned up at me.

"So what happened?"

I told her. "Shrimp Martin called me up a couple of hours ago and said he'd been shot. I called nine-one-one. They got him here, he lost a kidney and a lot of blood, but he's going to live." I left out the detail that it was a friend of mine who shot him. It's always good to hold something back, in case the conversation sags.

The damp head was tilted and she was squinting slightly. The woman seemed to be judging my credibility. "So where are the police?" she asked. Her tone was clearly challenging.

"The police?"

"He was shot. Where are the police?"

"A cop was here earlier," I said. "He left."

My little friend was unimpressed. "So who shot him?"

"Why would I know who shot him?" I said. I sounded defensive. Which I was. I'm usually good with my poker face. But for some reason the frank blue eyes already had me on the ropes. Also, my neck was cricking looking down at her.

She batted her critical blues. "You said Shrimp *called* you. Maybe he *said* something?"

"It was . . . everything's under control," I stammered.

"What's *that* supposed to mean?" She was making no effort now to conceal her disapproval with how things were being handled. Or not being handled.

"It was a domestic shooting," I said lamely.

The woman's eyebrows went up, like a stretching cat. "Uh huh . . ."

"The person who shot Shrimp is with my aunt." I added, "At the funeral home."

"Funeral home?"

"My aunt and I run a funeral home."

She studied my face. About a three-second deconstruction. The term "tough little cookie" was beginning to form in the judgment corner of my brain. Mary said, "Okay, so now what? You're here in case Shrimp dies? That's a little eager, isn't it?"

I took a step backward and kneaded my neck. Mary took it the wrong way. She took a step back as well. "What are you doing now, *measuring* me?"

"No. I just . . . nothing."

Mary shifted her weight over to one hip and tilted her head in the opposite direction. The eyebrows went up again—this time both—and a look of complete mistrust slotted onto her face. Now I know what Goliath must have felt like. This pipsqueak's body language was pebbling me to death before I even had a chance. I was reduced to a single bleat.

"What?"

"Would you mind not looking at me that way?" she said.

"What way?"

She made a huffy sound. "You big guys. You've got such a thing for small women."

"*Excuse me?* Who said I've got a 'thing' for small women?"

She uncurled her arms and raised a hand. "Down here? That was me?"

I pulled up. My lightning-speed calculation concluded that there was nothing to be gained in joining an argument with a total stranger with a height complex. At least not in a hospital waiting room. In a bar, maybe, but not here. She stood there, slingshot-ready.

"I think we're sliding off the track," I said. "Look. Thanks for coming down. Let me give you my card. When Mary Ann gets here, have her call if she wants. I might not be in, but she can talk to my aunt."

I produced a card and held it out. She glanced at it then tucked it into the rear pocket of her cutoffs. Any thicker and the card couldn't have possibly fit. She rubbed her bare arms. I hadn't noticed, but in fact it was pretty cold in there. They had the AC cranked and she was dressed for the sun. She squinted up at me again.

" 'Bye."

Like that, she turned and walked away. *Poof.* I raised my hand for a half-wave but it was to thin air and I let it drop. I did look to see if I could spot my business card. I couldn't, of course. But the effort was pleasing. My guess was that she knew I was looking. Julia tells me that they always know we're looking.

I traveled the length of the corridor and pushed the button for the elevator. As I waited, I glanced back. Mary was seated in one of the plastic chairs, trim tanned legs crossed, leafing through the magazine. She'd be learning those zing tricks for dulled marriages. I willed her to glance up from the magazine, but she didn't. The elevator arrived and I got on, squeezing in between a pair of gurneys carrying two pale vapors in human form. The doors were slow in closing. I faced front and again willed the irritating woman at the end of the hall to look up. She wet her finger and turned a page of her magazine. She didn't look up. Her foot waggled. The elevator doors slid shut.

I was in love.

Not really.

The doe-eyed boy in tights was shooting invisible arrows in all directions from an invisible bow. His victims clutched their hearts, their stomachs, their necks, flinging themselves to the ground and tumbling in somersaults, three, four, five rotations, then leaping to their feet to live another day. Or at least another several seconds. The doe-eyed boy himself was a show-off, leaping up onto a boulder, twirling his feet in midair, shooting off-balance, even tumbling along sometimes right beside his victims. His stash of invisible arrows was endless. In all, a very sprightly massacre.

"Here she comes."

"She" was a waifish girl done up in the same tights and the same doe-eyed makeup as the homicidal Cupid. She appeared atop the boulder, up on her toes, her pipe-cleaner arms snaking upward. In her hands was cupped a large opalescent disk. The moon. The nifty part was that when the girl came down off the boulder—her steps were like those of someone sticking their toe in the water to see how cold it is—the disk remained suspended in air. I tried, but I couldn't see the wires.

I'll skip the blow-by-blow. Bottom line is that the boy's invisible arrows had no effect on Moon Girl whatsoever. He fired away at an increasingly frantic pace while she pranced around mockingly, making an easy target of herself. Her invulnerability infuriated the boy, then exhausted him, then finally drove him to tears (invisible, like his armaments). Any minute I expected Moon Girl to sit down on the boulder and start doing her nails, ho-hum. In the end—I could have almost predicted this—the boy made a very melodramatic scene of handing over his invisible bow and an invisible arrow to the waif, and then he got up on the boulder and reached up to take hold of the moon, sticking his bony chest out so that the girl couldn't possibly miss the mark. She took aim and shot him. The moon came out of the sky in the boy's hands as he tumbled off the boulder . . . and the stage went black.

There was a finger-food-and-wine reception after the performance. The performers were there, looking like alien beings at a getting-to-know-you conference. My date for the evening— we'll call her Clarissa because that's what everyone calls her (she was christened Debbie)—spent nearly the entire reception with her fingers laced in a ball that she kept pressed tightly against her breast. Clarissa had only warm words for the performers, the most frequent one being "wonderful." Everything was *"Wonderful!"* Clarissa's face is one of the most expressive I have ever seen and she lavished it on the young performers, most of whom blushed and demurred at her fawning. This was what they had worked so hard for over the past several months. Clarissa had opened a dance studio over on Read Street early in the year and was trying to put a company together. Tonight was the premiere of *Dance of the Protégés* and the dancers had been so eager to please. If you could judge from Clarissa's liberal scatterings of *wonderfuls*, they had succeeded.

Clarissa reserved her largest fawning for the two principals, pulling out an entirely fresh set of superlatives for the doe-eyed boy and his twinlike murderess. Clarissa goosed up the boy in particular, who wallowed shamelessly in his teacher's praise. From the young girl, however, I detected a whiff of coldness. Competition, perhaps. The gristle of ego in a slow grind. The young dancer definitely had a bug up her ass about Clarissa. She was as skinny as a toothpick. Her eyes, which were lined like those of an Egyptian princess, were dark and mean. Clarissa smiled her effervescent pearlies right through the young dancer's pointed indifference, then didn't wait until we were out of the girl's earshot before saying to me, "So what did *you* think of the little bitch?"

Ah . . . showbiz.

This whole snap, crackle, pop was taking place in the lobby area outside the auditorium of the High School for the Performing Arts, where Clarissa had arranged to stage her show. Air kisses were flying with the frequency of the evening's invisible arrows. I wasn't having me an especially bang-up time. Could you tell? And it wasn't just the cheap wine. Part of it was my tooth, which had now begun to take on a personality all its own. And not one that I particularly liked. Khrushchev pounding his shoe at the U.N. comes to mind. But another big part of it was Clarissa. This was our third time going out together and the chemistry was still proving as so-so as on the first two shots. Even so, I had the sense that this was the evening where the mad blind plunge into the sack had now risen to the top of the docket. This was a big night for Clarissa, after all. God knows how much she had spent on the dress she was wearing, but elegance and glitter like that doesn't come cheap. For my part, I had come through in my big bad tux and I looked like a goodly portion of a million bucks myself. A couple as sharp-looking as the two of us—on a night of no small importance to one of us—is not a couple who are expected to peak at a Gallo and Gouda gala in a high school lobby. There are rules about these things, and it was only a matter of whether Clarissa or I—more specifically, I—were going to break them or not.

When the time came for the toasts and the little speeches, I took the opportunity to duck outside for some air. It must have been nearing nine-thirty. Venus and her friends were blinking and twinkling brightly in the night's blue veil. There was a pay phone near the corner. I stepped over to it and dug out a quarter. I dialed my number. After my own voice told me that I wasn't in, I cupped my hands to the mouthpiece and yelled, "Alcatraz! Sit!" Without a spy on the premises, I'll never know if my lowly hound dog actually does sit when I do this. I punched in the code to retrieve my messages. There was only one (besides the one I had just left). It was from Billie, telling me to call her. I had planned to do just that. And I did.

"Oh, Hitchcock, there you are. I've been trying to figure out how to find you." Billie sounded agitated. Billie is hardly ever agitated. "That woman you left at the hospital . . ."

"Mary."

"Yes. Mary. That's her. She called here looking for you. It's Shrimp Martin."

"What about him?"

"He's dead."

"He's *what*!" I switched ears. "What do you mean he's dead, Billie? He was fine when I left him. I mean, they told me he was fine. The doctor told me—"

Billie cut me off. "You'd better get down there, Hitchcock. According to— Apparently they had a little problem."

"A little problem? I'll say. The guy's dead, for Christ's sake. They had a *big* problem."

"That's not what I mean. According to this Mary, somebody went into Shrimp Martin's room and killed him."

"Billie, what are you talking about? Right there in the hospital?"

"That's what the girl told me on the phone."

"This is insane. Who the hell . . . Put Lucy on, will you?"

There was a pause.

"Hitchcock, Lucy's not here."

"Where is she? Did she go down to the hospital?"

"I don't know where she is, dear. I was in the kitchen making vichyssoise and she slipped out. I thought she was still sleeping."

I didn't like this. "Billie, did Julia come by?"

"No, dear. I'm afraid I haven't seen her."

Didn't like it at all. "When did Lucy leave?"

"It's close to two hours now," Billie said.

"And when did you say Mary called from the hospital?" I looked up at Venus. They say that the atmosphere on Venus is so thickly packed that light bends in ways we can barely imagine here on Earth. In theory, you can be looking straight ahead and staring at the back of your own head at the same time. That's about what I felt I was doing right then.

Billie answered, "That was about an hour ago."

I was halfway to Union Memorial before it occurred to me that I had forgotten to ask Billie about the gun Lucy had brought over. To see if it was still there on my desk.

I was three quarters of the way there before it hit me that I hadn't even said good-bye to Clarissa.

A hand grabbed hold of my arm the moment I stepped off the elevator.

"You're under arrest."

I plucked the hand from my arm as if it were a dead rat (which reminded me). "What's the charge?"

"Perfect attendance at all my murder scenes." John Kruk gave me the sneer that for him passes for a smile. He might even have chuckled. Kruk gave an up-and-down to my tux.

"I was just out for a jog," I said as I surveyed the scene. The intensive care ward was like a department store on Christmas Eve. People were going in all directions, yelling to be heard above the din, arms waving, urgent gesturing. If there was any order here, I was missing it. Uniformed police were milling about. Notebooks were at the ready. Questions were being asked. Some mild flirting with the nurses was going on.

Kruk rubbed a hand over his thick neck. "Let's hear it, Mr. Sewell. What do you know and when did you know it?"

"I thought those questions were reserved for the president."

John Kruk is largely banter-proof. He shifted on his flat feet and gave me his bored look. "I'm waiting."

"Who told you that I had any involvement in this whatsoever?" I asked. "Can't a man in a tuxedo just show up in a hospital on a Saturday night and not get harassed by the local constabulary?"

"Are you saying you don't have any involvement?"

"I didn't say that. I'm just curious how it is you're not surprised to see me."

Kruk consulted his notebook. "You phoned in the nine-one-one at approximately three o'clock."

"Yes sir, that sounds about right."

"Where were you when you made the call?"

"In my office."

"You didn't call from the victim's house?"

"From Shrimp's?"

"That's right."

"No sir."

"According to EMS personnel, someone was milling around outside the victim's home when they arrived. That's why I ask."

"Wasn't me. I was milling around a funeral home."

Kruk consulted his notebook. "So after arriving at the hospital, you passed the victim off to a Mary Childs late this afternoon."

"Ah, so it was good old Mary who gave me up."

"Miss Childs said that you knew who shot Mr. Martin." He gave me his whammy-eye. He's got a real winner.

"Miss Childs doesn't like me," I said. "We got off on the wrong foot. She'd say anything."

"Are you saying that she lied?"

"Well, no. I'm just saying the girl doesn't like me."

"So you withheld information about a shooting for . . . what do we have, going on ten hours now? Do you mind if I ask where you have been all this time?"

I thought about describing the dance performance to him, but that would have been cruel. And most certainly unusual. "I had a prior engagement." When he frowned at me, I added, "A hot date." Now I was giving false and misleading information. See how slippery the slope can be?

We were blocking the elevators. Sick people were trying to get off and on. A large hulking man was pushing a gurney. He was wearing a paper shower cap on his head. Anywhere but in here the guy would have looked like a wuss. Kruk and I drifted over to the waiting area. A woman and someone I took to be her daughter were huddled together on the plastic chairs. They looked confused and scared. A black kid in massive jeans and a do-rag was sitting across from them, frowning at his fists. He and Kruk shared a little staring contest as we carried past him and over to the window.

"I think he likes you," I said to the detective.

Kruk ignored me. Years of practice. The stocky detective squared off in front of me. "Let's start at the beginning." He pulled out his notebook. "I want a name, Mr. Sewell."

"You don't like Kruk?" Now I was in a staring contest. Which I lost immediately. "Lucy Taylor," I said.

He wrote it down. "Relationship?"

"Old friend."

"Old?"

"As in 'long time.' "

"How old is this Miss Taylor?"

"Around thirty. Thirty-one?"

"And her relationship with the victim?"

"Lady friend." Kruk scribbled something down. I added, "They met in March."

"And how well would you say you know Miss Taylor?"

"Pretty well."

Kruk asked again, "How well do you know Miss Taylor?"

"How do I answer a question like that?"

"You start with the truth and you end with the truth. Very simple."

"I know Lucy pretty well," I said.

He grunted. "Intimately?"

"Nothing like that. We grew up together. Lucy is like a sister to me." Kruk scribbled something in his notebook. I craned my neck to see if he had actually written "like a sister," but I couldn't make sense of his hieroglyphics.

Kruk asked, "Is there any reason why you would hold back from calling the authorities about this other than simple loyalty to an old friend?" He looked up at me. "Don't give me a glib one here."

"Reasons like what?" I said.

"I don't supply answers for people, Mr. Sewell. Do you need to hear the question again?"

"No sir. And the answer is also no, sir. Lucy was scheduled to show up at the funeral home to drop off a dress. Her grandmother died two days ago. We're handling the funeral. Just before she arrived, I got a phone call from Shrimp Martin. Shrimp was rambling. I had no idea why he was calling. In fact, I still don't quite understand it. But anyway, Lucy came in while I was on the phone to Shrimp. Shrimp told me that Lucy had shot him. Then it seems he passed out. Lucy proceeded to put a pistol on my desk and then pretty much went into shock. I didn't call the police because it didn't occur to me to call the police. I'm sorry. I called nine-one-one. I took Lucy up to my aunt's apartment, then I came here. Shrimp was worked on and then stabilized. The crisis was over, I thought. I phoned Shrimp's sister. Her lovely little housemate came here and took over the vigil. I proceeded to my hot date. The end."

"So your whereabouts the past few hours can be verified."

"I was at a dance program, Detective. I've got the scars to prove it."

"Why do you suppose Mr. Martin called you?"

"I told you, I have no idea. We weren't close friends at all."

He tapped his pencil against his notepad. "Here's a

thought, if he knew that Miss Taylor was heading over to your place, maybe he was calling you to warn you."

"Warn me of what?"

"That she had a gun."

"So what if she had a gun? Lucy wasn't going to shoot *me*. Lucy likes me. I'm her friend."

"And according to you, this guy was her boyfriend."

"Look, Detective, this is your area of expertise, not mine. But don't girlfriends shoot boyfriends all the time? And vice versa? Isn't that half of what keeps you in business?"

"I'm just trying to look at all the possibilities here," Kruk said.

"Well, I think you can scratch off the one that says Lucy was gunning for me. Lucy would never hurt me. We're friends. I told you, the first thing she did was hand the gun over."

"And where is that gun right now, Mr. Sewell?"

I wasn't proud of my answer. "I don't know. Last I saw, it was on the desk in my office." I figured he would ask me more about the gun, but he didn't.

"Okay. You said that Miss Taylor was due over at your place to drop off a dress. When had that been arranged?"

"Lucy called about an hour before she showed up. Said she was bringing the dress by."

"How did she sound?"

"She sounded fine."

"Fine?"

"Fine. Normal. Regular Lucy. There was nothing in her voice that suggested maybe she'd be plugging Shrimp with a bullet in the very near future."

"Sad. Upset. Angry. Distant. Confused?"

"You want me to pick one?"

"Only if you detected one in your conversation with Miss Taylor."

"Sad."

"Sad."

"Lucy had been close with her grandmother. Losing her was tough."

He was scribbling something down in his notebook when his attention was snagged by one of the uniformed cops who was over by the elevators. He was gesturing to Kruk with a cell phone. "Excuse me." Kruk went over to the cop and took the cell phone from him. I saw Shrimp Martin's sister wading through the crowd. Thankfully, not in my direction. I don't mean to sound crass, but it's my livelihood to deal with the recently bereaved. I really don't mind avoiding it when I'm off the clock. Mary Ann Martin blubbering against my chest simply wasn't my idea of a nice way to cap off the night. I could tell she was a blubberer. It was written all over her.

Kruk handed the phone back to his minion. The EMS worker I had spoken with earlier was being escorted over to Kruk. Kruk signaled me over. When I got to within about five feet of them the detective held out his hand, signaling me to stop. He turned to the EMS worker.

"Have you seen this man before?"

"Yeah. Right after I got here. He was asking me about the guy who was shot."

"Is this the person you told me about who was outside the victim's home? Who was asking questions?"

"Nah, I told you, that guy had one of those flattops."

"You're sure? This man's hair might have just been—"

"Hey," I interrupted. "Leading the witness."

"This isn't a courtroom, Mr. Sewell."

"Doesn't matter. I told you already, I called from my office. I was nowhere near Shrimp's."

Kruk dismissed the EMS worker. "I just took a phone call from one of my men, down at your place, Mr. Sewell. I sent a squad car over there the moment your name cropped up." He snapped his notebook closed. I remembered this now about Kruk. He had all the moves down pat. "You didn't tell me that

Lucy Taylor was no longer at your aunt's," he said. He didn't sound happy saying it.

"I was getting to that."

I could see that Kruk didn't care for my answer. "I asked my man to look in your office, to see if the gun was there. It wasn't."

"Somehow that's what I suspected."

"And why is that?"

"I don't know . . ." I let off a large sigh. "I guess I figured Lucy took it with her when she left."

"Do you have any idea where she might have gone, Mr. Sewell?"

"Off the top of my head, no."

"You will supply us with an address, I hope. Where Miss Taylor lives."

I did. Right then and there. Kruk passed it on to one of his men, who trotted off with it.

"I suppose that's all for now, Mr. Sewell. Naturally, if you hear from Miss Taylor again, I expect you to contact us."

"Naturally."

"Immediately. Not ten hours later."

"You think Lucy Taylor killed Shrimp, don't you?"

"We have the victim's own statement to you over the phone that it was Miss Taylor who shot him. We have your statement that Lucy Taylor came into your office, put a gun on your desk and then lapsed into shock. Or what you've surmised is shock."

"I mean tonight. Here. You suspect that she came over here to the hospital and shot him again."

Kruk rubbed his jaw with his stubby fingers. "Mr. Martin was not shot," he said. "Whoever did this used a sharp object. We've got the M.E. going over the victim. He was stabbed directly in the heart. Plus, all of his tubes were pulled out."

"He wasn't shot?"

"Guns make a loud noise, Mr. Sewell. If you were going to kill someone in a hospital, would you use a gun?"

"I guess not. Never really gave it much thought. So he wasn't shot. But you still think Lucy did it, right?"

Kruk tugged on his ear, passed the back of his hand along the tip of his chin, tapped a finger against his jaw. If crime solving ever sours for him, I guess the guy could always ask the Orioles if they need a new third base coach.

"What would you think, Mr. Sewell?"

I took a deep breath. "I'd wait until all the evidence had been collected and all the related parties had been questioned and their stories checked out."

Kruk grunted. "We could certainly use more fair-minded men like you in law enforcement."

"So what's your take on Lucy?" I asked.

"I'm issuing a warrant," the detective said flatly. "I think the lady's a killer."